Blue Heav

A playwright and lyricist, Joe Keenan re[...] Theatre from New York University. His [...] the Richard Rodgers Development Award from the American Academy and Institute of Arts and Letters as well as the Kleban Award from the Ed Kleban Foundation. *Putting On the Ritz*, which continues the escapades of Philip Cavanaugh, Gilbert Selwyn and Claire Simmons, is also published by Arrow. Born in Cambridge, Massachusetts, Mr Keenan lives in Los Angeles with his partner of nineteen years, Gerry Bernardi. Most recently Mr Keenan spent six years as a writer/producer for *Frasier.* His work on the show has earned him five Emmys and two Writers Guild Awards.

'Joe Keenan's first novel plunges headlong into a world of deceit, avarice and violence and it's all a scream... Keenan maintains impressive control over a wonderfully ludicrous plot...packed full of lines that are well worth memorizing...and with a finale that is staggeringly, hilariously contrived. Makes me want to leap onto the first flight to NYC.' *Time Out*

'Joe Keenan has put the 'high' back into high jinks. His send-ups of criminal nouveaux riches are biting and dead on...and his dialogue is refreshingly effervescent.' *New York Times*

'A prize as rare as hen's teeth...a genuinely funny gay comic novel that made me laugh so hard I couldn't dare risk the embarrassment of reading it on the subway...elegant, snappy, smartly constructed, narratively rich and consistently funny, Keenan's work is filled with sharpness and dazzling verbal felicity.' *Christopher Street*

'One of the funniest writers alive.' David Leavitt

'Try to imagine a remake of Frank Capra's *A Pocketful of Miracles*, directed by Harvey Fierstein as a homage to Noël Coward, with cheerful borrowings from *Some Like it Hot* and *The Sting* and even a faint echo of *Treasures of the Sierra Madre* – and you begin to get the flavour of Joe Keenan's fast, funny, knowing, and relentlessly hip, comic novel, *Blue Heaven.*' *Los Angeles Times Book Review*

ALSO BY JOE KEENAN

Putting on the Ritz

BLUE HEAVEN

Joe Keenan

ARROW

First published by Arrow Books in 2002

1 3 5 7 9 10 8 6 4 2

First published in the United Kingdom in 1988 by Black Swan

Arrow Books
The Random House Group Limited
20 Vauxhall Bridge Road, London, SW1V 2SA

Random House Australia (Pty) Limited
20 Alfred Street, Milsons Point, Sydney
New South Wales 2061, Australia

Random House New Zealand Limited
18 Poland Road, Glenfield
Auckland 10, New Zealand

Random House (Pty) Limited
Endulini, 5a Jubilee Road, Parktown 2193, South Africa

The Random House Group Limited Reg. No. 954009

www.randomhouse.co.uk

A CIP catalogue record for this book is available from the British Library

Papers used by Random House are natural, recyclable products made from
wood grown in sustainable forests. The manufacturing processes conform to
the environmental regulations of the country of origin

ISBN 0 09 943504 7

Printed and bound in Great Britain by
Bookmarque Ltd, Croydon Surrey

For Gerry

The author gratefully acknowledges
the support and assistance of Kevin Kynock,
Eric Dehais, Michael Pietsch, D. Fletcher,
Geri Thoma and Bruce Shostak.

One

Looking back on the whole ghastly affair, what surprises me most is that when news of Gilbert's plan first reached me I felt no sense of foreboding whatsoever. I didn't blanch, I didn't tremble, nor did I rush to a pay phone to call an airline and inquire about low fares to the Canary Islands. My early warning system, usually so reliable where Gilbert is concerned, had completely shut down. I was at a gallery opening, you see, and cheap wine will do that to you.

The gallery that evening was Concepteria on West Broadway in SoHo. It's one of those boldly experimental galleries, dedicated to the proposition that nothing is wholly devoid of aesthetic and, it follows, monetary value. The exhibit, entitled "Bags #3," was the work of a not unjustifiably obscure artist named Aldo Cupper. It consisted entirely of humanoid shapes sculpted from dark green Hefty bags stuffed with what the program described as "found objects" and what the world describes as several other things. Mr. Cupper could be seen bounding from one group of observers to the next, describing in copious detail the process by which he had "transfigured the disposable," and I was managing, through a vigilant eye and a willingness to end conversations abruptly, to stay one group ahead of him. It was while effecting a particularly narrow escape that I turned sharply and found myself face to face with Holland ("Holly") Batterman.

"Philip!" he shrieked, "I've been calling you and *calling* you! Where have you been?"

"Home."

"All day?"

"Well, I went downstairs for cigarettes around four."

"That's when I called and called! Listen, I am so mad at you!"

"Mad?" I inquired, perplexed.

"Furious! In fact," he added, gesturing toward the sculpture, "if I were any madder I'd *buy* you one of these!"

Holly, if you haven't met him, is five foot eight, totally bald, and weighs close to three hundred pounds. As such, he's not New York's most romantically successful homosexual. He derives what solace he can from being its most ostensible.

"Keep your voice down. What are you mad at me for?"

"Oh, I'm not really mad. I just hate to be the last one you call when you have such marvelous dirt! So, tell, tell! Who's the lucky girl? Is she pregnant—and if she is, how on earth did *that* happen?"

I stared, baffled. Extraordinary as it seemed, he could only be driving at one thing.

"Holly, did somebody tell you I was getting *married*?"

He screamed with laughter causing heads to swivel all through the gallery. Holly's laugh sounds like a getaway car rounding a corner on two wheels.

"*You?* Oh, pleeeez! I'm gullible, honey, but not *that* gullible!"

I stared coolly. Happy though one may be with one's sexual preference, one hates to be thought incapable of versatility.

"So, who are you talking about?"

"Gilbert, of course!"

"*Gilbert?*"

"Yes!"

"Gilbert *Selwyn*?"

"Who *else!*"

As I said, no alarm bells, no cold sweat. No sudden urge to see faraway places.

"Gilbert is getting *married*?"

"He didn't *tell* you?"

"No! Who is she?"

"I hoped *you'd* know!"

"I haven't heard a thing."

"Why that little trollop!" said Holly, heaving a sigh of indignation on my behalf. "Imagine him not telling you when you two go back so far! I would've thought he'd call you first thing and ask you to be best man!"

No quickening of the pulse. No swift lunge for the travel brochures.

"Well, I wouldn't worry, hon," said Holly maternally. "If you ask me, he was pulling poor Jimmy's leg about the whole thing."

"You're losing me, Holly. Could you give this to me from the beginning? Everything you know?"

"Just try and *stop* me!" he said, and plunged into his story, which, from the sparsely punctuated sound of it, had already been recited in full to at least three people.

"Jimmy Loftus who's looking just fabulous these days though you can tell he's spending a fortune on it was at Dunhill the other day getting something to wear to his kid sister's debutante ball can you believe their money when who should he see but Gilbert who's asking about get this morning coats! *So,* Jimmy who can't *stand* Gilbert at all since that really embarrassing business with him and that night club act of his and Gilbert and Phil Cavanaugh oh that's you sorry to bring it up honey walks up to Gilley and says, 'Well, hello!'— sweet as anything—'Going to a wedding, Gilbert?' 'Yes,' says Gilbert, '*mine*'—which confuses Jimmy no end 'cause he doesn't know if Gilbert's bi or what and how do you ask in front of a Dunhill salesclerk, right? *So,* he says, 'Nice girl?' and Gilbert says, 'Only the most wonderful girl in the world!' and Jimmy says, 'Oh really—as wonderful as that hunk I saw you dancing with last week at Rampage?' and Gilbert—giddy little Gilbert!—gives him this blank ever-so-serious look and says, 'You know, James, it amazes me that a man of your family background should possess no sense of decorum whatsoever. I suppose there are some things money can't buy.' 'Yes, but you're not one of them,' says Jimmy and walks away very pleased with himself until he realizes he forgot to ask who the girl was so he calls me— if anyone's gonna know, right?—only I'm as much in the dark as he is. So I say, 'Hang on, I'll find out,' and that's when I called and called! You really don't know *anything?*"

"No. I haven't talked to him in a month. Why don't you just call him yourself?"

"I have! I've called and *called* but—"

"You'll know when I know," I said and turned swiftly toward the bar. A bit rude of me to be sure, but I'd just spotted Aldo Cupper swimming toward us through the crowd. He was beaming as only an unknown artist can beam when he's just spent two hours in a room containing his work, much wine and a hundred people who can't be sure they won't someday need a favor from him. Flight was imperative.

Flight, however, was rendered impossible by the sudden attachment to my left wrist of three hundred pounds of implacable Batterman.

"Wait! Hold on! You must have a *clue!*"

"I told you, I—My God, look! Mary Tyler Moore!"

This ploy distracted him sufficiently for me to free my wrist, but it was too late. Aldo was upon us.

"Holland!" he cried ebulliently, "I'm so pleased you could make it. I've been wanting to tell you how much I enjoyed your set designs for Papp's all-Hispanic *Importance of Being Earnest.*"

"Aren't you sweet," said Holly, craning his neck madly.

"They really were marvelous," said Aldo.

"They were fun," agreed Holly, giving up the search and regarding me with a disgruntled look. "But *these*"—he gestured toward the bags—"these are just stunning. *Philip* here hasn't shut up about them for a minute."

"Really!" said Aldo, fixing me with a hungry, expectant look, like a vampire watching a hemophiliac shave.

"I've never seen anything like them."

"You missed 'Bags #1' and '2,' then?"

"Regretfully."

Silence fell.

"A lot of people have been asking me how I make them."

"Really?" asked Holly, suddenly concerned. "Have you been telling them?"

"Certainly. It may look complicated but it's a very simple twelve-step procedure. I'll explain if you like."

"Sure," I said. "We'd both love to—Oh, my God! Is that clock right?" Muttering the old standby about kidney dialysis, I hotfooted it out of the gallery and into the cool night air.

So buoyant was I over the timeliness of my escape that when I spied Gilbert half a block away on the opposite side of the street I did not duck into a dimly lit doorway; I instead called out his name. I might even have waved. Remembering this, I'm reminded of Claire Simmons's comment to me about my continued friendship with Gilbert.

"Philip," she said, "if there's anything at all to reincarnation, you're coming back as a lemming."

*   *   *

Perhaps you're wondering at this point why my wariness toward Gilbert is of the sort usually reserved for Jehovah's Witnesses and mushrooms in the wild. I'll try to explain.

You're perhaps familiar with the song "I Got Rhythm," the lyric to which, as sung by the late Ethel Merman, contains the lines:

> *Old Man Trouble,*
> *I don't mind him.*
> *You won't find him*
> *Hangin' round my front or back door.*
> *Oooooooooooooooooooooooh!*

Whenever I listen to this recording I feel certain that Merman must have known Gilbert, and that her confidence in the assertion was based on her knowledge that, so long as Gilbert was in town, Old Man Trouble would be far too busy at his place to give her own real estate so much as a thought.

That's not to say Gilbert is just unlucky. Oh, he is, but it goes beyond that. Gilbert manages always to be Old Man T's sorriest victim and, at the same time, his most indispensable collaborator. Fate and fate alone may place the banana peel in his path, but it is Gilbert who will every time make certain that at the moment of rendezvous he's carrying a tray laden with Baccarat crystal which he has, in order to impress a date, borrowed without the permission or knowledge of its owner, and which he'd been hoping to return in secret.

A lot of people are very fond of Gilbert because of just this. They tend to view his various outrages with, if not approval, a sort of bemused, tongue-clicking indulgence. This is because they've never suffered any of the consequences.

I'm not one of these people.

"Philip! I'm so glad I caught you! Claire told me you'd be here."

"Remind me to thank her," I said icily. My spirits were high and my curiosity boiling, but I was determined not to broach the topic of wedding bells until I'd given him a certain amount of grief. Our last encounter had been among our more memorably disastrous, and, while he was willing, as always, to pretend nothing unpleasant had occurred, he was not the one who'd spent three nights replastering his walls.

"It's been ages!" he exclaimed, hugging me.

"Twenty-six days and I still wake up screaming."

He drew back and gazed at me with that disappointed stare one gives to those of whom one had expected better.

"You're still thinking about that?"

"Yes."

"That was weeks ago! I can't see why anyone would want to live in the past."

"I can't see why anyone would want to live in *mine*."

"Anyway," he said, brightening, "you can't stay mad at me for long! I have news, Philip! Wonderful news! Now, I know this will come as a shock to you but—"

"You're getting married."

There's nothing quite like the face of a person who's just had his big scoop airily dismissed as yesterday's news. The combination of surprise and pique is one I never tire of, and Gilbert's face was at this moment a masterpiece of the genre.

"You've already *heard*? God, don't tell me you were speaking to Jimmy Loftus?"

"No. He told Holly. Holly told me."

"Holly!" moaned Gilbert. "Shit! Now whoever I tell they're going to say, 'Yes, I know, Holly told me!' "

Annoying, of course, but he brought it on himself. As he well knew, telling Jimmy is the next best thing to telling Holly, which is the next best thing to leasing the billboard over the Winter Garden.

"Ah, well," he sighed philosophically, "let 'em gossip! I don't care. I don't care about anything but her. I'm in love, Philip. For the first time! Deep genuine love."

"Good for you."

"I had no idea what it felt like."

"I dare say."

"I must admit, I thought you'd be a little more surprised."

"I might be if I believed it for a minute."

"Philip!" he cried, injured. "I mean it! I'm really in love with this girl. I want to marry her. I want to have children, buy a house . . ."

He continued in this vein for some time but I wasn't having any. "Gilley," I said, "I don't know what your angle is, but if you don't have one, then . . ." I stopped. I didn't know what, then. He'd never not had one.

He stared at me a moment then switched gears, opting for the low, measured tone used to convey sincerity in commercials for pain relievers.

"I hoped you'd be glad for me. I don't suppose I should blame you if you're incapable of feeling anything but skeptical contempt for your best friend's happiness. We all have our limitations. But nothing you say can—"

"All right! I'm sorry. Congratulations." I was by no means sold on any of it, but I could see there was no use pressing him for the truth just yet.

"So, who's the girl?"

"With your attitude I'm surprised you even want to know."

"Of course I want to know, you jerk!" I exploded. "I'm dying of curiosity." It didn't take two seconds for me to realize this was not a prudent admission to have made.

"You know, Philly, I just realized how thirsty I am. Maybe we can find someplace nice to sit and have a drink and I'll tell you all about her."

I had, as usual, just enough money to keep me alive for exactly half the period for which it would have to suffice. Gilbert's financial status could always be guessed, but I thought I'd ask anyway.

"Do you have *any*thing?"

"Sorry. Not on me."

"We could stop at your cash machine."

"We could," he agreed, "but it would only be a social call."

I turned and began walking west.

"One drink, Gilbert, I swear, that's all this is worth to me."

An hour later found us shivering under the stars at the Riviera Café in Sheridan Square. It was mid-October, but a fair number of Village bistro owners were still keeping their outdoor stations open in an effort to cash in on the die-hard alfresco crowd, people who, like Gilbert, find pneumonia a small price to pay for Maximum Visibility Dining. Our waiter was setting down the bill, along with the third round, and Gilbert was explaining, in uncalled-for detail, the reasons behind his conversion to heterosexuality.

"Women," he said, "are different. They're not the same as men. Women are . . . nourishing. No, hold on, that's not the word. They're *nurturing*. That's it. Women nurture you, Philip. Not like men. Men are selfish. They're always undermining you, resenting your success, bitching at you for wearing their sweaters." The waiter caught my eye, shook his head in quiet sympathy and withdrew.

Gilbert lit a cigarette and stared dreamily toward Seventh Avenue. "She's a remarkable girl."

"So I've heard. What I haven't heard is her *name*."

"I'm leading up to it. You know what's wonderful about women?"

"Yes! I do! I've heard nothing else for the last goddamned hour and I'm really getting sick of it!"

He smiled in what he imagined to be a winning manner. "Maybe I have gone on a little. It's just that I know how cynical you can be, and I want you to know how sincerely I feel about all this."

"Well, mission accomplished, okay? Now for Christ's sake, who is she?"

He finished the scotch in one gulp and, grinning from ear to ear, dropped the bombshell.

"Moira Finch."

I slumped back in my chair, overwhelmed by the sheer grisliness of the concept. If my eyes have ever in my life actually goggled, that was the moment.

"That *cunt*?"

He stiffened and regarded me with a steely eye. "Philip," he said slowly, "I'm going to forgive you for that."

"Well, I'm not forgiving you for *this*!" I said, waving our twenty-dollar check in his face. "Do you expect me to believe for one instant you really intend to *marry* that crazy bitch?"

"You can believe what you like, but if you call her even one more name I'm asking you to step outside."

"We are outside, you asshole! What are you trying to pull on me?"

He lowered his voice. We were back in the aspirin commercial.

"I realize you've never been very fond of Moira—"

"*I've* never been fond—!"

"But you don't know her the way I do. You've only met her a handful of times."

"That was enough! She's the most mercenary, cold-blooded bundle of affectations ever to—"

"I repeat, Philip, you don't know her."

"Maybe I don't, Gilbert, but most of what I've heard about her has come straight from you. I thought you hated her guts!"

He frowned and shifted his weight in the chair.

"I'll admit there was a time before I'd come to really understand Moira when I did, occasionally, find her outward manner to be . . . mildly abrasive. I may, at that time, have said things about her I now regret having said."

"You said she had a face that could poison a reservoir."

"That would be one, yes."

"You said when she sucks an ice cube it doesn't melt, it gets bigger."

"Honestly, Philip! Why do you have to dredge up things it pains me to remember! I don't care what I said before. Moira Finch is a wonderful girl and I love her deeply! You just have to believe me."

"No, I don't! I just spent twenty bucks I couldn't afford to get the truth out of you, and you're not leaving till I get it."

I glared implacably.

"Oh, all right," he sighed at length. "But it goes no further."

"It won't."

"I mean it. If word gets around, the whole thing's as good as ruined."

"Okay."

"You swear you won't tell? Anyone? Not even Claire?"

"With what you've got on me?"

He smiled, the notion filling him with security. "Yes, there is that, I guess. Whichever one you mean. I'm sorry I lied. I had to, really."

"I'm sure."

"No, really. I'll be talking about this to scads of people. I need all the rehearsal I can get. Was I convincing?"

"Up to a point."

"Moira, huh? I suppose I should have picked someone else, but I really couldn't have. Under the circumstances."

"I'm not sure I'm following this," I said, growing uneasy, for he was wearing the same smug little grin he always wears when he fancies he's thought up something monstrously clever.

"You admit you're not in love with Moira?"

"God, no! I mean, I'm fond of her, really!"

"Seriously?"

"Yes! I've spent a lot of time with her lately and she's not half as bad as we make her out to be. Well, maybe half, but not a bit more. She's actually a lot of fun once you get to know her."

"But why on earth are you going around telling people you're getting *married*?"

"Because we are."

And he meant it. I could tell because the grin had blossomed into a smirk. Whatever he was up to, he thought it was just brilliant.

He giggled wickedly at my confusion and said, "Well, go ahead— *ask*!"

"*Why?*"

"I'll tell you, but it's kind of involved and I'm getting a little chilly out here. Maybe we could go someplace warm and—"

"I'm not buying you another drink! I'm poor this month, really poor, and I don't—"

"Oh all right! I'll buy you one."

"I thought you didn't have any money!"

"Well, I don't have much."

The waiter arrived to collect and Gilbert, murmuring something about cigarettes, dashed off to find a machine. The waiter glanced after him and received what must have been the most unmistakable cruise of his life.

"Is he for real?"

"You don't know the half of it," I said, glumly forking over the cash. "He's getting *married*."

"I pity the poor girl."

I had to laugh at the notion of anyone pitying Moira. Then, noting the waiter's befuddled look, I explained.

"You don't *know* her—believe me, Moira can take care of herself."

He nodded, still puzzled, and began to move off. Then, turning abruptly, he asked, "*Moira?* Moira *Finch*?"

"That's the one!" I said, surprised.

"He's *marrying* that crazy bitch?"

He wandered off to the register shaking his head in disbelief. I added a dollar to the tip.

TWO

66"The beauty of it is that all it needs to work is for people to *think* we're in love. They may think we're insane, but that's all right. So long as they believe we mean it. Sincerity, Philip. If we can feign that, we're in the clear. Which is where you come in."

"Hold it right there . . ."

We were facing each other at a window table at the Jaded Palate, a recent addition to the Columbus Avenue cavalcade of chic, fun, short-lived eateries. Gilbert and I are both Upper West Siders and we'd agreed on the advisability of reaching home turf before the hour grew too late, or the number of our functioning brain cells too few. Anyone who's ever sat on an uptown express with a besotted Gilbert and heard him loudly whisper "What angelic boys!" in reference to the three Hispanic street-gang members seated opposite him will appreciate the wisdom of this decision.

"Just because you're letting me in on this, don't think for a minute I'm getting involved."

"I haven't even told you what it is yet!"

"Okay," I sighed. "What's the angle?"

"Well . . . three weeks ago," he began, "I went to a wedding. My stepfather's fat niece, Steffie. Have I told you much about my stepfather's family?"

"Just that they're Italian and there are a lot of them."

"Scads, Philip, scads! When they throw a reunion they have to rent Rhode Island. They're all very close and very Old World, if you know what I mean—big fat widows dressed in black, plaster saints all over the place. So, anyway, when I got the invite which said me and guest, I knew right off my guest should not be a 'special friend.'

That's why I took Moira. And don't roll your eyes at me—I'd already called every woman I know and one subdued transsexual."

"I'd have canceled before going with Moira."

"Well, I couldn't. I *had* to go. And I had to go with a woman. See, like it or not, I'm in a position these days where I simply have to make a good impression on Tony."

He was referring to Tony Cellini, a very rich businessman his mother had married two years ago following the demise of her second husband, the late Edward Harcourt.

"Ever since Mom married Tony he's *completely* controlled the purse strings. He gives her a fat monthly allowance, but she goes through it in no time and never has a thing to give me when I'm hard up, which is always. So I may go begging to her, but he's the one she has to get it from. That's why I have to stay on his good side. And it helps a lot if every now and then I show up accompanied by something presentable with breasts."

"He has no idea you're gay?"

"God forbid! I'd never see a dime! Fortunately he's thick as a phone book about these things and so is Mom. Every time I see him he draws me aside and says, 'Gilberto, you dog, you gettin' enough these days?' And I have to leer and say, 'More than I can handle, Tony! They're wearin' me out!' It's disgusting!"

"Then why do you do it?"

"Because if I don't he doesn't slip me the fifty. Anyway, I needed a lot more than fifty this time. I owed money to everyone, I'd just lost my job at Bloomingdale's—"

"You lost your job?"

"Oh, right, I haven't seen you. Yup, s'all over! My career as a floorwalker has ended."

"But you were only there a month. What happened?"

"Oh, this little misunderstanding," he said, fluttering his fingers to connote inconsequence. "I mean, there's no way I could have known it was *her* scarf she was putting in her purse. And besides, when you see a woman who looks like Jackie Onassis, you don't assume it *is* Jackie Onassis. You say, 'Oh, there's a woman who looks kind of like Jackie Onassis. And she's stealing a scarf.' At any rate, Moira and I showed up at the wedding right on time, but it turned out things were all delayed—please lift your head off the table, it's distracting—

things were delayed an hour because they were waiting for this old geezer. His name is Freddy Bombelli and he's eighty-six and sort of the patriarch, but they have to jump-start his kidneys and he's going to be late. So to keep everyone happy they opened the bar up. I thought, 'Perfect! Here's my chance to ply Mom with liquor until she agrees to go work on old Tony for me.' "

He paused a moment and sighed.

"I was *so* confident, Philly. You have to understand—the two of them *love* weddings. They eat like pigs, drink like fish and dance till they drop. If there was ever an ideal time to hit them up, this was it. So I looked for Mom, and there she was outside in a deck chair next to the shrine of the Blessed Virgin—conveniently located for poolside worship—and she was knocking back the daiquiris, so I went right to work. She was in a *wonderful* mood, and I was so eloquent! It was going perfectly! Then she did something incredibly stupid and ruined it all!"

This last was not hard to believe. I had only met his mother, Madeline ("Maddie") Selwyn Harcourt Cellini, a dozen or so times over the years since Gilbert and I graduated from high school, and not at all since her marriage to Tony. But, despite the infrequency of our friendship, I feel a great deal of affection for her, mixed with a dollop of envy, for she's a woman who has always managed to prosper and thrive while remaining serenely out of touch with reality. Reality, if determined to contact her, would search long and in vain for a forwarding address.

"What did she do?"

"Well, just as I'm about to warn her to wait till Tony's half in the bag before asking him, she suddenly stands up and starts waving her arms like a traffic cop. I turn around and there's Tony stomping toward us, and by the look on his face he's just passed a stone or something."

"Bad timing?"

"The worst! He hadn't had *one* drink, hadn't danced *one* hully-gully and hadn't even laid eyes on Moira (which, if I was going to make my pitch now, meant I'd brought the dumb bitch for nothing!), and to top it all off he's worried sick about this Freddy Bombelli character. Apparently everyone's nuts about the old guy, but he's just had some major operation and still insists on coming to the wedding. Everyone's afraid he's going to keel over in the reception line. So that was the kind of mood he was in when Mom staggered to her feet and said, 'Tony honey, would you believe it—Gilbert's broke *again!*' Some chance I had!"

"You didn't get the money?"

"No," he said and glumly downed his margarita in one gulp. "What I got was a lecture complete with a biography of the whole Cellini clan! Daddy getting off the boat with four cents and a dream. Working hard, building a business, yadda, yadda, yadda! And, of course, by not giving me the money he was doing me a *favor* because how would I ever learn resourcefulness and sacrifice—fucking sacrifice!—if he pulled me out every time I was in the hole? And by this point there were half a dozen fat old widows—they looked like bison!—standing there cheering for Tony and Italy and their hardworking dead husbands, and when he finished they applauded! Oh, Philip, it was *awful!*"

He shuddered once more at the memory and, signaling the waitress for another round, plunged in again.

"I was crushed, Philip, totally crushed, and all I wanted was to find someplace to be by myself and lick my wounds. So I wandered into the kitchen, and there was Moira, clutching that enormous bag of hers, hunting for Saran Wrap. Apparently she didn't want the caviar she'd stolen to get the cheese she'd stolen all fishy. Well, she was about the last person I felt like being with but I *had* invited her and I was stuck with her for the whole day, so I at least had to be civil. So we started talking and I wound up telling her all about it. And, you know, she was really nice. She empathized. She said that *her* mother has so much money she sculpts with it, but she never gives Moira a dime. I suppose she must figure Moira would only lose it on one of her brilliant investments. She always does."

That's a funny thing about Moira. In the field of personal relations she's known far and wide as Manhattan's foremost tactician. She gets what or who she wants, by whatever means she deems necessary, and she's not fussy about the body count. Her business dealings, however, are another matter. Give her a dollar and she will immediately rush off and invest it in some nascent enterprise which then declares bankruptcy within the week, if not the hour. My friend Claire once referred to her stock portfolio as the Misfortune 500.

"S'anyway," he continued, "what with our stingy parents and the fact that she's as broke as I am these days—she really lost a bundle

on that designer pasta—we started to feel a certain, y'know, cama-
raderie. Anyway, we decided to rejoin the party, but we took a wrong
turn somewhere and wound up in this ballroom that hadn't been
opened to the guests yet. The door wasn't locked so we just traipsed
right in . . . *and there they were!*"

He paused and a rapt beatific expression illuminated his face.

"There they were," he repeated with hushed reverence, "all spread
out on two enormous tables."

"The caterers?"

"The *gifts*, Philip! You've never seen so many gifts in one place!
Dozens and dozens of gorgeous white and silver boxes! Big ones with
VCRs and microwave ovens! Little ones with diamond cufflinks and
Cartier watches! And not just boxes, Philip—envelopes, too! A great
tall stack of them, and you just knew the stingiest contained at least
a hundred dollars! What a sight it was, Philip! What a breathtaking
sight!"

"Oh, *Gil*bert," I moaned, burying my face in my hands, for the
awful truth was at last apparent. "You can't really intend to marry
Moira Finch just for the *gifts!*"

He regarded me with a puzzled look.

"You make it sound like a bad idea."

"It *is*, Gilbert! It's the worst one you've ever had!"

"It isn't!"

"Gilbert—"

"No, really," he said with childlike earnestness. "We've thought
this through. We've looked at it from every angle and I tell you it is
golden!"

"Do you mean to say the two of you just strolled in there, took one
look at the loot and started right in proposing to each other?"

"Of course not. Don't make us sound impetuous. The idea may
have occurred to both of us then, but we didn't bring it up for another
three, four hours at least. Still," he added with a fiendish grin, "you
could tell our minds were on the same track because we both went
into action the minute the caterer kicked us out."

"Went into action?"

"Oh, you know, dancing together, holding hands. Letting people
think we were an item. And that was only half the campaign!"

"What was the other half?" I asked, not certain I wanted to know.

"Heavy ingratiating!" He giggled at the memory. "Oh, Philly, you should have seen me go after those people's hearts! I was shameless! You've heard of the legendary Selwyn charm?"

I had, I conceded, adding that I'd also heard of Bigfoot and the lost kingdom of Atlantis.

"I was magnificent! I danced with aunts and grand aunts and hideous cousins no one else would dance with! I laughed at jokes, I sang Italian songs! I let every fucking widow there tell me her husband's life story, and cried in the same places they did. I told fat Cousin Steffie time and again how beautiful she was, which wasn't easy to do with a straight face—dressed in a wedding gown she looks like nothing so much as an Alp.

"By the time we left I was the favorite relation by marriage of every Cellini, Bombelli, Fabrizio and—who are the other ones?—every Sartucci in the place. They were all begging me not to be such a stranger, to visit more often, and you can bet your ass that's just what I'm going to do! You can say what you like about this scheme, Philip. I'm telling you, it can't miss!"

I scrutinized his face which was positively radiant with greed. He was dead serious.

"Look, how many people have you told you're getting married?"

"Lemmesee—there's Moira, naturally, and Jimmy today—"

"Good, then it's not too late to—"

"Oh, and Mom, of course."

"You told your *mother*!"

"You bet! There's no going back, Phil. She's full of plans already. I'd break her heart."

"You're insane! You're going to go through a charade of this size just for some gifts?"

"You didn't see them! You weren't there when they opened those beautiful boxes!"

"You mean they opened the gifts? Right there at the wedding?"

"Sure. It's the big event of the day."

He explained that this was a family tradition started many years ago by some shrewd Cellini bride who deduced that if her guests knew in advance that all gifts would be held up to the merciless glare of communal scrutiny she wouldn't see quite so much cheap stemware as her elder sister had. Naturally, all Cellini brides to this day have refused to break with so sacred a tradition, for the competitiveness it inspires is all to the bride's advantage. It had certainly been all to

Steffie's, to judge from the catalogue of items Gilbert feverishly re-cited.

"Projection TVs, they got. Two of them! Stock certificates and crystal! Silverware, heirloom jewelry, cases of Dom Pérignon! A race horse, Philip! Uncle Chick gave them a fucking race horse! They cleaned up!" He admitted to feeling mildly embarrassed when they opened his gift, ten pounds of designer pasta, but insisted that most considered it very chic, and Steffie was nothing less than thrilled.

"And I'm not even counting the money. Tony the Tightwad forked out five hundred bucks. Freddy Bombelli gave them five grand. The total cash, Philip, came to thirty thousand dollars! I had no idea how much money Tony's family had! But next March I'm going to waltz down the aisle and grab my share!"

He took a big gulp of my margarita and smacked his lips in loud satisfaction.

"And that, honey, is only the half of it!"

"I don't want to hear the rest!"

"There's also," he continued obliviously, "the money from *Moira's* side. God, you've heard about her mother, haven't you?"

Indeed I had. Moira's mother, the former Mrs. Finch, left the States some years ago. She now resides in the quaint English village of Little Chipperton where she reigns socially supreme as the Duchess of Dorsetshire. If you've met Moira you are doubtlessly aware of this fact as it is one she has managed to work into the first five minutes of every conversation she's ever had. If you haven't met Moira I'll warn you that should this fate befall you you must not express any curiosity whatsoever. For even the most routinely polite inquiry—like, "No kidding? A duchess?"—will elicit an avalanche of self-aggrandizing details from Moira, including all the amusing things Prince Charles said to her when, as Mummy's guest, she attended the royal wedding. (One wonders how Princess Di liked the pasta.)

"Yes, I've heard about her mother. But I thought dukes are always poor these days."

"Not this one. They've got baskets of it. Now maybe they won't give any to Moira when she wants to invest in cosmetic pet surgery, but if she's actually getting married—well, c'mon! They *have* to fork over big! So with me bringing in the Cellinis and her roping in the duke and duchess and all their rich chums we have it figured at fifty thousand at the absolute least! Not bad for a day's work, huh? *Huh?*"

And with that, he laughed so hard he passed tequila through his nose.

I sat smoking pensively as our second round arrived. Ethical considerations aside—and aside is always just where they are when Gilbert makes plans—the whole thing did look pretty lucrative. Two stunningly unscrupulous people with rich but closefisted families could hardly devise a more surefire means of inducing them to hand over a sackful or two. There remained, however, a pterodactyl in the ointment.

"But *Moira*, Gilbert? Get married? To her?"

"We'll just be sharing an apartment for a year or two. God, Philly! For that kind of money I can deal with having Moira as a roommate for a while."

"But it's a legal bond."

"Just a temporary one," he said lightly. "We've already signed a prenuptial contract and when we break up we split it all down the middle. If we can't agree who gets something we'll sell it and divide the money. See? We've mapped this whole thing out, engagement to divorce, and it is perfect! 'It's tops,' " he sang, " 'It's first! It's DuPont! It's Hearst!' " He began clapping his hands and stomping his feet on the floor with glee.

"Will you stop acting like a queer leprechaun. People are staring."

He regained a measure of composure and raised his glass in a toast.

"Here's to you, Philip—my best friend, and now my best man!"

"No!"

"Philip!"

"I said no!"

"Why not?"

"Because it's dishonest and I want no part of it!"

This was not my real reason. I was convinced the whole thing would end in some unanticipated but hugely embarrassing way and, were I to take part, a good portion of the ultimate egg would be on my face. But if both the high and low roads go to the same place, one naturally takes the high one.

"Dishonest!" he said in a puzzled, hurt tone. "I fail to see how. Not," he hastened to add, "that I'd call it especially honest either. But, really! Where's the harm?"

"You're lying to everyone you know and cheating your family! Think of your poor mother!"

"She'll be thrilled to see me get married."

"And when she gets to know Moira?"

"She'll be thrilled to see me divorced."

"What about Tony?"

"Him!" snorted Gilbert. "I'm only following his advice. 'Be resourceful!' he said. As for the rest of them, they're *rich*. What's a couple of hundred to them for a really good time and a chance to see all their cousins?"

"You're swindling a duchess," I said, thinking as I did that it was not an accusation I often got a chance to make.

"Oh, honey!" he replied, rolling his eyes ceilingward. "You expect me to feel sorry for some woman whose biggest problem in life is fox hunts getting rained out? Don't be such a Pollyanna! You *have* to be my best man!"

He stared pleadingly at me. I knew from long years of experience what was coming next.

"After all, Philip—"

"Don't say it!"

"—you were the *first*. The first ever!"

And so, to my lasting regret, I had been. Mind you, this was ten years ago when we were both sixteen and treading the boards together at Our Lady of Perpetual Prayer High School. The romance began in the spring of our junior year and ended that July when Gilbert's penchant for tricking with wealthy older gentlemen ceased to be a mere suspicion on my part and became instead a medically incontestable fact.

I suppose ours was a fairly typical adolescent fling, complete with troublesome logistics, jealous fights and moist reconciliations. Nothing at all unique. But Gilbert has, in the intervening years, smothered it all in great winsome gobs of nostalgia. Which doesn't bother me. What bothers me is his habit of bludgeoning me over the head with it whenever he's trying to talk me into doing something I don't want to do.

He ogled me affectionately.

"Remember those days, Philly?"

"Better than you do."

"I didn't know what love was till that spring."

"I didn't know what crabs were."

"The things we did! The crazy promises we—"

"Oh, stuff it, Gilbert! It's not going to work."

"Okay, how much money do I owe you?" he asked, effecting the switch from paramour to pragmatist with the speed of a man born to finagle.

"Including the most recent damages?"

"If you insist."

"I do. About five hundred dollars."

"That much!"

"At least!"

"Well then, I'd think if anyone would have a reason to want this thing to come off it'd be you! C'mon! If you're not best man I'll have to pick someone else, probably some Cellini who'll be totally underfoot and I'll have to be acting the excited straight boy all the time. I'll go nuts! Besides, if you're in on all the planning and spending a lot of time with me and Moira, then people will be much more likely to believe you when you lie for me."

"But I don't want to lie for you."

"Philly," he said sadly, "I don't see that you have much choice. Think of the people who'll be calling you with questions—'Has he really gone straight?' 'Why *her*?' What are you going to say to them?"

"This is beginning to sound like a lot of work just to get back the money you owe me anyway."

"All right," he said, taking a nonchalant sip of his margarita. "Double it."

He smiled serenely.

"Are you serious?"

"Of course. You don't think I'd let you help me without offering you a share of the loot? Just be my best man, tell a few innocent lies to everyone you know, and the money is yours."

"A thousand dollars?"

"Oh, hell, let's make it fifteen hundred. I believe that would give you enough to buy that computer you've been salivating over for the last year and a half."

As he said this, he smiled broadly, for he could see my defenses crumbling before his eyes.

This was, you'll recall, the middle of October. Since the demise the previous December of my trusty Olivetti, I had been forced to make do with a manual typewriter left to me by Uncle Walter who had, I suspect, purloined it from the Smithsonian.

"Fabulous machines, aren't they, computers?" asked Gilbert. "Is it true that when you want to revise something all you have to do is change the parts you want on a screen? Then you push a button and it spits out a beautiful new copy of the whole thing while you have a sandwich?"

"Something like that."

"You don't have to stay up all night retyping?"

"No."

"And you don't have to keep glopping on that correction fluid that makes it look like you're typing on oatmeal?"

"All right! You win! I'll be your best man!"

"Oh, thank you, Philly!" he cried. "I knew you'd never let me down!" he added and, leaning over the table, seized my head in both hands and kissed me on the lips.

"If you're trying to convince people you've gone straight, you're off to a great start."

"Oh, c'mon! Who's going to see us at this time of—oh, shit!"

Gazing over my shoulder, he smiled half-heartedly and waved. I turned and saw Moira Finch standing out on the sidewalk, pantomiming surprised delight. When she noticed it was me in the other chair her pantomime doubled in intensity, suggesting almost unendurable elation. Moira, as you'll see, is not a girl to feign things halfway. Pausing only to fend off a passerby who was attempting to perform the Heimlich maneuver on her, she raced into the café and was upon us.

Three

"Gilbert, honey! And Philip! Oh, isn't this just too wonderful?"

She grabbed a chair from a neighboring table and shoved it under ours, banging our shins. "Imagine running into the two of you just out of the blue! And you're both looking so nice! I could faint with pleasure!"

"Congratulations, Moira!"

"Oh, he's told you?"

"Yes."

"Isn't it fabulous?"

"Literally."

"The two of us are so happy we can't stand it! We can't wait to tell everyone."

" 'Scuse me," said our waitress who'd been hovering since Moira had seated herself.

"We don't know whether we should just spread the word informally or wait a bit and have a huge bash and tell everyone at the same time. Maybe we should—"

"CanIgetyousomething?"

"Oh! Gee," said Moira, eyeing our margaritas and staring poignantly down at her purse. "No . . . nothing for me. I'm fine."

"I have plastic," said Gilbert, whose finances were improving with every drink.

"Oh? They didn't take it away then?"

"No, I sold some things and paid it off."

"Well," said Moira, suddenly parched. "Maybe a little wine. Or *champagne*! Oh what a good idea! Let's all have champagne and celebrate! Do you have Veuve Clicquot?"

"Yes."

"Fabulous! A bottle of that."

The waitress withdrew and Moira sat back in her chair, sighing contentedly. Immediately she sat bolt upright again.

"Oh, darling, I have the most amazing news!"

"What is it?"

"Not yet, love. Let's wait till Vulpina gets here."

Gilbert and I blanched as one.

"Vulpina?"

"Yes. I was supposed to meet her across the street. Don't worry though, I'll be able to see her from here and I'll run and get her."

Gilbert and I exchanged discreet glances of dismay. Vulpina (no last name, which, I suppose, says it all) owns and operates the SoHo boutique of the same name. She is among Moira's dearest friends, presumably because Moira finds it to her advantage to be seen regularly in the company of someone alongside whom she might be considered unaffected. Vulpina is six foot one, weighs maybe twenty-six pounds, speaks in a Hollywood Slavic accent, and dresses exclusively in her own designs. These designs, which have been spotted as far north as Houston Street, vary widely in cut, fabric and intended function, but they are all heavily imbued with Vulpina's unmistakable hallmark, overpriced hideousness.

"Oh, what fun!" chirped Moira. "We can all party together!"

"On my card?"

"Oh, you!" She laughed gaily. "My stingy baby! So," she said, turning to me, "were you surprised when he told you?"

"Not a bit. I'd had a feeling he was chasing you for years."

"Well, he finally caught me!" she said, laughing and pinching his cheek. "He finally caught me!" she repeated and it occurred to me that if a venereal disease could gloat, this was just what it would sound like.

"Of course, people are bound to call it a whirlwind courtship but I've always said when you find the right person you just know it. I mean, you really just *know*. Maybe not right away. Take Gilbert and me—we knew each other for years before it finally clicked, but when it did, well we just *knew*. It's like reading 'The Wasteland.' "

"Oh?"

"You know, the first one or two times you read it you're just bored and you don't get it at all. Then you read it again and *bang*, you're just sitting there thinking 'Yes, *yes*, oh my God, how true!' That's just how it was with Gilbert and me. We were lying there in this meadow, gazing up at the stars when out of nowhere we both started weeping with happiness! At the *exact* same moment! Now, I ask you, have you ever heard of two—?"

"Moira, I told Philip we're getting married for the gifts."

"Oh. Well, don't I feel silly!"

"I thought we needed someone else on the team. And if there's anyone on earth we can trust, Philly's the one!"

"I hope you don't object."

"Not at all!" she said, smiling toxically. "I just hope Gilbert means it when he says you're the only one. I mean, you know how things get around."

"Well, you can trust Philly. He's in for a cut."

"*Really?*" she asked and the people at the next table had to button their sweaters.

"Taken from my share, of course."

"Well, isn't that nice of you! He is *such* a sweetheart. He really is. I would never consider doing this with anyone else." She patted his hand affectionately. "Did he tell you he's moving in with me?"

"No kidding? When?"

"First thing tomorrow!" said Gilbert.

"We talked it over and decided the parents really expect it these days. We wouldn't want them to think we were tentative or anything. And there's plenty of space. Even a nice little room where Gilbert can work on his book."

"How's the book going?" I asked.

"Coming along," he said in bored, subject-closing sort tone.

"*Is* it?" I asked.

"Yes, it's about doubled in length since the last time I saw you."

"Added a dedication, did you?"

Gilbert, I should explain, fancies himself a writer. He wants desperately to be a world-famous, flamboyant, provocative novelist and will do anything to achieve this goal short of putting words on paper. Some authors procrastinate, others suffer from dry spells, but Gilbert, so far as I can surmise, is actually putting off writer's block.

He often claims that his furiously hedonistic lifestyle is merely research for the dazzling and profound page turner he'll someday complete, but I think the truth is somewhat simpler. We travel in circles where it's extremely difficult *not* to be an artist working on a project. Tell people you're a weekend terrorist with a sideline in necrophilia and you hardly risk disapproval. But say you have no ambition to create Art, not even prose poems, not even *collages,* and you're treated like some bizarre unsentient life form, a thing to be pitied but shunned. So Gilbert sat down a few years back and began a novel. Now, this odious task out of the way, he can go to parties every night of the week and complain bitterly about how his social obligations keep him from his work. I tease him every chance I get in the hopes that he may yet surprise me with a few pages.

"Don't start again, Philip. Just because I don't rush to show you every page doesn't mean I'm not doing it."

"Okay. Moira, you'll be living with him. If you hear typing, call me."

"I write in longhand."

"Oh, champers!" cried Moira, for the waitress was approaching bearing an ice bucket and a stand to put it on.

All hopes for a three-way split were dashed by the sudden appearance of Vulpina. Her outfit this evening was among the more outré she'd ever devised. It consisted of immense brown jodhpurs, a sort of black lace mantilla and a skin-tight white silk tube top. The total effect suggested a teabag in mourning.

"Pina! You found us. We were so worried."

"I'm sorry, I was delayed. It could not be avoided," she said darkly. Then, managing the merest wisp of a smile, she murmured, "Hello, Gilbert. Philip."

"We just love what you're wearing! Is it new?"

Vulpina thought for a moment as if wondering whether to trust us with sensitive information, then broke down and confessed, "No it's old. I did not wear it for three years. Too many memories."

"Of what?"

"A Tuesday. Long ago."

"You're so svelte these days," commented Gilbert.

"But I'm not. Only today I ate pizza. And last night . . ." Again she paused, then whispered cryptically, ". . . other things. Many other things."

As you've probably surmised, Vulpina's main stock in pretense is this habit of always speaking as if it were midnight and she was standing on a railway platform in Zurich, fingering the blueprints under her trenchcoat while waiting for the Belgian with the carnation. She can imbue the most commonplace utterances with the sort of throbbing intensity one should only be allowed to employ when saying, "The tip is poisoned, use it if you must," or, "Silence, you fool— his men are everywhere." I realize this habit may sound quirky and amusing, but after a while you just want to hit her.

Gilbert glumly requested another glass for Vulpina. It arrived in short order and we toasted the happy couple.

"So, Pina's here now," said Gilbert to Moira. "What's this big news?"

"I have it right here, lambkins," said Moira and, reaching down under the table, produced her famous purse and opened it. She'd clearly been to a party earlier that evening because the smell of ripe brie amidst the combs and cosmetics was hard to miss. She wasted little time in finding the item and closing the clasp. It was a letter.

"It's from Mummy," she said. "You know, the Duchess of Dors—"

"Yes, I know."

"You have to hear this!" she said and, affecting a slight British accent, read us the letter.

" 'Darling Moira, I know we spoke only hours ago but I just had to write and let you know again how thrilled the duke and I are over your delightful news. Of course, it is a big step and we'd have liked a chance to meet the young man first'—she is *so* overprotective— 'but Gilbert sounds like a wonderful and industrious boy and we have every confidence that in choosing him you've exercised your usual superb judgment.' " This struck me as an odd thing to say to a girl who once dropped three grand on theme funerals but this was not, I felt, the moment to say so.

" 'As for the wedding I'm simply bursting with plans and can't wait to get stateside and discuss them with you and Gilbert. *Malheureuse-ment*, I shall be quite stranded here at Trebleclef'—that's the an-cestral home . . . *gorgeous*—'till November when the Little Chipperton Medieval Festival is finally over.' That is such a bore," sighed Moira. "Every year the poor darling has to run the whole thing. Give speeches, award all the prizes, and pick the Damsel of the Day. You wouldn't believe the politicking that goes on! She'd love to just tell the whole lot of them to fuck off but what can she do? She's the only duchess for miles and miles so she gets stuck with everything!"

"Heavy lies the head, huh?"

"You have no idea. But listen to this!" she said and resumed reading—" 'I've booked rooms at the Pierre for eight weeks starting Friday, November 21. I'd love to see you married there but I suspect, *hélas*, that the ballroom there will be too small for our purposes. What do you think of the Plaza?' "

"I think it's wunnerful, Momma!" cried Gilbert, who can drink anything but champagne.

" 'Please jot down any ideas you may have for the ceremony and reception and send them to me posthaste. And remember, dear, you're my only daughter so please don't allow thrift to inhibit your natural good taste.' "

She smiled a small tasteful smile and, refolding the letter, opened her bag to place it inside. And as she did, her mother's words hung over the table like a perfume so sweet not even the smell of rotting brie (commingled, one now discerned, with spinach puff pastries) could foul its bouquet.

"What a lovely woman," said Gilbert softly.

"She's always been so good to me," said Moira, sniffing. She dabbed her eye with a hanky and some salmon fell out of it.

"Quite a mother-in-law you're getting there, Gilbert!"

"Congratulations," said Vulpina, rising. "I vill design the gown."

Before anyone could thank her, she announced that she had to leave to see a client. And you just knew from the way she said it she'd be met at the corner by a black stretch limo containing the vice president, a sultry female demolitions expert and Mikhail Gorbachev's long-lost identical twin.

Left now to its own our little syndicate fell into a rapture of conspiratorial glee. Moira and Gilbert ordered another bottle and proposed toast after toast, each profuse in its praise of the other's beauty, wit and ingenuity. Eventually their giddy attentions turned to me and I found myself happily buried beneath a mudslide of unction. Clever Philip! Handsome Philip! Helpful Philip! The effect of all this on what remained of my mind is not hard to imagine. My attitude toward the plan underwent a change.

"An' I dunno what these peeploo say you look awfuler talk about. You look wunnful. Dozeny look wunnful?"

"Yes! He's getting so hunky! You've been working out, haven't you? I can tell."

"He looks—wuzza were?"

"Boyish."

"Rye! You look boish."

"And to look so hot and write the way he does! That's just unfair! You're unfair, Philip, that's what *you* are!"

I smiled in tacit agreement and wondered if anyone had ever been blessed with two friends even half so charming or perceptive as the pair who sat before me now. The mere sight of them, hunched now over the pocket calculator Moira never travels without, filled me with the warmest of sentiments. How radiant they looked! Gilbert with his great blond forelock and impish choirboy grin. And Moira—poor maligned Moira!—how she glowed with madonnalike warmth as her fingers danced over the keys. Had ever a couple looked so made for each other, so totally and unassailably plausible? Had ever a scheme been so clearly destined to be crowned with success?

We stumbled out onto Columbus Avenue, our hearts as high as our bill, and marched jubilantly uptown singing show tunes full voice, as happily blind to the future as we were to crosstown traffic.

Given my impetuous headlong stride and a tendency to close my eyes while sustaining high notes it was a miracle that I wasn't hit by a speeding taxi. Indeed, in light of what followed it was not only a miracle. It was a shame.

Four

I'm not usually susceptible to hangovers. On the other hand, I'm not immune to them either. Although the Hangover Fairy is fairly indulgent of my occasional excesses and given to sparing the rod, this is not the case in instances of brazen provocation. On the morning following our celebration at the Jaded Palate, any doubt I might have had as to whether or not a combination of burgundy, scotch, tequila, triple sec and champagne constitutes brazen provocation was swiftly erased. I lay in bed till noon listening to the bloodcurdling screams of the pigeons on my fire escape, the relentless timpani of my pulse and a somewhat softer popping sound. Probably my cells dividing.

Gilbert and Moira, whatever their own agonies that morning, wasted no time in getting the nuptial ball rolling. Gilbert left his West Ninety-third Street shoebox and moved into God's Country.

God's Country is the name by which Moira's friends, associates and victims refer to her apartment. Located on Central Park West and Eighty-third, it boasts four bedrooms, five baths, a dining room, a study, a laundry and a living room the size of a small prairie. It's owned by a dear old thing named Gloria Conkridge whose husband died some years ago and, as Moira puts it, "left her a little patent on something"; blood, one suspects. Gloria now resides in Palm Beach but maintains the apartment as a sort of museum to house all the memorabilia accumulated during her glory days as a New York society hostess. She visits once a year in the spring, staying for just one week of extravagant party-giving before staggering back to Florida and a rejuvenating regimen of sheep glands, grapefruit and gigolos.

Moira, in a deal of the sort only she can finagle, lives there rent-free the rest of the year. All she has to do in exchange is keep the mementos dusted and tend lovingly to Gloria's menagerie of forty pet dogs, cats and birds. Lest you leap to the conclusion that, by agreeing to care for these animals, Moira has taken on anything vaguely akin to a job, let me point out that they're all quite dead and stuffed by a taxidermist, who, judging from the eerily realistic poses he's captured, really knew his sawdust.

However questionable one might find Mrs. C's taste in hanging on so tenaciously to her departed chums, she at least had the decorum to keep them out of view in a little shrine behind the kitchen. Moira, in contrast, finds it amusing to pose them in various nooks where guests can come across them unexpectedly. The effect is not pleasing. The whole place looks like some awful Hammer Studios film, the finale of which would have them all springing to demonic life and devouring the promiscuous baby-sitter.

Gilbert, however, was not the least put off by this macabre touch in the decorating scheme. So thrilled was he by the improvement spacewise over his previous quarters he wouldn't have cared if Moira had filled the bedrooms with wax replicas of the Manson family. And not only did he now have ten times as much room to kick around in, but a nice little income as well. He'd sublet his own studio, for which he'd been paying $325, for a larcenous $800. Moira naturally insisted on half of his profit and Gilbert, by telling her he was only getting $450, managed to clear $412.50 a month.

I didn't see much of them for the next week or so. Holly Batterman had spread the word with his usual efficiency, as a result of which they were besieged with invitations from friends eager to see the romance for themselves and pass judgment on its authenticity.

My only conversation with them that first week occurred in Zabar's. I collided with them at the cheese counter where they were purchasing something green-flecked and ghastly to take to a dinner party at the playwright Marlowe Heppenstall's Barrow Street lair. They apologized for not having called, but things had been "justyouknowinsane."

They said they'd been out to Long Island for a fabulous dinner with Maddie and Tony Cellini, both of whom were charmed by their daughter-in-law to be. The Cellinis had also received a warm letter from the duchess. Her Grace had expressed once more her entirely baffling delight over the marriage, and invited them all to dine with her at the Pierre the night of her arrival.

My own chores as third member of the syndicate had begun the day after our celebration, the very moment I'd felt well enough to place the phone back on the hook. I received that day alone eleven phone calls from people who'd spoken to Holly and were, like him, eager to know who the lucky girl was. I can tell you with some authority that there are few worse fates that can befall a hungover eardrum than to have the words *"You're kidding!"* screamed into it by eleven homosexuals in the course of one afternoon.

The calls continued unabated for the rest of the week, by which point they were mostly repeats from people who'd seen Gilbert and Moira with their own eyes but remained skeptical. Many thought Gilbert was merely trying to attract attention by becoming engaged to a woman—and not just any woman either but the most spectacularly unlikely one he could find. Others maintained it was all a hoax he had devised for the sheer fun of pulling everyone's leg, as had been the case back in 1980 when for two months he had many of us convinced he was pining away for a handsome former lover who was one of the American hostages in Iran. I did my best to persuade one and all that I myself thought he was dead serious and that theirs would be a marriage of true minds, but these assertions fell on deaf ears. Many just assumed, correctly, that I was in on it.

My task wasn't made any easier by Gilbert's insistence on maintaining that his conversion to heterosexuality was exclusive and permanent. I told him that to say this was to place more of a strain on the credulity of his friends than was either desirable or necessary. There's a limit to what people will believe and, while small adaptations of one sort or another are common, complete overnight transformations are not. You'll believe that the lion will lie down with the lamb. You may even accept that they liked it so well they're considering a permanent arrangement. But if you're told the lamb now gets up every morning and kills a zebra for breakfast, you know you're being teased.

I made this argument to Gilbert, but he remained intransigent.

"No! I'm sorry, but no."

"Why not? Why can't you just tell people you've become bisexual?"

"Because I've already told them I've gone straight—that I doubt I was really ever gay to begin with."

"Oh, honey!"

"Well, that's what I've said. And you don't start out with one story then change it all around. It destroys your credibility."

"But I've told everyone and *no one* believes it!"

A pensive silence fell.

"What are they saying?"

"Well . . . for one thing they all bring up your past affairs. Face it, Gilbert, you haven't exactly been the soul of discretion."

He couldn't argue with that. I've known a number of people who've held the belief that love is merely a game, but Gilbert's the only man I know who seems to view it as a spectator sport. Do you remember that Paul Simon song from some years back, the one in which he stated that there are fifty ways to leave your lover? Well, to Gilbert there's only one: bring him to the largest party you can find, down seven scotches in an hour while growing increasingly maudlin, wait for a lull in the noise level, then hurl your drink in his face shouting, "It's finished, you hear me! *Finished!*" People will approach you and ask what's wrong. Tell them.

"Let's not forget," I said, "that you've had three affairs and three breakups in the last year alone. *No one* fails to mention this. What am I supposed to say?"

"Tell them it proves I'm straight! My affairs never lasted because I needed something I could only get from a woman."

"From *Moira*? Why can't we agree to say you're bisexual! You know they'll believe that."

"Of course they will," he said testily. "That's because being bisexual isn't a change at all. It's a phase. Honestly, you're so thick sometimes! Think—how many people have we known who've at one point or another decided they were suddenly bisexual?"

I considered it a moment and found to my surprise that I could immediately think of four. Gilbert pressed on.

"Blair Monroe did. So did Andy Pommerantz. Briefly! It happens all the time. Some silly queen has one little fling with a woman and decides he's now an official bisexual. Then he drives everyone up the wall talking about how much *richer* his life is now that he's one of the sensitive few who refuse to confine their love to just half the human race. 'Straight men just love women, gay men just love men but *I* love *everybody*, nyah, nyah, nyah!' And it always blows over! Six weeks later you run into him and he's with some cute guy and you say, '*So!* How's *Lisa*?' and he just wants to *kill* you!"

"Okay, so people may think it's only a phase. What's the difference?"

"The gifts, Philip! The gifts! Look at this from their perspective. You're going to a wedding and you're convinced the marriage is going to last as long as a Radio Shack battery—how much are you going to spend? Huh?"

"Don't you think you're taking this just a bit far?"

"No. Whatever anyone says you just keep insisting I'm really and truly straight. I was never gay, I was trendy. Okay? Stick to your guns!"

"They're your guns, Gilbert."

"Whosever. Just stick to 'em and sooner or later people will start to buy it."

People, however, did not.

At least not until mid-November when Gilbert and Moira, annoyed by my reports of widespread skepticism, took matters into their own hands.

Nancy Malone, an actress friend of ours, had recently won the uncoveted role of Marie Curie in Marlowe Heppenstall's musical bio, *Eureka, Baby!* Word had it that the show was off-Broadway's answer to Valium, but Nancy's a friend so we accepted her invitation to attend the opening and subsequent obsequies. Gilbert, of course, took Moira, who has long been a pal of the perpetrator's. (During her brief career as an actress she appeared in his short-lived musicalization of *The Bell Jar*.) I asked my friend and collaborator, the composer Claire Simmons. Claire has shared my warm feelings for Marlowe ever since our days with him in the BMI songwriter's workshop, where our candid critique of his *Bell Jar* musical (*Bong!*) led him to retaliate by demolishing everything we wrote for the next two years.

Following the show our foursome nipped down the street to Vanessa's and had a good giggle reviewing the low spots of the show. Even Moira joined in on our effort to find still more rhymes for radium than Marlowe had employed in the show's rousing finale. Our mood throughout was highly convivial.

So it surprised Claire and me to notice, soon after we'd arrived at the cast party, that Gilbert and Moira were engaged in some strange silent row.

"What's with those two?" hissed the ubiquitous Holly Batterman.

He motioned toward the other end of the room where Gilbert and Moira stood about six feet apart glaring at each other.

"You got me, Holly," I said. "I don't know a thing about it."

"Oh, sure, Blanche! Just like you didn't know he was getting married—then that very night you had drinks with him at the Riviera before going uptown to meet Moira and Vulpina at the Jaded Palate for margaritas and Veuve Clicquot!"

There are moments, I confess, when I worry what would happen if Holly ever decided to work for the Soviets.

"Holly, believe us," said Claire. "They were laughing and joking not—"

She stopped short. Holly was staring raptly over our shoulders. We turned to see that Gilbert and Moira were now standing close together. Gilbert, his face red with anger, was holding Moira's wrists in a tight grip, whispering what did not appear to be sweet nothings into her ear. Moira, whose features at the moment called to mind those of a kabuki lion, hissed something into his ear, bit the lobe, threw scotch on it, and fled the room.

Many of those present had seen this and those that missed it soon saw Holly's vividly mimed reenactment. From then on there was only one topic of conversation on everyone's lips: the Fate of the Marriage. The joyous pair refused to discuss it at all. I asked Gilbert myself but he only promised to talk at a more opportune moment.

Normally, of course, I'd have dragged him into the bathroom and pummeled it out of him if I'd had to, but my energies that night were focused on the show's costume designer, a strapping youth with broad shoulders and a habit of sucking ice cubes provocatively. However eager I was to get the scoop on the sudden rift I was more determined still not to leave this lad's side till I was sure at least one of us would wake up the next morning wondering where the hell he was.

But while I was learning more about bustles than the average boy wants to know, things on the battlefront were getting stranger and stranger. Moira, who hadn't cried in public since her baptism, suddenly burst into tears and ran sobbing from the room. About midnight I glanced into one of the bedrooms and saw her sitting on the edge of the bed with Claire. She was sobbing quietly with her head on Claire's shoulder and Claire was murmuring "There there"s, looking sympathetic and utterly confused. Claire later joined me and Edith Head for a bit and we asked what she'd managed to learn.

"Not much, I'm afraid. She said it was too painful to talk about, she just wanted to be held. Then she kept crying and saying what a

fool she'd been. I don't know what happened but I've never seen
Moira so upset. I feel awful for her."

Not long after that Gilbert was seen in the kitchen making drunken
passes at the two actresses who'd played the roles of "Marie's Courage"
and "Marie's Doubt" (for it was that kind of a musical).

The exact sequence of events following this has been lost in a
morass of conflicting reports but there is one thing on which all who
were present later agreed.

At two a.m. or so people noticed that neither Moira nor Gilbert
was anywhere to be seen. It was assumed that they'd left quietly and
separately. But this assumption was proved incorrect when Jimmy
Loftus, entering Marlowe's bedroom to retrieve his coat, found the
two of them lying on top of it, half-naked and necking passionately.
Jimmy bolted from the room and with the fervor of a latter-day Paul
Revere began telling everyone what he'd seen. About a dozen revelers,
possessed of both swift feet and a devastating lack of tact, stampeded
to see for themselves. They were greeted by the sight of the happily
reconciled pair struggling into their clothes and blushing up a storm.
They emerged grinning sheepishly, apologized to Marlowe and disappeared, arm in arm, into the night.

I didn't witness this as I was in the kitchen learning all about
Velcro, but those who saw it assured me that the devotion that shone
in their eyes was indisputably authentic. These were the same people
who had until then been unwavering in their skepticism. But now
they busily informed friends who'd not been on hand that everything
was true. They'd seen it with their own eyes. And those who continued
to doubt Gilbert's sincerity did so merely because they Hadn't Been
There.

Gilbert phoned me the next morning to crow long and loudly about
the ingenuity he and Moira had displayed in bringing people around
in so devious a fashion.

"Wasn't it just perfect!"

"Sorry, I missed it."

"Oh, that's right. You were busy with Betsy Ross. You didn't waste
much time on him I hope?"

"Three hours. It turns out all the time he was stringing me along
he was just waiting for this hunky old friend of his named—"

"Barclay, yes, I know. I kept meaning to clue you in but I never
got around to it. Oh, I wish you'd seen our exit. We were just brilliant!

People were smiling at us and going 'Awwwwwww!' They bought it, they really did!"

"I'm so glad for you."

"Well me, too! We're in the clear now! I just know it's all smooth sailing from here on in."

"I hope so."

"I know so! Trust me, sweetie, our problems are over!"

Five

Our problems had not, of course, even started. But start they did on November 19, a rainy Wednesday just two days before the scheduled arrival of Her Grace, the Duchess of Dorsetshire.

Gilbert, Moira and I were sitting around the dining table at God's Country trying to be diplomatic with Vulpina who was showing us her sketches for Moira's wedding gown. Even Moira, usually Vulpina's most outspoken apologist, had been leery of accepting her generous offer to create gowns for the bridal party. Gilbert and I had urged her to decline politely, pointing out that there are only a few acceptable approaches to bridal design and that Pina's specialty, the attention-starved psychotic look, is not among them. Moira conceded this but felt that, given the wide consensus on the good taste of respecting tradition in these matters, surely even Vulpina would restrain any tendency toward iconoclasm.

Vulpina, however, had done no such thing, choosing instead to pull out all the stops and show the SoHo design gang just what she could accomplish when she really spit on her hands and got down to it. I lack the sartorial vocabulary to describe the result but perhaps you'll get the idea if I say that had it been Moira's intention to marry not Gilbert but instead, say, Destructo the Visigoth, this little dress would have been just the ticket.

"Oh, Pina!" said Moira at length. "It's so . . . *active*! I mean, wedding gowns are usually, you know, very passive. But this is so . . . so energized! I don't know if I can live up to it! What do you think, Gilleycakes?"

"I love it. But if *you* think it's maybe a little—"

"No! I love it, really I do! It's so primal!"

A long minute ticked by.

"Then I may begin constructing it immediately?" asked Vulpina.

"Of course," said Moira, ". . . the minute Mum gives the okay."

Vulpina arched her back in displeased surprise like a cobra that sees it's been trying to hypnotize a rubber mongoose.

"It is for *her* to decide?"

"I know it sounds incredibly old-fashioned but I did promise Mummy approval of *all* the details. Don't worry though, I'm sure she'll love this."

"I trust there will not be much delay," sniffed Pina. "I'll barely have time as it is. Locating the materials could take weeks."

"I can imagine!" said Moira, eyeing the sketch. "All those wolverines! Well, don't you worry, love, I won't waste a minute getting the verdict!"

Vulpina regarded her with narrowed eyes, then, turning away, picked up her portfolio.

"Now the bridesmaids—"

The phone rang. Gilbert and Moira nearly knocked each other over traversing the room to reach it. Gilbert got there first and, after listening a moment, turned to us and excitedly announced it was a transatlantic call.

"I'm not here," said Pina in the annoyed tone of a girl who wishes she'd never agreed to safeguard the darn microfilm in the first place.

"Oh, Pina," giggled Moira, "it's not for you. It must be Mummy!"

She reached for the phone but Gilbert hung on to it, covering the mouthpiece with one hand.

"Moy, put the phone on the speaker system! Philip *has* to hear her!" He turned to me and said, "She's a hoot!"

Moira hissed "No" and grabbed for the phone but Gilbert held fast till she groaned and, crossing to the sideboard, flicked a switch on the answering machine. Immediately the nasal voice of a transatlantic operator filled the room.

"Is innyone on the lion, please?"

Moira grabbed the phone from Gilbert.

"Yes, I'm here! Who is it?"

"I have a person-to-person call for Miss Moira Finch."

"This is she."

"Thenk you. You may proceed with your call."

"Moira?"

"Mummee!"

"I'm so glad I got you and not your dreadfully adolescent message."

The voice had an odd buttery rasp to it that no fan of *Gigi* or *A Little Night Music* could fail to recognize.

"My God!" I whispered to Gilbert. "She sounds exactly like Hermione Gingold!"

"I know!"

"But I thought she was born in America."

"She was—in *Pittsburgh*! That's what's so funny about it!"

"Listen, dear," wheezed the duchess. "I have the most dreadful news."

"Oh no!" said Moira, sitting. "It's not the duke, is it?"

"Would that it were! It's me, darling. I had a terrible accident and I'm lying flat on my back."

"What happened!"

"Queen Mab threw me into a ditch."

"She did! But she's always been such a sweet horse!"

"I know, dear. But some horrible little boy at the Medieval Festival threw a jousting lance at her and she went absolutely wild. It was horrid! She trampled a nine-year-old boy to death!"

"Serves the little hoodlum right!"

"Don't say that, dear. It wasn't the same one."

"Sorry, Mum. Are you all right?"

"Of course I'm not all right! I was hurled into a ditch! They tell me for the next three months I'm not allowed to do anything but lie here and eat all the fattening sweets my friends have been spiteful enough to send me."

"Mummy! I could cry!"

"And I so wanted to be thin for your wedding! I wanted people to look at me and say, 'Is that the mother or her sister?' Now they'll just say, 'My God—who's the dirigible in peach silk?' I wish I were dead!"

"Well, when can you get here?"

"I told you. Between my shoulder and my hip I'm not permitted to move for three months."

"Three months! Can't you recuperate over here?"

"No. I told Nigel I wanted to sail over in a week or so and then have the Pierre install a hospital bed. But he just wouldn't have it."

"He's so pigheaded! Are you in agony?"

"I was, but they've given me some lovely drugs and I'm much

better. I'm just upset I won't be there to get my nose into things. Then there's Gilbert, of course. I was so looking forward to meeting him! Couldn't you two fly over here for the holidays?"

Moira looked to Gilbert who shook his head madly then added some violent flailing lest his point be mistaken.

"Gosh, I don't think so. He's so busy with his novel."

"Oh, blast," sighed Mummy. "I'm sure he's wonderful as you say but I do wish I could meet him a bit sooner than it seems I'm going to."

"So do I, Mummy. I need you here! I don't know where to begin!"

"Nonsense. If you need me I'm only a phone call away. You'd be surprised how much I can accomplish with a few well-placed calls. Why, only yesterday I made arrangements for your wedding gown."

"My gown?" said Moira, casting a nervous glance in Pina's direction.

"Yes. Lady Pym's flying to California next week to stay with Jimmy Galanos. He owes her a favor and she owes me a dozen so it's good as done."

"That was very sweet of you, Mummy. But I've already taken care of the gown."

"*Have* you?" asked the duchess, with a throatful of dry ice. "And who, pray tell, is designing it?"

"A friend."

"A friend? Oh, Moira, *please* tell me it's not that horrid Vampira woman who made the monstrosity you wore to the Smythe-Northropson's party last time you were here!"

Moira smiled weakly at the three of us. I gazed over at Vulpina. Her face was completely expressionless as it always is when she's truly livid.

"*Mo-therrr!* She's my dearest friend—and a brilliant designer."

"Don't tell me such rot—I remember that dress far too well. It was mauve with glass eyes on it! If you think I'm about to spend a small fortune for the privilege of seeing my only daughter march down the aisle of St. Patrick's Cathedral looking like an opium dream you are tragically mistaken!"

Things continued in this sticky manner for some minutes. Moira squirmed, Gilbert and I suppressed giggles and Pina did her impression of an Easter Island stone deity. Moira attempted to mollify all parties by telling the duchess that Vulpina was so eclectic a designer that she could function brilliantly within any stylistic limitations imposed upon her. Eventually the duchess relented so far as to withhold judgment until Moira had mailed her some sketches.

"Listen, Mummy, I was just on my way out when you called, so—"

"I can take a hint, precious. Just one more thing."

"What?"

"Aren't you curious about how this is all to be paid for with me and my magic checkbook trapped over here?"

"Oh. I hadn't thought of that. Well—why don't you just send me a check large enough to cover whatever might come up?"

"Inadvisable, dear."

"Why?"

"You know what a tightwad Nigel is. Any check I sent for a large amount would have to be co-signed by him. And it wouldn't matter how frugal it was. He'd insist it was too much."

"What are you saying, Mummy?"

"I'm just trying to explain how your stepfather has to be handled. You see, Nigel doesn't mind spending money as long as he doesn't *know* he's spending it. The best way to get him to pay for something is to make it a fait accompli. He may complain, but he'll pay. So dear, you pay for everything yourself, then give me the receipts— whatever you do, *save* the receipts!—then I'll give them to Nigel, and he'll grumble a bit then give you a nice big check to cover it all. Believe me, it will save quite a few headaches."

From the look on Moira's face she was not in agreement regarding the scheme's analgesic advantages.

"But, how am *I* supposed to pay for things? This wedding will cost thousands and thousands of dollars! I don't have that kind of money."

"Yes, you do. In your trust fund."

"But, Mummy! You told me I'm not allowed to *touch* that money."

"Yes. And now I'm telling you you are. I'll send your trust officer a letter telling him to liquidate everything. That comes to about two hundred thousand. He'll open you a checking account."

"You want to liquidate my fund! How can you do that—I mean, I'm living on the interest."

"Well, you can live off the money itself just as easily!"

"But wouldn't it be much simpler if I just bought what I had to over here and had everyone send the bills over there?"

"Are you *mad*! Have you any idea what utter hell my life would be with a new bill coming in every day and Nigel making a great bloody fuss about it? Not a day would pass without him bursting into my sickroom screaming 'Look what came in! Does that girl think I'm made of money!' "

"He can't be as bad as all that!"

"He's worse! And I'm suffering enough as it is. I don't mind having *one* fight about the money this will cost but I'm not going to have one every day! There are limits to my affection for you. You just call Winslow at the bank next week. By then he'll have heard from me. Isn't that simpler?"

"Oh, much. Well, I have to run. I hope you feel better."

"So do I. Give my best to Gilbert."

"I will. I love you, Mummy."

"I love you too, dear. Sporadically."

And with that she was gone.

None of us said anything for a moment because none of us knew where to begin. Should we try to soothe Vulpina's bruised ego? Should we ask Moira to explain just why she'd kept secret the existence of a two-hundred-thousand-dollar trust fund? Or should we, more to the point, ask her why she was now staring down at her stomach as if she could see protruding from it the bloodstained handle of a butcher's knife. As it's the third of these issues which most concerns the outcome of our saga, I will dispense quickly with the first two.

Vulpina's wrath was easily assuaged. We told her she had every right to withdraw her offer rather than pander to so despotic a philistine as the duchess. But what would this accomplish beyond throwing Moira into the hands of some derivative bourgeois lacemonger? Wouldn't it be more satisfying to stay on and design a gown which would, to the unschooled eye, seem absolutely conventional, but which a discerning few would recognize as a wickedly subtle parody of the whole phallocratic bridal tradition? Pina nodded sagely at this suggestion and departed, muttering something about having to reach a pay phone and hoping it wasn't too late.

The moment Vulpina was gone Gilbert turned and faced Moira.

"You've got a fucking two-hundred-thousand-dollar trust fund!"

"Yes," she replied curtly, "what about it?"

"You might have mentioned it!"

"Did you ask?"

"How long have you had that little pile tucked away?"

"I don't see that it's any of your business. Now, if you two will excuse me I'm going to lie down. I have a splitting headache."

She turned and walked quickly out of the room.

"I don't get it," said Gilbert. "Why would she be *secretive* about a trust fund? I mean, she's always bragging about the duchess. You'd think she'd have rubbed our faces in it."

I agreed that Moira was not one to miss a chance to flaunt status symbols and that her secrecy regarding the trust was, as such, baffling.

After some reflection, though, it began to seem less so. Moira may be New York's most indefatigable social climber but she's also its biggest sponge. Wide knowledge of the fund would have done much to cramp her style. A girl known to have two hundred grand in the bank is not a girl to whom any starving author is going to loan twenty dollars "just until Friday."

Which left only the third question: Why was Moira so distressed by Mummy's insistence that she liquidate the fund?

"Christ," said Gilbert. "You know Moy—she's probably been itching to get her hands on that money from the minute the fund was set up."

"Oh, God."

"What?"

"What if she did?"

"Did what?"

"Got her hands on it! Maybe that's what's wrong. Mummy's asking her to spend money she's already gone through."

Gilbert apparently concurred as to the probability of this scenario, for he rose in silent fury, seized a stuffed Lhasa apso and drop-kicked it into the next room.

"Hold on!" I said. "We don't *know* that's what she did! I mean, how could *anyone* do it? The risk! The legal obstacles! You'd have to be . . ."

"Moira?" offered Gilbert, and within a moment we were standing at the doorway to her bedroom demanding she unlock the door.

"Go away!"

"This trust fund—you ripped it off, didn't you!"

The door opened. Moira stood there in a bathrobe, a towel knotted around her head.

"I don't have the vaguest idea what you're talking about."

"No?" he said. "Then why were you trying so hard to get your mom to pay for the wedding another way?"

Moira stared at him tight-lipped then, turning away, slumped back to the bed and sat. She pulled a pink cigarette from an ashtray and puffed moodily.

"Moira," I asked gently, "just tell us—is there any left at all?"

She burst into tears and buried her face in the pillows.

"Cut the boo hoo shit," snarled Gilbert. "You just call Mummy back and tell her you'll need more money!"

"I *can't*, you idiot!" she cried, rising. "If I do she'll know the trust is gone! I can't ever let her know I spent that money!"

"Well, brilliant, don't you think she's going to figure it out when she gets here and sees the reception's at fucking Burger King!"

"Oh, Philip!" she cried, hurling her arms about me and sobbing onto my sweater. "Was he this mean to you when you two were together?"

Not having realized the story of our little romance had reached a broad audience I could only stammer incoherently till she looked up from my chest and said, "But of course he was—he gave you crabs!"

"You tactless bitch!" said Gilbert.

"Moira," I said, "you really spent *all* of the money? Two hundred thousand dollars?"

"Well," she sniffed, "it's not as if I squandered it all on *la dolce vita*!"

"Oh, *no*!" sneered Gilbert.

"Sure, maybe a few thousand, forty or fifty. But the rest I invested. I thought I was going to make a *fortune* with that money! Then everything came crashing down and I was left completely penniless, and I don't get any sympathy from either one of you!"

"Look," hissed Gilbert sympathetically, "why don't you just call Mummy right now and tell her about the money? The sooner you get it over with the longer she'll have to cool down before the wedding."

"Gilbert, you are such a naïf! You heard her just now—she's still beating me over the head with dresses I wore two years ago. How soon do you think she's going to cool down over two hundred thousand dollars? She won't even *come* to the wedding, never mind give me anything!"

I glanced at Gilbert. It was clear that the prospect of entering into a marriage of convenience with Moira in which he would be the sole generator of income they'd agreed to split down the middle did not sit well with him.

"Moira," I asked, "how did you even manage to do this? And how have you managed to keep it from her? If she set the fund up doesn't she keep tabs on it?"

"Oh that," she said airily. "That's all taken care of by my trust administrator, Winslow. Winslow sends her a nice little statement every month saying it's all still there and I got my monthly interest check."

I stared, aghast.

"This man works in a *bank*?"

"Well, of course."

"And he's helping you defraud your mother?"

"Well, he hasn't got much choice!" said Moira, smiling girlishly. "He's the one who helped me get the money in the first place. See, about two years ago he'd written a play about these gay people who go to Guyana with Jim Jones. No one would touch it, but I thought it was fabulous and I told him I'd put up the money for a little showcase if he'd just fix it so I could get into my trust without Mum finding out."

"But, my God—didn't he realize what trouble he'd be in if she ever did find out?"

"Yes, he was concerned. He's that type, you know. High strung. But I told him a little white lie about Mummy having inoperable bone cancer and since control of the fund would revert to me when she died there wouldn't be any trouble. So, he got me the money. Then the show closed in New Mexico. And Mum's still in remission. He's been very sweet about sending her the statements."

"Jesus, Moy!" said Gilbert. "Is there anything you won't stoop to?"

"Oh please! Talk about the pot and the kettle!"

They continued in this vein for some time and I was about to tiptoe away from the wreckage when an unhappy thought struck me. If a way wasn't found out of this mess then the syndicate's income would be cut in half. Such a drastic reduction in the profit margin would certainly lead Gilbert to make a cold-eyed reappraisal of the entire budget, with particular scrutiny given to such items as perks for the best man. I could hear his arguments already: "Did Shakespeare have a computer? Did Chekhov?"

"Enough!" I shouted, interrupting a comment Gilbert was making about Moira's hair. "The question is, how do we keep Mummy from finding out about the fund and at the same time get *her* to pay for the wedding?"

"Well, it's obvious, isn't it?" sighed Moira. "We just get the money from somewhere else. Then when Mummy reimburses me for what 'I' spent, we reimburse whomever."

"So," Gilbert concluded, "all we gotta do is find someone willing to loan you the money."

Silence fell as we pondered our circles of acquaintance, searching for someone possessed of both the vast wealth and profound stupidity prerequisite to granting a loan of this size to Moira. The silence continued for long minutes, such people being neither plentiful nor, as a rule, unsupervised. At length, though, Moira brightened and said: "Of course! It's so simple—Winslow! I'll just throw it all in his lap!"

"You think he'd be willing to help?"

"Well I should think so! If Mummy finds out about our little shenanigans I may be in the dog house, but Winnie! He'll really have his fanny in the Cuisinart!"

"Does he have that kind of money to lend?" asked Gilbert.

"No, but he'll know where to find it. God, I should have phoned him before I even told you about it. I could have spared myself a lot of abuse."

"And you could have spared me a goddamn heart attack!" said Gilbert.

Moira, deciding a little rapprochement was in the best interest of the syndicate, fixed Gilbert with that same lost penitent look which has, over the years, melted the hearts of so many store detectives.

"Oh Gilley, you're not really mad at me, are you? I mean, you don't *hate* me? I couldn't bear for us to be married if I thought your feelings toward me were—"

"Yadda, yadda, yadda! Just get your bloodhound of a mother off the scent and make sure she gives us a bundle and I'll love you till the day we divorce."

"Oh, you're so sweet when you want to be! Say—I have just the best idea! Let's all go grab dinner at Burma Burma then dance it off at the Abbatoir."

"You think we can get in?" asked Gilbert eagerly.

"Pina gave me passes! Whaddaya say? Dinner's on me!"

While the phrase *dinner's on me* is one to which I usually respond with Pavlovian swiftness, I felt in this case that celebration was not only premature but counterproductive. This was, you'll recall, just two days before the duchess had been due to arrive, and Maddie had invited us all to lunch the next afternoon to plan her reception.

According to Gilbert, Maddie had wanted to get started with everything the very moment she'd heard the joyous news. The only thing that had kept her from doing so was her knowledge that traditionally the bride's family, in addition to footing the bills, supervises all planning and preparation. Now, with the duchess laid up, Maddie would waste no time in appointing herself surrogate and storming Fifth Avenue with her platinum card clenched between her teeth. How could we let this happen before we even knew how Maddie would be reimbursed?

"I'd love to party, too, but don't you think we should prepare a little? Call Winslow? Give him time to work something out?"

"For God's sake, Philip, we're not meeting Maddie till one o'clock. Winslow's at the bank every day at nine. I'll have plenty of time!"

"I've been dying to go to that club!" said Gilbert.

"You're such a worry wart!"

"It's been *days* since I've gone dancing!"

"Trust me! Winslow's brilliant!"

"What should I wear?"

"He'll think of something!"

He did.

Six

Gilbert glanced at his watch again.

"I'll kill her."

"Calm down."

"Well, how's it going to look! Mom'll be here any minute . . . 'Gilbert, where's Moira?' 'Oh, gosh, Mom, she's at the bank, black-mailing her corrupt gay trust officer and you know how long *that* can take!' "

We were nursing light beers in the bar of Maddie's favorite restaurant, Trader Vic's. We'd been here since twelve-thirty, the hour at which Moira had promised to meet us for a pre-Maddie debriefing on Winslow's plan of attack. Hopes that such a debriefing might yet occur were remote, and Gilbert's feelings toward Moira had grown darker than the bar itself. Not that I blamed him for being in a surly mood. Just twelve hours earlier he'd drained the bitter cup and the aftertaste still lingered.

During our celebration at the Abbatoir, our table had been visited by Erhart Lund. Erhart is an incredibly handsome blond model within whose pants Gilbert had for years campaigned to establish a beach-head. Erhart informed us that he'd broken up with his lover, then proceeded to make it abundantly clear through both word and gesture that any assault Gilbert might now care to launch would meet with swift and unconditional surrender. However, the immediate presence not only of Moira but of Billy Tengrette and Fay ("Marie's Courage") Milton, two of Holly's most cherished informants, left Gilbert with no choice but to give Erhart the cold shoulder, a mere fraction of what he'd have preferred to offer.

"Lighten up, Gilbert. I still say you're making a mountain out of—"

"Erhart Lund! Erhart Lund had his tongue in my ear and I had to sit there pretending to be *annoyed* while holding hands with that controlled substance I'm engaged to until he——! Well it's about time!"

I turned and there was Moira standing at the entrance to the bar adjusting her eyes to the gloom. She was wearing one of Vulpina's creations, a gaudy orange number with huge black polka dots and a tattered hemline.

"Oh, God! She looks like Wilma Flintstone!"

She spotted us and hurried to the table. Our hopes for a conference on the trust-fund conundrum were immediately laid to rest by the arrival, right on Moira's heels, of Maddie Cellini.

She sauntered in, spotted us immediately and waved as ebulliently as a shipwrecked islander greeting a rescue party. She wore a low-cut, rather festive black dress with a matching hat and veil. She started for our table but was intercepted by the hostess who embraced her as though they were not only the oldest and dearest of friends but had each till this moment assumed the other to be dead.

"Where the hell were you!" hissed Gilbert to Moira.

"Where the hell do you think I was?" said Moira, beaming and waving back at Maddie. "I was with Winslow."

"Did he have any ideas?" I asked.

"Yes! It's all taken care of. I love your mother's dress."

"And just *how* the fuck is— Hi Mom!"

"Hi, kids! Don't you two look wonderful! I was just telling Kungshe about you. I said, 'Can't you just tell they're in love?' and she said yes, she could. Philip, honey! Mwah! It's been ages but you look just as handsome as ever! It's a wonder some nice girl hasn't snapped you up, too! Or has one?"

"Not yet!"

"Too bad. You be patient, dear. How's your writing going?"

"Great!" I lied.

"How wonderful! I wish Gilbert here would get on the stick and finish his book. I have dozens of friends who can't wait to read it."

"Young friends, I hope."

"Mrs. Cellini!" gushed a sarong-clad waitress materializing by our side.

"Lelani! How nice to see you! How's your little boy?"

"He be six years old next week!"

"Well, you tell him happy birthday for me! We're here for lunch, hon, but I think we'll have us a nice cozy drink in the bar first. Just bring me something with a gardenia. How about you youngsters? Oh my goodness, boys! You can't drink beers at the Trader's! Not when there are so many more fun things you could have! Let me order, okay?"

We nodded in cheerful assent and she asked for a couple of Stinkers.

"And you, Moira, what'll you have, dear? And don't tell me Perrier! This is a party, you hear!"

"Whatever you're having will be fine with me, Momma Cellini."

Lelani departed but not before Maddie had introduced us all and volunteered the information that Moira's mother was, could you believe it, a real live duchess, which had to be the first time in Moira's life anyone had beaten her in the race to convey this to an uninterested stranger.

"I'm so sorry I came in this gloomy dress but I just couldn't help it. I had a funeral this morning and there wasn't time to run home and change."

"Another one?" asked Gilbert.

"Yes!" said Maddie, her eyes widening. "Isn't it amazing! I don't know what it is but ever since I married Mr. Cellini I go to more funerals!"

"Oh?" I asked.

"Yes! And always on his side of the family. I swear, Philip, they are the most accident-prone people in the whole country! There are some can't even operate a car without driving it off a cliff! This fella today, Joey Sartucci—very sweet man, cousin of Tony's—would you believe he drowned in a bowl of soup? I said to Tony, 'Tony, how could such a thing happen!' Tony said he fainted while he was eating his lunch and by the time his wife got home it was too late—the minestrone had gone right into his lungs! It was awful hard on her coming only six months after her brother Frank got run over by that runaway cement mixer. And just two weeks ago there was Tony's poor dead brother's oldest boy, Robby!"

"Robby died?" asked Gilbert, scanning the horizon for our drinks.

"Well, he might as well have!" said Maddie. "No one can *find* him! I saw his mother at the funeral. The woman's a wreck!"

"Uh, tell me, Maddie," I asked, trying to sound as casual as possible, "what business is Mr. Cellini in?"

"Tony? Oh, he's an entrepreneur. I must say the money's awful good but I wish the hours were more regular. As it is now he gets phone calls at three and four o'clock in the morning and the poor thing has to get dressed right that minute and run to some warehouse. 'Tony,' I say to him, 'for God's sake, you're the big cheese, can't you make someone else go!' But he always says no, it wouldn't be responsible. He's very responsible, Tony is, and very bright, too. All his relatives give him their money to invest because he can always tell just which stock is going to go up real quick. It's a gift he has. Oh, look! Here come our drinks! Aren't they beautiful! Thank you so much, Lelani! Oh, Gilbert, Moira, guess who says hi?"

"Who?"

"Freddy Bombelli!"

Moira looked puzzled briefly, then her eyes lit up in recollection of the man's age and economic status.

"Freddy! He's that rich that *sweet* old man we met at the wedding!"

"I saw him at the funeral. Isn't he something? Eighty-six years old and never misses a burial! Anyway, he sends you both his regards."

"Well, how *nice!*" said Moira, and if we'd been in a cartoon her head would have turned into a cash register, the drawer sliding out of her mouth with a *ching!* as big dollar signs popped in her eyes.

She asked Maddie to convey her warm regards to the old gentleman and Maddie said she could convey them herself at her annual Christmas bash on December 12. We were all cordially invited.

Maddie toddled off to ask the bartender how his divorce was going and I clutched Gilbert's wrist, wondering which of a thousand questions to ask first. Before I could decide, though, he turned to Moira with a few of his own.

"*Well?*"

"Well what?"

"What did Winslow say!"

"I told you—it's all taken care of," she said and giggled. "Winslow had the most fabulous idea! Take it from me, we're sitting even prettier than we were before."

"I'm sorry to butt in here, Gilbert, but how much do you really know about these people?"

"What people?"

"The Cellinis!"

"What about them?"

"Well, c'mon! Don't the things Maddie's been saying kind of suggest something about their line of work?"

"Philip!" said Gilbert, his lips blossoming into an incredulous smirk, "are you saying you think my mom is married to some . . . some *mobster!*"

"It's not funny!"

"Not funny? It's a hoot! Do you believe him!" he asked Moira.

"C'mon, Moira, you heard her, too. Runaway cement mixers, people disappearing . . . What do you think?"

"Dear Philip," she said drily, "you must stop reading so much Elmore Leonard. Why, you haven't even met the Cellinis! I have and I can tell you they are some of the warmest, most civilized people I've ever known."

Gilbert echoed the sentiment and before I could argue any further Maddie returned. I was annoyed but not really alarmed, as the dispute seemed purely academic. If Gilbert and Moira chose to believe Tony's family was one hundred percent thug-free, despite compelling evidence that it's a rare Cellini who departs this life unassisted, that was their right. A naïve conclusion, to be sure, but was there any real harm in it?

Yes, as it turned out. Buckets.

Upon her return Maddie ordered a second round and said how much she was looking forward to meeting the duchess the next day. Moira, smiling bravely, broke the sad news about the duchess's riding accident. Maddie, gasping and clucking, offered Moira her deepest sympathy, adding that, if it were any consolation, it sounded to her like "just about the classiest accident anyone's ever had." She assured Moira she'd be delighted to assist with any details the incapacitated duchess would now be unable to see to and Moira, brushing aside a tear, accepted the offer. Then, in a maneuver completely unforeseen by Gilbert and me, she departed violently from the script, revealing the exact scope and nature of Winslow's plan.

"Gosh, Momma Cellini," she said, lowering her gaze, "there is one little thing I suppose we should discuss."

"What's that, dear?"

"Well . . . oh gosh! I was going to leave all this to Mummy. She has this absolutely divine sense of tact. Me, I never know how to put things."

Maddie patted her hand and spoke in a gentle nunlike tone. "Spit it out, honey."

"Well, you see, Mum is proud, very proud—and very determined to do things the traditional way. So she absolutely insists that she and the duke pay for the wedding. Everything."

Moira paused.

"And?" prompted Maddie.

"I just hope you understand it will have to be a very small wedding."

"How small, dear?"

"Oh, just the immediate families, I guess, and a few close relatives and friends. Best man, of course," she said gesturing toward me, "and I'll have my friend Pina as Maid of Honor. But no bridesmaids or ushers. Just a small quiet affair in the best affordable taste."

"Moira, dear," said Maddie slowly, "I'm assuming the problem here—and you stop me if I'm putting my foot in anything—is money troubles."

Moira nodded tragically.

"When Mummy married the duke she knew she wasn't getting as much as people thought she was. Just a title, Trebleclef, and the man she loved. You know how the taxes are over there."

"No, how are they?"

"Oh they're criminal! And what with estate duties, and this special Duke Tax, there's never much to spare at all. Oh, they get *by*. They open the house to tourists and that brings a little in. Though, last year they were reduced to renting Trebleclef to dreadful people who filmed a horror movie in it. Did you see *The Thirsty*?"

Maddie shook her head and clucked sympathetically.

"Anyway, even with all that, they were determined to make it a big wedding, no matter how many jewels had to be sold. But then came this accident and . . ." She paused a moment as though struggling to hold back an impending torrent of tears. "Oh, she's *okay*, really she is! She'll walk again. With a cane. But the treatment, you see, it's the best money can buy. The duke insisted. So, we had a talk about the wedding and the duke and I agreed it would have to be small. Mummy was furious! 'How will it look!' she kept saying. But we finally convinced her her spine just had to come first and she agreed that a small wedding was for the best. I'm so sorry to bring all this up at such a festive luncheon. But I did think it had to be said right at the beginning so there wouldn't be any misunderstandings."

I'd seen Moira's performances before, and with the exception of those actually given on a stage, they'd all been very professional. This latest piece of work, though, transcended the lot. The warmth, the sadness and filial devotion all seemed so genuine, so sincere. It was terrifying.

Maddie wiped her eyes with a cocktail napkin and Gilbert took the opportunity to fix Moira with a stare of bug-eyed fury.

"I'm glad you told me this," said Maddie. "Now, honey, you'll forgive me for some plain speaking but all the tact I've got you could stuff in an olive and still have room for the pimento."

She took Moira's hands in her own and smiled beatifically.

"All I have is one son. I always wanted to have a daughter, too, but after a while I got over the hump, and I knew then the only daughter I'd ever have would be the girl Gilbert decided to marry—if he ever did, which I used to worry about on account of he was shy. So, I've been waiting for Gilbert's wedding for years and years. And it'd just about kill me not to be able to share it with all my old friends and my new family. Now, darling, you said yourself your mother was all in favor of a big wedding before that lousy horse knocked her silly. So, if a big wedding's what your people want, and it's what our people want, too, what difference does it make who pays for it?"

Moira opened her mouth to protest but Maddie held up a hand and plowed sweetly on.

"Yes, dear, I know what you're going to say, and it's just *dumb*. Sure your mother's a proud lady and sure she'd rather follow tradition! But Moira, honey, the traditions to worry about are the fun ones, not the who-pays-for-what ones! Listen, I got an idea—why don't I just fly over there tomorrow and have a nice little heart-to-heart—?"

"No! You mustn't do that! She'd hate it!"

Maddie stared bewildered.

"I mean, it's not *you*, Momma Cellini! She doesn't want to see anyone! Not until after the cosmetic surgery!"

"The accident was that bad?"

"Yes! When she fell her face hit a flagstone. She bit her own lip off."

"The poor *thing*!"

"Oh, they sewed it back on. But between that scar and all the other facial bruises and the broken nose she's not looking her best. And, just between us, Mother is terribly vain."

"Well, who isn't?"

"She'd feel wretched if you saw her for the first time looking like that."

"Well, I don't blame her! Not one bit. I'll just call her on the phone."

"She can't talk! She's not allowed to move her mouth until her doctors are sure the lip won't be rejected."

"How *awful* for her! Gilbert, are you all right? Quick, Philip, pound him on the back a few times."

"Are you okay, love?" asked Moira.

"I'm fine, dear. I must have choked on something."

"Poor lamb!"

"I'll tell you what then," said Maddie. "Why don't I just write her a nice long letter?"

"That really is very thoughtful of you, but I just know however tactfully you make the offer she's still going to be very upset. Oh, she may accept eventually, but she's going to feel embarrassed. I know it's silly but that's just the way she is."

"Proud," said Maddie, nodding sagely.

"And the doctors did say she should avoid any emotional stress whatsoever for the first six weeks of her recovery."

"Six weeks! Well, honey we can't wait that long to get started. There's too much that has to be done!"

They mulled it over and finally arrived at this accommodation: Maddie would go discreetly forward with some preliminary expenditures and then, at some point in January, Moira would gently break the news to poor Mother that the Cellinis had insisted on shouldering the expense of a larger wedding and hoped she would not take offense at their presumption.

"You've been so understanding!" said Moira. "And so generous! How can I ever repay you for being so kind?"

"Easy! Just let me get started the minute we stagger out of here! I just love to plan weddings! I know I'll never have another one of my own," she said, an assertion which, given her husband's line of work, struck me as unduly pessimistic, "so the nicest favor you can do for me is to let me help with yours!"

And with that, she rose and strode off to the powder room to repair the damage Moira's poignant tale had wreaked on her mascara.

Moira downed her drink and smiled triumphantly as though she expected us to fall all over her with congratulations on a job well done. She deduced quickly that no such reaction was forthcoming.

"What's the matter with you two?"

"What the hell do you think you're doing?" hissed Gilbert through a frozen smile.

"What do you think! I'm getting your family to pay for everything!"

"I know that, you lying bitch! How *dare* you soak my mother for all the money you blew on your goddamn assholic investments!"

"Well, there's gratitude for you!"

"Gratitude!" snarled Gilbert. "*Gratitude!*"

"You stupid twink! Don't you realize I just made you somewhere between twenty-five and fifty thousand dollars?"

The anger left Gilbert's face and was replaced with a look of utter confusion.

"Huh?"

"*How?*" I asked.

"Gawwd!" she whispered. "It's a good thing Winslow and I are the brains of this operation because you two are totally thick! Don't you get it? Mummy is going to *reimburse* me for everything that gets spent. Everything! If we borrow the money from someone we have to pay it all back when Mummy pays me. But if it's a *gift*—! We just get our hands on the receipts, give them to Mummy, she 'reimburses' us and it's all ours!"

Gilbert said nothing for a few moments. He just sat there transfixed in a state of religious ecstasy.

"Moira," he finally whispered, his voice thick with emotion and rum. "You are so wonderful!"

"That's more like it!" she said, kissing his cheek. "Mind you it wasn't *all* Winslow's idea. He came up with the part about getting your family to pay and my mother to 'reimburse' us, but *he* wanted me to use all the money to replenish the trust fund so *he'd* be off the hook. Which is just like Winslow! But I said, 'Don't be silly, Winnie, why put it back? Much better to find some good investment that will

triple it and then there'll be plenty to replenish the silly fund and
tons left over for—' "

"Are you two *serious*!"

Heads turned toward us from every corner of the bar.

"*Philip!*"

"Shhhhhh!"

"Honestly! What's the matter with you?"

"What's the matter with *me*? Are you two insane? You can't *do*
this!"

"I don't see why not," said Moira.

"Gilbert! Don't you see what you'd be doing!?"

"You bet I do!" he giggled. "Pulling a fast one on old Tony and
making a fortune while I'm at it!"

"But Gilbert—you just don't embezzle money from mafiosi! They
don't *like* it! If he catches on to what you're doing he might kill you!
He might kill all of us!"

Gilbert guffawed through his cocktail straw, blowing bubbles in
his Stinker.

"Oh, puh-leeeeeez!" groaned Moira, amused in spite of herself.
"You're not going to start that nonsense again!"

"Gilbert," I said, as close to apoplexy as one can be while managing
to remain outwardly composed in the bar of a Polynesian restaurant,
"I think you're making a very serious mistake. I know I've never met
the Cellinis but I don't care. They frighten me."

"Oh, *everybody* frightens you."

"Look!" cried Moira, lampooning my alarmist tendencies. "Lelani!
She's got a gun!"

Gilbert hooted and pointed to the South Seas landscape just above
Moira's head.

"That painting!"

"What about it?"

"The eyes on the native girl just moved!"

"Oh no! We're being watched by the Menahooni gang!"

This last sally did them in completely. They sat there clutching
their sides, convulsed with drunken laughter.

"Well, what's gotten into you two?" asked Maddie, plopping down
beside Moira.

"Philip's been telling the most wonderful jokes."

"Oh, you writers are so clever. Well, I'm glad to see you all in such a good mood again. I can't stand to see people get all gloomy over money—not when Tony has so much he hardly knows what to do with it! Why, only a month ago I saw him filling a suitcase with twenty-dollar bills—just for a weekend in the Bahamas! 'Tony!' I said to him. 'How much can you *drink* in two days!' Lelani! Thank you so much! Aren't these delicious?"

Seven

"I tell you, Philly," said Gilbert as we set off across Central Park, his mother and betrothed having parted company with us to enjoy the first of many shopping sprees, "there have been times when I've considered Moira just about the lowest form of life you could see without a really expensive microscope. There have been moments when just thinking about sharing a place with her for another year and a half has made my skin break out. But when I sat there just now listening to her talk about receipts and reimbursements I knew, right here"—he thumped his chest—"this was the girl for me!"

"Gilbert! Open your eyes, will you? That girl is pure poison. Don't you see what she's getting you into?"

"A higher tax bracket, that's what. She's magnificent, Philip. She just doubled our take from this, and all it took was one little lie."

"*One* lie? Maybe it's one lie now but keeping it up is going to take hundreds and hundreds more."

"We're up to it," he said, smiling confidently.

"Not me."

His smile vanished and he stopped in his tracks.

"I hope you're not thinking of quitting on me."

"I'm not thinking about it. I'm doing it. As of right now, you can count me out."

"But why?"

"Why! Gilbert, you're swindling the fucking *Mafia*!"

"Oh, that again," he said, rolling his eyes.

He seated me on a bench and addressed me as if I were a small child who refuses to give up the notion that his closet's inhabited by Dr. Blood and the Monkey Men.

"Philip, I really don't know why you're suddenly convinced my stepfather is some Napoleon of crime, but I wish you'd cut it out. It's getting old."

"Well, how do you explain all the things Maddie was saying? People drowning in their soup. And Tony with his suitcases full of money!"

Gilbert giggled and fixed me with a smile that was a perfect mix of affection and condescension.

"Phil! How do you explain *anything* my mother says? I mean, c'mon! You've listened to her for ten years—have you ever heard her get *anything* right?"

He had a point there. My mind strayed back to that excruciating night during Gilbert's adolescent golddigging stage when Maddie pulled me aside at a dinner party and confided how embarrassed she was that Gilbert was playing matchmaker for her. Why, in the last year he'd dragged home *three* refined fortyish gentlemen, all of whom had money to burn. Very sweet of him, she felt, but if she had to sit through one more opera she'd scream.

Gilbert continued:

"She said Joey Sartucci drowned in his soup. What do you want to bet he just had a heart attack at lunch? And someone had a car accident—big surprise! They drink like fish. It's a wonder more of them haven't driven off cliffs. And as for my cousin mysteriously disappearing, he's probably just run off to Vegas with some bimbo. A few silly coincidences and you're convinced you've just walked into *The Godfather, Part III*!"

"Gilbert, even if I agreed your family is harmless—and I don't—there's still that plan to consider."

"It's a beautiful plan!"

"It stinks! There are a million things that could go wrong and if I know you every one of them will. This whole thing is going to explode on you and I don't want to be there dodging the shrapnel."

The argument grew heated after that. He called me a traitor and a coward and threatened to tell Holly every embarrassing secret of mine he could recall including the time when I was seventeen and the copy of *Ranger in Paradise* fell out of my bookbag in full view of the glee club and Sister Joselia. He said Moira would be furious and do dreadful things to me. But I stood firm. For once in my long friendship with him I was going to do the sane thing and walk away while there was still time.

Then he offered me another five thousand dollars to stay and I said, in that case, yes, I'd do everything I could.

All right, yes, it was an incredibly dumb decision and I realize there's little I can say that will make me seem less greedy and stupid than I was. But let me mention a few things about my situation at the time to help you appreciate why greed and stupidity came so naturally to me that afternoon.

As you may have surmised, I am, by profession, a writer. In terms of income, the period when this was all happening was not quite my Golden Age. (Such an Age has yet to arrive and if it's now approaching it's doing so with remarkable stealth.) I had a part-time job as a secretary-cum-gopher for a writer named Milt Miller who, under the pen name Deirdre Sauvage, was the author of twenty successful romance novels. This job consisted of doing his shopping, answering his fan mail, making his lunch and running to libraries to find out "what the fuck they were wearing in the court of Louis XIV." This brought in about seventy-five to ninety dollars a week, which usually just barely covered the rent on my tiny semi-condemned one-bedroom on West Ninety-ninth.

My only other recent income had been a fifteen-hundred-dollar option paid me for a play I'd finished in August. The option had been purchased by a wealthy young woman named Pears Beaufort. Pears worked out of an office in her Sutton Place town house and had, so far as I knew, produced only one show, a "spring frolic" at Smith College. She'd rhapsodized over my little one-set comedy, *Shut Up and I'll Explain,* but, four months after purchasing a one-year option, hadn't exhibited the slightest intention of ever actually producing it. All inquiries were met with assurances that she was working on it, delivered in a voice which made it clear she considered it unspeakably grasping of me to have asked at all.

So, with my best play destined to languish unproduced for another eight months (at which time I could only begin to look for another producer), Gilbert's offer of five thousand was not one which could be rebuffed without due consideration. So consider it I did. My mental process went something like this:

"Five thousand dollars! Five thousand dollars! A decent stereo! Books, records, theater tickets! No more eggs! Okay, so I have some suspicions. Are suspicions facts? *No.* And what if I'm right and they're mobsters—does that mean they'll find out? *No.* And what if they do? We just give the money back, right? Five thousand dollars! New clothes! Restaurants! Scotch instead of vodka!"

"What's so funny?"

"You just should have seen the look on your face when I said 'five thousand dollars.' You looked like a Frenchman having an orgasm," he said authoritatively.

"Let me get this straight, Gilbert. That's five thousand *over* the cost of the word processor and the printer?"

"I don't remember any talk about printers."

"Well, I'm getting one. A fat lot of good the computer does if you can't print out what you've written."

"Sounds a little steep to me," he said in a weary nasal tone like Pears Beaufort haggling at Cartier, "but I suppose I can afford to be generous. Though if you're asking that much, you'd better be prepared to work for it."

"How?" I asked uneasily.

"Oh, hard to say just now, but I'm sure something will come up. We'll have to prepare more. You're right about our plan. It needs work—nothing we can't take care of. I may have you do a little marketing research."

" 'Marketing research?' "

"You know—make a list of everything we need then shop around to see who's going to charge us the most."

"Why would you want to pay—oh."

"Exactly. We're being reimbursed for every dime we spend. God forbid we should find any bargains. Oh, shit!"

"What?"

"Vulpina!"

"Ah."

His face was set in a tight wince as he contemplated being saddled with a gown that was apt not only to be hideous but free to boot.

"Christ! That no-talent swizzle stick is going to cost us a fortune!"

"How much could one dress cost?"

"Are you kidding? One of those beaded jobs that twenty illegal aliens go blind sewing? They cost thousands."

"Oh. Well, just tell Vulpina you refuse to accept it as a gift and let her charge you the same."

"Philip, you heard the duchess say what she thinks of Pina's designs. Do you think for one minute she'd agree to fork out thousands for one of her monstrosities? We need Galanos or Bill Blass or someone."

"Ah."

"Well, that settles it. Vulpina's out. I don't care how sticky it is for Moira. If she thinks I'm going to sacrifice thousands of dollars to avoid offending that little wombat she's got another thing coming."

"Never mind Pina. The thing we should be worrying about is how to keep the Cellinis from finding out that story about the duchess being poor is a complete crock."

"Hmm. You're right. We won't get anything at *all* if that happens. Any ideas?"

"No."

We mulled the matter in silence.

"Well," I said at length, "the main thing is to keep the two groups separate. The less they communicate the less chance of anyone letting something slip."

"What if something *does* slip?"

"Well, it can't! That's the whole problem."

Silence again descended.

"What if we tell Mom and Tony the duchess is just mortified about being poor? You know, very emotional. Breaks down into hysterical sobs if anyone mentions it."

"I don't know how much good that will do. Your folks are paying for a wedding she ought to be paying for, and they'll think she *knows* they're paying for it. How are they going to feel if she's not even grateful?"

"She's too embarrassed to say anything. Wait—even better! We say she's a bit crackers, too! She has all these delusions of wealth and grandness. 'The poor pathetic old dear. Please, *do* be tactful.' We'll rig it so everyone's walking around on eggshells so scared of saying the wrong thing they don't say anything at all! It's absolutely perfect!"

He giggled and, carried away with a spurious sense of achievement, hugged me madly while stamping his feet on the ground. I was not quite as convinced of the brilliance of this approach and began mentally cataloging things that could go wrong with it. But this train of thought was soon derailed when, embarrassed by the hug, I looked around to see if anyone could see us. And there, sitting on the next bench, was a worst-case scenario.

The man rose and, crossing to our bench, stood directly in front of us. Gilbert, sensing his approach, turned and squinted up. The face was hard to see, silhouetted as it was against the late November sun, but when he spoke there was no mistaking the voice.

"Mr. Selwyn," it cooed murderously. "How I've been hoping I'd run into you again."

Gilbert has, in the course of his exploits, stepped on an assortment of toes, acruing, in the process, an assortment of enemies and ill-wishers. While there does not, so far as I know, exist anything like a Society for the Suppression and Eventual Elimination of Gilbert Selwyn, I'd bet that anyone wishing to start such an organization would have little difficulty recruiting members or soliciting funds for badly needed research.

But of all Gilbert's enemies there wasn't one who viewed him with anything approaching the pure, nearly operatic hatred felt by the man who stood before us now. His name was Gunther Von Steigle.

"Gunther," cried Gilbert cheerfully. "Long time no see! Gosh, this *is* a little embarrassing isn't it? A little touchy? Ha ha! Well, what can I say! L'amour, l'amour! Sit down, Gunny. How've you been? No hard feelings, I hope?"

Eight

As a great admirer of strong, fast-paced story-telling, I'm entirely in sympathy with those of you who feel that there's no more irksome literary device than the flashback. Whenever I come across a bit of it lurking unsuspected in the middle of some otherwise gripping account it gives me that same ambushed feeling you get when you turn the page of a library book and find the margin caked with some dried murky substance, the origin of which you don't care to contemplate.

So, with this in mind, I'll try to briefly convey to you the facts regarding Gilbert, Gunther Von Steigle and the poet Paris Goldfarb.

Gilbert and I first laid eyes on Paris Goldfarb at Holly Batterman's second annual thirty-ninth birthday party last June. Gilbert stared at him across the room for about five seconds then turned to me and solemnly announced that he'd found the man with whom he wished to grow old. This didn't surprise me. Gilly has always been a sucker for a pretty face and Paris had cheekbones that would heal the sick.

Gilbert ran to Holly (if anyone's gonna know, right?) and asked for the complete poop. Holly informed him the boy was named Paris Ulysses Goldfarb, was twenty-six, came from Summit, New Jersey, lived on St. Marks Place, worked at an antique store on Madison in the seventies and was the most colossal bore in the solar system. For reasons no one could fathom, his great beauty had not prevented him from developing a morbid streak wider than the River Styx. When he wasn't discoursing on vivisection or the Tyranny of Time he was quoting great chunks of morose poetry from his own heavily remaindered collection, *Echoes of Nothing*. And if that wasn't enough to deter Gilbert, he had a lover possessed of an equally bleak disposition.

The lover, Gunther Von Steigle, was an actor of strikingly limited range who owned a hairdressing salon on Lexington Avenue. Holly pointed him out. It was easy to see why he might have had difficulty finding varied roles. He had that handsome monster look—thick wavy hair, piercing blue eyes, and a hawklike nose all set, unfortunately, just above a jaw so heavily pocked and cratered you thought if you looked closely enough you'd see tiny astronauts planting flags on it.

"Listen to your auntie," concluded Holly. "I know he's cuter than a baby duck but he's not worth the trouble!"

Gilbert disagreed with this assessment. He wanted Paris desperately and was sure that any darkness in his temperament was due to his being yoked to a moody, pockmarked Svengali of a lover. And so Gilbert made up his mind to "save Paris from Gunther."

His first step was to remove Gunther from the picture. Here luck was on Gilbert's side, for an old flame of his, a producer, was just putting together a summer tour of *Arsenic and Old Lace*. Gilbert informed him that the perfect actor to play the Boris Karloff role was in town and eminently available. The producer contacted Gunther's agent and Gunther, who hadn't worked since January when he'd appeared in ELT's *Oklahoma!* as Jud, gratefully accepted the job.

Not long after Gunther's departure Paris began receiving phone calls from a variety of Gilbert's friends. The calls went pretty much like this:

QUEER YOUNG MAN: Hi, is this 555-9026?
PARIS: Yes.
Q.Y.M.: Well, hi, Gunther. You probably don't remember me. We met two weeks ago. You said you liked my tan line?
PARIS: (*icily*) Who is this, please?
Q.Y.M.: *Oops!* Sorry! Wrong number! (*Giggle. Click.*)

A week after the calls began Gilbert saw Paris again at a little soiree arranged by Holly. At this party Gilbert presented himself as a serious-natured young man with passionate interests in antique furniture and rotten poetry. A week after that he began spending his nights on St. Marks Place.

Things proceeded smoothly till late July when Gunther, faced with an unexpected hiatus, decided to pay his melancholy baby a surprise visit. He popped in at eleven on a Sunday night and when the smoke had cleared Paris was ensconced in Gilbert's apartment (for the lease on St. Marks was in hubby's name) and Gunther was back on tour playing his lines with a heightened sense of menace. Two weeks later Gilbert, arriving at the conclusion that he could never be really happy with a boy who composed morbid free verse at breakfast, showed Paris the door.

The rift between Paris and Gunther was never patched up. The now homeless poet decided New York was too frivolous a place for one of his exquisitely somber nature, and he left town in search of grayer pastures. Neither Gilbert nor I had seen either of them again. Until now.

"No hard feelings, I hope? I mean, all's fair in love and war, right?"

"I think you know what my feelings toward you are, Mr. Selwyn."

"Still smarting, huh? Well, don't fret, you'll get over him. I certainly did! Oh, I'm sorry, you haven't met my friend. Philip Cavanaugh, this is Gunny Von Steigle."

"A pleasure!" I said, cheerfully extending my hand.

He ignored it and returned his grim stare to Gilbert.

"Holland tells me you're getting married. To a Miss Finch?"

"Yes. Wonderful girl. You must meet her some time."

"She doesn't care that you are a homosexual?"

"Ah!" trilled Gilbert, "but I'm not! I went through a phase . . . experimentation, you know. You hear so much about it in this town and my curiosity got the better of me but, no, it wasn't *right*. Not for me anyway. I've got nothing against you people, mind you—ask Philip. But I'm very happy with my dear Moira."

"I don't believe you."

"Believe what you like," yawned Gilbert. "It's of no concern to me."

"Just as, I'm sure, it's of no concern to you that this girl's mother happens to be a wealthy woman. A duchess, so Holland tells me."

"What are you saying? That I'm some sort of—*fortune hunter?*" asked Gilbert, smiling at the ridiculousness of the suggestion.

"Of course you'll deny it. But you don't fool me, Mr. Selwyn."

Gilbert sighed to indicate that while this may all have been amusing at the outset it was rapidly becoming tiresome. I didn't view it as lightly. Gunther's bearing, calling to mind as it did that of a guest

Nazi on "Hogan's Heroes," was pretty silly but I could see the malice behind it was genuine.

Gilbert, though, perceived no such threat or he would not have remarked: "You know, Paris told me you had all the charm of boiled meat but I didn't realize he was attempting to be kind."

I hoped Gunther would reply in the same snippy vein. Some good old-fashioned bitchiness would have been a welcome relief from his exterminating Druid routine. But he just stared at us and, taking a Swiss army knife from his pocket, began to clean his fingernails.

"Paris," he said at length, "loved me very deeply. If he said such things it had to have been because someone poisoned his mind against me. Who do you suppose could have done that?"

"Hard to say. New York is full of discerning critics."

"When we fought he told me about phone calls he received. Calls from men who claimed they'd tricked with me. But in the year I spent with Paris I was not unfaithful once. How do you explain those calls?"

"I don't have to explain anything, you Nazi trollop! Come on, Philip!" Gilbert said, rising. "I think we've heard enough nonsense for one day!"

"Nonsense, is it, Mr. Selwyn? You steal from me the one man I have ever cared about, you strip away his innocence and trust, and then you discard him the moment you find some rich pig woman who wants to buy your pretty simpering face."

"Hold on there, asshole!" said Gilbert in a manly voice. "You're talking about the woman I love!" Then it must have occurred to him he was talking about Moira because he burst into uncontrollable high-pitched giggles.

"It's all a great joke to you, isn't it?"

"It's not!" said Gilbert, clutching his sides.

"The pain you inflict, the lives you destroy—"

"Oh, shut up!" snapped Gilbert, his giggle fit over. "You just don't want to admit your big romance fizzled because your boyfriend was sick to death of you long before he ever met me."

"I loathe you."

"Yadda, yadda, yadda. Let's go, Philip."

"I'd like to fix that pretty face of yours. I'd like to take this knife and write his name across your cheeks."

"And they'd still look better than yours, volcano puss!"

"Gilbert, the museum's gonna close soon."

"What? Philip, you're not *intimidated* by this creep, are you?"

"No—but he's not threatening me."

"Don't be so certain of that. I'm sure whatever Mr. Selwyn did he was not without accomplices. You're his best friend, so I assume—"

"Don't assume anything! I don't know what he did and I didn't help him do it. So just leave me out of this."

"You seem nervous, Mr. Cavanaugh. Perhaps because—"

"Gil-bert!" I bellowed and began walking away.

"I'm coming, okay?"

He followed a few steps then turned back to Gunther and in a wicked impression of his accent said, "Undjoo, you wotten kwout herr-dwessah! You keep your dee-stunz or I vill be forz to do sumtink I vill wee-gwet!"

Gunther smiled for the first time. A sharp rigor mortis grin that made my flesh creep.

"But Mr. Selwyn, you've already done so *much* you'll regret."

The smile clicked shut and, turning sharply away, he strode off across the Great Lawn.

I wasted no time in confiding to Gilbert my concern over this new menace. I felt it unwise to underestimate either the sincerity of his desire for vengeance or his ability to act on it. As such, he should be either avoided or mollified—calling attention to his complexion was not the way to do this.

Gilbert blithely dismissed these concerns. He said Paris had told him plenty about Gunther and among the things he'd confided was that Gunther was all bark and no bite, a "paper tiger." I replied that I'd seen his fangs at close range and they hadn't looked like origami to me.

I dropped Gilbert off at God's Country and as I walked home up Broadway I noticed the Thalia was playing *The Godfather*, parts I and II. I nearly whimpered with fear, certain that this was God's way of letting me know I was a greedy shmuck destined to perish for his sins in a Mafia bloodbath. Silly of me, I know, but during periods of great anxiety, which is to say always, I'm highly sensitive to signs and omens. I can interpret virtually anything that crosses my field of vision as proof from heaven that all my darkest fears will come true, only sooner than I thought they would.

Passing the newsstand at Ninety-sixth Street I noted the headline on the *Post* which read TWO SLAIN IN MIDTOWN BLOODBATH and my panic grew. Never mind that my chances of seeing a similar *Post* headline on any day of the year were about three in five; this one was for me and me alone. I walked the rest of the way with my eyes cast downward lest I catch sight of another headline reading GREEDY GAY LYRICIST FOUND DISMEMBERED IN POORLY DECORATED APARTMENT.

On reaching home and finding the light switch near the door not working again, I all but collapsed with fear at the thought of crossing the darkened room to reach the lamp on the other side. I accomplished the task, however, without encountering a fat Sicilian clutching a yard of piano wire and, slumping into my comfy chair, I breathed heavily for a bit and began to ponder the increasing complexities of the situation. What were the possible rewards? The possible dangers? I thought long and hard and could reach only one conclusion: if I stayed in the syndicate we'd run up against the Mafia and I'd be viciously murdered for my complicity, and if I bowed out Gilbert and Moira would pull it off and make tons of money and I wouldn't see a dime.

As I sat there paralyzed with indecision my phone rang. I answered and heard the soothing voice of Claire Simmons.

"When, please, are you going to join the twentieth century and get an answering machine? I've been calling for days and you don't even know because I can't leave a message."

"Sorry. You want to leave me messages, buy me a machine."

"Greedyguts. Where have you been hiding yourself?"

"I've been spending time with Gilbert and Moira."

"How lucky for you. What's new with them?"

To which I heard myself reply: "Oh, they've got this insane scheme to swindle their families and I'm sort of helping them with it. I'm either going to make a lot of money or get killed by the Mafia. Can you come over?"

Nine

Claire arrived not twenty minutes later and the moment her ample form sailed through the door I felt hope kicking in like warm scotch on a cold night. Claire's one of those brisk, nanny-like women who have a way of immediately taking charge of any situation involving wayward children or adults behaving like same.

She asked for a cup of tea ("Real tea, please, not herbal. I'm sick of drinking warm meadows") and sipped it thoughtfully as I gave her the facts. To her credit, she didn't once interrupt me with any of the withering comments that must have occurred to her. She waited until I was through, then, fixing me a look of concern, said:

"Philip, be honest with me—are you on drugs?"

"No! I couldn't afford to be. Why?"

"Because I can't think of any other way someone could lose as many brain cells as you seem to have misplaced. How in heaven's name did you let yourself be talked into this demented scheme?"

"Well, it wasn't that demented to start out with. Gilbert just wanted someone to confide in."

"And someone to lie through his teeth to everyone you both know."

"Well, yes, that too."

"Including *me*. Don't think I appreciate that. I *asked* you what he was up to, getting married, and you vowed on your mother's grave—"

"I'm sorry! What should I have done?"

"You could have confided. You know I wouldn't have given it away."

She was right about that. Claire is the only person I know who can be relied upon to keep her mouth shut when asked to. Holly Batterman just loathes her.

"I'm sorry. I promised Gilbert."

"Please do yourself a favor and don't make promises to Gilbert. They just get you in trouble."

"Look, I know you've never liked Gilbert—"

"That's not true. I've always enjoyed his company. He's funny and very charming when he wants to be. He's also a complete idiot. I've never met anyone so determined to have tons of money and willing to do anything for it except work. One asinine scheme after another! And I've even enjoyed those—but from a distance. Which is how you should enjoy them, too."

"Are you through scolding me?"

"No. I doubt I ever will be."

"So, what should I do about this wedding?"

"I have no idea."

"You don't?"

"How could I? It all depends on things you don't know yet. Mainly the Cellinis. Are they mafiosi or aren't they? If they are, you're going to pull out immediately. I'm not suggesting, I'm commanding. You'll pull right out and from there on avoid Gilbert like the plague, because if you don't *I'll* go straight to Gilbert's mother and tell her everything."

"You wouldn't!"

"You know very well I would. I won't let you get yourself killed over a few thousand dollars."

"But what if they're harmless?"

"If they're harmless I don't see where I come into it. I'll recommend you get out of it because it's dishonest and not likely to work, and you'll ignore me as usual and go ahead and do it. Right?"

I conceded the point.

"But you wouldn't blow the whistle?"

"No. I only butt in when there are lives at stake."

"You really think it won't work?"

"I'm not saying it couldn't, but honestly! All those lies! It would take a genius just to keep track of them never mind keeping everyone believing them all. And *Moira*. Do you really trust her even for a minute?"

"Well, gee," I said weakly, my head spinning from this onslaught of realism. "We *are* all in it together."

"Philip, you idiot, she's defrauding her own mother, her stepfather,

her trust officer, her in-laws and her best friends. You think she draws the line at cheating *you*?"

"She's not paying me. My part comes out of Gilbert's share. *He'd* never cheat me."

"Yes, but who's to say Moira isn't planning to cheat *him*? Please, dear, for my sake, walk away. Even if they're not all Mafia. There's a very small chance you'll make some easy money and a very large chance you'll be terribly embarrassed, if not actually sued. If not actually killed."

"Claire, instead of telling me how rotten my chances are why don't you help me improve them?"

She arched her back slightly and pursed her lips as though she'd just spotted roaches in her silverware drawer.

"You know better than to ask me to participate in some silly hoax!"

"But I want my computer!" I whined. "Think how much faster we'd get a show written if I had a word processor!"

"Or a shred of discipline."

She had me there, of course, but I did my best to look surprised and injured and after a moment she sighed heavily and bent just a hair.

"Philip, to be honest, there's a part of me that would like nothing more than to see you pull this off. You've gone to bat for Gilbert dozens of times and never gotten a thing for your trouble. It's high time you did."

"Then help me out! You don't have to do anything. Just consult. I'll tell you what's going on and you tell me what we're doing wrong—"

"Now, just stop it—"

"Claire, who's really getting swindled? Maddie and Tony are rich as shit. And as far as the money Moira gets from the duchess, it's the same money she'll get when her mother kicks off anyway!"

"Philip! These are rationalizations!"

"And damn fine ones, too! C'mon, Claire, I'm just asking for your opinions. You're the sharpest person I know. You're so good at figuring people out—how they'll behave in a situation, what they're really thinking when they say one thing and mean another."

I knew if there was any hope of enlisting her this was the way to do it. Claire, though she denies it hotly, is extremely vain about her intellect, as well she should be. She's the only person I've ever met who can solve those maddening London *Times* crossword puzzles. You know, the ones where the clue is "hat for a princess?" and the correct answer is "carburetor." She can't resist a challenge. If she could be induced to view the situation not as an ethical but as an intellectual problem, the Byzantine complexities of which could only be solved by her awesome perspicacity, I'd be in business.

"Please! You said it would take a genius to keep everything straight, and I hate to bother you but you're the only genius I know."

"Oh, stop it. You're just trying to flatter me into it."

"There, see? You're so insightful!"

"You don't let up, do you?"

"Claire, you know I'm going to go ahead with it anyway. How will you feel if Moira does what you said she might? Pulls a fast one and walks away with all the money—just because you weren't hovering on the sidelines looking out for our best interests."

"*Our* best interests?"

"Of course," I added, modifying my tactic, "there's no saying you'd be able to outfox Moira, even if you did try. She's pretty sharp."

"I will not be goaded."

"Well, she's already fooled you once. At Marlowe's party. Even after we all had that jolly hour at Vanessa's she still had you cooing with sympathy over her shattered engagement. Boy," I lied, "she sure crowed about that!"

"Did she?" asked Claire through narrowed eyes.

I said nothing, but smiled and gave her a "Hey, happens to the best of us" shrug of sympathy which would, I hoped, infuriate her completely.

"Good Lord, what a bitch!" said Claire, thrilling me to the core, for it's an epithet to which she rarely resorts. It meant war in the offing.

"Gilbert's an utter fool to get mixed up with her and so are you."

"I know. But we *are*. That's why we need you."

"Well, let's get some things straight. First, if there's even the faintest whiff of the Mafia in any of this you're resigning immediately."

"Absolutely."

"And I'm not going to tell you how to swindle these people. I'll just keep an eye on Moira to make sure she's not swindling you."

"Right. Now, how do we figure out if the Cellinis are nice Italian businessmen or vicious murdering thugs?"

Claire frowned. "It will take some discreet sniffing around, I guess. *Very* discreet sniffing. We can check newspaper files, too. I don't suppose there's a chance I could meet Maddie? She sounds sweet but quite the blabbermouth. Might give me a clue or two."

I replied that she could meet them all. She could be my date at Maddie's Christmas bash on the twelfth. She frowned and said she'd have to rearrange some things as she'd planned to be out of town until the fourteenth. Claire works for a rising new greeting card concern and must occasionally descend on card stores about the land and persuade them that Hallmark has gone the way of the dinosaur.

"I didn't know you were going away."

"It's one of the things I've been trying to tell you for the last three days. I'll be gone two weeks, the first in Chicago, the second in Boston. Do you think you can stay out of trouble that long?"

I replied, too grateful to feign indignation, that yes, I could manage.

I resolved to entangle myself no further in syndicate business till Claire had passed judgment on the Cellinis. The next day I phoned Gilbert and told him Milt Miller had saddled me with an enormous research project and that for the next few weeks I was going to be busy learning all about Venice in the era of Casanova, with particular emphasis on those problems which might be encountered by a chaste servant girl who, condemned for a crime she never committed, must pose as a gondolier. He balked at the time lost from my syndicate chores but was assuaged by my assurance that the money earned would allow me to be unusually generous with his Christmas present.

He invited me to spend Thanksgiving with him and Moira at Casa Cellini. I declined, deciding at that very moment to take my sister, Joyce, up on her standing, if somewhat obligatory, offer to dine in New Rochelle with her and my brother-in-law, Dwight. Dwight's a very successful corporate investment broker and the country's leading example of acquisitiveness gone mad. He writes Hammacher Schlemmer off as a dependent.

Claire and I spent a pleasant and productive few days polishing up the outline for our new show, which concerned a Candide-like innocent's voyage through the world of network programming. Then on Turkey Day morning she set off for Chicago, Gilbert and Moira set off for Old Westbury and I slouched toward New Rochelle. My day went as drearily as expected. Between having to enthuse over the new electric cat door and listening to Dwight's concerned queries as to when I was going to wise up and get out of what he insists on calling "the songwriting game," I found myself feeling little of the gratitude appropriate to the day. I consoled myself with the thought that, having done my family duty, I could now pass on Christmas (which would, if past years were any indication, be an advertisement for Marxism).

Gilbert called the next day bursting with news.

"I've called you fifty times! Where have you been!"

"At the library," I lied.

"Almost done with your research?"

"I've hardly started. What's up?"

"Plenty," he said and dished up these developments.

The Duchess Conspiracy had gotten off to a smooth start. Moira had spoken to Mum and told her what a darling Maddie was and how helpful she'd be with a myriad of nuptial details. The duchess had immediately fired off a letter warmly thanking the Cellinis for the generosity they were displaying by "shouldering burdens" with which she herself was unable to cope.

The letter had reached Maddie on Wednesday and she showed it to Gilbert and Moira on Thanksgiving. Moira, realizing that her mother's expressions of gratitude were conveniently ambiguous, lied that she'd already told Mummy of her confession of the family's poverty and Maddie's subsequent offer to finance the wedding. Poor Mum, she said, had been crushed with embarrassment, but this letter proved how nobly she'd swallowed her pride and agreed to accept their generosity. And on Thanksgiving, too!

Tony, however, was less sanguine about the duchess's poignant capitulation to the famed Cellini munificence. True, he waxed magnanimous, repeatedly asserting that he thought of Gilbert as his own son. But when Moira casually wondered how many revelers the Plaza could accommodate, Gilbert couldn't help but notice a pensive look come over him. It was, Gilbert said, the look of a man beginning to feel that where ballrooms are concerned, blood is thicker than water.

This suspicion was borne out the next day when Maddie called

Gilbert to announce that Tony had had a wonderful idea. Why not have the wedding at Casa Cellini? It was large enough to accommodate the number of guests (estimated at 250), had a "sweet little ballroom" and a spectacularly equipped kitchen. Wouldn't that be nicer? More homey?

Gilbert fervently agreed with this suggestion, knowing that it was, so far as Tony was concerned, not a suggestion at all but an unconditional demand. But upon hanging up he woke Moira and as he brewed the coffee she sat with her trusty calculator bitterly assessing the damage to the syndicate's income. After all, the duchess could hardly be presented with a bill for the use of a private home. Moira wondered if Mummy would even agree to accept this kindness (for the duchess remained, of course, unaware of her crushing penury) but finally decided that Casa Cellini was impressive enough. Besides which it was hardly in the duke's nature to pass up a chance to save so hefty a sum.

But the episode illustrated that, however much Tony wanted to indulge his wife, his generosity was not without limits. They would have to tread cautiously and see how they might compensate for these unwanted economies.

It was in this spirit of tactical extravagance that Gilbert finally laid down the law regarding Vulpina. Whatever you could say about her designing skills, and he said plenty, she did not possess the sort of wide notoriety which could demand a truly exorbitant fee. Moira, in an uncharacteristic show of loyalty, fought this vociferously. It was only when Gilbert threatened personally to phone the duchess, decry Pina's vulgarity and beg Her Grace to talk some sense into her daughter that Moira finally relented.

"I don't see why she made such a big stink about it. I mean, she can blame it all on her mother. Pina knows what the duchess thinks of her."

"Still, they're best friends. Moira can't like having to disappoint her."

"Dear naïve Philip! Moira just resisted so *I'd* be the bad one. She'd disappoint Pina six times before breakfast if there were a few bucks in it. So I guess that's—no, wait! I forgot! Guess who Moy and I ran into Wednesday night at Marilyn's Grave?"

"Who?"

"Gunny Von Steigle!"

"No!"

"Yes! We were out dancing there with Nancy and this Dutch model friend of hers, and we were having a break in one of the lounges. Have you been there? It's all tombstones and erotic statues and they pay gorgeous people to walk around naked, covered in plaster. We should go."

"Gunther?" I said, gently easing him back toward the topic at hand.

"Oh, right. Well, we were sitting there having beers—six bucks!— and learning the Dutch for everything, then I looked up and he'd just sort of materialized."

"What'd he say?"

"What do you think? 'Hello Mistah Selvyn.' In that voice of his— you know, Arnold Schwarzenegger auditioning for Henry Higgins. So I say, 'Look cute stuff, I told you if you kept harassing me I'd sue the pants off you.' And he smiled and said, 'I'm not harassing you Mr. Selvyn. It's mere coincidence that brings us together.' Then he looked at Moira and said, 'I take it this is your fiancée?' "

"Did Moira know about it all? You and him and Paris and us meeting him in the park that day?"

"You bet! I told her the whole thing the night it happened. So Moira knew who he was and she was staring daggers at him, just daring him to try something, and he looks at her and says, 'Hello, Miss Finch. Zo joo are engaged to zis homazeggsual fortune hunter?'

"Then Moira stood up and glared at him and said, 'You listen to me, mister—I know everything about Gilbert! Understand? *Everything*. So you can't surprise me with the truth or fool me with lies. But if you try to do either one again I will personally take that sieve you call a face and bash it into the nearest brick wall. *Now beat it!*'

"And *every*one in the room could hear that, and they just stared at Moira staring at him till he finally just *slunk* away! You should have been there! She was great! I'm so glad to be in such good hands!"

That's what he said on Friday. The Thursday after that I received a call from him at about five.

"You've got to come over here right away!"

"What is it?"

"What do you think it is? It's Moira!"

"What about her?"

"The lousy bitch is cheating on me!"

Ten

He'd sounded upset on the phone but I hadn't realized just how upset till I reached God's Country and, entering the kitchen, saw the empty containers of Früsen Glädje butter pecan sitting in the trash. This is Gilbert's favorite treat, and while his obsession with maintaining his boyish figure prevents him from indulging too frequently, in times of great inner turmoil he consumes it by the pint without pausing to chew the pecans.

"The *nerve* of that bitch! After all her snippy little lectures to me about *controlling* myself and making sacrifices for the common good. 'One slip, Gilley Pie! That's all it would take and everyone would know the whole thing was a sham. We don't want that, do we?' And here she is starting some sleazy affair with God knows who!"

I asked if he was that sure she was having a dalliance and he replied that it was beyond doubt.

Moira, he reminded me, had affected great sympathy for Pina after Gilbert insisted she be fired from gown duty. Moira claimed to have spent several nights last week bucking up her friend's shattered confidence. Earlier that day, though, Gilbert had been in SoHo, checking out a shop called Albino.

"Albino?"

"Chichi stationery. One invitation will set you back five bucks. Anyway, it's right around the corner from Pina's shop so I thought I'd bop in and ask if I could take her to lunch. You know, a little conciliatory gesture to smooth things over? So, I waltz in and there's that Chinese boy who works for her. You know, Peter?"

"Real short, real pretty?"

"If that's what you like, yes. I asked him where Vulpina was, and he said, 'Oh, sorry, Peenie's in L.A.!' That punk group she designs for, the Entrails, they're doing their first video and she's out there to help. 'Well, when did she leave?' I ask. He says, *'Two weeks* ago.' So Moira couldn't *possibly* have fired her, and she couldn't have been busy consoling her all week either. So Petey says, 'She calls in every day. Any message?' I said, 'Yes tell her Mr. Selwyn stopped in to deliver a message from Moira Finch. Miss Finch is sorry but she will not be able to wear Miss Vulpina's bridal gown because Miss Finch's mother, the duchess, would rather see her married in a Hefty bag with arm holes.' The nerve of that bitch!"

"Calm down. So what if she is screwing around? As long as she's discreet about it, what's the difference?"

"Erhart Lund!" bellowed Gilbert. "That's the difference! If I can give up Erhart fucking Lund she can damn well kiss off whatever nearsighted pork roast she's boffing twice a week! There are principles here!"

"Ah."

"You don't know how horny I've been! There's been no one since Paris. No one! Three months it's been! Do you know what that feels like?"

"Yes."

"Oh. Well, it's different with you."

"Thanks a lot."

"Oh, you know what I mean! You're not like me. You're stronger, more self-sufficient. But me, I'm such a—"

"Slut?"

"Romantic, I was going to say. Because I am. Really, Philip, I'm only at my best when I'm in love. I didn't realize it till now because I'd never not been in love for more than a week or so, but these last few months have been just awful!"

We heard the front door slam and a moment later Moira danced in.

"Philip, my angel, it's been days! What have you been up to?"

"Oh, I've had this research project for Milt Miller. And I'm writing a musical with Claire. Lots of work."

"Work! Tell me about it! I never imagined putting a trousseau together could be so harrowing! I'd rather write a dozen musicals! Gilley dear, please don't be furious but I have to break our date tonight."

"Oh?" said Gilbert, giving me a deceptively casual glance.

"Yes." She addressed me sweetly: "We were supposed to be going to a little early evening cocktail party at Holly's. Were you asked?"

"No."

"Oh, that Holly—I can't imagine what he has against you. Anyway, Gilley, I won't be able to make it. Something's come up."

"What?"

"What is it ever? Poor Pina! She's done some work on her spring line and she wants my opinion. Dash, dash dash! That's all I do! I'll just go take a quick shower then I'll be off. Why don't you take Philip to Holly's? I'm sure he won't mind and if he does, fuck 'im, right? Have fun!" she chirped, and traipsed out of the room.

Gilbert regarded me grimly. We donned coats in silence and left.

I had a fair guess what he was up to. He was planning to hide outside the building and follow her. This struck me as a childish, melodramatic way to deal with the situation and I hoped he'd let me tag along.

As soon as the elevator doors closed he said, "Here's what we do . . ."

"I'm way ahead of you."

Upon exiting the building we gazed about and soon agreed that a spot across the street behind the wall of Central Park would afford a good view of the door and the desired minimum of visibility. We zipped across the street and scrambled over the wall, attracting the alarmed gaze of several respectable citizens who must have considered us either sui- or homicidal to be entering the park after sundown in December.

We crouched there in the darkness, breathing heavily from our exertions and feeling a sense of illicit cunning that was quite agreeable. It was like being plunged into one of those blithely improbable thrillers in which private citizens without a bit of military training elude and ultimately topple hugely sophisticated international crime cartels.

We raised our heads just above the top of the wall and fixed our eyes on the door. About twenty minutes later Moira appeared. She was carrying a large dress box and wearing a trench coat, both of which details gave the proceedings just that extra dash of Ludlum I'd been hoping for. She turned and began strolling briskly down Central

Park West. We followed behind the wall and saw her turn west at Eighty-first Street, which, fortunately for us, was where the wall stopped to permit entrance to the park.

We emerged and attempted to cross the street. Traffic, however, was completely against us, which struck me as monstrously unfair since in a proper thriller passing traffic is always on the side of the good guys, whizzing by at just the right moment to block the arch-assassin's aim and ruin his delicate concentration. We stood there a moment hissing through our teeth, then Gilbert grabbed my hand and, shouting "*C'mon!*" dragged me swiftly across the street amidst a volley of shrill horn blasts, screeching tires and taxi drivers accusing us of Oedipal tendencies.

We reached the sidewalk, slowed to a trot and, by the time we'd reached Columbus Avenue, caught up with Moira. She stopped quite suddenly at the corner, forcing us to dive for cover behind a large column at the entrance to an apartment building.

The scene's resemblance to a hackneyed suspenser was rendered complete by the sudden sight of an immense black limo pulling up directly in front of Moira. Gilbert gasped and I couldn't blame him. From the poker-faced driver to the smoked, presumably bulletproof windows, everything about the car reeked of ill-gotten gains. The sheer length of it was astonishing; I've seen limos with bars in the back seat but this one looked like it had a restaurant.

The driver emerged and opened the back door for Moira. She entered and the car sped off down Columbus.

"How could she?" said Gilbert, his eyes huge with wonder.

"Huh?"

"How could anyone sleep with—with *him*!"

"Gilbert, you know who that car belongs to?"

"Yes! It's Freddy Bombelli's!"

"Freddy Bombelli?"

"Yes!"

"Isn't he a little . . . mature for Moira?"

"Mature! He read the fucking Old Testament in manuscript! My God, I don't be*lieve* this!"

We turned and began the walk homeward, Gilbert ranting full voice and totally oblivious to the amused or offended stares of passersby.

"Do you believe that rotten little whore? To be willing to fuck a withered old goat like Freddy Bombelli!"

"Uh, Gilbert—"

"You haven't *seen* him! He's about five feet tall, reeks of cigars and has this white toupee that looks like it was made from dead hamsters! No one with an ounce of self-respect would dream of fucking him!"

"*Gil*-berrrt—!"

"Besides, he can't have half a hormone left! He probably can't even *do* anything! He probably sits there drooling while Moira shakes her titties at him and talks dirty—"

"Do you *mind*!"

"—And then he's so grateful he probably showers her with jewels and big fat checks, just for being nice to him and letting him look at her and—!"

He stopped in his tracks and emitted a sigh that seemed to rise up from the depths of his soul.

"God," he wailed. "Why couldn't he be *gay*!"

Moira returned to God's at twelve-thirty. She greeted us sweetly and, without waiting to be asked, launched into a detailed précis of her evening with Pina (who, having gone through life without a first name, seemed finally to have been given one: "Poor"). Gilbert sat listening in tight-lipped silence. It wasn't until Moira, finally taking note of his expression, asked why he was looking so crabbycakes, that he finally exploded, letting loose a torrent of sexual invective which absolutely stunned Moira, though not me as I'd spent the last several hours listening to him revise and polish.

When he was about done, Moira, seizing the woman's prerogative in these matters, burst into tears. How could she marry a man who would trust her so little as to follow her in secret and leap to such sordid conclusions on the basis of such flimsy evidence?

Certainly she'd been seeing Freddy Bombelli but she was not, by any stretch of the imagination, his mistress. Their relationship was purely professional. His eyesight was failing and he'd hired her to read to him.

"I read to Freddie three nights a week. He pays me twenty dollars an hour, which, as I'm sure experience has taught you, Gilbert, is not mistress wages. I wouldn't lay a finger on him, even if he asked me to which he wouldn't because he's a complete gentleman which is more than I can say for a certain rat-faced little snoop I have the misfortune to be engaged to."

Gilbert was not convinced. He replied curtly that a young woman whose chaste occupation it was to read to the aged had no reason to lie about her whereabouts, whereas a mercenary slut, willing to engage in sexual practices which might best be described as necrophilia with consent, would naturally take all steps to ensure that such activities should remain her own nasty little secret. Moira rebutted with an ashtray which missed Gilbert entirely and caught me on the right kneecap.

"You beast!" she cried. "If you don't believe me just ask your mother! She set the whole thing up!"

Gilbert stalked over to where Moira sat and, staring dangerously down at her, asked if she was calling his mother a pimp.

"Oh, cut the melodrama, you Airedale. If you'll just shut up and get me a drink I'll tell you about it."

Gilbert scowled mightily but complied with the request. She took a ladylike sip and began.

She said that the day she'd gone window shopping with Maddie after lunch at Trader Vic's, they'd gotten tired and decided to stop for refreshment at a charming bistro on Fifty-second Street.

"It's called Paradiso."

"I know. Tony's cousin Aggie runs it."

"We were having coffee and pastry and who should come in but Freddy! Your mother waved to him and when he got close enough to see who we were his face just lit up and he insisted we both come sit at this special table with him and his five lawyers. We had a *terrific* time. I don't know *where* you get your disposition from. Your mother's delightful."

I rose to replenish my drink and Moira continued to wax rhapsodic about the woman from whom she was extorting thousands of dollars.

"*So* genuine! You should have seen the way she charmed those six old men, telling stories and asking about their health and their grand-children and all that sort of stuff. I kept pretty quiet, as always, but by the end I was chatting away with Freddy. He asked me if I had a job and I told him how I used to be an actress but finally quit because the people were all so insincere. Well, he just got all excited and turned to one of his lawyers and started going on about how it was *fate* brought me to the restaurant! Then he explained about his eye problems and how he needs people to read to him. He'd tried a few but they turned out to be real duds. *No* expression. But with all my professional experience," (which, you'll recall, consisted of nine previews and one performance of Marlowe Heppenstall's *Bong!*) "I'd be absolutely perfect for the job! So, a few days later I had a little tryout and he hired me. I *read* to him, Gilbert. Period."

Well, countered Gilbert, if it was all so innocent why hadn't she, or for that matter, Maddie, ever mentioned this innocent job to him?

"I asked Maddie to clam up about it. I didn't want you to know I was working. I was going to surprise you with a Christmas gift— something really special and wonderful. Though, just what one should give to a fiancé who suspects one of prostitution won't be easy to figure out."

She glowered and downed her drink. Though there was no smile on Moira's face, her pout was the pout of victory. Then, without meaning to, I uttered five words which reversed the positions completely.

"What's in the box, Moira?"

I referred to the dress box which Moira had carried on her errand of mercy. She'd returned with it, but before entering the living room had put it down by the hall closet, almost but not quite out of our line of vision.

"What box?" she asked casually.

It was no good, though. Despite her vast stage experience she had not been able, in the split second following my question, to conceal the quick panic felt by a guilty thing surprised.

"This one," said Gilbert, dashing to the hall and returning with it.

"Oh that," she said, making a pathetic show of stifling a yawn. "That's nothing. Just my book."

"*The Forsyte Saga?*" asked Gilbert as he began prying it open.

"Gilbert, don't you touch that! It's Freddy's property!"

Gilbert gleefully opened the box, scrutinized its contents and burst into triumphantly bitchy laughter. He reached in and pulled out a paperback novel.

"Well, well! If this is what he's reading no *wonder* he's going blind!"

I could tell at first glance that it was one of those lushly packaged romance novels of the sort which have done so much to enrich the coffers of my employer, Mr. Miller. On second glance, I could see that it was by Deirdre himself, an early effort entitled *Cupid's Tender Bludgeon.*

The cover, in scrupulous adherence to the prototype, depicted a haughty raven-haired beauty standing on the edge of a moonlit cliff behind which rose the spires of an ancestral castle. Her face was contorted in the expression which seems de rigueur for these gothic covergirls, a sort of ecstatic wince. She was dressed in a long gown, the neckline of which swan-dived to one eighth of an inch above the nipples of her ripe heaving breasts. Behind her, one hand placed roughly on her pale moonlit shoulder, stood a tall bare-chested fellow who, judging from his appearance, owned not only the castle but one of the few Nautilus machines available in nineteenth-century Cornwall.

"Look!" hooted Gilbert. I glanced up to see him dancing about the room, holding before him a gown very similar to the one worn by the woman on the cover. Gazing again at the portrait I noted that the woman herself bore a resemblance to Moira, though it was hard to imagine Moira looking quite so rapturous in the company of anyone but a really good tax lawyer.

"Oh, God, Moira," I managed to gasp between guffaws, "he actually makes you dress up for him!"

"I don't see what's so goddamned funny about it!"

Gilbert grabbed the book from me and ran to a chair a safe distance from Moira's.

"You are both such children! Just because he enjoys seeing a story brought to life! I mean, God, it's the exact same principle as the Royal Shakespeare Company's *Nicholas Nickleby!*"

" ' "No! No!" I cried,' " read Gilbert, " ' "You mustn't Simon! It's wrong!" But though my words were strong my actions were weak. I made no move to resist the tender onslaught of his hot sinewy flesh.' "

"Shut up!"

" ' "Daisy O'Malley," cried a thin voice within me, "What sort o' woman are ye become in these three short months since ye left the cloistered halls o' St. Cecilia's?" ' "

Moira rose and, bounding across the carpet, snatched the book away.

"If either one of you tells so much as a soul about this—"

"Holly?" I cried snatching the phone up. "Holly Batterman? Have you got a pencil, honey?"

Well, that finished both Gilbert and me completely. We just sat there busting our buttons with Moira's demonically angry expression fueling our mirth.

"Are you quite through making asses of yourselves?"

"Are *we* through? Oh, honey," said Gilbert, "you've sunk low to make a buck before but . . ." He stopped in midsentence as his amused expression faded, a shrewd suspicious look taking its place.

"Wait one minute! You're telling us you go three times a week to this incredibly rich old man and read soft porn to him, in *costume* yet, and all he's paying you is *twenty* dollars an hour?"

Framed that way, it seemed suddenly rather difficult to believe.

"Yes," she replied primly as she packed her dress back in its box. "Twenty dollars seems more than fair to me."

"Oh, I'm sure!"

Moira sighed wearily and huffed off toward the hall closet. She returned momentarily with her trenchcoat over her arm. She removed an envelope and handed it to Gilbert.

"There! See for yourself!"

He gazed at it sourly and handed it to me. It was a check for seventy dollars made out to Moira.

"Satisfied?"

"No," said Gilbert and, grabbing her coat, began rifling the pockets.

"Give that back, you shit!"

He did but not until his hand had emerged clasping a small Tiffany blue box. Moira watched with a weary put-upon look as he opened it to reveal a dazzling pair of ruby earrings.

"Paste!" said Moira.

"*Really?* Well, give 'em to me! I'll donate them to the block association jumble sale."

Moira snatched them back, remarking on their sentimental value.

"You conniving little tart! These must be worth thousands! No wonder you've kept your mouth shut about Freddy! You're raking in a goddamn fortune and you don't want to share it with me!"

"If Freddy wants to give me an occasional gift, I don't see that it has anything to do with you."

Gilbert disagreed strenuously with this viewpoint. Fearing a long, violent and unresolvable argument of the sort in which the happy pair was beginning to specialize, I thanked them both for a lovely evening and let myself out.

A phone call from Gilbert the next morning confirmed that I'd been prudent to take my leave when I did. They'd argued the matter well into the small hours and neither had budged one bit. Gilbert felt that had it not been for their engagement Moira would never have met Freddy, so it was only fair that all profits from her position (over and above her hourly wage) should be considered syndicate income and split fifty-fifty. Moira had begged to differ.

This disagreement marked the abrupt end of cordial relations between the syndicate's two principal shareholders. What slight amiability they had ever displayed toward one another vanished entirely. True, they continued to socialize as a couple and on these occasions managed to present a sweet portrait of prenuptial infatuation. But that was only in public. Within the confines of God's Country the atmosphere grew more Arctic with each passing day.

At first Moira professed to be saddened by the rift and made a few stabs at détente. She was cheerful to Gilbert. She ignored his belligerent silences and bought him a pair of amusing ear muffs. When these efforts failed to bring about any thaw, she took the big plunge: she called L.A. and fired Vulpina, explaining that the duchess had put her foot down. Gilbert, far from being grateful, pointed out that she was only making good on the lie she'd fed him earlier, and that firing Vulpina would only increase the cost of the gown, an increase they would split equally when the duchess reimbursed them.

Moira, indignant over the reception accorded these peacemaking efforts, shifted gears. Overnight she went to the opposite extreme and began goading Gilbert at every opportunity. He'd stagger into the kitchen at ten a.m. and find her nonchalantly perusing the *Times* in her ruby earrings, pearl choker and Hermès scarf. Gilbert retaliated by splashing dimestore perfume all over her bedroom, then removing all the lightbulbs and replacing them with red ones. Moira, by way of response, left three lines of talcum powder on a glass coffee table in the study.

And so the Christmas season passed.

But this behind-the-scenes cold war was not the only consequence of Moira's new Rent-A-Wench franchise. Nor was it the worst. These hostilities, nasty as they seemed, were merely the Calm before the Storm.

The storm broke on December 12 at Maddie Cellini's Christmas party.

Eleven

The party was to begin at five in the afternoon and, in keeping with the innocent spirit of the holiday, the first two hours would be given over entirely to the junior members of the firm. Among the scheduled events were a snowball fight and a surprise visit from Santa, who would, one supposed, take the little Cellinis on his knee and ask them who they wanted hit for Christmas. We agreed that seven-thirty would be a prudent time to arrive.

This entailed leaving Manhattan by six, and since Claire's flight from Boston didn't get in till five I had only moments to fill her in on all that had transpired in her absence. She listened carefully and was particularly glad to hear that Gilbert and Moira were on the outs. It offered hope that he might yet wise up and back out. It also meant she'd get a chance to see Moira dissembling at full tilt. In this expectation she was not disappointed.

"Phil, my angel, how wonderful to see you. Mwah! Oh, your cheeks are so cold! Poor baby! You come right in and have a hot toddy!"

She turned to Claire who had gained a few pounds on her trip.

"Claire! It's been ages! You look different—I can't put my finger on it . . . well, whatever it is, it *suits* you."

Moira was wearing a festive red frock adorned with a small jeweled Christmas wreath pin, a gift from Freddy. Her wearing it was a calculated kick in the teeth to Gilbert, a nightlong reminder of her superior income and intransigent refusal to share it. Still, she betrayed no ill will but rather gazed at him with an affectionate smile that was never less than convincing.

Gilbert's performance, though competent, scarcely approached the virtuosity of Moira's. He chatted merrily enough with Claire and me but couldn't even look at his betrothed without his smile stiffening into a grimace. And my discerning ear could detect the pure malice churning beneath every "dear" and "honey" he uttered. Imagine Josef Mengele touring *Barefoot in the Park* and you'll get the idea.

Our drinks finished, we traipsed downstairs and into the car loaned to Moira for the evening by—who else?—Freddy Bombelli.

We arrived at eight.

Gilbert had once remarked casually to me that his mother was "into Christmas." I saw now just how staggering an understatement this had been. One glimpse of the house made it clear that Maddie's affection for the holiday surpassed even that of Charles Dickens and Mattell, Inc.

"My goodness!" said Claire. "People *live* here?"

"Oh Gilley, it's *fabulous*! Isn't it *fabulous*?"

Casa Cellini is in a style architects sometimes refer to as Very Big House. Or Norman, I suppose, if that's the word that means lots of gray stone, leaded glass and turrets liberally scattered about the top. Viewed by moonlight in November, say, it might take on the ominous aspect of a stronghold, something built by a feudal lord whose run-ins with angry serfs had left him security-minded. Tonight, however, under the benign influence of Lady Maddie, it was literally ablaze with good cheer.

White lights defined every corner and contour of the house and red-bulbed candelabra glittered in every window. A winding path lined with neon candy canes led to a huge front door flanked by two twinkling angels, like the ones in Rockefeller Plaza, only bigger. On the roof of the house was an astonishing tableau of Santa's sleigh; astonishing, I add, not because the figures seemed lifelike, though they did, but because they had been rendered *in flight*. The sleigh hovered some twelve feet above the roof and the reindeer sloped gently downward. Only Rudolph's left front hoof seemed actually to touch the surface. How this effect was achieved I can't say, for the mechanism was invisible to the naked eye.

And that wasn't the half of it.

Trees all over the grounds were festooned with lights, as were the shrubs surrounding the house. On one side of the lawn three mechanical elves skated on a frozen pond. On the opposite side of the lawn was a life-size nativity scene. Real sheep, kept warm by thermal lamps, stood alongside statues of the traditional figures. Suddenly the strains of "We Three Kings" were heard over the sound system and from behind the house appeared three resplendently draped manni-kins. They glided crècheward along a concealed track and as they did a bright star appeared thirty feet in the air over the scene. When they reached the crèche the music swelled into "Joy to the World." The elves stopped skating to watch. Then the lights dimmed on that scene and the wise men glided off around and behind the crèche to return, one presumed, to their starting point at the rear of the house. To distract the viewer's attention from this, the roof suddenly bright-ened and Santa began waving and wishing us all a merry Christmas.

And though the area had not yet had a single flurry the entire scene was blanketed in snow. We stared for long moments, aghast and delighted.

"There was more last Christmas," said Gilbert, concerned. "I hope Tony hasn't had a bad year."

We were greeted at the door by our hostess. She wore a gaudy red dress with a huge bubble skirt and looked very much the queen of this Christmas kingdom.

"Well, hi kids! Where have you been! You missed the snowball fight!"

"Hi, Mom. Where's Santa's workshop?"

"Oh, don't you *miss* it? I know I do. It got all wet. Some poor workman nearly electrocuted himself on Mrs. Santa!"

Two maids appeared and helped us off with our coats.

"Moira, baby, don't you look pretty! I love your pin. Gilbert give it to you? Philip, honey, so glad you could come! And who's your lovely date?"

I introduced Claire and Maddie hugged her like a long-lost daugh-ter.

"Claire and I have been collaborating for years."

"Ooh!" giggled Maddie. "Well, I'm sure it's no business of mine! Gilbert, are you sure you can afford to give Moira such expensive gifts?"

"Oh, Gilbert didn't give it to me," trilled Moira. "Freddy did."

"Oh, well *he* can afford it. So, the cat's out of the bag, huh?"

"Yes. Gilley's so clever he just wormed it out of me!"

"Isn't she sweet, Gilbert? Gettin' a job to pay for your gift!"

Gilbert replied that he didn't know what he'd done to deserve her.

"My goodness," said Claire, "that's quite a remarkable display you have out there, Mrs. Cellini!"

"Please, honey, it's Maddie! But I agree with you. Ain't it terrific? Do you know some old fogies on the town council tried to make us get *rid* of it? Said we weren't zoned for it or something."

"What happened?"

"Tony reasoned with 'em. Well, kids, are you gonna stand around in the hall all night or are you gonna come meet the family?" To this we made the only possible reply.

To the left side of the foyer I glimpsed a huge expanse of parquet leading to tall French windows. This was apparently the "sweet little ballroom" Gilbert had mentioned. Maddie, however, led us to our right into a large elaborately decorated living room. In one corner stood a huge flashy Christmas tree and in all the other corners stood huge flashy Cellinis.

It was clear that in describing the Cellinis as "an awfully big family" Maddie had not referred solely to their penchant for frequent marital relations with prayer the preferred contraceptive. Gazing about the room I saw a lot of Cellinis, most of whom were, themselves, a lot of Cellini. There were exceptions, younger men and women with slim builds and off-season tans, but for the most part groaning suspenders and billowing gowns were the order of the day.

Maddie, realizing that no one wants to meet a hundred heavyset strangers without first partaking of something alcoholic, steered us straight to a bar set up in front of a window overlooking those tireless little skaters. Behind the bar stood a tall chiseled cater waiter, the promixity of whom to so much liquor would present a challenge to both Gilbert's and my own limited self-control.

"Roger, hon, I want you to meet my son, Gilbert, and his lovely fiancée."

Greetings were exchanged.

"And this is his friend Philip and his date, Claire. Roger here isn't really a bartender. He just does it to make money. He's really an actor and next week he goes into rehearsal for an evening of one-act plays!"

Gilbert and I requested Chivas, Claire a glass of champagne. Moira, ever the professional, stuck to ginger ale.

"Gil, kiddo, how are ya!" boomed a voice from behind. We turned to behold a bald grinning behemoth, his arms flung wide in greeting.

"Chick!" squealed Moira. She flung her arms about his neck, a tactic we'd see repeated dozens of times that evening. But this first encounter provided our first inkling of just how meticulously Moira had prepared for this assault on the hearts, minds and checkbooks of her family-to-be.

"It is just so good to see you again!"

"Well, good to see you, too, Moira!"

Maddie introduced us. He was Tony's cousin, Chick Sartucci.

"How's Rosa?" asked Moira.

"Well, she's puttin' away the eggnogs like they was Perrier but apart from that I guess she's doin' okay."

"And how's Lina? Is she here?"

"Yeah, she's here. She's doin' great—on a diet so be sure and tell her how good she looks."

"And Ugo and Betty?"

"Couldn't be better."

"And how are the grandchildren? I remember you showed me their pictures at Steffie's wedding. They must be so excited with all this! Especially little Silvio—I think three is the first year they really start to understand who Santa is, don't you?"

"You bet he understands!" said Chick with a booming laugh. "He made a list long as the fuckin' 'spressway! Hey," he said, turning to Gilbert, "some memory this girl has? That's the last thing a red-blooded guy needs, huh? A wife with a good memory!"

"Hey, I don't mind, Chick! She never holds anything against me—unless I ask her to!"

Chick roared and Gilbert flashed a smile at Moira. She wasn't the only one who could play to the groundlings.

"Say, 'fore I forget," said Chick in a less jocular tone, "I wanna thank the both of you for sendin' that lovely card after my brother Joey passed on. Me and Rosa thought it was real sweet of you."

Gilbert glanced at Moira for a confused instant then said that it was the least they could do.

"We really appreciated it, 'specially with you two bein' so new to the family. There are a lot of 'em your age didn't take the time to write anything at all, never mind a poem."

Maddie began waving at someone across the room.

"Lunch!" she cried. "I have some friends you gotta meet!"

"Lunch?" I inquired.

"Dickie Fabrizio. 'Lunch' is just his nickname. That's him over there," said Chick pointing to a man wedged into a loveseat, a plate of hors d'oeuvres balanced precariously on what once might have been a lap. "He's called 'Lunch' 'cause if you call his office any time between noon and four you can't reach him. He's out to lunch. Look at him! Makes *me* look like a fuckin' go-go dancer!"

Lunch rose with some difficulty and oozed in our direction. He looked like a special effect.

"You shoulda been here today!" said Chick, nudging me. "He played Santa Claus!"

"What did you do? Butter the chimney?"

Chick roared.

"Hey, Gil, I like this guy! Butter the chimney!"

I felt Claire slip her arm through mine and glancing down at her (for I'm six inches taller) I noticed a strange fixed smile on her face.

"Well, if it ain't the two lovebirds!" wheezed Lunch when he finally reached us. "Maddie here's been telling me all about you. 'Gratulations!"

Maddie introduced Claire and me saying that I was Gilbert's oldest friend, a playwright.

Lunch immediately revealed himself to be that creature most dreaded and despised by dramatists the world over: the Amateur With An Idea For A Play. His involved a man who, in the midst of an affair with a gorgeous woman in her thirties, discovers he's also attracted not only to her gorgeous teenage daughter but ("Here's where it gets good!") her gorgeous fifty-year-old mother. This premise was, he assured me, autobiographical and mine for the taking. I replied that I'd give it every consideration.

"How's Samantha?" asked Moira.

"Sammy? You can ask her yourself, she's right over there. Hey, Sam!"

"What do *you* want?" quacked back a middle-aged woman standing some yards away.

"Come here an' congratulate the happy couple!"

She joined us.

"Look at you," she said to her husband, "crowding the bar as always! Gimme another gimlet, honey," she said to Roger, offering him her empty glass and an ill-disguised leer. "Oh, Maddie, isn't he a knockout?" she sighed.

Maddie giggled like a schoolgirl and said she was happily married but yes, he sure was a good-looking boy.

"What a puss on him!" Sammy said, squeezing his cheek. "Please, hon, tell me you like girls!"

"I worship them," said Roger in a voice which left no doubt in my mind that he was content to worship from afar.

"I'm just teasin' you, baby," said Sammy. "S'none of my business, I'm sure. Gilbert, you're looking very nice yourself. Give Auntie Sammy a kiss!"

Sammy Fabrizio was a large woman in her late fifties. She wore a tight strapless gown of electric blue and earrings which might, on a weaker woman, have caused spinal damage. Her hair was sculpted into a bizarre terraced beehive that made her head resemble an ancient Inca cliff dwelling. Her voice reminded me of a duck, and not a clean-living duck either but one that's been drinking gin and chain-smoking since it was a duckling.

Introductions were made and Lunch, who viewed standing up as a calisthenic, suggested we move to a recently vacated sofa.

Moira once more asked a barrage of questions about her future in-laws, recalling the names not only of Lunch and Sammy's brood but those of their eldest's husband and four children. They were delighted by the swiftness with which she had mastered the complexities of the family tree. Gilbert tried to compete but kept making errors after each of which Moira sweetly corrected him, calling him her "dizzy baby."

Now, at first, listening to this prodigious performance, I felt Moira had gone too far for her own good; that in laying it on so thick she could only raise questions as to what motivated so passionate an interest in people she'd barely met. But Moira, no fool, took care to defuse any suspicions with a poignant homily on the subject of Big Families.

"You see, I was a difficult birth and after me Mummy couldn't have any more. So when Daddy died—I was six—there were just the two of us. Oh, there were cousins somewhere but they were on Daddy's side and they'd disowned him for marrying beneath him. Well, when you only have one person in the whole world, naturally you dream about having a big family. When I'd see movies like *I Remember Mama* I'd pretend it was *my* family up on the screen. So now, when I look around here and see all these wonderful people all related to each other . . . well, I could just bust when I think that someday I'll be part of it!"

"You already are, honey," quacked Sammy, wiping a tear from her eye.

"Some girl you got here, Gil," sniffed Lunch.

"So, what about you two?" asked Sammy, turning to Claire and me, "you planning to tie the knot?"

"Yes," said Claire, taking my hand. "We just haven't set a date yet."

"You are?" squealed Maddie, delighted. "Well, I didn't know that! Did you know that Gilbert?"

"No!"

"I guess the cat's out of the bag," said Claire, digging her nails into my palm. "I'm sorry, Philly. You're not mad at me, are you?"

"Of course not, darling!" I said, my head swimming.

"Well, *I'm* not surprised," said Moira. "I could tell all the time."

"Could you really?" asked Claire.

"Of course. Women just know."

"There I go!" said Maddie, tears drizzling down her cheeks. "I see two young people find each other and bang go the waterworks!"

"Oh, Maddie," said Moira. "You're as bad as Freddy."

"Freddy who?" asked Sammy.

"Bombelli," cooed Moira. "Your uncle."

"You know Freddy?" asked Lunch, strangely interested.

"Oh, yes, very well. That's how I know so much about the family. He talks about you all the time. He is just so *proud* of you all."

She explained her job with Freddy, omitting reference to his taste in literature and curious demand for costumed reenactment. Anyone would have come away with the impression she'd been reading *Dombey and Son* to him in a vicarage garden.

"Some fuckin' coincidence," said Lunch, significantly. "Tony's future daughter-in-law working for Freddy the Pooch!"

"A little respect!" quacked Sammy, snatching the glass from his hand. "That's enough for you! Quarter past eight and you're already shit-faced. You watch your mouth in front of the little ones. They know you were Santa."

"Hey—speakin' of Lunch playing Santa, Phil here said somethin' that cracked me up—"

"Maddie, where's the bathroom?" I asked, rising.

"Go out in the hall, dear, and it's the first door on your left at the top of the stairs."

"Ladies first!" said my fiancée, popping up beside me. "You lead the way so I don't get lost!" She took my hand again.

"Whatever you say, hon!" I grinned and off we went, Maddie's voice trailing behind us.

"Aren't they adorable! Don't you two do anything I wouldn't do!"

Twelve

$\mathbb{B}$efore plunging you into that bathroom and the horrors with which Claire regaled me, I'd better stop and clarify a few points about the basic organization of what I have so far referred to as the Cellini clan. Sorry for the interruption, but this is all pretty essential stuff you'll have to know sooner or later and it'll be easier to grasp if I give it to you in one neat clump.

As you've already seen the "Cellinis" are not all Cellinis. They are, in fact, only one-third of a clan which might most accurately be called the Bombelli family even though Freddy and his widowed daughter-in-law Bruna are the only surviving bearers of the surname. But it's from Freddy and his three sisters that everyone else is descended.

Back in the early twenties Freddy started a little meatpacking business. Before long it had become a very big meatpacking business, owing in part to the silly habit his competitors developed of always having their factories burn down on them. During these happy years of growth each of Freddy's three sisters married. The names of their husbands were Enrico Cellini (Tony's father), Carlo Sartucci (father of Chick) and Tommy Fabrizio (who spawned Lunch).

All three hubbies went to work for their prosperous brother-in-law and as the business grew and diversified each became responsible for a different aspect of it. Enrico Cellini ran the storage and shipping concern, Carlo Sartucci took over the garment factory which a man named Klein had, in a fit of generosity, given to Freddy, and Mr. Fabrizio stayed in the beef biz. He had a growing boy to feed.

Freddy himself married in the late thirties, choosing as his bride Gina Latour (born Rose D'Amiglio), the singing star whose brief recording career and five-year reign as Queen of the Cayenne Club is remembered only by the most indiscriminate collectors of the chanteuse's art.

Simple enough, right? But now we come to Tony's generation and things get a bit more complex. All the above-mentioned were, whatever their other shortcomings, good Catholics. So take a deep breath, dog-ear the page for future reference, and I'll give you the roster of second-generation Bombellis.

The Cellini wing includes:

Tony Cellini (married, of course, to Maddie)
Steven Cellini (married to Lisa)
Theresa Cellini Pastore (married to Charlie Pastore)
Frankie Cellini (deceased; widow named Connie)
Carlo Cellini (deceased; widow named Marie)

The Sartucci branch includes:

Chick Sartucci (married to Rosa)
Manny Sartucci (and his wife Liz)
Sister Deena Maria Sartucci (Our Lady of Fatima)
Joey Sartucci (the minestrone fatality; widow named Anne)

The Fabrizios are:

Lunch and Sammy
Aggie Fabrizio (divorced)
Eddie "The Sausage" Fabrizio (and his lovely wife Mona)
Father Eddie Fabrizio, S.J.
Big Jimmy Fabrizio (deceased, never married)

As for the Bombellis, they are mercifully few. Freddy, like his siblings, longed for a large family but was blessed with but one son, Harry "Gotcha" Bombelli. Harry grew up and married Bruna. Of the clan, as I said, only Freddy and Bru remain, Freddy's wife having died in the sixties and Gotcha having gone to his reward two years before our story begins.

Now this second generation is comprised of men and women in their forties to sixties. They, in turn, have children of their own. But this next generations needn't concern you. They pop into things here and there but we'll deal with them as they do. The House of Bombelli is highly traditional as regards respect for seniority. Authority trickles down from the top so a basic grasp of the executive level is all you need to follow the motives informing the drama into which Gilbert and I, like a latter-day Rosencrantz and Guildenstern, were thrust.

As soon as Claire and I reached the bathroom she fixed me with a furious grimace similar to the one Sister Joselia had offered years ago when *Ranger in Paradise* fell out of my bookbag. My heart rose well into my throat for there could be no mistake as to what was behind so fierce a scowl.

"You can tell *already*?" I asked.

"Of course I can! And I could have told you two weeks ago if you'd bothered to give me any pertinent information!"

"I told you everything I knew. Is this why we're suddenly engaged?"

"Yes. They mustn't figure out what Gilbert is up to, and if they realize he's gay that's a good first step."

"What has that got to do with me?"

"Well, Philip, you are his best friend. If they know about you it might cast suspicion on him. How many straight boys have gay best friends? Some do, I'm sure, but if you'll forgive me for being blunt, Gilbert's performance as a lustful heterosexual is hardly so masterful that it could withstand the weight of much contradictory evidence."

"You're *that* convinced they're Mafia?"

"Philip, how naïve can you be! Dickie Fabrizio? And Moira suddenly best friends with Freddy the Pooch! Why didn't you *tell* me!"

"I never heard of Lunch till tonight. And Freddy I told you about."

"You said Freddy *Bombelli*, not Freddy the *Pooch*. It's like Jimmy the Greek. You only know him by the nickname."

"Well, *I* don't know him! Who the hell is Freddy the Pooch?"

She gave me the Sister Joselia look again.

"Philip, when you buy the *Times* what do you do, just incinerate everything but Arts and Leisure?"

She proceeded to inform me that Freddie the Pooch was one of the most legendary mobsters of the forties, fifties and sixties. There was scarcely a crime on the books for which he was not, at one point or another, indicted, but no DA ever managed to make a single charge stick. Witnesses against him were notoriously capricious, forever surrendering to bouts of wanderlust or hitherto unsuspected suicidal tendencies.

Early in Freddy's career one such witness, who was later to leap from his window after typing a self-critical note, told a reporter that those who crossed Freddy had been known to find a resting place inside a can of K9, the popular dogfood processed at Freddy's meat packing plant. The witness didn't last long but the sobriquet, Freddy the Pooch, stuck.

"If he's so goddamned important how come I've never heard of him?"

"Well, he hasn't been in the headlines for quite a while. They finally got him on tax evasion in the late sixties and he got a long jail sentence. I don't suppose he's been out now for more than a few years. I had no idea he was still alive. He was already old when they sent him up."

"Yes, and I was about ten, so excuse me for not having followed it all in the *Times*."

"Well, you weren't ten three years ago when Big Jimmy Fabrizio was indicted!"

"Huh?"

"You're hopeless! That whole FBI sting! They had him on videotape offering fifty thousand dollars to Senator Fowler if he'd agree to find no evidence that the B&F Meat Company was the front for a narcotics ring."

This rang the vaguest of bells.

"Oh, right. What happened?"

"It got thrown out of court—some technicality over the way evidence was obtained. Big Jimmy died about a year and a half ago. Car accident."

"How do you know these are the same Fabrizios?"

"Well, considering that their uncle is Freddy the Pooch I'd be surprised if they weren't!"

There was a loud knock at the door. We both froze in panic. I think for a moment we truly expected the door to be flung open by some roscoe-wielding plug ugly in a zoot suit who'd sneer and say, "So yez figured it out, didja?"

"Just a moment please!" said Claire.

"Have you got Philip in there?"

"Gilbert!"

"Come in!" I called.

He sauntered in and regarded us with raised eyebrows.

"Well, isn't *this* cozy!"

"Gilbert we have to talk."

"No kidding! What's all this stuff about you two being engaged?" he asked cautiously, unsure how much Claire knew. "Is it some kind of joke or what?"

Claire immediately laid this question to rest, informing him exactly why she felt it prudent that I acquire a fiancée.

Gilbert stood there dumbstruck for a moment, then spoke.

"Philip, you *told* her!"

"And a damn good thing I did."

"How *could* you! You promised me under no—"

"Gilbert, you fool," said Claire sharply, "that is entirely beside the point, which is that you're trying to swindle some extremely dangerous people!"

"Oh, please! Not this Mafia business again! I don't know why—"

"You certainly *don't*, so shut up and I'll tell you."

She repeated the story she'd told me, and by the time she'd gotten around to Freddy's unique place in the history of canine nutrition, Gilbert had taken on that pale, doomed look you often see in dental reception areas.

"You're making this up just to scare me."

"Gilbert," I cried, "wake up and smell the dog food! What we're doing here is *really dumb*."

"Yes," said Claire, "and it would be insane enough to do on your own. But to pick Moira as your partner! Do you trust her for a moment? Just look at the way she's sucking up to all of them! She's practically Freddy's mistress and she has the rest of them eating out of her hand. Why, if anything went wrong, what would she do? She'd play the injured lovesick woman seduced into crime by the slick gay con man to whom she'd lost her girlish heart. She'd throw the two of you right to the wolves!"

These words had a powerful effect on Gilbert. If before he'd looked like a man awaiting a dental appointment, he now resembled one awaiting a dental appointment in a clinic run by the Three Stooges. It was at this happy moment that we heard another knock on the door.

"Ye-es?" warbled Claire.

"Hi, hon," said Maddie, "are you all in there?"

"Yes, Mom!"

Maddie burst cheerfully in, clutching a crystal punch cup brimming with eggnog.

"I thought you might be. I don't know why it is but whenever I throw a party the young people spend the whole night going to the bathroom in groups."

Claire, with her usual presence of mind, explained that Gilbert had drawn us aside to ask our advice on what he might give Moira for Christmas.

On returning to the party we saw that Moira had shifted into high gear and was standing by the piano leading a group in Christmas carols. We noted grimly that she'd learned the Italian lyrics to "Frosty the Snowman."

Scattered about the room now were some dozen waiters instantly recognizable as employees of Marvelous Parties, the season's hottest caterer. They were all possessed of those attributes which were MP's trademark: thick wavy hair, jaws you could cut yourself on and a certain icy hauteur that made them seem less like waiters than unusually polite storm troopers.

Maddie left to greet some new arrivals and the minute she was gone Gilbert's stiff smile vanished.

"Oh, God, all the caterers in the world and she had to book them!"

"What's wrong?" asked Claire.

"Let's just say my past is catching up with me."

"Oh, dear! You had a romance with one of these men?"

"No," said Gilbert, gazing around. "Three of them."

The situation our little trio now faced was, you'll agree, a stressful one. And stress is a funny thing. People deal with it in different ways. Gilbert, as I mentioned earlier, sulks and eats Frïsen Glädje butter pecan. I tend to unplug my phone and lose myself in the pages of a good mystery, taking solace in the knowledge that, whatever my problems may be, I haven't just been found bludgeoned to death in a locked library no one could possibly have entered or left at the time of my death. But ice cream and mysteries are solitary comforts and not much good in situations where one must deal not only with stress but public scrutiny as well.

In these situations Gilbert and I usually cope in the same way: we clown. A psychiatrist, I suppose, would say that our anxiety induces great insecurity which can only be eased by massive doses of approval, and who the hell cares? Whatever the reason, we don the caps and bells and do our damnedest to be bright and charming and witty.

I was perfectly aware that on this of all nights, such behavior was not advisable. The sane thing would have been to keep a low profile, doing all I could to ensure that, come tomorrow, none of these dangerous people would even recall having met me. But no, I had to *entertain* them. They may all have been vicious thugs who sold heroin in schoolyards and murdered innocents just for practice but I wanted them to like me.

"Gilbert!" we heard and turned.

"Agnes darling!"

"I *hate* to be called Agnes!"

"I know!"

"Brat! Give me a kiss!"

She was a very put-together woman, the sort you first guess to be around forty then later decide is fifty and diligent. She was a far cry from the other women of her generation present at the party. She was svelte though not cadaverous, used makeup to flattering effect and wore a mauve silk dress which, while fetching, didn't challenge you to guess what it cost.

"Aren't you going to introduce me to your friends?"

"This is my old buddy Philip and his fiancée, Claire. This is my cousin Agnes—"

"Aggie!"

"—Fabrizio. Have you ever eaten at Paradiso on East Fifty-second?"

"No."

"Shame on you!"

"She owns it. She's Lunch's sister."

"Oh, dear. Then you've met Lunch, have you?"

"Yes. He was charming," said Claire, without a trace of sarcasm.

"*Was* he?" asked Aggie, glancing over to where Lunch had parked himself to devour a fresh plate of lasagna. "He always runs when he sees me because I'm always after him to lose some of that weight. Don't you think he should?"

"Yes," I concurred, "if he could just lay off those between-meal meals . . ."

"Exactly! I think he should try one of those appetite suppressants."

"Aggie, dear," I said, "the government of Poland couldn't suppress that appetite."

Aggie beamed and said I was wicked.

"He certainly is," agreed Claire. "Has Lunch always had this weight problem?"

"Ever since high school."

"Yes," I said, "his yearbook picture was an aerial photo."

Aggie let out a sharp staccato "Hah!" that sounded less like mirth than karate. "Gilbert, who *is* this boy? He's a scream!"

"Oh, Philip and I go way back. He's a writer."

"A writer? How marvelous! Are you famous?"

"Not quite," I blushed.

"He has a small following," said Gilbert.

"They meet once a year in a Volkswagen."

"Hah!"

"He's really very talented. He's just not known yet."

"That's a shame. What does an unknown writer make?"

"Excuses."

"Hah!"

Aggie's distinctly audible laugh had caught the attention of half the room. A couple drifted over to us now and were introduced as Ugo and Betty Sartucci, Chick's son and daughter-in-law.

"What's so funny, Aggie?"

"Gilbert's friend, Philip um . . . ?"

"Cavanaugh."

"Cavanaugh. He's terribly clever."

"Oh, are you the one that made that great crack about Lunch playing Santa Claus?"

"What, what?" asked Aggie, eagerly.

Ugo chortled and repeated the mot. Then he added: "You better watch out for Lunch. He heard someone telling it and he's a little steamed!"

"That's okay," said Gilbert, "his wife's a little fried!"

"Darling," said Claire, desperately trying to extricate us from our new admirers, "could you get me another glass of champagne?"

"Of course, dear. Too much blood in your alcohol system, is there?"

Claire smiled and dragged me away but it was too late. The fan club followed us to the bar and Gilbert and I kept cutting our capers while knocking back double scotches to further demolish our inhibitions.

A certain portion of my shtick derived from gleeful exaggeration of the hardships endured by the struggling artist.

"Thank you!" I said, accepting a crabmeat puff from a passing Nazi. "I really need this. My last square meal was a saltine."

Before long our little audience had doubled in size. Then, after casually letting it slip that Claire and I were the authors of several comic ditties, I allowed Aggie to drag us to the piano. The bench was at the time occupied by Sister Deena Sartucci, a round little nun who was, from the sound of things, either playing brilliantly with mittens on or ineptly without them. Aggie sweetly informed her that she need no longer shoulder the burden of entertaining all by herself. I conferred briefly with Claire and took care to choose only three or four of our very best. The response was more than gratifying. Even Claire, who'd nearly fled at the thought of playing, couldn't help but be warmed by the waves of laughter and applause and soon we were both, along with Gilbert who knew the words, rollicking through our boogie woogie salute to the *New York Post:*

> *"Tot Is Crushed Under Daddy's Wheels!*
> *"Three Dismembered As Nut Goes Wild!"*
> *Jury Reels*
> *As Mom Reveals:*
> *"Voices Told Me To Eat My Child!"*
> *In the* Post
> *The* Post!
> *The* New York Post!
> *Sex and death with your morning toast!*

That one left them all so eager for more that nothing could induce me to continue. The egomaniacal beast within knew that my victory was complete and that by continuing I could only dim its luster. I begged off politely but firmly and sauntered away to the ballroom where the dancing was just getting underway. Claire soon appeared at my side.

"You really are a jackass!" she whispered through a tense smile.

"Give me a break, okay?"

"Why? I drag you aside to inform you that we're in a room full of racketeers and hit men. So, of course, you immediately go out of your way to make sure that each and every one of them knows who you are, excuse me, who *we* are. I don't understand you sometimes, I really don't!"

"I'm sorry. I was nervous and when I get nervous—"

"Be quiet."

I followed her gaze and saw Moira and Gilbert approaching.

"You two were wonderful! How sweet of you to entertain when you're not even getting paid. Everybody's talking about you."

"How nice," said Claire.

"But dear, what's all this about your being engaged! It's a joke, right?"

There was a slight edge to her voice. I could see she suspected, correctly, that our sudden spurious romance was in some way related to her own, which would mean Claire knew. And Moira wouldn't like that one bit. But Claire covered beautifully.

"Oh, Moira," she said, suddenly just a bit drunk, "I don't know what came over me! When Chick asked if we were tying the knot I was suddenly just full of the devil! I had to see the look on Philip's face if I said yes! And now I'm embarrassed to say I was fibbing 'cause they might think I was making fun of them. Because I *wasn't* really, I was just—"

"—Full of the devil . . . and champagne, too, I think!" said Moira with a gay little laugh. She'd bought it.

"Yes, I'm afraid so. I'd better call it quits after this one!"

"Nonsense! Have fun! That's what we're here for!"

Maddie entered the ballroom and swept over to our corner, atwitter with excitement.

"Good news, kids! Freddy's up!"

She ushered us back into the living room and there, sitting on a sofa by the tree, was the archfiend, Freddy Bombelli. Aggie sat next to him on one side and on the other sat Chick Sartucci.

Directly behind Chick a well-dressed goon stood casting a suspicious eye on Freddy's loved ones. He had a low square build topped by short dark curly hair and a face only Darwin could love. Maddie later told me he was Serge, Freddy's "nurse." The title was not wholly facetious for he did, in fact, have charge of the old man's complex schedule of pills and was, in addition, prepared to swiftly diagnose

any unforeseen impediment to Freddy's health and respond immediately with massive doses of lead therapy.

As for Freddy, my initial impression was not one of age but of
diseased youth. Sitting there, his feet not quite touching the floor, he
didn't look like an old man as much as one of those children stricken
by that horrid disease which causes them to age prematurely and die
of senescence at nine.

"Freddy, hon, look who's here!" cried Maddie.

Freddy the Pooch looked up and his face blossomed at the sight
of his favorite wench. "*Cara!* You came!"

"Of course I came! Didn't I say I would!"

"But you young people. So many parties. You forget."

His voice only added to this macabre illusion of an ancient child.
It was wheezy but at the same time cheerful and loud, an exuberant
death rattle.

"Freddy, you remember my Gilbert."

"Of course. Steffie's wedding. So nice to see you again."

"Nice to see you, Uncle Freddy! You look great!"

"I take care of myself. Lotta naps."

"And *this*," said Aggie, smiling significantly, "is his very talented
young friend, Phil Cavanaugh. Oh, and that's his fiancée, Clara."

"Yes, Aggie," he said, "I won't forget. Hello, young man, a pleasure
to meet you."

"Oh, the pleasure's all mine! I've heard so much about you . . . from
Moira! She told me how much she enjoys her job."

"Did she? That's nice. I'm afraid sometimes she'll get bored, maybe
want to quit."

"Quit! Oh, you silly, you! All I worry about is that you'll find
someone better and give the job to her."

"Is no one better! This girl," he said, turning to Charlie Pastore,
"Moira, she's engaged to Maddie's son Gilbert, I hired her to read to
me. My eyes, you see, the doctor said no more reading. And I love
my books, you know. All my life, every night after dinner I take a
good book and read it. What am I supposed to do now, watch TV?"

"What's wrong with TV?" asked Maddie.

"You like it, you keep it, dear. Pfff! Every channel, nothing but
police and car chases. I had enough of that when I was young."

Everyone laughed at this, and no one louder than Moira.

"Oh, Freddy!" she trilled, scandalized.

Claire and I stared at Moira then at each other. The same bloody thought had erupted in both our minds:

She knows! She *knows* they're all Mafia and Freddy is Freddy the Pooch and they deal drugs and bribe senators and kill people and she doesn't care! *She wants to swindle them anyway!*

"Oh, Freddy!" she sang, "did you see? I'm wearing your Christmas gift. It is just *so* cheerful! Isn't it cheerful, Gilley?"

"Very!" said Gilbert, casting a nervous glance to his left. He was looking at a petulant traybearer from Master Race Caterers whose eyes, in turn, were fixed implacably on Gilbert. The anger that glinted in them was unmistakably that of a man who had been Done Wrong.

"Say! I haven't shown you two the house yet, have I, Philip?"

"Oh, let me!" said Maddie.

"That's okay, Mom. I can do it. See you in a bit, Freddy!"

He dragged us off through the arch into the foyer.

"Close one?"

"Oh, you don't *know*, honey, you just don't know!"

He took a cigarette from his jacket, lit it with a trembling hand, inhaled deeply, and moaned: "I *knew* I should have given that asshole his stereo back."

"Did you two notice what I noticed?" asked Claire.

"You mean Moira busting a gut over Freddy's joke?"

"Yes! I didn't like the sound of that. It almost seemed as if she knows all about them."

"Of course she *knows*!" hissed Gilbert. "You can tell the bitch has studied the family tree right down to its roots! Grandchildren, birthdays, blood types! She knows it all—you think she missed the fact they're all vicious criminals?"

Claire stuttered incredulously. "But I—I don't understand. If it's— I mean—if she *knows* what they are how can she still be planning to swindle them?"

"Because she's fucking psychotic, that's why! And besides, like you said, anything goes wrong, who's Freddy-poo going to believe? Her or me?"

"Oh, good Lord, it's worse than I thought!"

"Ain't it always!"

"Shhhhhhh!"

I glanced behind me and saw Tony Cellini approaching.

"Tony!" said Gilbert, heterosexually.

"Gilbert!"

Tony Cellini was, uniquely among his generation of the family, a handsome man. He had a trim build, topped by a lean face with a strong aquiline nose and a square jutting chin, the whole of it glowing with an off-season tan. His hair was thinning on top but this was flattering too, providing the viewer as it did with another inch or two of gleaming bronze. His teeth were perfect and he flashed them readily in a smile that, even in the throes of panic, I found thoroughly disarming. This first sight of him was disorienting since Gilbert's imitations of him had suggested a man far more coarse, bald no doubt, overweight almost certainly, and given to blowing his nose on table-cloths. It occurred to me only later that Gilbert had unconsciously devised this alternate version of Tony to avoid facing the distressing fact that his mother had married a man he'd sleep with in a minute.

"Gilbert, you never told me you were a singer."

"You never asked! Have you met my friends?"

"No, but I've had the pleasure of watching them perform."

He shook our hands, warmly complimenting our songs, adding that we were the talk of the party. "It's Philip, right? And Clara?"

"Claire."

"I'm sorry. Claire. I think you'll both go very far."

We may have to, I thought.

"I'm Tony. Maddie's husband—and this one's stepfather."

"Nice to meet you, Tony," said Claire. "Wonderful party!"

"You can thank yourselves for that. If you hadn't taken over the music when you did we'd have had Sister Deena for another hour! And best of all, she's too embarrassed to go back now that everyone's heard what real playing sounds like."

"Oh, dear, I didn't mean to—"

"Don't apologize! No one can *stand* her piano playing. But how do you tell a nun she stinks on ice?"

I noticed that Tall, Blond and Vindictive was once again passing the salmon in dangerous proximity. Gilbert noticed too and, making his apologies, scampered off to the john.

Tony asked us about our work together and hopes for the future. I sensed he was leading up to something, and he was.

"Say," he said, snapping his fingers in an unconvincing show of spontaneity, "there's someone I know here who'd love to meet you."

He led us back through the living room and into a large paneled dining room, the table of which groaned under a buffet of Lucullan proportions. Off in one corner a soulful stripling stared down at a plate of scampi on his lap. He wore a rather wistful look as if all the shrimp had been personal friends. His hair was brown and wavy, and if the length of his nose prevented him from being really handsome he still had a sweet off-centered quality that was pleasant to look at.

"Always daydreaming!" said Tony, gazing fondly at him.

We approached his corner and he looked up like a startled fawn. Introductions were made. He was Leo Cellini, Tony's godson and nephew by his late brother, Carlo. Leo was seventeen, a senior in high school, an honor student and just crazy about musicals, especially the works of Stephen Sondheim.

Now, as a recent Gallup poll has shown, there are perhaps as many as ten seventeen-year-old honor students who are crazy about Stephen Sondheim and heterosexual as well, but nothing in Leo's bearing led me to suspect that he was among them. There was nothing so overt as to be noticeable to the average straight adult. But he had a tendency to run his words together when excited, and a way of always italicizing the modifier *so* which left no doubt in my mind that a thorough search of his room would turn up copies of *Christopher and His Kind*, *Mandate* magazine and the works of Gordon Merrick.

"Leo writes music, too," offered Tony. "Wonderful stuff."

"Do you really?" asked Claire.

"Well, uh, kind of," said Leo, torn, it seemed, between a desire to race to the piano and an equally strong impulse to crawl under a rock and die.

"I mean it's not nearly as *accomplished* as yours."

"Good," smiled Claire. "I don't think I'd like you much if it were."

Tony laughed at this and Leo also let go a nervous nasal burst which, I supposed, was also a laugh.

"Right. If I were good as you that'd be pretty obnoxious!"

"You betcha."

"I thought your songs were *so* good. I mean, the lyrics were *so* funny!"

"Why, thank you, Leo."

"I mean, I could see where you stole some of the ideas from but it didn't matter because the jokes were all new ones."

"The soul of tact," said Tony.

"No," cried Leo, anguished, "you know what I mean! Did I say something wrong?"

"Not at all. You were just being observant," I said, then turning to Claire, added, in a mock sotto voce, "Who *is* this brat?"

"Don't you hate him?"

"Who does he think he is?"

"Exactly."

"Of all the miserable little adolescent know-it-alls!"

Leo was hiccupping with mirth, delightedly aware that we would never have insulted him if we didn't actually like him.

Just then Sister Deena Sartucci descended and began genuflecting at the shrine of Claire's talent.

"I'm afraid you made my own paltry efforts seem quite pathetic!"

"Oh, no! You play very well!"

"Nice of you to say so, I'm sure, but I know you must have noticed how very many *mistakes* I make."

"Not so many at all."

"Sweet of you to spare an old woman's feelings, dear, but . . ."

She continued in this vein for long minutes, and when she finally asked Claire if she'd come to the piano and give her some pointers, that was, if Claire didn't feel she was too inept and arthritic and old to entertain the smallest hope of ever improving even the tiniest little bit, poor Claire had no choice but to leap at the chance to prove her mistaken. Tony joined them, leaving Leo and I to discuss "our mutual interests."

We stood there chatting pleasantly about the sorry state of musical theater, Leo trying mightily to impress me with his discriminating taste. He wanted so to be taken seriously and assumed I was ready to dismiss him entirely if I detected the slightest lapse in his scholarship or standards. This combination of brazen egotism and naked self-doubt reminded me of the way I'd behaved at his age so I found it extremely endearing.

For the first time that evening I forgot that I was surrounded by thugs and cutthroats. My thoughts were suddenly full of Leo. Or, rather, Leo and me . . . the shows we might see; the discussions we might have over quiet dinners; the experiences of mine he could benefit from; the lessons, many and varied, I could teach him as he was taking those first brave steps toward maturity, self-acceptance and—

Ding! Ding! Ding! Ding! Ding!

What on earth was I *thinking* of! How could I allow myself to dream of an illicit romance with this Mafia Child? Why, it was madness just to be standing here discussing *Pacific Overtures* with him!

"Oh, and don't you love the way in "Please, Hello" he takes the same metric scheme as the Major General's song in *Pirates of Penzance* then complicates it with the interior rhymes? It's my favorite lyric in the show."

"Mine is 'A Bowler Hat.' "

"Oh, isn't that *great*?"

In his enthusiasm he clapped a hand on each of my shoulders and stared directly into my eyes. The stare lengthened.

DING! DING! DING! DING! DING!

How to escape? Imperative though it was to avoid this youth and all the ruinous possibilities he represented, my regard for him was already too warm to want to risk hurting his feelings. Remembering Gilbert's earlier ruse I feigned a sudden desperate need to use the nearest john.

"You doing coke?" he asked, contradicting somewhat my naïve Norman Rockwell image of him.

"No, I just have to pee."

"Oh. I'll show you where it is."

"That's okay, I know. Hey, finish your dinner before it gets cold, nice meeting you maybewe'lltalkagainlaterbye."

In my haste to quit the scene I forgot one of the primary rules of successful party evasion: if you say you have to go to the bathroom, *go* to the bathroom. But so ravaged were my nerves that I'd only gotten as far as the next room when the sight of dependable Roger, ready, as ever, to provide succor to the afflicted, caused me to stop in my tracks. Ordering a double scotch, I took up a position by one of the tall windows. There I could gaze out at Maddie's Wonderful World of Christmas and begin trying to sort through the nightmare of complications which had arisen in the last hour.

"Hi," said Leo.

"Hello! Quite a line for the bathroom," I said.

"There are lots of bathrooms. I can show you where."

"That's okay, I can wait. Builds character."

"Oh . . . okay."

There was a baffled tentative look on his face that was heartbreaking to behold. He knew I'd tried to avoid him and, unable to see why, could only assume that I found him boring and immature and that I'd only been nice to him at all because my host had requested I do so.

Gripped suddenly by an intense need to rectify this misapprehension I began asking him all about his music and soon enough the conversation was bubbling along merrily once more. Too merrily, in fact, for Leo managed twice in the space of ten minutes to snag glasses of champagne from passing trays. What was worse, he imbibed them both in great greedy gulps.

As a result, his laugh, disconcertingly high in pitch, was coming more frequently now and whenever silence fell between us he was fixing me with increasingly provocative smiles so that I was forced to say something, *anything*, to avoid noticing the come-hither looks.

The worst of it was that my feelings toward him were so dreadfully obvious. He knew I was responding nervously to his advances not because I wasn't interested but because I was. He'd smile wickedly and I'd return the smile, involuntarily, for a fraction of a second before looking away or down. And then, attempting to pretend it hadn't happened, I'd look him in the face and ask somewhat stiffly what he thought of *Flower Drum Song*, which would only cause him to laugh again, only louder, which would cause me to shut up, giving him the opportunity to leer some more.

"Leo!" I said, blushing prettily.

"What?" he grinned.

"Cut it out!"

"Cut *what* out?"

"You know!"

"No, what?" he said, leering.

"Those looks you're giving me."

"What kind of looks?"

"You know what kind of looks!"

"I'm just looking at *you* the way you're looking at *me*."

"I am *not* looking at you that way!"

"*What* way?"

And so on.

Suddenly we were joined by a short ferret-faced man in his sixties who was smoking an immense foul-smelling cigar.

"Hey, Leo, how they hangin'! Gilbert's buddy cracking you up, huh?"

"Yes!" throbbed Leo, grabbing champagne from a passing tray.

"Hi there, I'm Charlie Pastore. Married to Tony's sister, Theresa."

"Nice to meet you."

"Nice meeting you, too. Heard you at the piano. Great stuff!"

"*Won*derful," agreed Leo, draining the glass.

Escape was more imperative than ever. I looked around for someone who'd offer a pretext to excuse myself and saw Claire at the piano struggling vainly to improve the good sister's technique.

"Gosh, I'm afraid I'm really neglecting my fiancée."

"Your fiancée?" asked Leo, stricken.

"Hey, leave her alone," said Charlie. "She's giving Sister Deena lessons and if anyone ever needed 'em, she's the one!"

"You're engaged?"

"Yes."

"To *her*?" asked Leo, unkindly.

"Hey, congratulations. You got yourself a talented girl. So, Leo, how's school? You finish this year, don't you?"

"Yuh."

"Been applying to lotta colleges?"

There was my cue.

"'Scuse me," I said, pretending to recognize someone across the room. "Nice meeting you both."

"Same goes! So your mom said somethin' 'bout Princeton or . . ."

I sped off, waving frantically at a nonexistent figure in the hall. On reaching the front door I paused but not for long as a quick glance over my shoulder revealed that Leo had taken leave of Charlie and was rapidly downing yet another champagne. Our eyes locked across the distance and he mouthed the word "Wait" as he placed the dead soldier on an end table.

Having witnessed how subtle he could be on two glasses, I had no desire to see what miracles of overtness he could achieve under the influence of four. I considered the stairs but decided that to do this was to risk the disastrous possibility that he would corner me in a bedroom. This left only two options: the ballroom or the corridor that ran parallel to the staircase on the ground floor. I sped down the hall. There were several doors and I reasoned that if I popped through the wrong one and witnessed a murder in progress I could always say I was just looking for the bathroom.

I ducked into a door at the end of the hall on the ballroom side and as coincidence would have it, it *was* a bathroom. I glanced behind me just as I shut the door to make sure that Leo hadn't seen me enter it. He hadn't.

I sat a moment and felt wonderfully relieved. Then it dawned on me—I was trapped. He would investigate all possible routes of escape including this one. He would knock on the door and ask if it was occupied. I could try to disguise my voice, which probably wouldn't work. I could lock the door and keep quiet in which case he'd be sure I was inside and wait me out, or I could not lock the door in which case he'd merely burst in on me.

For a moment this last option seemed most desirable for it would at least afford us a little privacy while I explained that I was a rapturously happy heterosexual deeply in love with a short one-hundred-and-sixty-pound female composer.

But then I thought, what if he just jumps my bones? What if I find myself unable to resist? This was hardly out of the realm of possibility, for the mere thought of such an assault had rendered me excited in a way that Leo, were he to burst in, would not fail to detect. And what if we're overheard by someone in the hall? How do I explain what I'm doing in the john with a seventeen-year-old—

"Knock knock!" sang Leo, rapping at the door.

So soon! I looked about foolishly as if there were any possibility of an escape route.

And there was! The bath was connected to another room! I lunged for the doorknob and, turning it as silently as my haste would permit, slipped into the room beyond, closing the door behind me.

Judging from the sound coming from the wall to my left the room was at the back of the house, behind the ballroom. The wall to my right had two tall windows and there was enough pale red light from Maddie's Winter Wonderland for me to see the room was a study. I turned and stood with my ear to the bathroom door. I heard another knock, louder it seemed, and Leo's voice asking if anyone was there. Then I heard him enter the bath.

It occurred to me that he would certainly note the door to the study just as I had, and I began looking frantically for a place to hide. There was a desk to my left. In front of it were two huge easy chairs facing perpendicular to the desk and across from these was a big leather sofa. There seemed to be room between the sofa and the windows so I dashed across and crouched behind it. And not a moment too soon, for immediately the door to the bathroom opened. Leo flicked a switch and the room filled with light. There was a pause as he surveyed the scene.

"Oh, caca!" he moaned at length and, flicking the light off, vanished once more into the bath.

I exhaled with relief and decided to wait just a moment or two till I could be sure Leo's search had moved upstairs, at which point I would find Claire, manacle myself to her wrist, and kiss her neck all night long. After crouching some moments my legs began to ache and I decided the wait had been sufficient. I rose with a little leap, feeling quite satisfied with myself.

Then I heard the doorknob turn; not the door to the bathroom but the tall paneled door which opened out into the room next to the study. I dove back behind the couch, landing flat on my knees and sending up and down both legs spasms of pain so intense I feared they'd be visible, like the stars that whirl around Wile E. Coyote's head after his rocket skates have malfunctioned. I stuffed my knuckles into my mouth and quivered in agony.

The door opened and the lights were turned on once more. I heard the voice of Freddy Bombelli.

"No, Serge," it wheezed, "we'd prefer the privacy. Wait outside."

"Oh . . . sure," said Serge mistrustfully.

"But Sergio—tell me when you hear the tarantella start. I don't want to miss that, okay?"

"Sì."

"You will remember?" asked Freddy dubiously.

"I'll remember!" said the injured primate.

The door closed. Two pairs of footsteps crossed to the sofa and stopped.

"Forgive me," hissed Freddy. "I hate to drag you away from such a delightful party but you know how families are—such big ears! Such gossip! You have a quiet chat in the corner and a half hour later everyone knows what you said. And I want this to be private. Is nobody's business, just yours and mine. Right?"

"Sure," said Gilbert, just a bit nervously. "What's up?"

Thirteen

I lowered myself inch by torturous inch till I was flat on my stomach and the pressure was off my poor battered knees. It wasn't long, though, before the pain in them was the furthest thing from my mind.

"I'm old," said Freddy, "but I'm not always so old-fashioned. You live a long time, you see the world change. If you're wise you change a little, too. I have many opinions that would shock my sisters if they knew I held them. So I don't tell them!" he added with an asphyxiated chuckle.

"Good approach!" said Gilbert.

"Gilbert, you must forgive me please, if I offend you—"

"Don't worry!"

"But one thing I have changed my thinking about very much is gayboys."

"Oh?" coughed Gilbert.

"When I was young, like you—way back, Prohibition—if I met someone I thought was a gayboy, automatically I hate his guts. I call him nasty names and maybe punch him a few times. If there was water nearby I'd throw him into it. I do not say this with *pride*, you understand. But at that time, in my world, which was very small, this was the correct thing to do. Such needless hatred! Such unprofitable cruelty! Today, I look back and I don't understand. Why should we behave so?"

"Well," said Gilbert, suicidally, "you were probably scared to death that if you didn't someone would think you were queer, too."

I cringed as best I could in that position and awaited Freddy's geriatric wrath. But he wasn't angry. He laughed.

"You know, I think you're right. We *were* afraid. But we had reason. At that time, someone thought you were a gayboy, it meant you were not a man, you were weak. Someone to cheat, take advantage of. Of course, if some unscrupulous person were to think of you in this way, you could show him he was wrong—but maybe you get in trouble showing him, right? Better he should never think such things to begin with. So—if you met a gayboy, you punched him. Foolishness."

Freddy paused and I prayed that Gilbert, having scored with the Fear of Association Postulate, would not now press his luck by voicing the still more popular gay theory that ninety-eight percent of fagbashers are repressed homosexuals.

"I am happy to see that in my lifetime, this has changed. The gayboys got tired of being punched so they stop hiding. They say to the world, 'Yes, we're gayboys and we're going to stay that way an' you don't like it, you can eat shit. You punch us, we punch you right back. And they're right! Whose business is it what they want to do? Is a free country, isn't it?"

"Absolutely."

"As long as you're good to your parents and honorable in business, you should be able to fuck anyone you want. Long as they're over eighteen. I do business with a couple of gay gentlemen, Alan and Derrick. Good people. Always meet obligations, pay their bills on time. We exchange Christmas cards. So, you see, I have nothing against gayboys."

"Well, I can see that! You're obviously a *compassionate, fair* man—"

"I think perhaps you know what I'm getting at."

"Well, I would guess that, uh, maybe someone or other has perhaps told you that I'm, uh, that is, that I *was,* at one time, briefly, gay."

"Yes. Moira did."

"No kidding?" choked Gilbert.

"Please, do not feel angry toward her or imagine she was disloyal! She loves you very much! You know this, don't you?"

"Never doubted it."

"She did not *volunteer* this information, you understand. It was I who brought the subject up. Why would I bring up such a subject? Well, it's embarrassing but I'll tell you . . . As I said, my family is full of gossips. One of these gossips (*who* is not important) was having lunch with me just after Moira began reading to me. I told this person of Moira's kindness and mentioned, in passing, that she was engaged to my nephew Tony's stepson. This gentleman was very surprised to hear this. You see, he used to work for me in a discotheque I own called Rampage. He said he had seen you there many times in the company of young men and that you were behaving—how should one say?—affectionately.

"I confess, this upset me very much. And I tell you why. Years ago a relative of mine (*who* is not important) but a nice young woman, she married a gayboy. He did not tell her about himself. He lied to her and made promises that he would be faithful. He was not. He broke her heart and brought disgrace upon the family. A terrible and dishonorable man. At the end even he could no longer bear his shame and he killed himself in some unusual fashion, I don't remember how.

"So when I hear these stories about you I assume—you must forgive me—that Moira knows nothing about it. So I tell her what I have been told. And then . . . she smiles! She smiles and she tells me everything."

"Everything?" asked Gilbert.

"Yes. And right away I like you much better than my niece's gayboy. You were not dishonest like him. You told your woman things she had a right to know."

"Well, sure I did!" said Gilbert. "I mean . . ." he began, and, not having the first idea *what* he meant, trailed off.

"Please. You mustn't be embarrassed. I am an old man. There's little I haven't seen in my life. You may not know it but many men have experienced the same problem as you, though not usually so young, of course. That is very sad."

"Terribly sad!" agreed Gilbert, baffled. What on earth had Moira told him?

"I have had this problem myself. Not often! A few times."

"Oh?"

"Though to be impotent so young as you were! A young man barely twenty. Most upsetting! I can certainly see why a boy who was in your position would prefer not to risk the humiliation of . . . failing with women. It's not easy at any age but the young are so sensitive. And, of course, times being the way they are, why not . . . experiment? Try things another way?"

He rasped in a low obscene chuckle.

"You see? I'm really not old-fashioned! I know a man needs to do *something*. If one thing doesn't work, try something else, yes?"

"That's *my* motto!"

"But what a joy it must have been to meet a woman with whom it was—different! I must tell you, Gilbert, how touched I was when she spoke of how grateful you were to her that she could make your problem suddenly vanish. How happy it made you to know at last you had found what you truly wanted, and you would never need anyone else for the rest of your life. I am a romantic, you see, so such stories give me great delight. You, too, I see. Just to remember it your eyes fill with tears of joy. *L'amore!* Such a beautiful thing, is it not?"

Gilbert was too choked up by the loveliness of it all to manage a reply and Freddy wheezed mercilessly on.

"So this is why I asked to speak to you. I heard things about you which alarmed me. Then I spoke to Moira and she said other things which made me happy. It would make me happier still to hear them from you.

"I suppose you must think I'm a nosy old man, eh? Butting in where I don't belong. But, please, indulge me. I have no children of my own left and Moira is such a dear child. I have come to think of her as my own granddaughter. Her unhappiness would be my unhappiness."

"That's just how I feel!"

"You're sure you love her? Enough to marry her?"

There was a pause then of not more than two seconds' duration. I lay there behind the sofa, desperately channeling every ounce of mental and spiritual energy I could muster in an effort to make extrasensory contact with that dark uncharted territory that is the mind of Gilbert.

Pull out! Say you've had doubts! And you realize now that you must for her sake—

"Of *course* I'm sure! She's everything to me!"

Nooooo!!

"I knew that, Gilbert. Just as I know you would never do anything to hurt her."

"Never!"

"Then we will say no more. You're a good boy! There is no reason to doubt your word. You would not lie to me like my niece's husband, who, as I now recall, set himself on fire and jumped off an apartment building."

"And just what he deserved, too! Breaking a woman's heart!"

"Thank you for your time. You've helped an old man sleep easier. The question for me is, how to return this favor?" He paused for effect, then said, "I think, perhaps I know a way."

"Oh?" asked Gilbert, pathetically. Clearly, he hoped that some small munificence of Freddy's might, like a frail ray of sunlight, pierce through the avalanche of woe Moira's vicious lies had sent cascading down upon him. A case of good scotch, perhaps, or a pair of diamond cuff links. A car, maybe?

"Moira tells me you're looking for a job."

Silence fell for a moment as Gilbert reeled from this, Moira's lowest, most perfidious blow yet.

"*Does* she?"

"I sympathize with your difficulty. Such hardship a young writer must endure while awaiting success! So I have tried to think of some pleasant occupation for you. And tonight, thanks to your delightful friend and your cousin Aggie, I think that perhaps I have found one."

At this reference to me my head shot up involuntarily. Whether he considered me delightful or not I trembled to think I could have any part in whatever he was devising for Gilbert. I held my breath, the better to hear the next fateful words he should utter.

At that precise moment, however, the door to the anteroom opened.

"*Scusati*, Signore Bombelli," said Serge, "but the tarantel—"

He stopped suddenly and yelled:

"*Jesus fuckin' Christ!* Down! Both of you! *Down!*"

Suddenly the room thundered with explosions and the window directly behind me collapsed into jagged shards. Terrible thoughts raced through my mind. How could he have *seen* me? What did it matter how—he had! Death was at hand! I should have fucked Leo! My heart leapt into my esophagus and fearful that I'd go to my grave disfigured by flying glass I crammed my face as far as it would go into the narrow space between the floor and the bottom of the sofa. I'd instinctively closed my eyes and, opening them now, I saw Gilbert's face, also pressed to the floor, staring at me in astonished terror from the other side of the sofa. He couldn't, of course, ask me what I was doing there aloud, but he bugged his eyes interrogatively. I attempted a response, but to convey, through facial expressions alone, that you've hidden in a dark room to escape a sexually precocious gay teenager and were then forced to remain hidden to avoid being noticed by an elderly crime czar is difficult in the best of circumstances, and impossible under gunfire.

I heard footsteps. It sounded as if two or three large men had raced into the room. There was a confused jumble of speech, the general trend of which was an inquiry into what the fuck had happened. Footsteps came closer to the couch.

"My God, Freddy! Are you okay?" said a voice I recognized as Tony's.

"I'm always okay!" cackled Freddy. "Sonsabitches never got me yet!"

An alarmed babble of voices drifted in from the anteroom.

"Three guys!" said Serge emotionally. "In the window! They came running up outa nowhere and pulled guns on Freddy and—"

He was cut off by the loudest laugh I'd ever heard. It was Tony.

"*Gunmen*, were they?"

Suddenly the laugh caught on. It grew louder and louder.

"What an asshole!" cried someone.

"They pulled *guns*, huh?" guffawed someone else.

"S'okay, folks!" said Tony, withdrawing. "No one's hurt. Gilbert! You look pretty bad, son. What can I say? High-strung family!"

"Freddy, that's some nurse you got. Doesn't miss a trick!"

"Don't tease poor Sergio," exhorted Freddy. "Just doing his job."

"C'mon, Gilbert. Close the door behind you so we don't freeze the place out. Maddie, baby! Don't worry, no one's hurt. We'll have Giuseppe board it up after the party. Hey, back up, Lunch! Show's over!"

The lights were turned off. I heard the door close and, after waiting a moment, poked my head around the corner of the sofa. The room was empty. Dizzy with relief I stood, turned around and saw the two slaughtered Magi lying in the snow, their arms still pathetically clutching their gifts for the birthday party they would never reach. The third was still erect and on its track but had been neatly decapitated. As I stood a moment frozen at the sight I heard the familiar carol start up again and the headless king, ghoulishly clasping its frankincense, glided off to give Baby Jesus a nasty surprise.

I ran into the bathroom and locked both doors. Five minutes later the tremors had almost entirely subsided and I rejoined the party.

Credit the Bombellis with a sense of humor. News of Serge's triple regicide spread quickly through the house and everyone thought it was the funniest thing since thumbscrews. Fresh explosions of mirth could be heard coming from every corner as new people were apprised of the details and fresh witticisms were coined. No sooner would the laughter begin to fade than someone or other would loudly announce he was going out to the crèche to frisk the shepherds and the whole thing would begin anew.

I heard the story from Aggie who cornered me the minute I entered the ballroom. She was drunker than when I'd seen her last but still in command of her consonants which was not the case with many others.

Someone looked out and noticed the headless king and suddenly there were about fifty people all crowding round the ballroom's French windows staring at the scene, splitting their sides. Under more stress than ever, I started making jokes, calling it the Brian DePalma Nativity. Given that my audience was comprised entirely of drunks who'd all been busting their guts before I'd even started I had little trouble inducing fresh gales of mirth.

In the midst of this Gilbert elbowed his way through to me.

"Hi!" he said manically. "How are *you*!"

"I'm *great*! How the hell are you!"

"Couldn't be *better*!"

We both broke down in helpless laughter and everyone else was already laughing so hard they didn't bother to wonder what it was all about. Then the crowd parted respectfully and Freddy came forward leading Moira by the hand. He'd apparently not spoken to Gilbert since the shooting, for he said, "Ah, here you are, Gilbert. I believe we were interrupted."

Everyone guffawed at the pleasantry, and Freddy beamed.

"I was about to make a request of you on behalf of your cousin Aggie. I see your friend is here, too. Good, good!"

"Oh Gilley!" said Moira, "you're just going to love this! You too, Philip!"

"Perhaps, you should ask them, Aggie," said Freddy.

"Love to! Listen, you two," she said, taking us both by our hands, "you're both a couple of starving artists and you both need something to keep bread on the table till you're both as famous as I'm sure you're gonna be. Now, my little restaurant has immediate openings for a host and a bartender, or rather it will have when I give the two I've got now the old boot. Hah! Well, they deserve it, they're bores! What I need is a couple of young charmers who can keep my surly relatives smiling even when they have to wait for a table they don't want to begin with, and the cook is smashed and burning the pasta! I had two princes with me for years but they left, and since then no one has worked out at all. I need you Tuesdays through Saturdays; we're closed Mondays and I rent it out Sundays for parties. You don't have to be there till five and you're always out by one so you have *all* day to work on your writing."

"Isn't it perfect?" said Moira.

"I don't care who tends bar and who hosts. You can flip a coin! So, kids, what do you say?"

"Well . . ." I began and was immediately drowned out by a chorus of lethal admirers coaxing us into submission. What could I say? That I didn't need work? After my merry quips about my poverty-stricken existence? And what could Gilbert say with Freddy standing there grinning munificently? That he didn't care if his wife and children starved while he finished (or, rather, contemplated beginning) his great novel?

We conveyed our grateful acceptance to the delighted applause of the assembled, and after much shaking of hands I excused myself, pleading that I had to seek out my fiancée and give her the joyous news.

I found her in the living room where she was still gamely coaching the good sister. She saw me and, excusing herself, ran to my side.

"Philip!" she whispered. "Where on earth have you been? I've been worried sick! Do you know what's been going on here? Gilbert went for a chat with *Freddy*. And in the middle of it that psychopath who works for him fired shots at Maddie's Christmas display! These people are poison, Philip! At least you can thank God you're not in too deep yet. Tomorrow morning, you tell Gilbert you're sorry but you are *out* of it. You don't intend to lay eyes on any of these hoodlums ever again. Is that clear?—Shhh! Such a nice party, isn't it, dear? Why, hello, Leo! How are you? So good to see you again!"

Fourteen

The next day Gilbert, Claire and I met at Claire's Riverside Drive apartment. The weather that day seemed deliberately chosen to intensify our mood. It was cold, gray and drizzly, and Claire's studio, which on a nice day looks small and cheerful, looked small and bleak, a place where pawnbrokers might go to die.

We hadn't discussed the situation since the party when I'd stammered out the news of our sudden career opportunities. The complications had become so overwhelming that there seemed no point in trying to sort them all out right there in the enemy camp. Claire just pulled us aside to secure our agreement on one thing: that from here on in Moira was to be told nothing. *Nothing*. She was not to know Claire was in on it, nor that any of us had the first idea we were dealing with the Mafia. Moira could turn any information to her own foul purpose so secrecy was the only advantage we could hope to cultivate.

We saw the wisdom in this plan and wasted no time in putting it into effect. The môment we left Maddie's we began waxing rhapsodic about the party and the family's boundless charm. As for the Massacre of the Magi, it was hard to affect a naïveté so thorough as to have been left intact after that bit of carnage, but we tried. Wasn't it natural that a man of Freddy's wealth should have an armed bodyguard? Rock stars had them, after all, and so did politicians. And how frightening those Magi must have seemed out of the context of the manger, swinging into view with their long robes and tall hats like some strange band of transvestite assassins. Still, how funny it had been when they'd all realized Serge's mistake! How Gilbert had laughed!

*   *   *

"Well, Gilbert," said Claire, locking her door, "I've been reading up on your family all morning and I can't say I'm encouraged for you."

We noted her small dining table was piled high with library books and copies of *New York* magazine. Various pages were marked with paper clips.

"God, where did you get all these back issues?"

"They're mine. They've been sending it to me for six years. I keep winning the contests. They do a lot of mob pieces, so I knew I'd find something. The books are worth looking at, too. Feast your eyes."

She disappeared into the kitchen alcove. Gilbert and I seated ourselves and, with trembling hands, began inspecting the evidence.

There was a book called *The Blood Broker*. I could see from the imitation *Godfather* lettering on the cover that it was one of the spate of tell-all Mafia books rushed into print in the wake of the fabulous success of Puzo's novel and its celluloid offspring. This one was about a Philadelphia racketeer named Louis Lucabella who'd flourished in the fifties and sixties.

Claire had marked a page. It recounted an incident that took place in the late thirties when young Louis was taking his first baby steps toward infamy. In brief, he and three enterprising cohorts had begun a small pharmaceutical concern, the purview of which overlapped that of a similar enterprise operated by Beefman Bombelli (for this was in the days before he was called the Pooch, or they'd never have been so rash).

Soon one of their little band disappeared and a week later the rest were summoned to Freddy's slaughterhouse for a few friendly hands of poker. Louis and his friends, however, had some difficulty enjoying the game for it was repeatedly interrupted by the sounds of blood-curdling screams and cracking bones, all coming from the next room. At each of these pesky interruptions, Freddy apologized, explaining that this was, after all, a slaughterhouse with a daily quota of cattle to dispatch—though which rare breed of cow was capable of screaming, "No more, please, just kill me!" he didn't say. In a mere three hours poor Bossie fell silent and Freddy, who was behind, let the three depart with their chips, saying he'd be only too happy to cash these in whenever they cared to return.

I looked up from this cheering account to see Gilbert staring at an article as if it were the last chapter of a Stephen King novel. Silently we traded off.

It was a piece about Freddy, written two and a half years ago when he was released from prison. It painted a frighteningly inaccurate portrait of a sad little man, debilitated, chastened, "tired of the bloodletting" and close to death. There was a picture of a tiny hunchbacked figure dolefully leaning on his cane in a small unweeded garden, a man who couldn't have been more unlike the horridly robust homunculus I'd met at Maddie's party. My heart sank as I thought of that shrewd lizard, gulling the public into thinking he was a spent force when he was still bursting with malignant energy.

Claire reentered with coffee for us.

"Did you *see* this?" I asked.

"Yes. Stupid journalist. Completely taken in!"

"Oh my gawwwd," moaned Gilbert, immersed in Freddy's slaughterhouse shenanigans.

"And that's hardly the worst of it," said Claire with a nod to the books and magazines we hadn't yet perused. "They're dreadful people. And there are more of them than you can shake a stick at."

"I don't get it. That day at Trader Vic's Maddie made it sound as if the Bombellis were dropping like flies. What's that all about?"

"Who cares?" moaned Gilbert. "I don't want to know!"

"That's exactly the sort of attitude that got you into this mess to begin with."

"Do you want to pick on us or do you want to help us?"

"*Both,* if it's all the same to you. I mean, I've seen idiocy before, but nothing to compare with the sheer witlessness of your behavior last night. Running around begging for attention! And you, Gilbert! Why on earth did you have to make such absurd promises to Freddy?"

"Fuck you, Miss School Marm. I just told him what he wanted to hear. You going to tell someone like that what he *doesn't* want to hear?"

Claire agreed he had a point.

"And besides, there was Moira out there sucking up to everyone like crazy just so they'll give us good wedding presents. What's she going to do if I turn around and tell Freddy I'm calling it off? She's going to get furious, that's what, and say, 'Oh Freddy-poo, that lousy faggot broke my heart! Cut his nose off for me, would you?' "

"But the *jobs,* Gilbert. You can't actually go to work for these people!"

"What could I say, honey? Look, s'no big deal. We'll get out of them!"

"Should we?" I asked. "If we renege we'll only make them mad. Besides, if we turn down jobs, especially when we're so broke, that'll just tip Moira off that we know they're Mafia."

"Why are we letting Moira call the shots anyway?" fumed Gilbert. "She's just as guilty of trying to swindle them as we are! It was *her* idea!"

"Try telling Freddy that," I said. "He thinks she's Anne of Green Gables!"

"Well," said Claire, "clearly we have to do something to see this whole double payment swindle doesn't succeed. That's the worst of it. Making Tony pay for a wedding Moira's mother thinks *she's* paying for."

"How do we stop it?" asked Gilbert.

"We could tip off the duchess," I offered.

"Just what I was thinking," said Claire. "Write the duchess a little anonymous note. Then leave it to her to step in and quietly set things right."

"Anonymous note? Grow up! Moira will *know* we wrote it. And if we sic Mummy on her what do you think she'll do to us?"

"But *will* she know you wrote it? I mean, she doesn't think there's any *reason* you'd want to pull the rug out from under her, does she? She thinks you're all in favor of swindling them, right?"

"She thinks I'm thrilled about it."

"Well, see she goes on thinking that. Stay gung ho. And remember you don't know your stepfamily is Mafia! Not a clue! Because if you start fretting about them being criminals, then the duchess gets an anonymous letter—well, she could certainly put two and two together. So you *love* the family. You too, Philip. They're colorful and harmless."

"Which means we definitely take Aggie's jobs."

"Why?" asked Gilbert, alarmed.

"Why *wouldn't* we? She knows how broke I am. Besides, you're supposed to be sucking up to your family to get them to spend more on wedding gifts. Why pass up a chance to see them all the time unless you're suddenly scared to death of them?"

"He's right," frowned Claire.

"Shit!"

"Look," said Claire, "it's not as if you have to keep the jobs forever. You can look for something else while you're there, then in a few weeks say you got a better offer and you're sorry but you have to quit. The point is to keep Moira off the scent. You might do even more to confuse her."

"Like what?"

"The letter to the duchess—fill it with nasty things about the two of you. Make it look like it was written by someone who hates your guts."

"Good idea."

"She's still going to wonder about it."

"Let her. Brazen it out. Be as mad about it as she is. You have as much to lose, don't you? Who told Freddy you were gay? Mightn't *he* have sent it? And again, if she doesn't know *why* you did it, she can't really be sure you did."

An awful thought hit me.

"What if the duchess decides to go straight to Maddie and Tony?"

Claire inhaled sharply as the horror of the thought washed over her. She chewed her lip a moment.

"Well . . . I don't think she would. It'd be highly embarrassing to tell the Cellinis her daughter was swindling them. I think her inclination would be to hush it up, not bust it wide open. She might call the Cellinis and say she and the duke had suddenly come into money and could now afford to pay for everything. But, to be on the safe side we'll do this: make two copies of the letter and hold on to one so if the Cellinis are furious and want to take it out on you, you can prove that you were the ones who moved to *prevent* the swindle from happening."

We pondered it a bit and agreed that this plan, while not entirely bug-free, was the only one we had. Claire fetched some plain white typing paper and we drafted the following letter:

Dear Duchess,

 I am not by nature a meddlesome person but I feel it would be wrong of me not to inform you of certain unsavory facts which have recently come to my attention.

 Your unscrupulous daughter, Moira, has squandered all the money in her trust fund (probably on drugs) and is now attempting

to conceal this from you with the help of her sniveling fiancé,
Gilbert Selwyn. If that's not bad enough, this Gilbert is a homosexual who flaunts this fact to the world by spending all his time
in the company of a man named Philip Cavanaugh who is a well-
known fag and the author of several disgusting plays. Your daughter
and Gilbert have led Gilbert's very rich family to believe YOU
have no money at all! They think you and your husband, the
Duke, are greedy snobs who expect the groom's family to pay
for the wedding and, you can believe me, their opinion of you
is PRETTY LOW!

I have always had great respect for British royalty and when
Charles married Diana I bought many souvenirs. It would break
my heart to stand by and see the reputation of a real American-
born royal woman (like Mrs. Simpson) ruined by the disgusting
lies of her greedy daughter and a pair of alcoholic pansies!

> Yours regretfully,
> A Wellwisher

Claire made two copies in a childlike scrawl very different from
her own elegant hand. She placed one in a plain white envelope and
copied the address of Trebleclef from Gilbert's address book. In the
middle of this she stopped and said:

"How do I know this?"

"Know what?"

"The address? How many people know her mother's address? Because if you're the only one, dear, it won't look good for you."

Gilbert thought about it a moment and said that his mother and
Tony were the only ones he could be sure of. However, Moira was
forever going on about the beauty of Trebleclef and the charm of
quaint Little Chipperton. Surely dozens of friends had heard her sing
their praises. The address could read simply Trebleclef, Little Chipperton, and we could trust the local postman to know that the house
was located on St. Crispen Road.

Claire agreed and addressed the envelope.

"There. I'll send it DHL so we can be sure it doesn't get lost and
lose us valuable time. Remember to be cheerful about your plan. If
she senses you want to bail out it won't be hard to guess who sent

this. Oh, about the job, Gilbert—pardon my frankness, but you loathe work of any sort, don't you?"

"Not at all! I've always been prepared to do a good day's work if the job isn't some tedious—"

"Gilbert," I interrupted, "you know you can't bear working."

"Well, who can? What's the point?"

"The point is Moira *knows* that. So how did you react about her helping you find work? I mean, after the party, when you were alone?"

"Oh. Well, she immediately asked me how it went with Freddy and I said he told me all that bullshit she'd given him—*her* saving *me* from impotence!—and that I'd said it was true 'cause what *could* I say? Then she said, 'Oh, I thought it was ever so clever of me to come up with that story right on the spot when he said he'd heard you were queer.' Then she went on about how she kept meaning to tell me but *I'd* been so nasty lately she'd hardly had a chance. She had no idea Freddy was going to drag me aside for a man-to-man talk about it. Then she said, 'Oh well, all worked out for the best, didn't it?' and I said, 'Yes, thanks for the job, you miserable cunt,' and went to bed."

Claire winced but allowed that this was in the appropriate spirit.

"If you'd said you were glad or actually thanked her she'd have known you were intimidated because you'd figured out who Freddy really was and were scared of what she might have him do to you."

We agreed there was nothing more we could do till the duchess reacted to the letter. The ball was in her court.

"I hope she kills her!" said Gilbert. "I hope she goes at her with a chain saw and disinherits the pieces! That vindictive bitch deserves every ounce of misery she's got coming to her!"

He paused and gazed up at the clock.

"God, is it two already? I've got to go meet her. We're picking out our silverware pattern."

Fifteen

The Christmas season is usually among my favorite times of the year. Many of my friends would scoff to hear me voice such sentiments since I so often grouse about the season's more odious characteristics; the vapid, obligatory cheeriness of TV anchorpersons, the impossibility of finding nice inexpensive presents that don't *look* like nice inexpensive presents and, most of all, those mercenary tree sellers who flash gap-toothed smiles and say, "Seexty dollar! But for you feefty!" in reference to some spindly coniferous eyesore which, prior to being cut down, had been the embarrassment of the whole forest.

And yet every year by the middle of December a certain goopiness steals pleasantly over me. I festoon the apartment with decorations and take out a mortgage on a tree. I put on albums I've held on to since childhood and listen to the likes of Andy Williams and Dinah Shore singing traditional carols, as well as sixties holiday anthems which have, for obvious reasons, failed to achieve perennial status. I check out the Fifth Avenue windows. I send cards. I have been known to mull wine.

Not this year. Oh true, I went through some of the motions. I even purchased a little tree. But none of my efforts to achieve holiday cheer had much effect on my frazzled nervous system. Each day passed in an agony of suspense over what the duchess would do when she received the letter.

Claire had sent it off the Monday after Maddie's party. She'd used DHL, the good folk of which assured her that it would arrive the very next day. So from Tuesday on the three of us lived on tenterhooks. Meanwhile fresh complications descended like so many seasonal flurries.

Tuesday afternoon my phone rang.

"Hello?"

"Is this Philip?"

"Aggie!" I said, my blood pressure zooming. "How ya doing!"

"Fine. You sound sick, hon. Still hung over from Friday?"

"No, from Wednesday. I haven't even gotten to Friday's hangover yet."

"Poor thing. Have you tried some hair of the dog?"

"Yes. In fact, I just threw up a fur ball."

"Hah!"

What was it, I wondered, about this woman that caused me to wisecrack so desperately whenever I spoke to her? Why did I insist on walking the wag's tightrope?

"Listen, adorable, I have some bad news about the job."

"Oh?" I said, trying not to sound as hopeful as I felt.

"I know you were planning on starting this week but Maddie called me and pointed out, lamb that she is, that it would be dreadful of me to fire George and Sylvester the week before Christmas. I hadn't even thought of that but she's right, of course. I'm heartless but I'm not *that* heartless. So, do you mind waiting till January?"

Not a pardon, then, but a stay of execution. I leapt at even this.

"Not at all!"

"I'm sorry, but listen—since I'm asking you to keep yourself free till then I think it's only fair of me to put you on a little retainer."

"Aggie—!"

"No, I insist! Really, I do."

"I'm not protesting. I'm asking how much."

"Not a lot, hon, but you can buy yourself something nice for Christmas. Gotta run, baby. You have yourself a merry one!"

I sat a while with the phone in my lap, calculating the pros and cons of Aggie's largesse. I could certainly use the money, particularly this close to the holiday, but I couldn't help feeling there were strings attached. And while it was too early to be sure, I couldn't shake the unsettling feeling that Aggie's interest in me was not entirely platonic. Even if this suspicion proved inaccurate, accepting a retainer meant I'd be obliged to stay on the job for more than just the few weeks Claire had suggested.

The phone rang.

"Hi hi!" said Gilbert. "Guess who I just spoke to?"

"Aggie?"

"You, too? Well, *that's* good news, huh? It's about time we started getting some loot out of this family!"

I expressed my opinion that Aggie's bounty was a mixed blessing since it rendered our early-retirement plan obsolete. Gilbert, of course, hadn't thought of that, but agreed the more generous she was, the stickier it would be to duck out after a mere few weeks on the job.

I rang off and phoned Claire to sound out her views on the retainer conundrum. Claire, with her usual mental prowess, considered the problem for three seconds and offered a perfect solution. I should deposit the check but not spend a dime of it. Then when I quit I could write Aggie a check for the full amount, explaining that I could not, in good conscience, keep a retainer for a position I'd held so briefly.

That night Gilbert, Moira and I attended Holly Batterman's annual Christmas party. Our host greeted us at the door and ushered us into his loft which was decked with boughs of holly.

"*Get it?*" he shrieked.

Within minutes he'd dragged me into his bedroom to pump me with questions about Gilbert and Moira. Were they still in love? Were they fighting, as was rumored, and if so, over what? Was I there when Gunther and Gilbert met in the park? Was I, really? *Tell!* Was it *sordid?* Was it true about Moira meeting him at Marilyn's Grave and calling his face a sieve and screaming her lungs out at him with Cher standing not twenty feet away? And Vulpina! Why had Moira fired her? Was it *really* the duchess, or was Moira afraid she'd design something horrendous? Did I know Pina was livid? *Livid!* Almost as furious as Gunther. Why, Holly had considered not inviting *either* of them tonight but it seemed such a nasty thing to do just before Christmas.

"Holly, you didn't!"

"You bet I did! Moira never tells me a thing. I always get it secondhand. If she wants to tear Pina and Gunther's eyes out at least let her do it where I can *watch!*"

I ran to warn Gilbert and Moira what lay in store but this proved unnecessary. Both Pina and Gunther had arrived during my interrogation by Holly, whose eyes were now bulging with anticipation. There was no doubting what *he* wanted for Christmas.

Alas for Holly, this simple wish was not to be granted. Although the delicious tension engendered by such proximity was felt by one and all, the warring parties took advantage of the spaciousness of Holly's loft and kept their respective distances all evening. Gilbert and Moira were cheerfully oblivious to Gunther who glared from a distance with a gaze that reminded me of a vulture flying impatiently over a desert full of indecently healthy hyenas.

Pina made no such overt scowls, nor did she have to, for her dress seethed with a malevolence all its own. It was a full-length sheath with triangular panels of black silk crisscrossing down across her breasts and congealing into a tube that constricted her from midsection to ankle in the style favored by Morticia Adams. Adding to the drama of it were aluminum epaulets which, while rounded, seemed very sharp, like pizza cutters. More lethal still was a huge metal corsage she wore on her hip which looked like a child's pinwheel constructed of Cuisinart blades.

Holly's guests greeted this cunning number with wide stares and an equally wide berth, but Moira and Gilbert pretended to be quite unaware of Pina even when Holly screamed as she tripped and fell, blades first, into his peach velvet love seat. Not even the sight of her standing in the opposite corner chatting with Gunther himself elicited any response. It wasn't till Marlowe, emboldened by drink, demanded the scoop that Moira even acknowledged the situation.

"My, what a gossip you are! We haven't fought at all! It was just that Mummy, you know, the duch—"

"Yes, yes, I *know*, dear."

"She wanted to see me married in something very traditional and froufrou. So, even though Pina offered very graciously to whip up something *fun* I decided it would be criminal of me to ask her to work within any limitations at all. I'd be the last person to ask her to submerge her design personality!"

Holly had floated by to catch the end of this and swiftly let it be known that Moira's version of events did not entirely coincide with Pina's. *Pina* said she'd been fired in the midst of a second design she was executing to Moira's *specifications*, one which Moira hadn't even *seen* yet, and that, to add insult to injury, the dismissal had come not in person but in a long-distance phone call during which Moira, asked to justify such treachery, had responded with a bad imitation of telephone static before saying, "What, dear? I can't hear you!" and severing the connection.

"Holly, you silly!" said Moira, kindly, "I think Pina was just joshing you. You see, we all know what a gossip you are so we invent malicious things just to see if you'll believe them. And you *always* do! We lie to you all the time and it's terrible and we really must stop! But I love your tree!"

And, having thrust a hot poker into the very soul of her host, Moira laughed lightly and drifted off to sing a few carols round the piano. Some time later after we'd finally convinced a nearly apoplectic Holly that Moira's assertion was unfounded, Gilbert and I found Moira and suggested it was time to go. We were halfway to the door when we ran smack into Vulpina.

"Oh, Pina, love! Were you *here*? I didn't see you! I love your dress. *So* Christmassy."

Holly saw us and sped over.

"Gosh, kids! Leaving so soon?"

"We'd love to stay really but we're all of us just coming down with colds, so—"

"Yes, well, before you go, dear, remind me again—my memory's so bad these days—who did you say was designing your wedding gown now?"

"I didn't say at all, dear one."

"See? No memory at all. Who do you *think* though?"

"I couldn't say, Holland. It's quite up to the duchess. She insists on having her way about it. And stubborn! Philip, did you hear she wouldn't even let me use Pina? Pina, darling, I am still *so* sorry about that! You do forgive me, though?"

All eyes were on dear Pina, Holly's aglow with the hope of some withering comment. But Pina only offered a typically incoherent sentiment. "But, dear, it's all perspective. Perspective is like fashion, always changing. How soon everything is different than it was."

"You are *so* right, dear. Perspective! Gilbert, do we have any Contac at home? I'm sure this is going to be a cold."

Aggie's note arrived the next day. It read simply, "See you in the New Year." Enclosed was five hundred dollars.

In cash.

My heart was on a trampoline, leaping and sinking all at once. Such a generous sum and all for *not* working for two weeks! And yet I'd be a fool to spend even a penny of it!

I became pensive.

I'd opened the letter while sitting at my desk and I now found my hand straying to the drawer where I kept my checkbook—not a prudent move since the figures contained there could do little to bolster the moral courage I'd require to leave such a windfall untouched.

I had less than sixty dollars to my name. I checked my wallet, which was hardly necessary. The rich may walk around with no idea how much cash they have on their person but the poor know the exact figure at all times, and I can usually quote the serial number on anything larger than a five. I knew my billfold contained exactly seven dollars in singles, one subway token, and a sixty-dollar check from Milt Miller. The check plus whatever else I could earn from him by the end of the month would cover the rent. Maybe.

And what about Christmas gifts? Cards? The phone bill? Booze! How would these things be paid for?

Hmmmmm.

I decided that Aggie's money, unspendable though it was, could at least be pressed into service to keep my account at a reasonable balance so that I could spend every meager penny of my own resources without getting overdrawn. So, I traipsed off to East River Savings to enrich my account by some five hundred and sixty dollars of which, of course, only sixty was ever to be spent.

Or, since it was Christmastime (how pretty the store windows looked), let's say one hundred to be spent. The forty-dollar difference could easily be made up out of pocket when the time came to bid the job adieu.

Actually, I could probably spend even two hundred and still pay it back.

It was with this disastrous train of thought chugging through my head that I reached the bank and, snatching up a deposit slip, took my place in line.

When I returned to my apartment some three hours later the phone was ringing. Hastily depositing my bags and packages on the sofa I snatched it up and murmured a breathless hello.

"Where have you been?" said Claire.

"Out."

"I am getting you an answering machine for Christmas. It's more than my nerves can take these days to listen to your line ring while

I sit here wondering if you're trussed up in Freddy's slaughterhouse."

"Must you?"

"Sorry. What's the word from Gilbert? Did the duchess call?"

"I was just going to phone and ask myself."

"What about Aggie's check? Did it come yet?"

"Yes, as a matter of fact," I said, guiltily eyeing the cast albums.

"How much?"

"Five hundred."

"Good gracious! Well, you'd better put it in the bank. If you return the same check she'll know you were planning to quit right from the start."

"Actually, it wasn't a check," I said, beginning to feel that, while it would certainly be nice to have some scotch in the house again, Ballantine's would really have done just as well as Pinch and, similarly, that two liters might have sufficed to see me through the season.

"She sent cash?"

"Yes."

"Oh, dear, Philip. I hope you won't get angry with me but I think it might be a good idea if you gave it to me."

"Claire!"

"You know how money burns a hole in your pocket. And if you have all that cash on hand the week before Christmas you'll be tempted to spend it. And you *do* see how enormously foolish that would be, don't you?"

"Of course!"

"And you know it will be safe with me. Please. For your own sake."

"I'd really rather not."

A telling silence ensued.

"Okay," sighed Claire, "how much is left?"

"Uh, I'm not sure," I said pulling my wallet from my coat pocket. I checked the contents and gasped with surprise. I had spent like some mesmerist's dupe under a posthypnotic suggestion to squander. Now, the trance broken, I could scarcely believe the extent of the damages.

"I've got sixty-two bucks."

"*Please* tell me you're joking."

"Look, I can still pay her the money back! I'll be making plenty and if I put so much aside every week I can—"

"But you *won't*. You have never put money aside in your life! When you make it, you spend it! You'll be going to the theater and restaurants and buying expensive liquor and when it's time to quit you won't be able to without making that cobra woman feel you've played her for a fool so you'll have to go on working at the damn place for at least half a year or till someone puts a bullet in your head, which at the moment I'd be all for!"

"Well, Merry Christmas to you, too!"

"I am trying to save your life, you dolt, and the job would be much simpler with even minimal assistance from you."

"I can take perfectly good care of myself!"

Her reply to this was lengthy and masterful but limitations of space prevent its inclusion in this account. Suffice it to say that after I hung up the phone and glanced once more at the sofa, the six pounds of coffee, the gourmet mustards, oils and vinegars, the selection of cheeses, the side of Scotch salmon, the baguettes, the chocolates, the four cast albums, the champagne flutes, the Christmas cards, the four hardcover novels, the six plays, the two film star biographies, the carton of Merits, the colored Christmas lights, the three bottles of Pinch, the four bottles of champagne and the *Men of Provincetown* calendar all seemed to have lost their lustre.

I glumly refrigerated the foodstuffs as it occurred to me that even *half* of what I'd spent could have purchased a decent electric type-writer. This thought plunged me into an abyss of self-loathing where I remained till Gilbert called. He sounded in an even worse mood than me.

"Well, still no word from Mummy!"

"Well, she'll call tomorrow for sure. What about Aggie's money? You get yours?"

"Yes. You?"

"I've already spent it."

"Lucky you. Guess what happened when I got mine."

"What?"

"Well, of course, Moira had to be the one to get to the mail first and she positively glued herself to me till I'd opened it. And what did she say? 'Oh, Gilley, how *perfect*! Now you'll be able to afford to fly to England and spend Christmas with Mummy and the duke!' "

"Oh, Jeee-sus!"

"Yes! Won't *that* be fun! Spending Christmas in some big drafty house with a frenzied harpy who's just received *my* letter informing her Moira's ripping her off and I'm a sniveling pansy!"

"You've got to get out of it."

"Thanks a lot, Sherlock! *How?* She went on and on about how she's sucking up to my side and I've hardly done a thing to win over hers. I didn't know *what* to say."

We pondered it in silence a moment, then, as I gazed distractedly at my booty, a thought hit me.

"Do what I did."

"What?"

"Spend it. Blow the whole five hundred so you can't afford the plane fare. If I know Moira she'd sooner die than pay for you."

"What if she offers to? If I make too big a deal about not wanting to go then when the duchess lowers the boom she'll know I sent the letter."

"Just spend the money. We'll deal with any offers as they come."

Fortunately the contingency did not arise. That night was a Freddy night for Moira and when she returned home, Gilbert sheepishly informed her that he'd gone out for a spot of Christmas shopping, got carried away and blew his plane fare. Moira immediately let it be known that she had no intention of subsidizing his extravagance with her hard-earned dollars. Rather than search for an alternate means of financing Gilbert's fare she devoted her mental energy to devising a suitable excuse as to why he had to stay home. She decided Job Responsibilities would do, and retired to pack. Her schedule called for her to depart Friday and return the following Saturday, the twenty-seventh.

The next day, Thursday, was fraught with tension. We knew the duchess *had* to have received our note and yet she had made no response.

Why?

"Tell me," asked Claire that day, "does the duchess *know* Moira's going there tomorrow? I mean, it's not a surprise visit is it?"

"Not as far as I know."

"Well, that's it then. The duchess wants to confront her in person and she's afraid if she warns her what's coming Moira will keep her distance."

The day passed still without word from England, and the next morning Gilbert saw Moira off at the airport. He let Moira feel this was a conciliatory gesture after a month of tense relations, but he mainly went out of a desire to make sure she was truly leaving the country.

We knew that it was only a matter of hours now till all hell broke loose and we decided to take our minds off it by finishing up our Christmas shopping. Gilbert bought Tony a box of his favorite cigars and for Maddie he picked out a set of ceramic coconut cups for her beloved tropical-style drinks. Gilbert didn't buy for Moira. They'd agreed some weeks ago to exchange gifts after Christmas when they'd both, they'd hoped, have fat checks from their folks. Though, of course, the likelihood was now remote that Moira would find anything at all in her stocking, excepting, perhaps, a subpoena.

These chores completed, we went back to God's Country around six to sit amongst the stuffed kitties, sip scotch, watch movies, and wait for the Inevitable.

By midnight we'd seen *Gentlemen Prefer Blondes, Dinner at Eight* and something dreadful called *Xanadu*. Moira still hadn't called and we sat there amidst a rubble of takeout cartons, wondering what had happened. Gilbert begged me to stay the night so I'd be there if the call came early the next morning. I agreed to.

But the call didn't come that day.

Nor did it come the next.

By Sunday night we were half frenzied but managed to calm ourselves. Moira was being watched perhaps, or feared she was, and was waiting till she could get away and make the call from outside the house. Surely we'd hear from her Monday.

I went over in the morning to keep the vigil but by one o'clock (six duchess time) nothing had come and I had to leave for Milt Miller's to answer fan letters and mail out autographed photos of Deirdre Sauvage (who is, in fact, Milt's blowsy sister Dolores posing for the Vaseline-coated lens in the same gown she wore as Desiree in the Teaneck Mummer's production of *A Little Night Music*).

I finished up around seven and rushed back to Gilbert's to find him sitting in the kitchen glumly finishing a pint of butter pecan. No call had come.

We passed the evening in a frenzy of speculation. We had antic-

ipated every conceivable reaction both from Moira and her mother—
every reaction, that is, except this baffling silence. Had the duchess
even received the letter? Had she received it but not told Moira
till inquiries could be made and the trust fraud confirmed? Had
they simply killed each other? Should Gilbert call or would that tip
her off?

We'd each planned to spend Christmas Eve with family and the
day itself together with Claire since Maddie and Tony would be flying
off to the Bahamas bright and early Christmas morning. However,
agonizing suspense and holiday cheer are not compatible and as the
morning of the twenty-fourth crept by with no word from Moira we
were both so demoralized we'd have preferred to give the whole thing
a miss. But that afternoon we trudged dutifully off to our respective
loved ones. Glasses were raised, trees complimented, and presents
exchanged. Gilbert was given a five-hundred-dollar gift certificate for
Brooks Brothers so he could buy clothing for his new job. Maddie
and Tony opened Gilbert's gifts and others from the duchess and
Moira. The duchess had sent them a Waterford jam jar and half a
dozen crocks of gooseberry preserves made by her cook from berries
picked on the verdant grounds of Trebleclef. Moira gave them a framed
picture of herself with a touching inscription. Meanwhile in New
Rochelle Joyce and Dwight waxed rhapsodic about their gift, a tiny
electric mincer, and I did likewise about my mezzanine seats for *Cats*
which I had seen in previews and loathed.

The evening was not without its news value, however. The minute
I got home Gilbert called.

"Hi, how'd you make out?"

"Don't ask! They gave me a fucking Brooks Brothers gift certificate!"

"Sounds generous to me."

"Sure, if you want to run around looking like some little yupster
climbing the ladder at Citicorp! That's not why I called, though. Guess
who gave us a ring about six?"

"Who?"

"The duchess!"

"My God! Did she spill the beans to Tony?"

"No! I don't think she ever got the letter! She was just chipper as
anything, wishing us all Merry Christmas and thanking Mom and Tony
for her gift and saying how she can't wait to meet us all."

"You talk to Moira?"

"No. I asked to but Mummy (*God* she sounds like Hermione Gin-gold!) said she'd gone out caroling with 'some nice young people.' I swear, Philly, she never got it. She couldn't have."

The next day the three of us gathered together at God's Country and did our best to put aside our tensions and enjoy the day. We partook heavily of spirits, even Claire who is usually the soul of moderation. I suppose we all felt that, under the circumstances, a mood of festivity would not be achieved without copious assistance. We began the celebration by helping Gilbert stuff a small turkey and then retired to the tree to exchange gifts. Claire, as threatened, gave me an answering machine and Gilbert gave me a first edition of a Wodehouse novel. I gave Gilbert two film-star biographies and Claire a tape I'd secretly compiled of various gifted friends singing her songs. Claire and Gilbert exchanged recent albums. Maddie and Tony had given Gilbert a bottle of Chivas for me and we wasted not a second in toasting my benefactors. We then watched *It's a Wonderful Life*, at the conclusion of which, awash in sentiment and Chivas, we stag-gered out to the kitchen to tackle the rest of the meal.

The food diminished our tipsiness somewhat and a good thing it was, too, because just as we were finishing dessert Moira called.

The minute the phone rang the three of us looked up from our plates and stiffened like those nervous gazelles on "Wild Kingdom."

"Put the speaker on!"

"Already is," said Gilbert, and picked up. "Hello!"

"Hi, honey! Merry Christmas!"

"Merry Christmas to you! Isn't it late over there?"

"Yes, it's one in the morning! How was your day?"

"Terrific! How was yours?"

"Fab! Ever so traditional."

"Great!" said Gilbert, shrugging his shoulders and raising his eye-brows. What was going on? Had nothing happened at all?

"Chestnuts roasting and all that?"

"Oh, the works! Do you have company?"

Claire pointed to herself and shook her head frantically.

"Just Philip!"

"Tell him Merry Christmas for me! You two make a nice dinner?"

"Yes! We stuffed a turkey and had lots of vegetables and some absolutely delish—"

"*Did you do it, you son of bitch?*"

"What!"

"*Did you do it?*"

"Did I do what?"

"*Fess up you asshole! I know you did it! I have proof!*"

Claire stood and, catching Gilbert's attention, began frantically miming confusion, shrugging her shoulders wildly while adopting a facial expression of daft, almost deranged, incomprehension. She looked like a charades player who'd been assigned *One Flew Over the Cuckoo's Nest* and was going for "whole idea."

"What the fuck are you talking about?" said Gilbert, getting the message. "What am I supposed to have done?"

Silence fell on the other end.

"Moira? What's the matter? What happened?" And then, in a concerned tone: "Are you all right?"

"Yes," she sighed. "Okay, I guess you didn't do it. I was just testing you."

The three of us exhaled mightily and slumped back in our chairs. Seizing my glass with a trembling hand, I guzzled the last of my chablis.

"Testing me?"

"Well, if you'd said, 'I didn't do it!' or 'You can't prove it!' before I even said what I was talking about then I'd know you did it."

"Did what?" said Gilbert, with just the right blend of perplexity and pique.

"Well, some absolutely vicious person sent my mother a letter telling her everything."

"Everything?"

"Well, just about. Here, listen—"

Her voice dripping with toxins, she read the letter.

" '. . . Yours regretfully, a *Wellwisher*'! Have you ever heard anything so hateful in your life!"

"Never! This is all your fault, you stupid bitch!" said Gilbert, brilliantly seizing the offensive.

"*My* fault!"

"Well, you must have told someone about the trust fund! I certainly haven't breathed a word of it!"

"Neither have I!"

"Then it must have been your stupid Winslow!"

"Winslow! What about Philip?"

"Don't be ridiculous! He's right here, I'll ask him. Philip," he said holding a finger to his lips—if I were to answer she'd know the speaker was on—"have you ever breathed a word about Moira's trust fund to anyone? . . . He says don't be ridiculous!"

"Well, you just have his word for it!"

"Which is good enough for me!"

"Don't shout at me, you beast! You don't have the first idea what I've been through!"

"Oh. Well, sorry," said Gilbert. "Your mom come down hard on you?"

"No, not *her*. Don't worry. She knows *nothing* about it."

On hearing this happy bit of news I shot forward once more in my seat and poor Claire choked on her trifle. Gilbert paused for the merest instant before bellowing:

"Well, if she doesn't know anything what the hell is the problem?"

"What's the problem? God, you are so dense!"

She proceeded to tell us her tale, and a pretty tale it wasn't.

Not long after her accident the duchess had received a letter from a poacher who'd been shot in the pants by the gamekeeper and was now threatening to sue her for two million pounds. The duchess has extremely high blood pressure and the tantrum induced by this missive had struck the duke as inconducive to her recuperation. So the duke discreetly charged his loyal butler, Murcheson, with the task of screening the duchess's mail. Anything which struck him as potentially upsetting was to be referred to the duke who would deal with it as he saw fit.

But when Murcheson, whose loyalty to the duke was not, it seemed, unwavering, laid eyes on the letter about Moira's trust fund he decided immediately that, although it fell squarely into the category of "potentially upsetting," he would not show it to the Duke. He would, instead, wait a few days and show it to Moira. He felt certain the young lady would be grateful to him for standing between her and a most unfortunate exposure. And Murcheson, who was fifty-seven, had little hair, a bulbous nose, dental problems, and perhaps seventy pounds more on his short frame than medical specialists deemed advisable, had not been on the receiving end of a young woman's gratitude for quite a few years.

And so, shortly after Moira's arrival, Murcheson drew her aside, showed her the damning letter and assured her that neither her mother nor the duke had been apprised of its contents. Moira, in a rare show of naïveté, threw her arms about him and exclaimed, "Oh, Murcheson, how can I ever repay you?" Murcheson replied frankly and Moira, despite her skills as a strategist and many years of stage experience, could not induce him to accept an alternate payment plan.

"You didn't!" gasped Gilbert.

"What else could I do!"

Fortunately, she said, by the night of their second assignation she'd managed, through the time-honored tape-recorder-under-the-bed method, to get the goods on Murcheson. Thus armed with incontestible proof of his blackmail, she secured his promise not only never to touch her again but to seek out and destroy any further letters from the author of this one, for, she assured him, her downfall would be his.

"So at least we don't have to worry about anyone tipping off Mummy!"

"Thank God for that!"

"Still, do you believe it? Of all the slimy mean-spirited things to do!"

"But *who* could be on to us? Who could have done it?"

"I don't know, dear, but when I find out I'm going to bury the fucker."

Sixteen

Was Moira a supernatural force? It was beginning to seem so. How else to explain the frightening ease with which she could juggle countless lies, extract jewels from murderers, suck trust funds dry and thwart all efforts to expose her? A little sober reflection might have led us to see that a real supernatural force would never make stupid investments, read Deirdre Sauvage aloud, or fuck butlers who'd let themselves go, but our reflections that night were anything but sober. We sat in the light of the tree, obsessing about Moira until in our minds she was an ageless indestructible she-thing who'd begun her career in the Eumenides, coached Torquemada, and given Hitler the idea.

By morning cooler, if slightly throbbing, heads prevailed. We talked it through from all angles, even seeing the bright side. Hadn't Moira at least ruled us out as authors of the letter?

We agreed the basic plan should remain unchanged. The duchess had to be informed of the swindle, for only she could discreetly put a stop to it. It was clear even Moira knew this, or why would she have gone to such distasteful lengths to see the duchess was not shown the letter? But if Murcheson was standing guard over the post, we'd have to resort to phoning. It was less desirable than the mail since a voice could be recognized or even, as Moira had demonstrated, recorded. But what was the alternative?

We dialed directory assistance for the appropriate county and found that although the Duke of Dorsetshire was unlisted there was a number for Trebleclef in Little Chipperton.

"So, who should make the call?"

We agreed that since Moira's forced assignations with Murcheson had left her with a thirst for vengeance even Sweeney Todd might have found immoderate, it was vital to keep suspicion deflected from us. Claire remembered that a co-worker of hers, a fellow named Peter, was moving to Texas in January. His imminent departure made him a safe choice and he could, she promised, be relied upon to do it if she assured him it was for a good cause.

He would simply phone and ask to speak to the duchess, saying that he was a reporter writing a piece about the tragic events at the Medieval Festival and the duchess's brave recuperation. Once he had her on the line he'd ask why she hadn't responded to his letter? What letter she would say, and he'd read it to her. We agreed the danger to Peter would be minimal so long as he made sure to disguise his voice. As extra insurance for *us*, the call could come when Moira, Gilbert and I were all together, so she'd see there was no way either of us could have made it.

Saturday morning Claire called Gilbert and me to tell us Peter had proved willing. He'd join Claire at her place Sunday and the call would be made promptly at one. So the next day around noon I showed up at God's Country for brunch, bearing a gift for Moira. It seemed a good idea to keep her as off guard as possible, and the personal sacrifice involved in offering it was extremely slight.

"Oh, Philip dear, how thoughtful! Tickets to *Cats*! But I feel just awful, I haven't gotten yours yet—but I will! It's just been so crazy!"

I said Gilbert had told me of her ordeal and I offered my sympathies.

"It really was too dreadful! I mean, I've known Murcheson for years and years and I never dreamed he was capable of such low, disgusting—well, anyway, he's working for us now. He knows Mummy would strangle him with her own two hands if she heard what was on that tape!"

"Can we hear it?" asked Gilbert.

"No," said Moira with great finality.

We retired to the dining room for brunch. Moira insisted on cooking so it was frozen waffles and something vaguely meatzoid called Sizzlean. As we ate we discussed the informer's identity and it became clear to Gilbert and me that, in firing off our little salvo, the Allies (as I'd begun to think of us) had not considered the full ramifications of our actions. Our concern was so focused on deflecting suspicion from us that we'd given no thought at all as to where it might ricochet.

"*Vulpina?* Moy, hon, are you *sure?*"

"Yes! She's the only one who knows the trust exists at all. Except for Winslow Potts, and he has as much to lose as I do."

"Pina knows about the trust fund?"

"Of course," said Moira. "Don't you remember? The day she brought those revolting designs for my gown and Mummy called and said she'd had the accident and I'd have to use my fund? And I went on and on about how I lived on the income and couldn't it all be paid for some other way? Pina was right here, soaking up every word of it."

"But she wasn't here when you told us you'd spent the money."

"So, she figured it out. I mean, she *knows* I've made some bad investments in the last few years. Pina's very clever in a low vicious sort of way. Then when I fired her the spiteful bitch decided to get back at me by spilling the beans. God, I'm *sure* it's her! You heard her at Holly's! All that nonsense about perspective and how soon everything will be different!"

Of course, we knew these comments had just been Pina being her usual cryptic self, but how could we say so without seeming to know things we couldn't unless we were the responsible party? We agreed Pina's remarks certainly *seemed* to take on new significance in light of the letter, but added that the situation demanded more study.

There was, I suddenly realized, one ray of exonerating sunshine still waiting to beam down on Vulpina, and that was Peter's call to the duchess—which, a glance at my watch confirmed, had taken place only moments ago. It would confirm that the informant had been a man, not a woman, and a man, at that, whose identity would be comfortably ambiguous.

Just then the phone rang. Moira answered, listened a moment and said, "I accept the charges!"

At once a look of distaste came over her.

"Yes, it's me, Murcheson. What do *you* want?"

The full impact of this greeting took a moment to sink in on me. If the call was from Murcheson and not her mother this was probably because he was standing guard not only over the mail but over incoming calls as well. Peter had never gotten through.

"*When?*" asked Moira, ruthlessly. ". . . Oh, he *did*, did he? Thank God you answered! What did he say? . . . Oh, Gawd, how positively *lame*! . . . What did the weasel sound like? . . . He *did*? Well, well, *well*! . . . Yes, *damned* important! Listen, anyone else calls, she's got laryngitis! . . . Thank you, Murcheson. Keep up the good work!"

"Well," said Moira, hanging up, "she tried again! Or *they* tried again, I should say, because she's not working alone."

"She's not?"

"No. She's in cahoots with *Gunther!*"

It was sickening, really, that, the destructive forces of Cause and Effect having already pummeled us half senseless, Coincidence should now rush to get a few lumps in too. But that was just what had happened.

Peter had shown up at Claire's right on schedule and begun rehearsing his role. She'd told him to disguise his voice both for his own protection and ours. Naturally, she'd recommended a British accent and it was in such an accent that Peter dutifully rehearsed. His wasn't a very good British accent, though. It was tentative and combined improbably the voices of Alistair Cooke and Stanley Holloway. Peter was something of a perfectionist and painfully aware that his characterization lacked the ring of authenticity.

Which was why, the moment Murcheson had answered the phone, some drive deep within Peter told him to abandon the voice and switch to a German accent. He'd performed *Stalag 17* in high school and his rendition of an overbearing Nazi was a model of the impressionist's art.

Peter's artistry, however, was confined to accents and stopped quite a bit short of improvisation. Faced with a barrage of questions regarding his journalistic credentials, Peter had waffled pathetically, going so far at one point as to cite the publication he worked for as *Duchess Monthly*. Murcheson had angrily demanded his name and it was at that point that Claire had reached over and depressed the receiver button.

Claire had seen the episode as no more than another round lost in the battle to break through to the duchess. She couldn't perceive the consequences of Peter's last-minute accent switch. I'd told her about Gunther when I'd first filled her in about the syndicate but I hadn't mentioned his accent. After that I hadn't made too much of him at all, since, in the aftermath of Maddie's party, he'd seemed the least of our problems.

But now, with Moira convinced he and Pina were behind the smear campaign, what horrors might she perpetrate against them? And how horribly might they retaliate? How could we stop Moira? Indeed, how could we not *assist* her? For with this new evidence, could we really pretend to be unconvinced by her conspiracy theory? It was too damned plausible.

After the way Moira had dressed him down in public, wouldn't Gunther be eager for revenge? Vulpina, too, had been given a motive for vengeance when Moira had rejected her designs. And hadn't we seen them chatting away at Holly's party as though suddenly the best of friends?

Clearly they'd met, compared grievances and, pooling Vulpina's inside information about the trust with Gunther's Aryan wiles, had reached the correct conclusion that Moira had spent the money and was trying to hide this from her mother. Then, in their rush to taste blood, they'd sent the poisonous note to Trebleclef.

"What should we do?" asked Gilbert, dreading her reply.

"Isn't it obvious? We have to fuck them over and let 'em know if they try it again we'll fuck them even worse!"

"Moira," I said, "we're trying to avoid trouble, not get into it!"

"Wimps! Honestly, what I wouldn't give to have a couple of *men* working with me!"

"Eat shit, toots!" said Gilbert. "We just don't want you to do something demented that's going to get them so mad they decide to stop bothering the duchess and squeal to Tony and Mom instead!"

"Gilbert," she said condescendingly, "don't you think I've thought of that? That's why we have to *scare* them! So they won't dare do anything more at all! And if you don't agree with me fine. I'll do it myself."

What could we do but agree? Only by staying involved could we keep her revenge from getting too crazed, or worse still, tipping Pina and Gunther off to damaging information which Moira believed they knew but which they, in fact, did not. Besides, if we showed any reluctance to get back at them, that would only make Moira suspicious of *us*.

It was all hideously complicated, but every speculation led back to the same fear: that Moira, the moment she smelled treachery from our side, would sell us out and claim the whole thing was our idea. This fear overrode all other considerations. Placed against it any mild (or not so mild) havoc wreaked against Pina and Gunther seemed quite inconsequential. My talks with Gilbert regarding their fate went something like this:

"I feel so terrible."
"Me, too. They don't deserve this."
"I know. I feel awful."
"But whatcha gonna do?"
"Exactly. Can I freshen that?"

We at least managed to convince Moira that whatever we did should be done surreptitiously. Moira, being an artist of the vindictive gesture, hated to see what would probably be some of her best work go unsigned. But she agreed that since we had no concrete proof of what they'd done, it was best they have nothing to pin on us. We knew who was trashing us and, by the same token, they would know who was retaliating.

Of course, they *wouldn't* know. They wouldn't have the vaguest idea who was threatening them or why. They'd simply be plunged into some Hitchcockian nightmare of mistaken identities, with unknown malefactors meting out unearned retribution for unspecified grievances.

"Poor Pina. I always sort of liked her."
"Me too. She's strange but—"
"Engaging?"
"Yes. Fun to be around."
"She'll be so frightened!"
"And so confused! I'm sick about it."
"Me, too."
"Say when."

Seventeen

The worst of it, of course, was that it left us powerless to try to reach the duchess again. Any attempt would be blocked by Murcheson and communicated to Moira who would then turn up the heat on Gunther and Vulpina. And, with the temperature already just shy of combustion, this was not to be desired. Only by abandoning all efforts at contact could we convince Moira that her anonymous warnings had served their purpose and could be abandoned without loss of face.

As for the nature of these warnings, this had yet to be decided. Moira said only that they should be as grisly as possible but it was, after all, still the holiday season. January would be soon enough to get down to work.

Claire was furious. The thought that Moira could, without even realizing it, foil two consecutive plans and force her to be a silent but consenting party to a terror campaign against two relatively innocent people was more than Claire's pride could bear. Her determination to stop the Moira machine grew daily but she didn't have the first idea how to do it.

Another dreadful side effect of Murcheson's interception of the letter was that the copy we'd kept to prove we'd tried to stop the swindle was now worthless. How could we prove the original had even been sent? Moira and Murcheson would deny having seen it and it would once again be our word against hers. And what chance did the truth stand against Moira?

To further brighten the picture, the Aggie dilemma, which I'd resolved not even to think about till January, reared its head three days early. Any doubt as to whether her retainer came with strings attached was removed when she called to invite Claire and me to "a little New Year's Eve orgy." Her silkily commanding tone reminded me of Catherine de' Medici inviting a favorite jester to some court shindig. She casually mentioned having an "adorable baby grand" if we "felt like singing" in much the same way Kate might have said, "Oh, and Foole, dear, you *must* bring that pig's bladder you're always doing such amusing things with."

Claire wasn't thrilled.

"What right have you got to go accepting invitations on my behalf?"

"We're engaged, remember? Besides, you've got to be there to protect me. I think she wants my body."

"Keep it up and so will half a dozen organ banks."

The night of the thirty-first I donned my threadbare best and like a good little Mafia lapdog squired my date to Park Avenue and Seventieth. The crowd was a mix of Bombelli clan members and other moneyed Manhattanites—ad men, brokers, a hefty gaggle of lawyers and, for seasoning, two artists, a short-story writer and that most ethereal of beings, the avant-garde choreographer. We didn't see Aggie upon arrival but she soon smelled us out and swooped down for welcoming kisses.

"Thank God a few *amusing* people are here! Philip, what a stuffy crew I've managed to assemble! All very successful and sweet. But so dreary!"

"Yes," I said, gazing around. "They look like Friends of Thirteen."

"Exactly! But what can I do? They're too damn rich to snub!"

A waiter approached with a platter of upscale munchies.

"Goodness," said Claire, "what's all this?"

"Sauteed baby eggplants with an apricot glaze, and baby zucchini stuffed with young lamb."

"Who's catering? Gerber?"

"*Hah!* Oh! Gotta run! Fifty million just walked in with a new wife."

She assured us we would not be *too* bored if we confined our conversation to the short-story writer and Demo Glish, the choreographer.

To this last fellow I took an immediate dislike. He was standing languorously in the center of Aggie's white and gray penthouse wearing a ponytail and electric blue pajamas, and feeling miffed at how many of those present failed to recognize him from the cover of last July's *DanceMagazine*.

"Exotic creature!" said Claire.

"And *very* big this year. He choreographed that antinuclear ballet at BAM, the one where no one moved."

"Oh, dear! If I'd been there I'd have moved soon enough."

"I was, and couldn't. My date refused to budge for fear of being thought 'unreceptive.' "

We watched Moira approach this lethargic genius and declare herself a big fan. Moira's such a celebrity worshipper that if Richard Speck had been in the room she'd have walked right up and said, "I'm sorry, you don't know me but I *loved* your killing spree. And all nurses! How *did* you think of it?"

She caught our eye and waved us over. We steeled ourselves and joined them.

"Philip and Claire! I want you to meet Demo Glish. He choreographed *Shards* at BAM!"

"Yes, I saw it."

"Really?" said Demo, brightening. "Opinions?"

"I'm sorry, but I didn't much enjoy it."

Demo's lips puckered with amusement.

"I should hope not. I never set out to make global suicide 'enjoyable.' "

"*Well* said!" gushed Moira. I wanted to strangle them both.

But with rage came inspiration. If Aggie was some great admirer of this twit, mightn't I nimbly disingratiate myself from her by raking him over the coals? With any luck she might fire me before I began work!

"Ah. You set out to be '*un*enjoyable'? How nice to have such realistic ambitions."

Aggie, who'd been standing a yard away, joined us. Here was my chance.

"I think," purred Demo, "that your problem is preconditioned expectations. You expected something safe and accessible and I gave you a disturbing glimpse of what our world will be after the apocalypse."

"If that's truly the case, Dummo, I suggest you tour Russia with it. If you can really convince the Soviets that a postnuclear future will consist exclusively of bad dance at inflated prices the arms race will end overnight."

I turned and strode briskly away. Reaching the bar I ordered a double Chivas, feeling immensely pleased with myself for having gotten my best shot in while she was there to hear it. Surely so blatant a display of tactlessness would give her second thoughts about my suitability for the job. She would seek me out later and inform me in frosty tones that—

"You *darling* man!"

"Oh, Aggie! Listen, I'm sorry about—"

"Please! I've been dying to hear someone put that twit in his place all year! He used to be fun but he's gotten so *full* of himself! That crack about the Russians! Priceless! I'm going to tell *everybody*!"

At one a.m. Aggie got around to asking Claire and me to perform. I was so exhausted from trying to live up to the waggish reputation Aggie had bestowed on me that I leapt at the chance to abandon spontaneity in favor of more rehearsed jests. Gilbert joined us on a few numbers as did Moira who, entirely to our surprise, had memorized all our songs. Claire, at my instigation, finished up with a little something from our show in progress. The song, "Cold Comfort," was the lament of a powerful woman who can pay for whatever she desires. And usually has to.

> *I've sable-filled closets, all larger than Saks,*
> *In mansions much grander*
> *Than Vanderbilt's shacks—*
> *Cold comfort!*
> *When all that I want is love!*
>
> *I've chauffeurs and butlers, all handsome and tall.*
> *I've lackeys and henchmen*
> *And Frenchmen on call—*
> *Cold comfort!*
> *I'd gladly trade them all*
> *For someone who's gentle*
> *And isn't a rental.*

The response from the besotted revelers was highly gratifying and sped right to my head like the better sort of drug. All the problems facing me suddenly seemed as minimal as Mr. Glish's choreography. Moira, Aggie, the Mob, the duchess and all the perils they represented were mere trivial inconveniences a man of my intellect and boundless charm could set right in a minute. If it had ever seemed otherwise it was because I had given in to my only flaw, which was my tendency to underestimate myself. I smiled over at Moira who was accepting the congratulations of our adoring fans. She pointed at me, saying, "But *he's* the one who deserves the credit!"

Indeed I was! Who did she think she was? A clever little minx, to be sure, but a match for Cavanaugh? Never!

And there was Demo, the poor wretch, slouching in a corner, coughing up little clots of envy. I'd shown that poseur what it meant to satisfy an audience! He'd seen what happens to those who cross swords with Philip Francis Cavanaugh, just as Moira would see! Just as Gunther would! Just as the Mafia would, were they so foolish as to take me on!

I snatched a glass of champagne from a passing traybearer who smiled and said, "Funny stuff!"

"Thanks!" I replied, flashing a smile intended to excite his hopes, for he was a fetching sort if you like wavy, chestnut hair and museum-quality cheekbones. Perhaps if I felt magnanimous I'd catch him in some private nook and offer him a night with next year's Tony winner. I downed the champagne and picked up another from a blond mid-western type, giving this boy a similar grin, for it paid to keep one's options open. I bathed in drunken compliments from my fans, taking care to ask their names and occupations, for one's public does so appreciate these little shows of interest if they're persuasively feigned.

Soon I had to relieve myself. Leaving the bathroom I walked smack into Aggie who was even drunker than me. She thanked me for my performance, saying it had simply made the party. Then she threw her arms about me and kissed me on the lips.

Poor lovesick old darling! I thought to myself. How she pines for what she can never have! A brief kiss is all she can hope for! But, I thought, shouldn't I at least make it one she would remember? A kiss she would treasure through her declining years, think of on her death-bed and, so doing, die with a smile on her lips? I clasped her in my arms, lost my balance and fell forward, smashing her head against the opposite wall. I apologized drunkenly and she replied drunkenly that she'd enjoyed it. We kissed again briefly and, smiling wickedly at each other, rejoined the party.

I basked more in the attention of my public, particularly a charming redheaded waiter whose name now eludes me. It was this last encounter that led Claire to grab me by the elbow and inform me, in her most headmistressy voice, that it was time to go. We gathered up Gilbert and Moira and shared a cab to the West Side. I got off at God's Country telling Claire that I wanted a little nightcap with my two best friends.

We collapsed on the sofa, lit cigarettes, and uncorked champagne. Even Moira was slurring words, something I'd never heard her do. We toasted ourselves for having stolen the party and agreed it had been a phenomenally successful evening.

"And the bess part," said Moira, "is while we were havin' the time a our lies at Aggie's, rotten little Gunser was getting a beeeeg nasty shock!"

"Oh?" I asked, suddenly soberer.

"Wudjado?" inquired Gilbert.

"Well!" she giggled. "Firs' I bought a doll, a man doll, 'bout this big," she said, indicating something a foot high, "then I took a fork 'n' poked holes inna face so it looked jus' like Gunny-bunny. Then I stuck a beeeg knife inna chest 'n' smeared it with ketchup! Then I wrapped it all up inna Natsy flag and pinned a note on it said, 'Ya loss *that* war, Hideous, 'n' yer not gunna win *this* one, you blackmailing Shithead'—signed 'a *Wellwisher!*' Then s'afternoon 'bout five I wrapped it in pretty paper 'n' I took it to his place 'n' I jimmied the front door open 'n' left it right ou'side his door! S'top floor walk-up so nobody will see it but him! Wuzzen I good?"

We agreed through thin smiles that, yes, it would show *him*. But, mightn't it also prompt him to go to the police?

"Let 'im!" hooted Moira. "Wudda the pleece gunna say? *They're* gunna say, 'Okay, we'll fine the culpriss! Jus' tell us who yer *blackmailin*'! Wuzzy gunna say t' *that*? Huh?"

We agreed this was an interesting point.

"An' nex week, Vulpenis!" she crowed, giggling at her pun. "Nightnight, sweetums."

She kissed Gilbert on the forehead and zigzagged off to bed.

Amazingly, my brain was still functional enough to realize there was a chance Gunther hadn't yet seen the doll. He might be out of town or at a late party. We called him, holding the receiver between our ears. It rang eight times and, just as it seemed there was reason to hope, he answered.

"Hello?"

We said nothing.

"Hello? Who is this? . . . *Who is this!* Vy are you plaguing me? Vat blackmail? I'm going to the police, you hear me!"

We hung up.

"Oh boy," said Gilbert, and I nodded.

For a while we just sat not saying a word. I could feel my earlier happiness and confidence draining away like water from a tub. I thought back to my performance at Aggie's. What an egomaniacal ass I'd been! And necking with Aggie! What had possessed me?

I gazed at Gilbert. I'd never seen him looking more lost and pathetic.

"How could this all have happened?" he said. "It was such a *good* idea!"

"It was never a good idea."

"It *was*. So easy! All I had to do was pretend to love Moira and be nice to everyone and in a few months we'd get lots of neat presents. And now we're threatening people and they're calling the police, and the Mafia's going to find out and we're going to be killed! Oh, God!" he whimpered, his head sinking onto my chest. "Are you as scared as I am?"

"Yes."

"Are you as horny?"

"Gilbert!"

"Philip—it's been so long for me! It's been a long time for you, too. I know it has! Don't we care for each other? Haven't we always? And what could be worse than getting killed when we haven't gotten any for six months? I mean, picture it! Think how we'd feel standing there in some garage, blindfolded, thinking about the last precious taste of love that could have been ours if only we'd taken it! How would you feel, Philly? Wouldn't you feel just *awful*?"

I conceded the point.

Eighteen

Over the next weeks, in those moments when I wasn't busy quivering in terror, I couldn't help but be ruefully amused that the affair Gilbert and I shared in our twenty-sixth year was in so many respects indistinguishable from the one we'd shared at sixteen; it was less a sequel than a revival.

There we were again lying to friends about our whereabouts, making discreet phone calls to confirm the schedules of those in a position to burst in on us, gesturing rudely at each other the moment people's backs were turned, and living in perpetual dread of discovery. Of course, the price of discovery now could be death, as opposed to counseling.

It was foolish, yes. What can I say? I knew that it was, as the song says, the wrong time, the wrong place and, given Gilbert's promise to Freddy, the wrong sex as well. I won't defend myself by saying it was Love compelling me to risk Death, because it wasn't. It was Death compelling me to risk Sex. How often my thoughts went back to that awful moment in Tony Cellini's study when I heard the thunder of Serge's gun. With death looming as a certainty had I regretted the good deeds undone, the places unseen or the plays unwritten? No. I thought mainly of Leo, the rosebud I didn't gather while I might have. Not the noblest of sentiments, I admit, but one I was determined not to experience again.

Also in common with that long ago fling was our insistence on pretending we were in love, that the seeds of passion long buried below the surface of friendship had blossomed into the Real Thing. True, we'd admitted that first night that basic lust and the fear of losing our last opportunities to get laid were the only forces driving us. But as the affair dragged on and the joint agreement that "this one'll be the last time, really" ceased to be made, Gilbert's natural tendency to romanticize came to the fore and I succumbed to it rather than face the tawdry fact that I was not stealing afternoons of sweet oneness with my soul mate, but merely grabbing another nooner on my way to the cemetery.

Our secrecy about the affair extended even to Claire. The tongue lashing she'd given me when I told her I'd spent Aggie's retainer had been memorable, but nothing compared to the one I'd get if she learned Gilbert and I were emulating that "dishonorable gayboy" who'd broken Freddy's niece's heart and, in consequence, ended life as a human firework. I did, however, update her on the Gunther situation.

"What a twisted mind she has, Philip! It worries me more every day!"

But what could be done to set things right? We could hardly just send him a new little mannequin with the wound healed, the face cleared up, and a note attached reading "Disregard previous doll."

On the plus side there seemed little reason for Gunther to suspect we were behind it. Why would Gilbert or Moira accuse him of blackmail? It didn't begin to make sense from his standpoint, so our policy was to wait and keep our fingers crossed.

On January 4, the duchess celebrated her sixtieth birthday. Gilbert reluctantly shelled out the funds to pay a photographer for a sensitive study of Moira and him. Moira supplied a lovely silver frame (though she was unable to satisfactorily explain why Bloomingdale's had been unable to provide a gift box or, for that matter, a sales slip). Tony and Maddie sent a pair of bed trays to enliven her recuperation, and Freddy, surprisingly, sent best wishes and a stunning emerald brooch, offering still more proof of the extent to which Moira had infiltrated his affections. Moira crowed that Mummy had called Freddy to thank him and Freddy had been "simply dazzled" by the duchess's charm. They'd spoken at length and she had invited him to visit if he ever found himself in Little Chipperton.

It was at this time that Gilbert and I began our jobs at Paradiso.

How best to describe that bistro so highly touted in the Mafia Michelin? The first word that leaps to mind is dark. You enter through a small dark vestibule, pass through a long dark bar and then, if you haven't stumbled and broken your neck, you enter a square dark dining room that seats about fifty. Beyond this there's a private room that seats twelve. The floors are black marble and the walls are lacquered black panels separated by red stripes. The tablecloths are the same deep bloody color as the stripes. The lighting is a masterpiece of high-tech senselessness, dramatic little pinspots throwing circles of light onto the strangest places, the side of a table or the floor, anywhere except where someone might actually put a plate of food.

The lunchtime clientele, which I seldom saw, consists primarily of executives having Power Lunches. The evening crowd is more relaxed, a mixture of Bombellis, tourists, and moneyed sorts who think nothing of paying twenty-two dollars for pasta and considerably more for anything that used to be alive.

That first night Aggie greeted us effusively and introduced us to the "family," a very mixed bag, all of whom had been working there at least five years. There were two waiters, Mike and Christopher, and they could hardly have been more dissimilar.

Mike was a short, plump, middle-aged man of limited mental resources but infinite good cheer. It was impossible not to like him because he liked you, whoever you were, immediately and without reservation. His standard comment on everyone was, "He's all right."

Christopher, by contrast, was fortyish, thin, fastidious and reptilian. He was, I swiftly perceived, homosexual and no credit to the fraternity. You got the impression that when he was at a formative age something terrible had been done to him, leaving him with a jaundiced view of humanity and a tendency to talk like George Sanders. If Mike's invariable comment on his fellow man was "He's all right," Christopher's was "He doesn't fool *me*."

Rounding out our little community were the kitchen folk, Lou, Marcello and Mario. Lou, our chef, and Marcello, our prep chef, were friendly enough, but given to undue generosity with the details of their sex lives. Mario was our monosyllabic dishwasher. I heard rumors his reticence was due to his having refused the state's hospitality some ten years sooner than the state had been inclined to withdraw it. Since I worked behind the bar I saw little of this trio and that was fine by me.

I was grateful to have chosen the job of bartender as it seemed fraught with fewer perils than Gilbert's position as host. It was up to him to take reservations and choose where to seat people, often a matter of great delicacy since many "priority regulars," as Aggie called them, had the unnerving habit of walking in unexpectedly and demanding the table of their choice. On nights when the reservation book was full and the PRs descended fast and thick the atmosphere produced was a diplomatist's nightmare.

"Don't worry, boys!" said Aggie. "All it takes is a little charm, and you've certainly got that. You just smooth the feathers, Gilbert, and send 'em over to the bar for free drinks and Philip you keep the zingers coming."

"No problem!"

"Piece of cake!"

Nothing like a nice low-pressure job!

The first night was mercifully slow, giving us a chance to get accustomed to our roles. Unfortunately the slowness of the evening gave Christopher plenty of time to ooze around to the bar and get acquainted.

"Welcome aboard."

"Thanks, Chris. Or do you prefer Christopher?"

"Christopher. You're an old friend of Agnes's?"

"Not an old friend. We met last month. She's Gilbert's cousin, sort of."

"*I* see. *Gilbert* knows Agnes."

"Right."

"And you know Gilbert?" he asked with flawlessly calibrated insinuation.

"Yes." I refused to hear the implied question. A straight boy wouldn't.

"How sweet. Agnes tells me you write songs?"

"Yes."

"Words and music?"

"Just words. I have a terrific composer named Claire Simmons. In fact, we're engaged."

"*Really?*"

"Yes."

"Just like Comden and Green."

"No," I said, falling right into it, "Comden and Green write book and lyrics together. Neither one composes. And they're not married. Betty Comden used to be married to Steven Kyle. Adolph Green is married to Phyllis Newman."

"My," he cooed, "what a firm command you have of theater trivia."

He glided off. I could see this charmer had it in for me but I didn't know why until Mike innocently drew me a picture.

"You're gonna like it here. It's a great place to work. Great people. Just takes time to get to know 'em. Chris, he can be a little cold at first but after a while he warms up just like anyone. In fact, last guy who worked the bar, Sylvester, swell guy, he and Chris got on like gangbusters. He was only here three months but they got to be real pals always going out after work. They even went away for Christmas. To Florida. Whuzza place? Key West."

Wonderful! I thought. It's not bad enough I'm pretending to be straight while working in a Mafia restaurant, the owner of which thinks I'm hot for her. I also have to contend with an evil queen to whom I'm the second Mrs. deWinter.

Still, if that first night had its unforeseen perils, there were unforeseen benefits as well. I soon learned that though mafiosi are heinous sorts with no respect for law or the sanctity of human life, they do, as a class, tip well. While most patrons bypassed the bar for their waiting tables, those that paused for a quick one were so generous I could count on making at least a hundred a night over and above my fifty-dollar shift pay. At that rate I'd be able to repay Aggie's retainer and scram in no time.

Or so I thought until the end of the night when Aggie asked me to bring her a spritzer in her office.

"Darling, forgive me for being direct but are those the *best* clothes you've got?"

" 'Fraid so," I blushed.

"Oh, dear. Now I've embarrassed you. Tell you what, hon—you go to Paul Stuart first thing tomorrow. Pick out a couple of suits, three pairs of slacks, some nice silk ties, say a dozen shirts. And shoes, of course, and belts and whatever else you'll need. I'll phone ahead and have them put it on my account."

"Aggie," I cried, alarmed. If her retainer had come with strings attached, this offer seemed fully equipped with leather straps and a branding iron. "I can't let you buy me all those clothes!"

She protested that it was merely a necessary business investment but I held firm and she relented, telling me I could pay her back whatever I could afford each week till the debt was settled.

The next day, my list in hand, I trudged into Paul Stuart. Aggie must have described me well because as soon as I entered a coiffed young smoothie hastened to my side, asked my name and said that Ms. Fabrizio had requested he "look after" me. Fixing me with that tiny smile salesclerks reserve for the Kept, he shepherded me through my selections, offering many tasteful suggestions and subverting all efforts at economy. I emerged two hours later some twenty-five hundred dollars poorer. Even were I to repay Aggie at the rate of several hundred a week, I would be trapped at Paradiso at least through the wedding.

After our second, more hectic night at Paradiso, Gilbert and I returned to God's Country a bit after midnight. Moira was on the phone. She hushed us, then flicked on the speaker. We heard the line ring as Moira smiled with evil glee.

"Hello?" said a frightened voice. It was Vulpina.

Moira moaned gently, pitifully.

"Who *is* this?" asked Pina with an urgency which made me certain this wasn't the first such call she'd received.

Moira spoke in the hoarse elongated drawl preferred by nine out of ten psychopaths.

"It won't hurrrrt . . . I promisssse."

"Who are you?"

"It will be verrrry quick . . ."

"*Who are you!* Why do you want to hurt me?"

"You knoooooow!"

"I don't!"

"Yes, you doooo! But it will be quick!"

"What have I *done*!"

"It won't hurrrt! And then you'll be miiiiine! Foreverrrrr!"

This cheerful little earful delivered, she hung up and smiled broadly.

"God, she's a sissy! How was work?"

"Swell, honey!"

"Was that the first call you made?"

"No. I called twice in the middle of last night. Once I was quiet, the second time I breathed a little, and then I called her about an hour ago and breathed again. But wait! The really good one's coming!"

She reached down beside her chair and picked up a little tape recorder I hadn't noticed there. It was connected by a cord to the phone.

"This won't take long," said Moira and left the room. In about five minutes she returned holding a ghetto blaster.

"Watch this!"

She dialed Vulpina a few times but the line was busy. Then she called again. Pina answered and in a pathetic little voice said, "Hello?"

Moira smiled saucily but said nothing.

"Stop this! You hear me! I've phoned the police and they are going to tap my phone and find you and—"

Vulpina was interrupted by the hysterical sound of her *own* voice booming from the ghetto blaster.

"Who are you!! Why do you want to hurt me? What have I done? What have I done? What have I done? What have I done?"

And as this ghastly loop repeated, Moira took a starter's pistol from her pocket and fired it. She then laughed maniacally and hung up.

"That ought to do it. But if she tries one more stunt, I swear I'm going to get nasty."

I stayed at GC that night to watch a "must see" late movie, waiting all the while for Moira to drowse off so Gilbert and I could enjoy our "absolute last time" together, for the affair was still in that stage. In the morning I nipped out before Moira rose and called Claire to give her the poop on the restaurant and poor Vulpina's plunge into the twilight zone.

"God, she has got to be stopped! I'm ashamed of myself, I really am."

"Ashamed?"

"I haven't applied myself enough. It's clear that Moira is thinking things through night and day, planning it all to the last detail. You don't beat someone who's working like that unless you work just as hard or harder. When can we all talk? The three of us?"

I suggested she meet us after work that night for a drink.

I was glad I did. Aggie spent the whole night sitting at the bar flirting as if she'd taken Leo's correspondence course. And no sooner had she left than Christopher oiled up to the bar, dropped onto a stool and began sighing so dramatically that there was no doubt but he wished to be asked what the matter was. I made concerned inquiries and soon learned that his beau, my predecessor, Sylvester, had disappeared into the night, taking with him Christopher's reason to live, not to mention several pairs of gold cufflinks.

"Of course, at my age," he sighed, "I don't suppose I'm apt to find anyone again."

Here, I thought, was my chance to improve relations and render the workplace atmosphere a bit less cool than it had been. I assured him that a man of his suave good looks and keen intellect should have no trouble attracting dozens of would-be replacements for this cad who had so foolishly failed to see what a prize was his.

It was not long, however, before things got sticky. He contradicted all my compliments thus goading me on to still more fulsome efforts and soon he was staring at me in a way that frankly challenged me to make good on my blarney.

So it was no small relief that Claire chose this moment to saunter in.

"Baby, what a surprise!" I said, leaning over the bar for a big wet one on the lips which took her quite by surprise.

"In the neighborhood, were you, and decided to see me home? Gosh, I've been thinking about you all night, Babe! My place or yours?"

We departed, Gilbert joining us, and as we strolled up Park Avenue in the cold night air Claire outlined her new plan of attack.

"What we need if we're going to get around Moira and this Murcheson are some well-placed allies. Now, who's as eager to see Moira knocked off her perch as we are? People who've also been victimized by her?"

"You mean like Pina?"

"I was thinking of Winslow Potts."

"Winslow? But he's the one who broke the law by giving Moira the trust money. He'd rather die than spill the beans."

"No, he wouldn't rather *die*. And if we explain that that's his option I think we can induce him to cooperate."

"You mean we threaten him?"

"If you want to put it that way. I think we'd mainly be enlightening him. Do you suppose he knows the Mafia is involved? I doubt it. Moira hasn't admitted that to you two. Why would she tell him when it would only scare him to death? From what I've heard he sounds like a timid man who made a greedy decision he'd do anything to reverse. When we let him know he can't, but he has a choice of whether he takes his licks from the Duchess of Dorsetshire or Freddy the Pooch, I think the choice won't be difficult."

Gilbert said he'd try to find Winslow's phone and address in Moira's book but that she tended to keep it in her purse which was seldom out of her sight. We agreed that we could afford to wait a few days if need be. Moira's vengeance against Pina and Gunther was finished so there were no fresh horrors looming on the horizon demanding to be fended off.

Which shows you how much *we* knew.

Nineteen

"Sorry to wake you. Bad news."

"Whah? How bah?"

"Time will tell! Moira met Gunther last night."

"Hwhah?" I mumbled, dislodging horrid little things from the corner of my eye so I could read the bedside digital. It was two-twenty.

"Moira! Met Gunther! At the movies. She was having a girl's night out with Babs Destefano."

"Babs?"

"Lunch's daughter. Moira's working her way through the family. We've got Chick's son Ugo and his hairy wife coming to brunch this Sunday. Anyway, they're in the lobby and there's Gunther and some friend of his and he smiles at Moy and says how is *she* tonight? And she says, 'I don't think we have anything to say to each other Mr. Von Steigle.' So he just sneers and says, 'Give my regards to your faggot fiancé.' *Right in front of Babs!*"

"Oh no! What did Moira tell Babs?"

"Oh, she said Gunther was this guy who'd tried to get into my pants only he couldn't, of course, so he hates my guts. Babs bought it but, *Jesus*, honey, Moira was fuming! Don't you see? She thinks Gunther knows *we* sent the doll and he said it just to prove he's not scared of us one bit. As far as she was concerned, it was a fucking declaration of war!"

At ten a.m. the phone woke me from a night of Technicolor sequels to "Little Caesar." It was Holly Batterman.

"This must be juicy if you can't wait till after lunch."

"It is, honey. Vulpina's cracking up!"

"Cracking up?"

"Completely! She's running around telling people that some horrible maniac is out to get her!"

"Oh?" I asked lightly.

"Yes! She says she gets phone calls where she hears her *own voice* begging for mercy!"

"Golly!"

"She even went to the police!"

"How 'bout that! Uh, what'd they say?"

"Well, I don't think they took her very seriously. The silly bitch went to the station wearing the same dress she wore to my Christmas party."

"Oh *no*—!"

"*Exactly.* In walks Batwoman at ten in the morning! They just about told her to go back to her home planet and leave 'em alone. So, whaddaya think? *I* say she's making the whole thing up for attention!"

"Me, too!"

"Really?"

"Absolutely! Did I tell you I once went to one of her fashion shows with a friend, a psychiatrist, and he could tell from her designs alone that Pina was *delusional*. Of course, I'm telling you this in confidence."

"Right. Gotta go!" he said and hung up.

Seconds later my phone rang again.

"Hi, Gerry, s'me! You'll never guess! Pina's gone off the deep end!"

"Holly?"

"Oh, you again? I must have pressed redial."

That night at work Gilbert glumly reported that Moira had secured the services of Jean-Louis Mallard to design for the bridal party. I'd never heard of him but Gilbert assured me he was *the* rising star of fashion and that it was quite a coup for Moira, which was why Tony and the duchess both consented to pay twenty thousand for the dresses. Tony had also forked out seven hundred dollars for invitations, plus hefty advances for the caterer and musicians. Money was already being spent and in quantity. The swindle was happening. We were doomed.

*   *   *

The next day Gilbert managed to obtain Winslow's phone number and address from Moira's book. He lived on West Eighty-first, only blocks from God's Country. Gilbert called to convey this, and also informed me that Moira had requested we meet her at a café called the Happy Grouse on Lexington Avenue. She refused to divulge the reason, saying it was a surprise and that we should sit at a table in front by the window. She had a gown fitting nearby but would meet us there at three sharp.

We reached the café at three on the dot and, taking our seats in the window, realized to our horror that we were directly across the street from Gunther's hairdressing salon, Capelli. The large-windowed façade afforded a good view of the inside where five women sat being attended by two besmocked women and a tall man with a red beard.

"Oh, no! Is he in there?"

"Not that I can—*shit*! There he is!"

The unmistakable features of Gunther Von Steigle had hovered into view right behind the chair closest to the window.

At that moment a tall striking woman with a wide-brimmed black hat walked briskly through the door of the salon and straight over to Gunther. She seemed to be screaming at him. Suddenly she tore off her hat and we saw that she was entirely bald underneath. Indeed, she was not only bald but had red scars crisscrossing her scalp. Just then someone entered the café and while the door was open we could hear her shouting, "You did this to me! You!"

The other women in the shop were understandably perturbed. One old darling leapt from her chair and started putting her coat on. Gunther began shouting back at Baldie, trying to escort her out, and Baldie began beating him with her purse. Screaming some parting shot at him, she stormed out of the shop, hailed a cab and sped off down Lex.

Seconds later the door opened again and Gunther's horrified patrons began scampering out, even a plump woman whose hair was still covered in shampoo. She just clamped a kerchief over her head and dove into a cab.

"Do you sense the subtle hand of Moira in this?" I asked, rhetorically.

"Jesus Christ, Philly! We better go before he sees us!"

We dashed for the door and looked out to make sure the coast was clear. It was. But no sooner had we stepped out than Gunther and the redheaded man appeared out of nowhere, desperately beseeching the last departing matron not to go.

We ducked down into our coats and began walking quickly downtown, but it was no good.

"You two!" he shouted. *"You two!"*

We ran for the corner, turned west and scrambled into a cab. Turning as we sped off, we could see him standing in the street, shaking his fist in the best melodramatic fashion.

Heading west, we saw Moira rushing east toward the café and the front row seat she'd hoped to share with us. Gilbert leaned out the window.

"Get in! You missed it!"

Moira heaved an exasperated sigh as she entered the cab.

"Oh, pooh! How'd it go?"

We filled her in.

"Wasn't she good? She was in Marlow's *Bong!* with me years ago. She usually wears a wig but when I offered her a few hundred for two minutes of performing without it she couldn't resist. But I'm furious I missed it! I should have told her to make sure we were all there first."

"Moira—Gunther *saw* us!"

"He was supposed to! I mean, why be *coy?* The gloves are off! I just wish I'd seen it! Was it funny? Was it delish?"

"Hello, Gunther? This is Philip Cavanaugh."

"You! Do you realize what you have done to my business!"

"Yes, actually, that's why I'm calling," I said, lowering my voice. I was on the pay phone at Paradiso and feared being overhead. "Gilbert and I had *nothing* to do with that."

"Of *course!* It was just a coincidence that you were watching from across the street!"

"No, it wasn't! Someone *told* us to be there. We got an anonymous phone call telling us where to go. So you see we're also victims of this . . . nasty person! He wanted you to see *us* and *blame* everything on—"

"Do not waste my time with ridiculous inventions, Mr. Cavanaugh. You thought you could enjoy my humiliation unobserved and now that you're caught you're trying to weasel your way out with talk of conspiracies. I suppose you also had nothing to do with that demented doll I received?"

"Huh? *Doll?* You mean, like Barbie?"

Click.

"Was he mad, honey?" asked Gilbert.

"Guess. And don't call me honey!"

"I'm sorry," he said petulantly.

"Well, it gets to be a habit, Gilbert, and you don't realize you're doing it. Like that time in the cafeteria in high school. 'Do you want some Jell-O, darling?' You never know who's going to hear and— So! How's the reservation book look tonight, Gil?"

"Gil?"

"Sorry if I'm interrupting something," throbbed Christopher, draping himself over the bar. "Dewar's rocks, soda back."

"Coming up."

"Customers!" cried Gilbert, bustling off to greet an arriving deuce.

"You boys don't have to whisper around me. I can keep a secret."

"Dewar's, right? Damn, we're out. Why don't you come back for this?" I said nipping around the bar and heading for Aggie's office. "It might take me a bit to find some more."

"I'll help!" he said and followed me in, closing the door behind us.

A delivery had been made that day and the small office was crammed with boxes, rendering the Dewar's difficult to find and a certain degree of physical intimacy difficult to avoid.

"Do you still think I'm suave?" asked Christopher.

"Chris!" I laughed, trying to pretend I thought he was joking. "You flirt, you!"

"I'm incorrigible," he said, mussing my hair. "Doing anything tonight?"

"Christo-pherr! Why are you wasting your time on me? You know I'm straight."

"And if you weren't? Would you be interested in me?"

"If, yes. Absolutely."

"You're not just saying that?" he asked winsomely.

"No, not at all! You're an attractive man!"

"If you ever had doubts would you tell me about them?"

"You'd be the first."

"I can keep a secret," he said, smiling.

"I'm sure you can."

"Unlike Holly Batterman," he added, the smile swinging shut like a bear trap.

"You know Holly, huh?"

"Very well. We were chatting about you just last night. He says he knows Jesuits straighter than you are."

"What a kidder!"

"You must take me for quite a fool, mustn't you? Coming on to me that way then hiding behind your chubby girlfriend."

"Christ! I wasn't coming on to you that night. I just wanted to make you feel good!"

"Oh, well, if that's what you want to do," he said and fell toward me, his hands hitting the wall on either side of my shoulders. He smiled and inclined his head toward mine, his thin lips parting as his eyes closed like a gothic covergirl's.

I shimmied down the wall, scooted around him and lunged for the door. He spun, lost his balance and fell face-first into a case of Smirnoff. I heard him squeal in pain and indignation as I nipped out the door. He emerged five minutes later wearing a Band-Aid on his temple and a look of utter loathing that made Gunther Von Steigle's worst efforts look like a chorus boy singing a title number.

On our next free Monday night, Claire, Gilbert and I met in front of Shakespeare and Co. We called Winslow Potts from a booth and Claire asked sweetly to speak to Audrey.

"Terribly sorry. My mistake," she said and hung up. "He's home."

We trudged the few blocks to his brownstone and rang the bell.

"Hello?" crackled a voice.

"UPS," said Gilbert.

He buzzed us in and we hurriedly climbed the stairs to his second-floor apartment. Claire and I stood off to one side of the door and Gilbert waited in front of it.

The door opened.

"Why, you're not UPS at all!" said Winslow, though from his tone he found Gilbert comely enough not to mind the deception by which he had gained entry.

"No, and neither are we," said Claire, appearing from the left as Gilbert neatly slipped his foot in the door.

"I'm Gilbert Selwyn."

"Moira's fiancé!"
"That's the one!"

Winslow Potts seemed to have been born nervous. Even in his calmer moments he reminded me of a hummingbird awaiting biopsy results.

"I have nothing to say to you! Nothing to say to any of you!" he shrieked.

"You don't have to say anything. Just sit down and listen."

We introduced ourselves politely.

"We're not here to hurt you. Just to tell you some things you should know."

"Can I take a Valium first?" he asked, edging toward a door.

"Certainly," said Claire, "but if you're thinking of calling Moira, don't bother. She's not in and we can erase your message before she gets back."

"Who are you—Miss Marple? Why are you people bothering me? I haven't done anything to you, have I?"

"No, but we're all in a fine mess and we can't get out without some cooperation from you."

"What mess! Moira said everything's going fine!"

"She lied."

"Oh, the *letter*, you mean? I know all about it. Those two friends of hers that are trying to reach the duchess—Vulpina and—"

"Winslow," said Claire, "*we're* the ones who sent the letter."

He gasped.

"But, that doesn't make sense! Why would *you* want the duchess to know about the trust fund."

"We'll explain,"said Claire.

"Can I take that Valium first?"

"Just bring the bottle out," said Gilbert.

He disappeared through an adjoining room and into a bathroom.

"Gawd! What a nervous queen!" said Gilbert.

"He has every reason to be," said Claire, intently perusing his bookshelf.

On leaving for the john, he'd left the door to some middle room ajar and peering into it now we saw a room very different from the subdued antique-filled chamber we were waiting in. It appeared to be some sort of laboratory. On second glance we saw that it was the apartment's kitchen, but the table and counters were laden with tubes,

178 / Joe Keenan

beakers and strange little gadgets. There was even a cage with white rats.

Winslow emerged from the bathroom.

"Well, we're not a *bit* nosy, are we?"

"What is all this?" asked Claire.

"I'll be damned if I know. It's my *roommate's*, all right? He does medical research. Completely ruined my kitchen but I can't cook for shit anyway. So!" He smiled shakily. "Why are you nice young people trying to tell the duchess more than she has to know?"

We told him, Claire backing up the mob details with the same selection of books and articles she'd shown to us.

He didn't take it well. He fluttered and twitched. He also cowered, goggled, gasped and, at one point, simply sat in a chair and vibrated. It was like watching Marcel Marceau mime an entire day at Disney World.

"You had *no* idea the Mafia was involved in any of Moira's plans?"

"Are you *insane*! I hadn't an inkling! She's told me nothing about this! Nothing! That despicable girl!"

"Then you see what trouble we could all be in?" I asked.

"What do you mean, *we*?" yelled Winslow. "I had nothing to do with it! How can I be held responsible when I didn't even know?"

"But you know *now*, Winslow, and we'll personally see to it you *are* held responsible if you don't help us put a stop to the whole thing."

"What do you mean, hold me responsible?"

"I mean," improvised Claire, "that we've left letters in the safe-keeping of our lawyers, letters explaining Moira's role in all this—and yours. If anything happens to us those letters will be mailed to Freddy the Pooch."

That was when he vibrated. We had resolved to be firm, even merciless, with him but I couldn't help feeling a pang of sympathy. Winslow is a large man in his late forties. He has a potbelly, a double chin and hair that is sadly, because improbably, blond and curly. And when the hair and the chins and the belly all begin shaking with cowardice it's not an edifying spectacle. I wondered what his "roommate" was researching and hoped for Winslow's sake that he was on the verge of a breakthrough in sedatives.

"These people must not be swindled!"

"Well, what am *I* supposed to do about it?"

"You have to call the duchess and tell her about the trust fund."

"That's *impossible!*" he shrieked.

"Please, try to calm down," I implored him. "We're on *your* side!"

"Sure you are!" he blubbered. "You burst into my house, scare me to death, then tell me I have to do what you say or I'll wind up as Alpo—and I'm s'posed to say, 'My, what nice new *friends* I've found!' "

Framed that way, of course, we seemed less than benevolent, but we did our best to persuade him that it was Moira who'd put us all in the positions we now occupied.

"We realize you'll catch hell from the duchess and the bank. But who would you rather deal with? Them or Freddy the Pooch?"

"I don't want to deal with anyone!"

And with that he burst into tears and rocked back and forth, keening like all the Trojan Women rolled into one.

"I better get him a glass of water," said Claire, and ran off to the bathroom. We did our best to calm him until she returned after a suspiciously lengthy interval.

"Please, Winslow," said Claire as he drained the glass, "whatever you do, don't call Moira. She is not to be trusted. She played you for a fool about the trust fund and she told you nothing about the risks of swindling Tony Cellini. She'd sell the lot of us out with no compunction if she thought it was the only way to save her own skin."

Winslow sat there almost motionless for the first time since our arrival.

"This is very upsetting."

"Yes, we know."

"I need time to think."

"Not too much," said Gilbert. "Tony's already spending it in gobs!"

"Well, I'm sorry, dear, but it's going to take me a few days to figure out how to approach all this. You can't dump a mess like this in my lap and expect me to sort through it all just overnight! And I have a very busy week at the bank. I'll call you Saturday."

"You won't call Moira?"

"I never want to speak to that miserable girl again! She's been stringing me along for months and I've been foolish enough to think she was sincere. It's the trusting people in this world who suffer the most!"

"You can trust *us*, Winnie," said Gilbert, rubbing his shoulders and speaking in a husky voice that percolated with false promises. "We're as scared as you are. We just want to get out of this in one piece."

We donned our coats and assured him that he could call Claire or me, though not God's Country, if he had any questions or suggestions.

As we strolled up West Eighty-first we agreed that it was in Winslow's hands now. At least he seemed thoroughly disillusioned with Moira and terrified of the Cellinis.

"Gilbert," said Claire, "what's the duchess's first name? I may be dropping her a line soon."

"It's Gwendolyn. What are you up to?"

"I'm not sure yet."

"You took a long time getting him that water. Were you snooping?"

"Of course."

"See anything?"

"It's what I didn't see that interests me. I want a few days to check into some things and then I'll tell you. Okay?"

"No! Tell us now!" whined Gilbert.

"No. It's a dumb idea. Unless I'm right, then it's brilliant. But if I'm right, I want proof. I want to present it to you all neatly wrapped up and beautifully summarized like Hercule Poirot."

"Or Nero Wolfe."

"Watch it."

We were disgruntled that Claire had suddenly chosen to withhold her theories. It seemed to show a want of team spirit. But eager as we were to discover the nature of these theories it wasn't long before fast-breaking stories consigned them to the back page. Wednesday night Gilbert and I arrived at work to find that Jimmy Pastore had died that morning.

Jimmy Pastore was a "Cellini" since his mother is a sister of Tony's. He was the son of Charlie Pastore, who, at Maddie's Christmas party, cut in on me and horny little Leo, giving me the chance to scram. Jimmy was also the brother of dear chubby Steffie.

Jimmy's life, while fondly remembered by Steffie, is of little concern to us; it is only the manner of his death that touches obliquely on the fates of the Allies. Jimmy met his end in the bathtub when a thirteen-inch Sony he'd been watching plunged into the suds, resulting in

Jimmy's tragic, if hygienic, demise. The coroner's verdict was death by misadventure.

It didn't take long that night, though, for Gilbert and me to see that this verdict was not unconditionally accepted by Jimmy's numerous relations. Many family members dined at Paradiso that night and they were more than bereaved; they were unsettled. Mistrustful. Cousins stared at cousins and whispered in little cabals; it reached the point where I was afraid to ask groups or pairs at the bar if they wanted another drink for the way they'd look up sharply from their whispers, wondering How Much I'd Heard.

Aggie wore black that night and, consigning Gilbert to assist me at the bar, hosted the evening, which became a sort of pre-wake. She spent most of the night in the small dining room in intimate confabs with various Cellinis, Fabrizios and Sartuccis.

At one point Chick Sartucci was at the bar with his son Ugo when Steffie and her husband walked in. They took one look at Chick and marched right out of the restaurant. Chick watched and then turned back to his beer saying, "They're fuckin' crazy!"

Late in the evening I pulled Christopher aside. The chilliness he'd displayed toward me in the wake of our little contretemps had subsided somewhat and I hoped he would not pass up a chance to prove himself in the know.

"Chris, what's going on here tonight?"

"Who wants to know?" he asked evenly.

I stiffened. The most casual inquiry had raised issues of allegiance and complicity. What *was* going on?

"Just me. I'm sorry, I was curious. This is usually a cheerful little place but tonight everyone's skulking around like . . ."

"Like what?"

"Forget it!"

"Take my advice, Philip. Don't ask questions. The less you know about people's private feuds the better off you are."

"What people? What feuds?"

I attended the funeral at Aggie's suggestion. The whole Paradiso "family" was going and my absence might have reflected a callousness she was sure I did not feel. It was the second time I'd seen the clan en masse and the difference could not have been greater. At Maddie's the various branches had mingled freely and with great conviviality.

But now in grief they did not band together as might have been expected, but remained isolated in three contingents. Of all those present only Gilbert, Moira and Maddie seemed oblivious to this air of division. They wandered freely through all groups offering condolences and touching reflections on the evanescence of life. Gilbert was more or less dragged through his paces by Moira, who knew that a few poignant words in the ears of the widow and parents could substantially increase the value of the gift they would select a mere two months down the road.

When I returned home I checked my machine and found a terse message from Milt Miller informing me my services were no longer required.

My feelings were mixed. On the one hand I hadn't relished juggling two jobs, but Jimmy's suspicious demise had strengthened my resolve to leave the restaurant as soon as Aggie was repaid. Now what would I fall back on? And why had he fired me anyway? I called him and asked.

"I'm sorry, Philip, I just don't need the help," he said nervously.

"But there's tons to do. You have a new book coming out and that always means *more* work for me! Why fire me now?"

He sighed with a mixture of discomfort and pique.

"I had a little call from the police."

"The *police!*"

"Surprised, are we! How dare you expect me to give you an alibi for a night when you were nowhere near my place? Do you think I appreciate being dragged into a drug investigation? I have nothing more to say!"

"Wait! There's some mistake here, Milt. I don't even use drugs!"

"Balls! You're using them now! I can tell! Don't call me again!"

I was baffled but not for long. It was Gunther, no doubt, getting a bit of his own back. You damage my livelihood, I eradicate yours!

As I sat there fuming, the phone rang again. It was Claire.

"Hello, sunshine! How goes it, my little co-conspirator?"

"I just lost my job with Milt Miller. Gunther apparently called and said I was prominent in narcotics circles."

"The fiend," she said lightly. "Buck up, darling, there'll be plenty of other jobs on the road to fame and fortune."

"*You* sound chipper."

"I am, Philip, I am! I've spent the last week dragging Moira up a steep hill to a lonely cross to which I will attach her as soon as I can find nails that are rusty enough."

"You're kidding!"

"I never kid, my pet. Trust me. If Moira tries to double-cross you now, she'd better grow gills and fast."

"What is it?"

"Patience, dear, I'm just putting the last few brushstrokes on my masterpiece. I'll give you the whole thing tomorrow."

"Claire, don't do this to me! I've seen enough movies to know that when someone says, 'I've exposed the villain but I can't tell you how till tomorrow,' that person will be found the next morning at the foot of a cliff in a mangled Buick!"

"Not this girl, dear."

She asked if tomorrow was a Freddy night for Moira. I said that yes, it was, and she said Gilbert and I could expect her at God's Country around eight.

"C'mon, Claire! At least give me a hint!"

"Philip, my dear," she said just before hanging up, "Satan may be the Father of Lies, but when Satan's busy, Moira baby-sits."

Twenty

I'd never seen Claire look more radiant than she did the night she vanquished Moira. She wore a pretty dress of deep blue and I think I spied a hint of the makeup she rarely wears. As she sailed through the door into God's Country she exuded equal measures of strength and femininity, like a Valkyrie just back from the hairdresser's.

"*Well?*" we said as one.

"There's hospitality for you! Aren't you going to offer me anything?"

"What do you want?"

"Something exotic, I think. Do you have any cognac?"

Gilbert dispensed beakers of the warming fluid and we sat around the fire he'd lit in the living room, waiting breathlessly for Claire to unfold her tale.

"Well, boys, the first thing I want to say is don't get too excited. We're not out of the woods. Not by a long way, I'm afraid. But we had two things to be frightened of before: the Mafia and Moira, and the more dangerous of the two, Moira, is now eliminated. Consider her permanently declawed."

"What have you got on her?"

"Patience, dear. It's a twisty path I've been down and I prefer to take you step by step.

"When we left Winslow's the other day there were a few things I couldn't quite figure out. The first was Winslow's profession, or rather, his avocation. You told me he was a playwright. In fact, such a dedicated and driven playwright that Moira had successfully exploited his ambition. She offered him a production of his work if only he would provide her access to her funds. And so desperate was his desire to be produced that he aquiesced, putting himself in a very precarious position.

"Well, I looked around that man's apartment and there was no evidence that he was a playwright at all! No theater books, and not so much as a single published play. Not in the living room and not in the bedroom either—I checked. There were no theater posters or prints, no souvenirs of shows he'd been involved in. Most significantly of all, there wasn't a desk or a typewriter anywhere in view. I don't think he could write at that kitchen table . . . it's too cluttered with his roommate's test tubes and chemicals. Now it's possible the type-writer might have been put away when not in use, but I ask you—a writer without a desk? Possible, but not likely. So if that part of Moira's story was invented, what else might be?

"Then there were the curious things he said—and the curious ways he said them. When you told him he had to confess to the duchess he said, 'That's impossible!' At first, I thought he was being rhetorical, that he was just unwilling to face the consequences. Then later I thought maybe he meant it literally. Now, under what circumstances is it impossible to confess to someone?"

"When they already *know!*" I said, leaping to my feet.

"What are you talking about?" said Gilbert.

"Gilbert, don't you *see?*" I said. "The fucking duchess is *in* on it! She's known what Moira's been up to all along!"

"I don't believe it! That *bitch!*"

And no sooner had Gilbert uttered these words than the lady in question burst through the front door and flew into the living room, the tails of her long black trenchcoat snapping viciously behind her. She glared hydrophobically at us, and Dr. Watson, without the slight-est assistance from Holmes, could have guessed that she'd seen Wins-low and he had Told All.

"You *traitors!*" she bellowed.

"Look, who's talking, bitch," snarled Gilbert and, with an athletic dexterity of which I'd not have thought him capable, snatched up and hurled a stuffed dachshund, catching her squarely on the jaw and knocking her flat on her behind.

"I'll have you *killed* for that!" she shrieked, sprawling on the carpet. "I have friends that will cut your legs off and beat you to death with them!"

"Oh?" said Gilbert, dumping a vase of wet tulips on her, "does this mean we're not in *love* anymore?"

"That's it!" she shrieked. "You're *dead meat*, Selwyn!"

Claire stood and addressed them primly.

"That's enough, you two. We have a lot to discuss."

"*You!*" hissed Moira, rising to her feet and backing up. "You think you're very clever, don't you, missy? Well, you're not! I've had my suspicions about you right from the night of Maddie's party and now Winslow has confirmed them all! How dare you try to tell my mother things that are none of your goddamned business!"

"We didn't have to tell her, did we?" I said coolly. "The duchess has been in on it for some time! Maybe since the beginning?"

"*What?*" said Moira.

"Don't play innocent," said Gilbert. "Claire figured it all out."

Moira looked to Claire, and howled with derisive laughter.

"Oh, *please!* Spare me your detective work, you cow. My mother knows nothing. *Nothing.* And she's not going to find out, either. You listen to me, you idiots! Freddy Bombelli is a very powerful, very *violent* man—you're right about that much anyway—and he's just crazy about me. He wouldn't believe in a million years that I've done anything crooked. But *you*, Gilbert, and your queer friends—he doesn't trust you at *all*. He's only willing to try because I ask him. So, from now on, *I* call the shots. If any of you try to fuck up this plan *ever* again I will run to Freddy, blow the whole thing wide open and tell him it was your idea and *you* talked me into it! Then he'll personally see to it the three of you are next week's gourmet special at Bide-A-Wee. Do we understand each other?"

"Sit down, Moira," said Claire, her voice loud with righteous authority, like Van Helsing telling Dracula to relocate.

"Don't talk to *me* that way, you mailbox!" screamed Moira. "I don't think you realize the position you're in!"

"Ditto, my pet. But, if you can keep that sewage pipe with lipstick closed for five minutes, I'll tell you exactly where you stand."

Moira stared haughtily but seated herself.

"Before you interrupted," said Claire, speaking very slowly as one who wants the moment to last, "Philip, Gilley-poo and I were discussing something Winslow said. We told him he had to tell the duchess about your plan and he said it was 'impossible.' Was he being rhetorical or did he mean it literally? I proposed the latter. But *why* was it impossible? These two leapt to the conclusion that it was impossible because the duchess already knew. But we know that's not the reason, don't we Moira?"

"I don't know what you're talking about."

"Poor naïve darling. Well, how does this sound: Winslow could not spill the beans to the duchess because the duchess does not exist. The duchess never existed. The duchess is a pretentious fabrication you concocted quite some time ago. An amusing, cheeky little lie that posed few practical problems. Then suddenly Gilbert wanted you to help him bilk his big wealthy family and you desperately wanted your half of the money. Only you were saddled with this imaginary mummy across the sea who was supposed to pay for the whole thing.

"You couldn't tell Gilbert the duchess was a fiction because he would never have dreamed of yoking himself to you if he didn't think your side was good for at least as much as his. So you kept it a secret. But there was one rather large problem. How could a nonexistent duchess pay for everything? So, you invented the riding accident so she could ask *you* to pay for it yourself out of a trust fund which, of course, never existed either, and which you had conveniently, and improbably, spent. How to get around that? Have Gilbert's family pay. How to get around Gilbert's objections to this? Convince him it was an elaborate swindle which would in the end double his income from the wedding. How's that so far? Rebuttal?"

"Gilbert," throbbed Moira, "you don't believe this evil woman, do you?"

"Moira," said Gilbert, his voice calm as death, "I don't know what to call you anymore. I'm out of words."

"But the calls from the duchess," I said. "We've all heard her. People have spoken to her."

"Of course," said Claire, "which brings us back to where we started; the real reason Winslow couldn't confess to the duchess was that he *is* the duchess. *He* made the phone calls and played Mummy. Am I right?"

"Don't grin that way, Claire. Your bridgework shows. I was *going* to tell you, Gilbert. I was looking for the right way."

"A posthumous letter, perhaps?" said Claire. "So, Winslow was Mummy, which is why he simply wailed when we said the duchess would have to pay for the wedding. He knew *that* was impossible, too."

"How did you work this out, Claire?" I said, dizzy with admiration.

"Well, once I assumed that Winslow wasn't a playwright I decided to see what else he wasn't. He wasn't a banker either. I called him two days running and he was home during banking hours. So if he wasn't a banker maybe there wasn't a trust fund, and if there wasn't a trust fund, just maybe there wasn't a duchess either. So I called the duchess using the old wrong-number ploy. I pretended to be looking for a bookstore called Trebleclef. I insisted my number was correct and the gentleman at Trebleclef, 'Murcheson,' I assume, insisted, of course, that it wasn't. Well, if this Trebleclef wasn't a bookstore, I asked, what was it? He informed me that it was a country inn with a charming little restaurant. So much for the ancestral home. I asked him if there was an old woman named Gwen there and he said, no, there was only one woman working there and she was a teenager. Here's where it gets good, boys! I decided that if Moira's real mum wasn't at Trebleclef maybe she was still in the States."

"All right, Claire," said Moira, "that's *enough!*"

"No, it isn't," said Claire, sweetly. "Philip, I remembered your joking that the duchess sounded awfully posh for a woman from Pittsburgh so I got a Pittsburgh directory and started calling all the Finches, asking if anyone could help me find a Gwen Finch, about fifty. I said if it was any help I knew she had a daughter named Moira. I finally reached her sister-in-law—your Auntie Mavis, Moira."

"A hateful woman!"

"And *talkative!* She told me I'd have no trouble finding Gwen if I just called California and asked for a list of women's correctional facilities. Even as we speak, Mummy is living in one, learning respect for other people's property. Like mother like daughter. Excuse me, Moira, I'm not usually this mean-spirited but you do have a way of bringing out the worst in people."

"Oh, that's right! Everything's *my* fault!"

"Listen to her!" thundered Gilbert, leaping up from his chair. "You prove right to her face that she's been lying to everybody she knows for years and she sits there pouting like we're the bad guys!"

"Oh, hush up, you. Is it *my* fault you were so greedy you wanted *me* to bring in a fortune too? You weren't satisfied to let me help you get presents from your family and split it up. No! You wanted dukes and princes showering us with money and ancestral jewels!"

"But you *told* me we'd have fucking dukes and ancestral jewels!"

"With your greed did I dare say otherwise? You'd have called it off and I'd have gotten nothing at all. And I *need* the money, Gilley. I need it desperately! I have a chance—*we* have a chance, if you want—to get in on the ground floor of the most profitable—"

"*Nooo!*" screamed Gilbert, falling onto a sofa and beating the arm rest with both fists. "Not another one of your stupid fucking *investments!*"

"Winslow!" I said, in one of the few flashes of insight I'd displayed in my recent career as a full-time dupe. "That lab was his!"

"I was getting to that," sniffed Claire.

"He's absolutely brilliant!" said Moira, "and he's working on an idea that will revolutionize—"

"I don't want to hear it! Whatever it is, I'm not interested!"

"You're *so* close-minded," sighed Moira.

"How did you handle the contacts?" asked Claire, with a trace of admiration. "Who was your man in Little Chipperton and how did it work?"

"Oh, it was pretty simple," said Moira, unable to conceal a touch of pride. "Bri, he's the one at Trebleclef, is an old flame of mine from years and years ago. I just told him I was having a little joke on some friends so if anyone called asking for the Duke or Duchess of Dorsetshire, say they were indisposed, take a message and call me reversing the charges. I have a private line in my room, of course. If he couldn't reach me, he could leave a message on my secret answering machine. (It's hidden under the nightstand, Gilley, so don't tear the place apart, okay?)

"Whenever Bri gave me a message for the duchess I'd call Winslow and tell him who the duchess had to phone back and what she had to say. The same thing went for letters. When the duchess got one Bri would call and read it to me. Then I'd dash off a reply, have Winnie copy it onto my duchess stationery, then send it express over to England to be mailed back here so the postmark would be right.

"Actually, the duchess got to be very convenient. Like when Pina came by to show me her sketches. I made sure Mum would call while she was here and say poisonous things about her. That way if the designs wound up being too much, which they certainly did, I'd have a dodge all nice and ready. And Pina couldn't blame it on me—I was just humoring Mummy!"

"And how were you planning to get out of Mummy coming to the wedding? What were you going to do, bump her off?"

"What else? Both Mummy and the duke will be having a little car accident three weeks from now. Mummy's first motor jaunt after her convalescence! *Très tragique!* A little close to the wedding, of course, but I'll be ever so brave, and, if you ask me, the sympathy should be worth a fortune in added revenue."

"But Gilbert thought your mother was a rich woman. What were you planning to tell *him* about your inheritance?"

"The duke's nasty cousin gets it all and won't give me a dime."

"Why not the goddamned truth for a change?" asked Gilbert.

"I didn't want our marriage to be unpleasant."

"My God, Moira," I said, "you're amazing!"

"Nice of you to say so, Philip, but it was all *far* from perfect. Take the business of the duchess reimbursing us for what Tony spent. It never occurred to me that Gilbert would decide we had to go try and get Tony to spend as much as possible because we were getting it back. I mean, I knew we weren't getting a dime back but how could I tell you, Gilley? Then *that* meant firing poor Pina, since who's going to pay thousands for *her* name? And, my gawd, all that messiness with you people trying to tip off Mummy because you guessed the family was full of wise guys and you were too wimpy to just go *through* with it anyway! I *had* to tell you about the letter and someone being on to us, but how come Mummy never *saw* it? So, I had to invent Murcheson! Then I thought Pina and Gunther sent the letter and you didn't dare tell me it was really you, so I took it out on *those* two! Like I said," she concluded, lighting a cigarette, "it wasn't perfect but I still think on the whole it was very well executed."

"Yes, Moira," said Claire, "and so will you be if Freddy finds out."

"I'm trembling, Claire."

"Moira, love, Gilbert tells me your mother, the one in England, not jail, just had herself a birthday and that Freddy sent her an expensive brooch. Mummy even called to thank him. Now correct me if I'm wrong, but I think if Freddy found out he sent that jewel to a woman who doesn't exist and received his thanks from a two-hundred-pound homosexual gentleman he would not appreciate this. He would feel you had played him for a fool, had *been* playing him for a fool as long as you'd known him. What do you suppose he'd do about that?"

"I'm not scared of you, Claire," said Moira shifting her weight in her chair. "You couldn't tell Freddy a thing without implicating these two!"

"Same goes, Moira. You try to pin anything on these fools and Freddy will get an earful from me, *or*, if you have any dark thoughts about removing me from the scene, from a friend of mine who's been given a letter to mail if I die, so you had better just pray I'm not hit by a bus."

"You have an evil mind, Claire. I'd never dream of hurting my friends! If I threaten them sometimes, well, that's just my way! I have to tinkle," she said and, with great dignity, left the room.

You'll notice that Gilbert and I didn't say much during all of these revelations and accusations. So mixed and jumbled were our thoughts that we were unable to find words to express them. Claire had had a few days to ferret out and assimilate the magnitude of Moira's deception, but Gilbert and I had gotten it in one massive dose and the effect left us reeling.

How had she done it! How had she dared *try*, for she had known *since Steffie's wedding* that her intended embezzlees were mafiosi! What enzyme was either lacking or superabundant in her brain that she could pit herself against such people, casually enlisting accomplices and deliberately failing to inform them of the risk they were taking? And the final mind-boggling absurdity was the cause for which these crimes had been perpetrated.

She wanted to invest in a new *cologne*.

"Don't scream at me, Gilbert! It's more than just a cologne!"

"Oh! A dusting powder too, is it!"

"If you'll stop ranting I'll explain. Winslow is a brilliant chemist! I mean, really brilliant. He graduated Phi Beta Kappa and went right to work for some pharmaceutical company working on one of those telethon diseases. Anyway, while he was there he had a sideline in creative chemistry. He did some very seminal work without which we wouldn't have Ecstasy today—"

"Oh, my," said Claire. "Put him on a stamp!"

"Anyway, he cut that out after a while because he couldn't stand the fear of getting busted. He's high-strung."

"*No!*"

"Then diseases started to depress him, so he got into cosmetics.

He worked for years—Chanel, Estée Lauder, everyone, and he was behind all their hottest scents. But people kept ripping him off. He never got the credit. So when he hit upon something really big he decided to quit for fear his idea would get stolen and someone else would make the billions and billions it's sure to bring in."

"What's so special about a cologne?" I asked.

"Well! For one thing, it's the world's first cologne in *pill* form!"

"What?"

"It's a pill. And it doesn't cover up the way you smell. It *changes* it. It actually chemically alters your perspiration so it smells like something else! Perfume, or citrus or nothing at all! Can you believe it? It's going to revolutionize the industry!"

"You're joking!" said Claire.

"I'm not! I've seen it! I've smelled it! It's wonderful! He just needs time and money so he can work the bugs out. I have an agreement where if I give him forty grand by a certain date I have fifteen percent of the patent. Do you know how much *money* I'll make!"

"None, Moira," I said. "You never do."

"Fuck you, Charlie! You shits can make fun of me the way you always do! I don't care! Scentinels are going to be the biggest thing ever and this time next year I will be spitting down at you from my penthouse!"

"Moira," said Claire. "You're free to invest in what you want to and to raise money for it any way you want to—except by risking these two jackass's lives. You see this?" she said, producing a slip of paper. "This is your mother's current address. How would you like it if she were sent Gilbert's number and advised to call him? What if she did and Gilbert ran to Freddy, crushed because the girl he loved had been deceiving him and his family? Because that's just what will happen if you don't go to Freddy and tell him you've changed your mind about the marriage. You're too young, or anything you want, so long as you don't blame these two."

"That's telling her!" said Gilbert.

Moira yawned contemptuously.

"Amateurs! Go ahead! Call Mom. Call Freddy! You know what I'll say? 'Oh, Freddy, I'm so ashamed! Yes, I lied about my parents! Gilbert is such a *snob* I was afraid he'd reject me if he knew Momma was a jail bird. So in a moment of madness I told him she was a duchess and he's such a *snob* he bragged to everyone and I've had to go on pretending 'cause I didn't know how to get out of it and, oh *Freddy*, it's been *awful*!' "

"Moira," said Claire, "how can you tell Freddy you lied for Gilbert's sake when you've been telling duchess stories for years."

"Oh, right. Well, I'll just think of something else then! I *always* do."

"We'll refute it."

"Go ahead, dear. You spill your beans, I spill mine. And I'll lie. I'll say Gilbert's fucking boys again. My word against yours. You really want that?"

Silence fell. We all gazed imploringly at Moira who just stared back implacably.

"Moira," said Gilbert, "please don't take this personally, but I don't want to marry you."

"Tough titty."

She puffed haughtily at her cigarette while we of the Allies exchanged troubled glances. It was a stalemate. Moira couldn't betray us without betraying herself and we couldn't force her out of the engagement without her wreaking havoc on us.

I looked to Claire who sat back on the sofa, her lips resting lightly on her fingers which were pressed together and pointed up, as if in prayer. I could almost hear that mighty brain of hers whirring away. After a moment she spoke.

"Moira," she said, "seeing as you can't stop lovin' dat man of yours, let me propose this. You go ahead with your plans. Kill off Mummy on schedule, mourn her convincingly, marry Gilbert, divvy up the loot and invest it with your customary shrewdness. But from now on, I'm in on it."

"You're not getting a cent from my half."

"I don't want any money. I just want the opportunity to do what I can to see these two fatheads don't get themselves killed. A few days ago I'd never have imagined you could get as far as the wedding without the whole thing falling apart. However, that was when I believed your success depended on the duchess and Tony never figuring out they were both paying for the same wedding. Now that I see this isn't and never was a problem, I think you have a chance of getting out alive so long as you can dispose of the duchess credibly.

Since you refuse to abandon the plan you give me no choice but to offer my assistance—my *reluctant* assistance—in helping you pull it off."

"Well in that case," gushed Moira, "welcome aboard!"

Claire naturally insisted that her aid was contingent on a policy of absolute openness on the part of all syndicate members. Nothing was ever again to be held back. Moira assured us she'd never lie to us again which was, of course, just too soothing for words, but what could we do?

Gilbert was understandably stung by the scope of Moira's treachery and the thought of actual marriage to her was one he viewed with mounting trepidation. The result of this was a concurrent increase in his affection toward me. I was his hope, his salvation, the only thing standing between him and insanity. The flattery was not without its effect on my great thirsty sponge of an ego, but even as I became tempted to reciprocate these sentiments and say, What the hell, let's call it Love, something held me back. Namely a vivid recurring image of Freddy Bombelli merrily igniting the fuses on row upon row of pyrotechnic gayboys.

We all met over the next week to plan the duchess's demise. We agreed the primary problem in eliminating her was documentation. Fortunately, Claire had access through her greeting card concern to printing machinery, and, though newspaper stock might prove difficult to obtain, we could at least fake Xeroxes of British obituaries and newspaper accounts of the tragedy. That left the problem of keeping Gilbert's family away from the funeral. If this couldn't be managed a funeral would actually have to be staged, a prospect which offered innumerable perils.

We were doing our little best to work it out speedily when one night Moira and Claire showed up at Paradiso just as we were leaving. We all climbed into a cab and Moira said, "We have a little problem, kids!"

"Oh?" said we.

"I read to Freddy tonight. He told me he's going away next week on a business trip to England and Switzerland and since he won't be far from Little Chipperton he plans to take Mummy up on her invitation to visit."

"Oh *no!*"

"Sticky, huh? Well, I *knew* we could never have the accident ready by then and even if we did he'd be there in time for the funeral. How could we possibly throw a whole funeral together over *there* in a week? So what could I say?"

"What *did* you say?" I asked, dread coursing through my veins.

"I said, 'Freddy you can't visit her there! She's going to be *here* a week from today. She's done recuperating and she's coming over!' And he was all excited and I said we'd have a little party the Monday before he leaves so he could meet her. So kids! Looks like we have to find ourselves a duchess! Any ideas?"

Twenty-one

Claire stared at us as if we had all completely lost our minds.

"But surely a *woman* would be preferable!"

We readily conceded that in the best of all possible worlds a competent self-assured actress in middle life would be a much better choice to play the duchess than a neurasthenic male perfumer, but this, alas, was not such a world and we had no choice but to go with Winslow.

"It's the *voice*, Claire. You've never heard it but we have—and so have Tony and Maddie and Freddy. Trust us, it's completely unique. If we used anyone else they'd know in a second."

"Can't we find a woman who can *imitate* the voice?"

"Claire!" said Moira. "We have a week! Where are we going to find a middle-aged woman who can talk like Hermione Gingold and who won't mind risking her life to help us swindle the Mafia?"

We agreed sullenly that even the most widely disseminated classified would yield few serious responses. It was Winslow or nothing.

"But can he *do* it?" said Claire. "It's one thing to do a vocal impersonation but it's quite another to pull it off in person with drag and everything. On top of which, there's the man's nerves to consider. I mean, this will take *enormous* poise and—"

"I know," said Moira, "I worried about that, too, when I had him do it on the phone. He *really* didn't want to. I mean, he was a basket case over it. But he came through right on schedule and he was brilliant! Not frightened at all."

"But he didn't know who they *were* then. Now he does."

"And whose fault is that, dear?"

"Look," said Gilbert, who'd kept more or less quiet till now since it's difficult to air one's views while swallowing pecans whole, "this whole discussion is pointless till we find out how Winnie looks in a prom gown."

We agreed there was no sense debating whether he was up to it emotionally till we knew if he could pull it off physically. We agreed to drop by on him the next afternoon with makeup, wigs and whatever assortment of frocks we could scrape together.

"Oh, dear," said Moira. "I haven't a thing that would fit him. Claire, darling, would you mind taking something of yours out? Just a tad?"

The next day Claire came by at noon. She had, to her chagrin, found several items in her wardrobe that seemed like they might fit Winslow, unaltered. They were relics from a year ago when, in the aftermath of a soured romance, she swiftly gained and torturously lost twenty-five pounds. She also brought a blond wig and a small supply of makeup.

Moira had no clothing to offer but donated a virtual steamer trunk of cosmetics with every shade of base, eyeliner, eye shadow, mascara, rouge, blush, lipstick, lip gloss and Georgette Klinger Gooke de Femme ever to be foisted upon a glamour-starved populace. Armed with this formidable array of feminine necessities, we marched the few blocks to Winslow's, noting, as we did, that this would be the first time anyone had ever come to transvestism via conscription.

"My! . . . what's all this?" asked Winslow.

He received the news with his usual sangfroid, and after we'd detached him from the ceiling we forced a Valium down his throat.

"I'm, I, I can't *poss*—I mean, I, I couldn't! I just, I'm, I,I,I *won't!*"

"Please, Mr. Potts! Try to control yourself!" said Claire. "We're merely here to investigate the possibility! No one's *forcing* you to do anything!"

"Speak for yourself, Claire," said Moira. "Winslow, we are all in deep shit and you put us there with your entirely too unusual rendition of my mother! You're the only one who can get us out of this, and you're going to—or, trust me, Freddy's pals are going to take you to New Jersey, tie you to a pole, and *peel* the skin right off you!"

"Moira! That's hardly—"

"Shut up, Claire! Winnie, you're nearly fifty years old and it's time

you grew up a little! You are going to stop this blubbering, dry your
eyes, and put on this fucking dress! *Now!*"

This strategy had far from the intended effect. He did not rise to
his full height and inform her, chins quivering with dignity, that he
would show *her*. He just sobbed convulsively and threw his arms
around Gilbert, begging for reassurance that, whatever came to pass,
he would not be peeled. Gilbert soothed him while the rest of us
glared at Moira, wordlessly conveying our opinion that such tactics
were not again to be used on a man who possessed all the fortitude
of a soufflé.

Claire again assured Winslow that we merely wanted to examine
our options and that impersonation was but *one* of these. She ne-
glected, of course, to say that emigration and suicide were the others.

"These three told me how dazzling you were on the phone!"

"He was!"

"Amazing!"

"Took me in completely."

"Did I, really?" asked Winslow, daubing an eye.

"Absolutely. Were you ever an actor?"

"No."

"Go on! Never?"

"Only once."

"Broadway?"

"Grammar school. I brought corn to the Pilgrims."

"Well, you've come a long way! Your portrayal was a masterpiece!"

"Stunning!"

"Can't you just see him as the duchess? With the right wig?"

"He'd be perfect! A little dusting powder and penciled-in eyebrows
and a beautiful high-necked pea-green gown—"

"Actually," said Winslow, "red is my color."

It didn't take long for us to see that, as regarded the proposed mas-
querade, Winslow was torn between warring instincts. On the one
hand, there was his extraordinary cowardice. The mere thought of
matching wits with the Mafia left him all but liquefied with terror.
Balanced against this, however, was his sincere desire to be a duchess.
Success depended on bringing this second tendency to the fore.

Moira and Claire shooed Gilbert and me out to buy lunch so they
could get to work on Winslow.

"You understand," he said, as we were leaving, "I'm not agreeing to go *through* with anything. This is just . . ."

"Experimental."

"Right. No dear, that's hideous, what's the beige thing?"

We deliberately dawdled so that Moira and Claire would have more time to effect the transformation, and the results, when we returned, exceeded our most optimistic forecasts. Even dressed in a drab, unbecomingly snug red evening dress Winslow exuded a frowsy poise that was, if not exactly feminine, still utterly *female*. With his heavy eyebrows and hairy arms plainly visible he still looked more like a mannish woman than a womanish man. It was in the attitude, the way he shaped his mouth and slumped comfortably in the chair. Often when you see transvestites (anyway, when *I* see transvestites—you may have led a cleaner life) there's something *too* feminine about them. They share a tendency to equate womanliness with an exaggerated elegance of gesture; most of us need only think of our mothers to realize that womanhood and elegance are not inextricably linked. Winslow had grasped this.

"At lahst!" he wheezed, regally. "I wondered where you boys had gotten to. I was about to send Murcheson out to the park to poke all the shrubs with a sharp stick!"

"Winnie!"

"My God!"

"You're fantastic!" said Gilbert, kissing his cheek. "My folks are gonna adore you!"

"*Hold on!*" cried Winslow, leaping up and tearing the wig off. "Who said anything about doing this for your folks? Not me! Did I say that? *I* didn't say that! I've agreed to nothing, you hear me? *Nothing!*"

"Mr. Potts, you have nothing to worry about! You're very convincing. Really, you are. All you have to do is conquer these nerves of yours!"

"I can't!"

"Of course you can!" said Moira. "What are drugs *for*?"

"Moira," said Claire, "Winslow will need all his wits about him, so I hardly think it prudent to resort to—"

"Claire," said Moira wearily, "the man is a chemist. He'll *know* what he's doing."

*   *   *

By the time we left, Winslow had reluctantly agreed to impersonate the duchess, but only under strict limitations.

He would appear at the party for exactly one hour. We would see to it that the party was crowded since this would reduce the time he'd have to spend with any one person. His entire conversation could be confined to introductions and apologies for not having had more time to chat. After an hour of this Moira would remind him that the doctors had prescribed heavy bed rest. The duchess would then bid all a good night and retire. The following day, she'd suffer a mild relapse and be forced to spend the weeks until the wedding recuperating in bed.

Visitors would be allowed in no more than twice in this period. The duchess could terminate any visit at will by falling into a peaceful doze, leaving her daughter to see the visitors out.

The question remained of just where the duke was through all this. We decided to put the old boy in Africa where he was desperately trying to sell the family's only asset besides Trebleclef, a run-down coffee plantation. Perhaps, if he refurbished it a bit, the meager few pounds it would bring in would help offset the duchess's medical expenses. At least we could comfort ourselves with the thought that, while Freddy's illicit business seemed to take him to many locales, we could be reasonably sure he did not operate casinos in Equatorial Guinea.

With less than a week to organize the duchess's coming-out bash we were kept pretty busy. There were invitations to extend, food to plan and prepare, wardrobe and makeup to select, and, most taxing of all, daily Winslow duty. Not a day passed without him phoning and declaring hysterically that he'd changed his mind. He could not possibly go through with it; he just wasn't good enough. No legendary star or diva could possibly have had half the thirst for snake oil that Winslow possessed. He had to be constantly soothed, flattered and assured that his duchess was a dramatic tour de force that put the paltry efforts of Dame Judith Anderson entirely to shame.

Wardrobing the duchess turned out to be far less troublesome than we'd feared. Searching for suitable accesories in a walk-in closet of Gloria Conkridge's things at God's country, Moira discovered a trunk full of old dresses. Gloria, even as a young woman, had cherished her carbohydrates, and most of the dresses were actually too big for

Winslow and had to be taken in by Claire, who spent the better part of the week sewing. Moira was unable to help, having always lived by the theory that sewing is a pointless skill, needed only by those who lack the ability to befriend designers.

Shoes, luckily, were not a problem, either. Sometimes female impersonators, regardless of their dramatic gifts, are given away by the sheer immensity of their feet and the incongruous spectacle of size twelve EE's wedged into mauve pumps. But Winnie's feet were quite small for a man of his size and he discovered, to our glee, that all Moira's shoes fit him perfectly.

Winslow shopped for costume jewelry and complained that the depilatories were giving him rashes. He experimented with wigs and finally settled on a rather grandiose gray one which set us back nearly three hundred dollars (my share coming from the money I'd sworn would go to repay Aggie).

It was decided that the duchess would walk with the aid of a cane, a vestige of her riding accident. A suitable stick was purchased and Winslow practiced hobbling about on it. He became adept at making tiny winces which suggested great pain, stoically endured.

One afternoon, in the middle of these preparations, Gilbert called and asked if I could meet him in front of the building. I agreed and arrived to find him standing under the canopy wearing a boyish smile and clutching, in one red-mittened hand, a large manila envelope. He asked me to walk with him in Central Park and we strolled toward the Ramble.

The Ramble is one of the loveliest areas in the park, a charming tangle of twisty overgrown paths and cul-de-sacs, offering an endless series of scenic little vistas. It's also among the park's more notorious sections, well known, especially in the warmer months, as a place where gentlemen go to meet other gentlemen with similar interests; i.e., a high esteem for physical fitness and a love of movie trivia. On this afternoon, though, the place couldn't have looked less carnal. A fresh snow had fallen overnight, the sun shone brightly, and even the few cruisers strolling about, glancing over their shoulders at you, had a quaint Currier and Ives sort of quality.

Gilbert and I chatted of this and that till we reached a fairly tranquil little spot. He asked me to sit and, like a boy giving flowers to the teacher, handed me the envelope.

"I want you to read this, Philip."

"You *wrote* it?"

"Yes, it's the start of my novel."

I opened the envelope and removed thirty typed pages.

"I've been writing almost every night, Philip. I sit at my typewriter till three or four and sometimes nothing comes at all. But I always try. I know you'll never respect me till I stop talking about being a writer and start actually doing it."

Well, that finished me, right there, right then. The thought that Gilbert's love for me could be so intense as to overcome even his dread of composition left me intoxicated with pride, gratitude and happiness.

Of course, at the time I didn't know that he had written only three of the pages since the onset of our romance, the other twenty-seven having been composed over the previous four years. That little detail he confessed much later. By pointing it out to you now I don't mean to suggest that Gilbert's vow of love for me was a calculated lie; it wasn't. Gilbert's passions are always as sincere as they are ephemeral. I'm sure he considered the three pages he actually did write "for me" a considerable tribute, coming, as they did, from a boy who'd rather tangle with a dragon than an Olivetti. But if he could beef it up with another twenty-seven prewritten pages, was there any reason not to do so? None, certainly, that would ever cross Gilbert's mind.

But as far as I knew that day every page, every paragraph, every imaginatively spelled word was testimony to a pure and deeply felt love, a love I had been too blind to see and too cowardly to reciprocate. Shame and joy in equal measures coursed through me as I clasped Gilbert in my arms and kissed him passionately . . . in full view, as it turned out, of Gunther Von Steigle, who was wandering through the Ramble for reasons of his own. He was standing about ten yards away, staring down at us from a little hill, his face aglow with evil satisfaction.

"Christ! Does he *live* in the park?"

"Let him stare!"

"I'd rather not."

"I love you, Philip!"

"I love you, too, Gilbert. Walk faster."

* * *

Unsettling as the incident was, we didn't give it a great deal of thought. There wasn't time to. All our energies that week were focused on the duchess's premiere, and all other concerns, even our blossoming romance, took a back seat to the complex battery of physical and psychological preparations.

Mother and daughter sat for hours, going over their imaginary history; how Mummy's first husband had died, how she'd met the duke, when they were married, and, of course, all the amusing things Prince Charles had said when Moira and Mummy attended the royal wedding.

As opening night drew closer, Winslow's conflicting attitudes toward the charade both intensified. His portrayal of the duchess grew sharper, more nuanced and assured, even as his attacks of panic became more frequent and acute. By the eve of the party, these schizophrenic mood swings had the rest of us on the verge of nervous collapse, completely unable to guess whether he would carry it all off majestically or melt into puddles of hysteria the moment the first guest arrived.

The Monday of the party dawned cold and gray. I spent the day at GC stuffing mushrooms while Claire pulled Winslow duty at his apartment.

The plan of attack called for Claire and the duchess to arrive an hour late. They would say they'd spent the day sightseeing and just as they were about to return home, Her Grace had met a dear old friend and lost track of the time. This way, when they arrived there'd already be a crowd and Winnie would be spared having to chat endlessly with solitary early-comers.

Half an hour before the party, Claire called.

"Listen, I have a crisis on my hands!"

"I knew it! What now?" wailed Gilbert.

"He's in bed under the covers, clutching a stuffed giraffe. He refuses to move. He won't go. He won't even get dressed."

The phone was on speaker and Moira said, "Well, MAKE him get dressed."

"Moira, I have been *making* him get dressed for an hour and he hasn't got so much as an eyelash on!"

"*Amateurs!*" hissed Moira. "Look, just don't let him leave. I'll be right over."

Moira left and twenty minutes later Claire returned. A few minutes after that, as we were all pacing apoplectically about the kitchen, guests began to arrive. First Maddie and Tony, then Marlowe Heppenstall and his wife, Nancy (Marie Curie) Malone and her boyfriend, Aggie, Lunch and Sammy, Holly Batterman and a redheaded man, Ugo and Betty Sartucci, Tony's sister Marie, Jimmy Loftus and a female friend, Chick and his wife Rosa, Father Eddie Fabrizio, Sister Deena Sartucci, dear cousin Steffie and her hubby, more Sartuccis, Fabrizios and Cellinis, other friends of Gilbert and Moira, Freddy Bombelli and the ever-vigilant Serge.

We greeted everyone with frozen smiles then ran to Gilbert's bedroom and called Winslow's for a progress report.

"I'M WORKING ON IT!" yelled Moira, without asking who it was, and hung up. Thereafter all calls met with a busy signal.

Gilbert, Claire and I passed food, made drinks, poured champagne and fended off questions about when the guest of honor would arrive with a cheerful insouciance that belied our panic.

By nine-thirty the questions concerning the duchess's arrival were so frequent, the suspense so unendurable, that I felt at any minute I would bolt out of the apartment, change my name, and learn to farm. Then, just after ten o'clock, Moira and the duchess arrived.

Twenty-two

Aggie and Maddie were nearest the door when I answered the bell, though it wasn't long before Claire, Gilbert and Holly Batterman stampeded over for a first look at Her Grace. Moira was standing there in her trenchcoat, smiling sweetly, and next to her the duchess stood resplendent in mink. Beneath this she wore a scarlet dinner suit that Claire had taken in a little too far for comfort. A matching pillbox hat completed the ensemble. She was smoking a Dunhill in a holder and dripping with jewels, mostly costume, though Freddy's brooch was the real goods. The cane, not to mention the infirmity that demanded it, was nowhere in evidence.

"Gilbert, *darling*! Can you ever forgive me! One hour late for my own party! *Dread*fully uncivilized, I know, but Moira and I were just leaving the Oak Room when who should I meet but Mrs. Everett Carlyle Pemberton! Hadn't laid eyes on her since Pittsburgh when she was Sophie Bukowski. Dreadful snob she's become! Would not *stop* talking!"

"Ever so dull," smiled Moira.

"She doesn't make comments, dear, she *extrooodes* them like a pasta machine. Went on about her new husband for an hour before she even thought to ask me if *I'd* acquired one. 'Oh, how *nice* for you, Gwen,' she said, rather condescendingly. 'And what does he *do*?' I told her. *Most* satisfying. Be a lamb, Gilbert, and take my coat. Moira, dear, Mummy wants champagne!"

"In a minute, Mummy. First I want you to meet Gilbert's mother. Maddie, this is my mother!"

Maddie took Winslow's pudgy hand and pumped it energetically.

"Pleased to meet you Your—oh, gosh, what is it, Highness or Grace or what?"

"Please! You must call me Gwen. I can't stand to be called Your Grace, except when it's by someone I dislike, then I rather enjoy it."

"And this is Maddie's cousin, Aggie. She owns the restaurant where Gilbert hosts."

"Do you *really*? Would you be an angel and give him a raise? I don't know what he makes, but the way my daughter spends money it can't possibly be enough."

"*Hah!*"

"Mummy!"

"Moira, did I say something about champagne? I'm not sure—it was so *long* ago."

"I'm getting it, Mummy. Now you behave!"

Gilbert and I followed Moira to the bar and whispered through tense smiles.

"What the fuck happened to the cane?"

"She didn't want it. Said she felt too good."

"Obviously! What is she *on*?"

"Not much! A bottle of wine, a few lines of coke."

"That's all?"

Moira sighed heavily.

"Well, just the teensiest bit of Ecstasy. Don't gawk that way, please. It's improved her mood enormously. Trust me, she'll be fine!"

"Mr. *Bombelli*!" shrieked Winnie from across the room. "I knew it had to be you, you dear, *generous* man! So nice to meet you at last! Come sit by me and turn my head!"

From that point on all bets were off, all ground rules abandoned. Our fate was now in Winslow's hands and he played with it as exuberantly and recklessly as a toddler wielding a pistol. All the stories so carefully concocted by Moira were either discarded or else embroidered beyond recognition.

A number of these embellishments were designed specifically to cast Moira in an absurd and unflattering light. I suppose it was Winnie seeking revenge for all Moira's lies and threats. Whatever the reason, he seldom missed an opportunity to paint Moira as a foolish, vain, thoroughly incompetent girl whom Mummy couldn't help but adore despite her countless inadequacies.

The rest of us might have been more amused by Moira's comeuppance had it not been for the fear that gripped us every time Mummy opened her mouth. There was simply no guessing what she would say next.

"So," said Maddie as she sat on the sofa with the duchess in a group that included Tony, myself, Claire, Holly, Aggie, Moira and Freddy, "pardon me for coming right out and asking, but I figure someone's got to, right? What is it like being a real duchess?"

"Maddie, dear, I should be lying through my teeth if I didn't admit to you that it is the most fun a woman my age can have with her eyes open. You get to swank around at charity bazaars, cut ceremonial ribbons and have people fawn all over you for doing nothing at all! I suppose a better sort of person would despise the endless flattery of social-climbing snots but, thank God, the Lord made me no better than I am and *I lap it up*!"

"*Hah!* You're my kind of duchess, Gwen," said Aggie.

"Why, thank you, Aggie, dear. How sweet of you to say so. Gilbert! Come sit next to your mother-in-law. Isn't he too charming? I was so relieved to see Moira had finally found someone with a little *breeding*. You should have seen the specimens she dragged home back in Pittsburgh. Darling, do you ever hear from that motorcyclist you rode with for a year?"

"No, Mummy," said Moira through clenched teeth.

"Thank heavens! Hideous thing!" clucked the duchess to Maddie. "Even the least finicky of grave robbers would have taken one look, slammed the lid, and refilled the hole."

"Mummy, you're terrible! Oh! Look at the time! Remember what the doctor said about getting to bed by eleven."

"Eleven?" moaned Maddie. "Oh, come on, hon. That's much too early!"

The others quickly agreed that it was the shank of the evening.

"But she tires so easily. We don't want a relapse, now, do we, Mummy?"

"No, dear, what *we* want is another glass of champagne. *We've* never felt better in *our* life!"

"*Hah!*"

"But Mum—"

"I think I'm old enough to determine my own bedtime. Besides, I saw the doctor just hours before my flight here and he said I was fit as a fiddle."

"How wunnnderful!" wheezed Freddy.

"Yes. Said it was the most astonishingly swift recovery from a riding accident he'd ever seen!"

"I'll say!" said Maddie. "You'd never know you'd bitten your lip off!"

"Lovely work, isn't it? I may be written up in a medical journal. So!" she said, turning her attention to Freddy, "you fascinating man! One hears the *strangest* things about you—!"

"*Who wants champagne?*" I asked.

"Moira tells me you've rescued her from a life of bonbon eating by actually giving her a job. Most brave of you!"

"But, Your Grace—"

"Gwen!"

"Gwen—she is a delightful girl! Such warmth and high spirits!" He proceeded, as usual, to convey his esteem for Moira and her skill as an interpreter of great literature.

"She can *act*?" said the duchess with frank astonishment. "Well, if that's the case, she's certainly come a long distance. The only time *I* ever saw Moira act was when she was in high school and she played the role of Wendy in *Peter Pan*. Forgot all her words and wet herself right there onstage. Ruined the entire—"

"*Mummeee!*"

"On*stage*?" asked Holly.

"Gwen, honey, do you like Polynesian food?"

"Only if it's accompanied by Polynesian drinks."

"Count on it! What say you let me take you to Trader Vic's for lunch this Tuesday?"

"I'd be delighted! We have *so* much to talk about!"

It wasn't till twenty minutes later when Maddie and Winslow were discussing the childhoods of Gilbert and Moira, debating which of the two had been the more difficult birth, that Claire, Gilbert, Moira and self managed to slip away to the kitchen for a crisis conference. By that point the duchess had accepted invitations to Paradiso, dinner at Casa Cellini and Holly's Valentine's Day bash.

"Good *Lord*, Moira," hissed Claire as she pulled a tray of artichoke bottoms wrapped in bacon from the oven, "what did you *give* the man?"

"It's called Ecstasy, Claire! It's just a harmless euphoric!"

"I'd hardly call it harmless! He's completely out of control. Isn't there some antidote for euphoria?"

"Just *you*, Claire," said Moira as she stalked away with a bowl of dip.

The rest of us conferred and decided that if we couldn't control Mummy, we could at least distract attention from her. We would ask Nancy Malone to sing. Nancy has a great voice, and the admiration she'd garner would take the spotlight off the duchess while we plotted our next diversionary tactic.

Things did not work out quite as planned. Nancy, after a bit of cajoling, agreed to sing a few numbers, but before Claire could ask her what standards she knew by, say, Porter or Gershwin, Marlowe Heppenstall had seized the keyboard and launched into the opening chords of a terrible ballad from *Eureka, Baby!* called "Why Am I Me?" Nancy had no choice but to gamely dredge up her Marie and by the time she'd reached the lines . . .

> *Why zis urge to explore*
> *Where no woman's gone before?*
> *What's within us that ze microscope can't see?*
> *Why do I care?*
> *Ah, Pierre,*
> *Why am I meeeee?*

. . . interest had waned considerably.

Interest soon perked up, however, for no sooner had Nancy finished the ballad, to polite applause, than the duchess swaggered over to the keys and said, "Dear boy, you play like an angel! Do you know 'To Keep My Love Alive'?"

Marlowe did, and he accompanied the duchess in a flawlessly timed performance of the Rodgers and Hart classic.

The reception was enthusiastic and cries of "Encore!" filled the room. The duchess bowed grandly and obliged her public with a few more selections, including "Makin' Whoopee." She finished the set with "My Blue Heaven" and, after singing it through once, called upon Gilbert and Moira to help her out with a reprise. They tried to wriggle out but the bibulous throng would not hear of it and they finally joined her in front of the baby grand. Their faces frozen in hideous mirth, they stumbled dissonantly through that hymn to young love and the joys of marriage. The duchess stood between them, an arm around each of their shoulders, singing boisterously as she prodded and pulled them through hastily improvised choreography like some deranged transvestite puppeteer.

The crowd ate it up. Not just the duchess, but Gilbert and Moira, too. Had ever young love seemed so giddy, so sweet and carefree? Even Holly, who was not very fond of Moria lately, remarked what an adorable picture they made.

"You must let Geoff take some photos!"

"Geoff?" I asked.

"Over there," he said, pointing to a handsome redhead. "Met him a few days ago at a dinner party. Marvelous photographer. Isn't he yummy?"

I replied politely and inquired if it looked serious.

"Well, nothing's happened yet—he's one of those old-fashioned types. Y'know, into *courtship.*"

Geoff sauntered over and Holly introduced me saying I was Gilbert's best man. Then he gamboled off to congratulate the duchess, leaving Geoff and me alone. We chatted a bit about photography. He kept smiling flirtatiously and I kept wondering why it is that when you're alone and horny you have no luck at all, and the minute you're attached to someone the world beats a path to your futon. He finally asked if I'd like to have dinner sometime and I said, or rather stammered, that I was involved.

"Nice guy?"

"Yes."

"Good. You deserve it."

I excused myself and sought out Gilbert to discuss strategy. I found him in the kitchen giving Mummy hell.

"Jesus Christ, Winnie, will you cut it the fuck out!"

"Gilbert, I'll thank you not to employ—"

"*Stuff* it, you demented queen," whispered Gilbert. "What do you think you're doing? Making lunch dates and dinner dates and—"

"My social life is my own concern, you impudent child!"

"Listen, toots," I said, "that stuff you're on is going to wear off in an hour or two. You're going to wake up tomorrow with a vicious hangover and a full engagement book! Do you realize what you gonna have to *do?*"

"Buy clothes," said Winnie, and he flounced majestically out of the room.

And so it went for the rest of that cursed evening. The duchess held court like the grandest of dames, and not a soul present failed to be charmed by her, or at least intrigued by the way in which all manner of opposing traits collided within her. She was refined, yet amusingly vulgar; ladylike, but earthy; imperious, solicitous, vain, self-denigrating, waspish and affectionate all at once. We gave up all efforts to steal her thunder, feeling that such attempts would only goad her on to new heights of flamboyance.

By eleven-thirty or so, when the party had shrunk to about half its size, she was holding a little group of us spellbound with the details of her riding accident. Freddy and Serge were listening, as were Tony and Maddie, Moira, Claire, Gilbert, Holly, Geoff, Chick and Rosa.

"I shall never forget how I felt hugging that damned horse's neck as the crazed beast stormed about the fair, knocking over displays and trampling that child to death! 'Stop her!' I cried to my husband, buy Nigel was never very good in a crisis. He goes to pieces. Like Moria. Finally I was hurled into a ditch! I remember lying there thinking, 'Oh dear, I shall never dance again!' I adore dancing. We must all go very soon!"

"What about now?" said Maddie.

"Now!" said Gilbert.

"Well, no time like the present, is there? The Gardenia Club's open till two! Whaddaya say, Gwen?"

"What a simply splendid idea. We'll all go dancing! My treat!"

"Mummeee!" said Moira, but her feeble protests about mending bones were silenced by Mummy who rose and robustly executed a buck and wing to the delighted applause of all.

Tony, Chick and the others all agreed that dancing sounded like a delightful way to cap the evening off.

"But, please, dear lady," protested Freddy, "you must let *me* be your host tonight. You are *our* guest!"

"You dear generous man! Of course you can pay! I was rather counting on it!"

"Mummy," said Moira, "we still have guests, and they're not all dressed for the Gardenia Club. Why don't you bring Gilbert and I'll stay here and—"

"No, honey, I'm happy to stay! I'm bushed! You go! Have a *great* time!"

"Aren't you sweet!"

Claire and I also begged off, claiming early morning appointments. Within moments their little group departed, giggling in anticipation of the terpsichorean joys that lay ahead. Claire, exhausted, told us she'd call first thing in the morning for a damage report and staggered off home.

That left me and Gilbert, Holly, Marlowe and spouse, Nancy and date, Ugo and Betty, and another three or four pals of Gilbert's and Moira's. Holly was sulking because somewhere in the flurry of recent departures his Geoff had slipped away without even saying good-bye, a sure indicator that the prognosis for romance was gloomy. We consoled him, insisting that Geoff was a bore and a floozy to boot.

Gilbert and I conferred briefly in the kitchen and decided there was no sense waiting up for Mummy, and no sense either in sitting around fretting over what fresh horrors Winslow's performance would spawn. Tomorrow would be soon enough to sift through the wreckage. Tonight we would drive it from our minds, get plastered and enjoy the company of friends and the absence of Moira.

For the next hour or so we played charades and sang around the piano. Ugo Sartucci, who had found himself stunningly ill-equipped to mime *The Rise and Fall of the City of Mahagonny*, pulled out a fat joint, feeling that this would go a long way toward equalizing the odds.

Marijuana is not usually my dish; it makes me forget jokes and eat whole chickens without bothering to sit down or close the refrigerator door. But on this particular night I wanted all the oblivion I could get and so smoked my share of the joint, which, Ugo assured us, was of a quality available only to the most well-connected. The party broke up not long after that, owing, I suppose, to the sudden inability of all those present to remember any consonants.

Gilbert and I waved them good-bye and stumbled off to bed.

Pot is, of course, renowned for its powerful stimulative effect on the libido, and Gilbert and I were by no means immune to this side effect. No sooner had we extinguished the lights than we fell upon each other, tearing at clothes in a way guaranteed to distress not only the Moral Majority but ourselves the next day, for neither of us can sew buttons. Our recreations, however, did not last very long. About five minutes after we began it, our little love feast was interrupted. By a flashbulb.

Geoff, who had not left at all, burst out of Gilbert's closet and, after blinding us with the first flash, flicked the overhead on and began snapping away, getting, at the very least, one recognizable shot of us before we could disentangle ourselves from one of those positions that don't seem especially complicated till you try to get out of them in a hurry. By the time we'd gotten off the bed he'd raced from the room closing the door behind him.

We chased him as far as the apartment door, further than which we were not, in all modesty, able to venture. He decided not to wait for the elevator but instead took the stairs. As he entered the stairwell he turned and flashed a triumphant sneer, and in that terrible instant I knew just where I'd seen him before.

The reason I hadn't recognized him was that the last time I'd seen the face it had been camouflaged. But there was no doubt now that that same face, under a beard, had been hovering next to Gunther Von Steigle's as he'd beseeched his last departing patron not to believe the vicious lies of the bald woman who'd stormed into his salon.

"Gilbert," I said, closing the door. "Do you know who that *was*?"

"No," said Gilbert, stoned out of his mind.

"He works with Gunther!"

"Oh!" said Gilbert, sliding down the wall and plopping bare-ass onto the floor of the foyer.

"Remine me again. Who's Gunser?"

Twenty-three

It was not a cheerful group that assembled the next morning at God's Country. Gilbert, Claire, Winslow, Moira and I stood in the rubble of the party looking like a tableau vivant based on *Guernica*.

"You crazy faggots!" sobbed Moira. "You'll pay for this, you hear me! You'll pay for all the suffering you've caused me!"

"Moira," said Claire, "you got us all into this to begin with and you're no longer in a position to threaten anyone. So unless you have something constructive to say, please keep your venomous mouth shut."

"You're fat, Claire," yelled Moira. "You're fat and you write shitty music and nobody likes you!"

Our discourse continued in this lofty vein for some time, everyone getting their licks in. That is, everyone but Winslow who just sat with his head on the dining table, suffering as a man only can when he's enduring a coke, Ecstasy and champagne hangover while contemplating two months of social engagements with the Mafia, all of which he must attend in a dress.

"Winnie," said Claire, "you mustn't be so upset. You can always get out of these appointments. We can say you're sick, that you've had a relapse."

"Naaaah! Naaahahahahahaha!" he replied.

"No," said Moira, "we can *not* say he's sick! He fixed *that* but good!"

"How? What happened?"

Moira explained biliously that Freddy, concerned by Moira's constant references to Mummy's frail health, had asked the duchess if she had a good doctor in this country. No, she'd replied, and Freddy had eagerly offered the services of his own team of skilled resuscitators, which services Mummy had gratefully accepted. Any relapse would cause these noble healers to descend and they would return to Freddy with a striking diagnosis.

"That was smart!" snapped Gilbert.

"*Smart!*" said Moira. "I don't want to hear *SMART* from either one of you, you dumb sex-crazed fruits!"

"Oh, fuck off, Moira! That creep was here all night and you didn't guess what he was up to any more than we did!"

"What I don't understand," said Claire, "is how he knew enough even to *try* to catch you in flagrante. I mean, if *we* didn't know you two were having yourselves a romance, how did he?"

I turned a pretty shade of vermilion and told them of that day in the Ramble when, transported with joy over Gilbert's return to literature, I'd kissed him in full view of Gunther.

Claire and Moira stared in appalled disbelief.

"And you didn't *tell* us!"

"It didn't seem important at the time. We had the duchess to get ready, and I forgot all about it."

"Good Lord! Couldn't you two control yourselves until after the wedding?"

"Claire," I said indignantly, "I'm sure you're terribly above such things, but I have to go where my heart leads me."

" 'Heart' seems hardly the organ in question. You two fools have had all of ten years to find each other. Why you had to put it off until Gilbert had promised Freddy the Pooch never to sleep with a man is more than I can begin to comprehend!"

"Please, don't be mad, Claire!"

"*Mad?* I am livid. Correct that, I am *fucking* livid! I have a good mind to walk out of here right now and never speak to any of you again!"

I had never heard Claire say "fucking" in my life, so I was deeply relieved when the phone rang before she could make good on her threat to abandon us. I didn't stay relieved for long, though.

"Hello?" said Gilbert, flicking the speaker on.

The sinister tones of Gunther Von Steigle filled the room.

"Mr. Selwyn?"

"Gunther! I was hoping to hear from you—you scamp!" he added in a pathetic attempt to put the whole thing on a lighter footing.

"I wished to thank you and Mr. Cavanaugh for posing for Geoffrey. I have the results before me."

"Do you!"

"Yes. You're most photogenic!"

"Hah, hah! I have to hand it to you! That was some practical joke! I mean, you've got style. No, there's a better word. Panache! Yes, Gunther, you've got panache!"

"You thought it a good joke?"

"The best!"

"Then wait, Mr. Selwyn. It gets better."

Click.

Moira erupted at length, assuring us that if this proof of our romance reached Freddy and forced the cancellation of the wedding, she would personally request he send two deaf assassins so we couldn't talk our way out of it. The rest of us nervously asserted there was little danger of this happening; Gunther didn't even know Freddy, much less the details of his chat with Gilbert regarding homosexual didoes. The real danger was in Gunther giving the pictures to Holly, in which case Freddy would hear about them when Holly bought commercial time during "60 Minutes."

In the midst of these cheery conjectures, the doorbell rang and Gilbert, after massaging the bruise he received when Winslow knocked him over running to the bedroom, answered it. Standing there was a scrawny delivery man from FTD.

"Hi. The Duchess of Dorchester live here?"

"She's resting just now."

"Swell. So you sign it."

Gilbert signed and took possession of a flower box the size of a steamer trunk. Tipping the fellow two quarters and a subway token, he closed the door and brought the box to the dining room. Inside were three dozen long-stemmed roses and a note which read:

Many thanks for the honor of your company. Might I hope to enjoy it again soon? I will call from Europe this week.

Your servant,
Frederick Bombelli

"Oh *Mummeee!*" sang Moira.

The voice of the duchess issued weakly from behind the locked door.

"I don't feel well, deah!"

"Winnie, it's okay. It was just a delivery."

Winnie emerged from his room, bit his lip, and tottered down the hall. In that moment he looked to me like an enormous child of four. All he needed was pajamas with feet.

"What lovely flowers!" said Winslow, daubing his eyes with a hanky. "Who sent them? Your parents?"

Moira glowered and handed him the card. He scanned it quickly and dropped it as if it were on fire. He sank into a chair, shook his head madly and required three dozen syllables to convey the word "No."

"Winnie," said Gilbert, "you'll be fine! Really you will. Don't you know how good you were last night?"

"No. It, it's all a big blur."

"You don't remember *anything*?" asked Claire.

"I remember the end of the night, dancing. I remember thinking how hard it was to let Serge lead."

"Well, you were just fine, Winnie," said Claire, maternally. "There's no need to panic. He knows you're a married woman. I'm sure his intentions are honorable. Stop giggling, Gilbert."

"The hell his intentions are honorable!" said Moira. "The old fool is smitten! Don't you two get it!"

"Get what?"

"It's like one of his stupid romances! Deirdre Sauvage and all the rest of them! They're all full of lords and ladies and countesses falling for high-spirited commoners! When the duchess started flirting with him the romantic idiot felt like he was in the middle of one of his books!"

"Oh, dear," clucked Claire.

We all looked to Winslow who was staring at the roses and sucking pensively on his index finger. No one said a word for a moment. Then Moira got up, strode purposefully to the phone, flicked the speaker off and dialed.

Winslow spoke softly.

"You know, when I was ten, in Bayonne, I used to have a dog named Lana. Mom fed her K9 because it was cheap and all my friends used to tease me that I was feeding my dog informers. Then, when I got older I read stories about Freddy the Pooch and all his gambling parlors and prostitutes and all the people he killed and made dog food from."

He picked up a rose and sniffed it.

"I never dreamed that someday I would date him."

"Hello, Brooks, darling?" chirped Moira on the phone. "I was just calling to thank you for the Ecstasy. It was *marvelous*! Just what my little soiree needed . . . Well, yes, I *do*, you mind reader you!"

She paused and cast an appraising eye at Winslow and the roses.

"Brooks, dearest, I hate to be tacky, but do you offer a discount if one buys in quantity?"

Our little meeting broke up not long after this. The remaining bone of contention concerned Claire's refusal to stay involved if success was to hinge on turning Winslow into a "drug addict." She would not be a party to such callous victimization. Winnie would face the Cellinis and Freddy unopiated, or else. Moira agreed to this, though the minute Claire's back was turned she gave Winnie a smile which succinctly conveyed that she'd secretly supply him with Ecstasy, coke and, should he request it, the blood of unbaptized infants—anything that would get him through the trials ahead.

The only remaining question was what to do about the Gunther threat. The answer for now: nothing. He was hell-bent on vengeance; pleas for mercy would only enhance his appreciation of the awful destructive power he possessed.

Gilbert walked me home that day. If our sense of a shared romantic destiny had been growing gradually till now, these latest events had made it swell to Shakespearian dimensions. We were star-crossed lovers, beset on all sides by treacherous enemies and unfeeling friends.

"We're alone, Philip! No one understands what we feel, what we mean to each other!"

"I think Gunther's figured it out."

"That's right, Philly! Make jokes! Be brave!"

The next day, the duchess made her second appearance. She shared a pleasant lunch with Maddie at Trader Vic's, where they discussed catering plans. Maddie's swift consumption of three zombies, combined with her natural naïveté, rendered the challenge to Winslow's nerve and acting ability so minimal that Moira decried the exercise as a waste of good drugs.

The more serious challenges lay ahead. Dinner at Paradiso on Thursday, lunch at Casa Cellini on Friday and dinner at Freddy's Long Island stronghold upon his return from Europe Saturday. Freddy's invitation was extended by phone from Switzerland while the duchess was lunching with Maddie. Moira graciously accepted on Mummy's behalf.

"Saturday, six o'clock, his place. All right?" Moira had said when Winslow staggered in from the Trader's.

"Ducky, my idiot child," Winnie had replied, tottering off to take a nap from which he awoke five hours later, unrefreshed.

The next day I opened my mailbox and inside, along with the usual bouquet of bills, subscription offers and flyers for shows featuring friends who haven't called in two years, there was a flat twelve-inch manila envelope with no return address. I knew at once what it was.

My heart pounding, I raced the three flights up to my apartment, peeled away the Scotch tape that covered the little clasp, and opened the envelope. Inside was the photo of me and Gilbert.

There we were, naked and busy, looking mildly stoned and extremely recognizable. The camera had caught us in that brief muddled instant before we realized the camera was catching us. Our expressions, as such, betrayed not shock but bovine bewilderment, like a pair of Trobriand Islanders getting their first look at television.

There was no note in the envelope, only the photo. Why, I wondered, were there no threats, no dark hints of what he intended to do with his pornographic trophy? Perhaps he just wanted us to know that any hopes we may have had about unfocused lenses were unfounded. And perhaps the stomach-churning suspense I was feeling was itself the point of the exercise. He wanted us to sweat.

I duly phoned Gilbert to tell him the photo had arrived and that, if it was any consolation, Geoff had caught his good side. Then Moira took the phone and asked if Claire and I could stop by God's Country for a drink after work. I accepted and called Claire, who kvetched a bit about the lateness but said she'd be there.

*   *   *

Winnie was already there when Gilbert and I arrived and Claire came a few minutes later. Moira ushered us into the dining room where we noted, to mild murmurs of surprise, she had prepared a light supper. A watercress and endive salad, slices of peasant bread, a piece of chèvre and a pâté with pistachios in it. A magnum of wine was chilling in a bucket.

"Well! How nice, Moira!" said Claire through a cautious smile.

"What's all this about?" asked Gilbert, not bothering, as Claire had, to conceal his suspicion that we were in for a major performance.

"Well, I just wanted . . . " she said and paused. For effect? Probably, but it was hard to say for sure. She seemed different in a way I couldn't put my finger on. Subdued and embarrassed.

"What's the matter?" I asked.

"Nothing. It's just . . . well, it's hard to talk when you know in advance that everyone's going to think you're full of shit."

"Moira," said Gilbert shrewdly, "are you trying to tell us you're sorry about everything you've done and you want us all to be friends now?"

"That's *exactly* what I'm talking about, Gilbert!"

"Now, Moira," said Claire. "You can hardly blame any of us for refusing to take anything you say without a shaker or two of salt."

"I know. That's what depresses me," she said and sat, her eyes cast downward and her hands folded daintily in her lap. "Because I *am* sorry. I really am. I *know* I've been dreadful. I've done awful things and I've said even worse things. But there were reasons for all of it. I'm not saying *good* reasons. I'm talking about problems of mine and these . . . fears I have."

"Fears?" asked Claire, casting a dubious glance in my direction.

"I've been thinking it over since that fight we all had after the party. And I've finally realized what it all boils down to is . . . I don't know how to *trust* people. Don't roll your eyes, Gilbert; it's the truth. I always assume people are going to take advantage of me unless I outmaneuver them first. So I lie, and I make up stories, and I do everything I can to preserve some kind of advantage. And I *always* get found out, and people scream at me, and I scream back at them and try to make out it's *their* fault when I know perfectly well it's mine. But I have to be honest, now. Really honest. I *hate* fighting you guys. I hate knowing you're all together against me because you're scared of what deceitful thing I'm going to do next."

"We're not crazy about it either, hon," said Winslow, his mouth full of pâté.

"I don't get it, Moira. Why should *you* find it difficult to trust *us*?"

"It's not just you guys. It's everyone I know. Like I said, it's a problem of mine. Always has been. I mean . . ."

She paused and smiled in that twisty sort of way people only smile when they're absolutely mortified.

"Well, as you can probably figure out from my mother's current address, my 'formative years' weren't too heavy on stability. We moved all the time and it seemed like anyone I got to like cheated me or disappeared overnight and . . . Oh, fuck it! I don't want to get into that. It's none of your business. And it has nothing to do with *us*. Now. All I'm trying to say, guys, is I want a truce. It's been four against one and I'm sick of being alone in this thing."

"Moira," sighed Claire, "if you want to convince us you really mean well—call it off."

"*No*, Claire. I've been through much too much to quit when we're this close to it. Winnie's an absolute genius and Scentinels is going to make a fortune. I'm putting every dime I make into it and if you're smart you'll do the same. Isn't that right, Winnie?"

Winnie agreed that when they write the book on body odor control in the twentieth century, the name of Winslow Potts will be writ large.

"Look," said Moira, "I don't expect you to get gushy and hug me all over. You'd be idiots to trust me after what I've done. Be as careful as you want to, but please stop hating my guts. Just give me a *chance*, okay?"

We could only agree, and we did. But as we ate and joked and chatted the same questions loomed in all our minds: What the hell was she up to? Or was she actually being sincere? And why was the second option somehow more displeasing than the first?

Gilbert and I talked it over late that night and realized it came down to this: Moira was our villain and, so far as we were concerned, she had no right to abdicate the post. For her to suddenly beg to be seen not as some imp of Satan, but as a poor greedy mortal, prey to all sorts of fears and needs, struck us as a horrid breech of etiquette. Listening to her plea, we'd felt the same resentment you'd feel if, in the middle of a *Star Wars* film, Darth Vader sat down and began to recollect his sad childhood at the space orphanage while clutching the locket his mother had pressed into his hand just before she'd attached his bassinet to the asteroid.

While we're usually willing to see others as, like ourselves, a mixture of faults and virtues, some people seem so utterly bad (or good) that we're refreshed by their unity of nature and loathe to admit into evidence anything that contradicts it. Moira was such a person. You thought you could know her for a hundred years and never once be compelled to empathize.

Now we had to wonder to what degree our Moira was just that: *our* Moira, a creation of our own fear and paranoia. Oh, there was no doubting she was a lying, mercenary, social-climbing bitch, but did this mean she was completely incapable of anything like affection or loyalty? We preferred to think so, but it was this very preference which made us now question our judgment.

Over the following weeks she did nothing to make us feel that our old image of her as a woman of complete self-sufficiency and unlimited mendacity was the real Moira. To the contrary, she was considerate and helpful, and displayed an almost embarrassing eagerness to be liked by us. Gilbert and I were touched, greatly relieved and bitterly disappointed.

Twenty-four

With the wedding now a mere eight weeks away, preparations accelerated into high gear, posing fresh perils and conundrums for our jittery quintet. Invitations were due to go out that week, which forced us to confront the problem of the duchess's guest list. Moira's immediate family, as she'd so touchingly explained at Maddie's Christmas party, was minuscule, but surely the duchess had *some* friends she wished to invite, either here in the States or off in Little Chipperton.

The duchess, of course, being imaginary, had few friends indeed. But how could we ask Maddie and Tony to believe that a woman of her gregarious charm lived a monklike existence, never venturing beyond the walls of Trebleclef to enjoy the mad social whirl of Little Chipperton?

The first thing we did was have the duchess seize control of the invitations. The invited would be asked to RSVP to God's Country. The duchess would keep her guest list to a minimum since those on it would also be fictitious and unlikely, as such, to attend. Over the following weeks the duchess could inform Maddie that none of her twenty or so overseas chums would be able to come, owing to as many reasons as we could dream up. The general excuse would be age. The duke, or Nigey as she took to calling him, was an old poop in his sixties and their social set was confined to even older poops, none of whom was much disposed toward transatlantic travel.

Claire gamely agreed to be Moira's maid of honor. She was leery of putting herself into so active a role but it seemed the safe thing to do. The fewer "outsiders" underfoot the better.

Besides, following Moira's "Hath not a bitch eyes?" speech, an atmosphere of détente had developed. Real trust was still out of the question; we'd seen too often what Moira could accomplish given only the benefit of a doubt. But some degree of civility and team spirit was a welcome alternative to the rancorous infighting which had characterized relations so far. So, when Moira asked Claire if she'd consider bouquet duty, Claire shuddered briefly and said she'd be honored.

The duchess dined at Paradiso with Moira, Maddie and Aggie. They took a table in the small room and, while I was not in on the girl talk, it seemed to go swimmingly if the staccato outbursts of mirth from Aggie were any indication. Mummy, without Claire's knowledge, did Ex again, though not coke, as the last time she'd combined the two Maddie had said, "My goodness, Gwen, do you have trouble digesting? I've never seen a woman chew her food so carefully!"

Christopher waited on the table, which did little to ease my mood of apprehension. He'd been much friendlier of late but his frequent smile was the smile of a man relishing some delicious private joke and, given our history, I couldn't shake the suspicion that the joke was on me.

At one point that night he slithered up to the bar and motioned for me to lean forward.

"She's a fake!" he hissed, through a thin-lipped grin.

"Who?" I murmured, seconds away from renal failure.

"The duchess! Do you know what's underneath that flashy dated dress and the wig and the jewelry and the six pounds of makeup?"

"What?"

"A fat broad from Secaucus who made good! Well, she doesn't fool me. Not one bit. Are you coming down with something, dear? You look dreadful."

The meal went off without any snags or false eyelashes falling, like Joey Sartucci, into the soup. Brunch at Casa Cellini also passed without incident, except for some brief confusion on Mummy's part regarding the geography of Great Britain. Tony, baffled, had asked her how Little Chipperton could be both *south* of London and *north* of Liverpool.

"No, dear," the duchess had replied patiently, "the *other* Liverpool."

You might suppose that this string of successful appearances did something to diminish Winslow's overwhelming bouts of stage fright. You would, however, suppose wrong. No amount of success could shake his belief that discovery and death were imminent and, while he always came through and seemed, indeed, to be having the time of his life when playing Her Grace, hysterical crying jags preceded and followed each performance. Every day on which the duchess appeared was a comedy parenthesized by tragedy, and the effect was, to say the least, harrowing.

One result of Moira's rehabilitation was Vulpina's reentry into the picture. Moira claimed to be consumed with guilt about the phone calls she'd made when she believed Pina was responsible for the letter, and now she began seeing Pina again. Pina told Moira of the agonies she'd endured not only as a result of the psychopathic phone calls, which had haunted her sleep for weeks, but also of the amused disbelief of her so-called friends. Moira assured Pina that she believed unquestioningly in the truth of her tale, and told Pina that if the calls were to recur, she would have her powerful employer pressure the district attorney to see that the matter was investigated and the culprit apprehended before tragedy struck. Pina was so grateful that when Moira asked her to be a bridesmaid she accepted, even though this entailed her wearing a gown not of her own design but one identical to that of the other bridesmaids, Betty Sartucci and Cousin Steffie.

Things, in short, were proceeding with a smoothness that was too good to be true. Then Gunther tired of waiting and pounced.

A letter addressed to Gilbert arrived at GC late Saturday morning. The envelope, which bore no return address, was printed in nondescript block letters. The note inside, in keeping with years of extortionist tradition, was composed of letters cut from newspapers and glossy magazines. It read:

MR SelWyn and mR CAvanauGH,

YOU have had SOmE Time nOw To ADmire yOUR *por*TraITs. HOW would *you* L.I.ke yOUr MAFIA friENDs to SEE THeM? Ag*n*ES FABrizio? Mo*THE*r and toN.Y. CellIni? FRED*dy* the POOCH?

MAil $1500 in 100 bILLS to p.O. BOx 723, TImes sQ. station. IF *money* NOt reCeived by MonDAY FEb 9 PicTures GO O*ut!!*

THE AVENG*IN*G ANGEL

Gilbert called me at noon and by one we'd all convened at God's Country, except for Winnie. It was felt that with dinner at Freddy's scheduled for that evening there was little to be gained from rendering him comatose with fear.

"It doesn't make sense!" said Moira. "Gunther doesn't even *know* these people—Freddy or any of them. He's never met them."

"But his friend Geoff did," said Claire. "It's entirely possible that Geoff recognized them. I mean, *I* recognized them at the Christmas party. Freddy fawned all over you, saying you were like a daughter to him. If he told Gunther about that, Gunther could easily have seen that there's a very important and *violent* mobster who'd be less than thrilled to find Gilbert was cheating on you—with another man."

"Who cares how he worked it out!" said Moira. "It's blackmail and we're not going to pay it!"

"Right," said Gilbert, uncertainly.

Moira took Gilbert's arm in hers.

"If Gunther sends the pictures to Freddy, *I'll* stand up for you. Freddy would never hurt you if I begged him not to."

But, argued Claire, it wasn't that simple. Gilbert had broken a promise not merely to Moira but to Freddy, too, and there was no guaranteeing Moira's pleas could persuade him to overlook this personal affront. And even if she could intercede on Gilbert's behalf where did that leave *me*?

"But what are we supposed to do? *Pay* him? That's . . . that's *unfair!*" said Moira, overcome suddenly by the realization that there is injustice in this world.

"Unfair or not, we may have to!" I said.

"Not *me!*" fumed Moira, heading for the phone.

She opened her purse, checked her book and began dialing furiously.

"Moira, do *not* call Gunther!"

"I'm not calling Gun— Hello? Ugo? Hi! S'Moy! . . . Great! How's Betty? . . . Fab! Listen, there's this creepface goon who is really busting my chops and I was wondering how I might go about giving him a present—like six months of traction . . ."

"*Hi Ugo!*" said Gilbert after he'd barreled over and grabbed the phone. Moira lunged for it but I seized her in a hammerlock and escorted her back to the table.

"No, *no!* No one's on our case! It was a *joke!* Moy meant *me!* We were just having a few words about clothing expenditures! . . . Hoo! You, too, huh! . . . Right! Can't live with 'em, can't live without 'em!'"

He explained Moira had called to invite him and Betty to lunch and a Knick's game next Saturday. Ugo enthusiastically accepted and Gilbert, trembling slightly, hung up.

"Are you fucking *crazy?* Breaking his legs! That's *really* going to make him play nice!"

"God, you're all such sissies! Don't you see? We've got to let him know he can't fuck with us!"

"*You,* he can't fuck with," I shouted. "*Us,* he can fuck with! We're the ones who'll be puppy chow if Freddy sees the pictures. We don't want to make him madder, we want to shut him up!"

"Well if you want to shut him up—"

"Moira, we are not going to *kill* anyone!" snapped Claire. "Can we please calm down and examine our options rationally before we act!"

Examine them we did, only to discover that we didn't have any. The risks of further antagonizing Gunther were simply unacceptable. He would have to be paid. Moira was adamantly against this, and argued almost tearfully that we hadn't worked so hard in order to surrender our profits to a "vindictive Kraut." Claire replied that we hadn't worked so hard to get ourselves killed either, though this was perhaps hard for Moira to see as she was in the least danger. Moira then remembered she'd turned over a new leaf and apologized, explaining that her reluctance to pay was based not on any callous disregard for our safety but on the principle of noncapitulation to terrorism.

We decided that one of us should at least attempt to secure the negative in exchange for the payment and I volunteered for the mission. It wouldn't have been right to involve Claire more than she was already, and Gilbert and Moira were out of the question, their dermatological jibes at Gunther's expense having greatly reduced their chances of achieving much in the way of entente cordiale.

"Something just occurred to me," said Claire. "This little crush Freddy seems to have on the duchess."

"Yes," I said to Gilbert and Moira, "you'd better do everything you can to nip that in the bud tonight."

"No, Philip," sighed Moira condescendingly, "Claire means we should *encourage* it. Right?"

"Exactly. Not too *much*, of course. Just enough to lead him on. That way, if push comes to shove, Mummy's intercession will be more valuable."

At that point Winslow arrived feeling just the slightest bit tense about dinner with Freddy. Claire and I decided to leave the preperformance ministrations to Gilbert and Moira. We wished Winnie the best of luck and scrammed for the foyer.

It was a chilly day but we both felt more like walking than taking a cab. The lightest of snows was falling and Central Park looked beautiful and quiet and serene, everything that life wasn't at the moment. We strolled wordlessly uptown for a few blocks before I broke the silence.

"You think I'm irredeemably stupid, don't you?"

"What, for not checking the closet before you went to bed?"

"No, for going to bed in the first place."

"Philip, what my own love affairs have lacked in frequency they've made up for in misery, so I don't consider myself in any position to give advice to the lovelorn."

"Okay."

"*If*, however, you had troubled to consult me about these sudden feelings you'd developed toward Gilbert, I'd have advised you to defer acting on them till the danger in doing so was past. Then you might have been better able to decide how real they were."

"What, you think we're only having an affair because we *shouldn't?*"

"What I think doesn't matter. What do you think? Oh, excuse me, I've forgotten—you don't think. You feel!"

I said nothing but made every effort to look wrongly accused.

"I'm sorry. They only reason I'm being a bitch is because I'm so damned mad at myself for having gotten into this mess to begin with."

"Don't be mad at yourself. You were only trying to help me."

"That's a crock, dear, and you know it. It was nothing more than ego masquerading as altruism. You got sucked in by greed and I followed out of vanity. I couldn't bear the thought of Moira playing me for a fool as if I were just *anyone*."

"When did she play you for a fool?"

"At the *Eureka, Baby!* party. When I was so sympathetic toward her because she'd fought with Gilbert. Then afterward she crowed victoriously to you two about what a chump I'd been."

"Oh. Actually, I made that part up."

"God love you."

That night I called The Avenging Angel.

"Um, hi, Gunther?"

"Mr. Cavanaugh, I do not appreciate these simpering phone calls. You have done me enough harm. If and when I wish to speak to you I will call."

"Right. I just wanted to say we got your demands."

"Demands?" he said innocently.

"Yes. We think they're a little steep but we're prepared to meet them provided you give us the nude photos *and* the negatives."

There was a long pause.

"Do not play games with me, Mr. Cavanaugh. I know nothing about nude photos, I know nothing about money and nothing about negatives! This is harassment, Mr. Cavanaugh—and whoever is listening in— and I demand you desist immediately."

"Can't we negotiate?"

"There is nothing to negotiate about! Do not call me again! Good-bye!"

I called Claire.

"Oh, hi—can you call me in the morning!"

"I'm sorry. Someone there?"

"Yes."

"A *date*?" I asked, then, realizing I'd let myself sound a bit too surprised, said, "I mean . . ."

"Yes, I know what you mean. 'Leap year so soon?' Good-*bye*, Philip!"

"Hold on! I'm sorry, okay! I just wanted you to know I called Gunther and he played dumb."

"What do you mean?"

"I told him we'd pay his price but we wanted the negatives and he played dumb. He knows nothing about the pictures or anything. And he thought someone was listening in, too."

"Oh, dear. Well, we should have expected that. You don't take the trouble to cut out letters for your blackmail note then cheerfully confess to the dark deed on the telephone when anyone can record it. He's a crafty one and . . . What, love? . . . Oh, don't be silly!

Of course not! We're writing a mystery . . . Look, Philip, *tomorrow*, okay?"

Gilbert stayed at my place that night. He rolled in about one-thirty looking grim and bedraggled.

"How did it go?"

"It was ghastly, Philip! Ghastly!"

I made him hot tea with a splash of Remy, and he spun his tale.

"We did what Claire said and told him to lead Freddy on a bit. We didn't say *why*. I mean, we lied. We said it would make him more generous at the wedding. But we told him to be careful. 'Tease him,' Philly. Those were my exact words. 'Tease him'!"

"He went overboard?"

"He's *divorcing* the duke!"

"A divorce! But he can't do that!"

"Can't? Philip, he *has* to!"

Twenty-five

This is how the five-year marriage between the Duke and Duchess of Dorsetshire came to its rancorous, if unanticipated, conclusion.

Winslow, coked to the tits and under advisement to tease Freddy's hopes, leapt to the task with all the abandon and misplaced self-confidence the drug is known to inspire. He cooed endearments, fluttered his eyelashes, and heaved his false boobies in a manner he thought guaranteed to incite passion in even the most geriatric of bosoms. Then, after the meal, as they sat sipping Sambucca, he delivered his masterstroke. Turning the subject to literature, he proclaimed Barbara Cartland to be the finest prose stylist of our century. Freddy, while he begged to differ, feeling the distinction belonged more rightly to Messalina Joyeuse, said nonetheless that the duchess's preferences labeled her a woman of great sensitivity and refinement, increasingly rare commodities in these vulgar times.

Moira, beginning to feel that Mummy was within inches of commandeering her still lucrative job as Freddy's reader, slapped her hand and cautioned her not to be such a flirt. What would the duke think?

"The duke," said Mummy frostily, "is hardly in a position to decry my harmless flirtation with a kindred spirit!"

She proceeded to paint the duke as the basest of philanderers and herself as the long-suffering wife, striving always to stave off self-pity by channeling her spurned affections into good works.

Mummy later asserted she'd chosen this tactic so Freddy would assume he had a better chance of successfully wooing her. Freddy would hope her contempt for the adulterous duke might lead her to repay the duke in kind. There was no possible harm in this since the duchess would, of course, remain loyal to her straying husband in the face of all provocation.

What Mummy hadn't counted on was Freddy's murderous side. Even at his advanced age he possessed a robust hatred for dishonorable behavior and a firm belief that bullets speak louder than words. He listened to the duchess's lament in silence and when she'd finished, his guests were startled to see a flintiness had come into his eyes. He began discoursing on the sanctity of the marriage bond. Only depravity of the most unforgivable sort could lead a man to defile this bond, especially if the woman were half so fine and noble as the duchess. While he did not come right out and say so, he seemed unmistakably to imply that death was not too extreme a penalty and that he was just the man to arrange the irksome details.

Winslow was stunned by Freddy's sudden vehemence and could only stammer that men were weak and had to be forgiven their excesses. Freddy replied gently that he hadn't meant his words to upset her and that perhapes fate or God's mysterious ways would soon alleviate her suffering.

Moira and Gilbert were quick to see just what stickiness might arise if Freddy sent his henchmen to England to bump off a nonexistent duke. But it seemed the only way to avoid the duke's murder was to render it unnecessary. They began beseeching Mummy to divorce the cad. They'd had no *idea* his infidelities were so flagrant! Self-respect demanded she end her sad charade of contentment and begin a new life!

Their insistence eventually made Mummy realize they meant her to agree to this sudden and drastic departure from the shooting script. Yes, she said, they were right! The time had come for a parting of the ways! She had only been timid because she felt there was little hope for a woman her age to start afresh. Freddy took her hand and assured her this was not the case.

"The worst of it," moaned Gilbert, "is it puts us in such a bad position with Gunther!"

"With Gunther?" I asked, unable at first to see any connection.

"Think about it! If he ever gets those pictures to Freddy now we're really dead! You should have heard him ranting about infidelity and cheating on 'good women.' What'll he do now if he finds out about *us*?"

"Sure," I said, desperately searching for a bright side, "but now that we know he's so gaga about the duchess she can plead for us!"

"I *know* that, Philly. And what if she *does*? What will *he* say?"

I mulled it over a moment then shuddered with dread.

"*Exactly!*" said Gilbert. " 'Marry me and I'll forgive them!' "

This was only speculation, but the scenario looked frighteningly plausible. And when we talked it over the next morning with Claire and Moira they too agreed that Freddy's passion might induce him to do virtually anything. Mummy could divorce the duke and still successfully fend off Freddy's advances. But the fending off would be much harder if Freddy had Gilbert's and my fates to use as bargaining chips.

It was all a terrible muddle, but one thing was clear: Freddy must never see the photos. Gunther's demands, present and future, would have to be met.

Further weight was lent this decision the next Monday when I returned from a trip to the supermarket to find another note from Gunther. This one was not mailed but simply folded and jammed into my mailbox. It read:

YOU ConVey MucH MR. CavaNAUgh *AND* learN LiTtLe! I wILL NoT bE EnTraPpEd. MY *PRICE* has JusT. R.I.seN $500 and *will* Rise anNotheR $5oo *ever*Y TIME you attEmPT to DEceiVE M*e*. JUstiCe WiLL BE *DONE!*

I brought it to God's Country that night when we all met for what was becoming a daily event, the Six-O'Clock Bad News.

"What does he mean, 'You convey much and learn little'?" asked Moira.

"Well," sighed Claire, "he apparently knows something after speaking to Philip he didn't know before. Philip, what exactly was said?"

I did my best to reconstruct the conversation but couldn't do better than a rough paraphrase which differed in no substantial way from the one I'd already given. She just sighed and said that I had to be as guarded as possible next time I spoke to him, which we didn't imagine would be soon since five hundred dollars was fairly pricy for what was, after all, a local call.

I gazed around the room, noting the fabulous arrangement of out-of-season flowers on the sideboard.

"Freddy?"

"Who else?" said Moira jealously. "You should see the earrings!"

We discussed payment of Gunther's demands. Moira was furious at the idea of contributing anything but we managed to shame her into putting in two hundred dollars, leaving Gilbert and me to pay nine hundred each. This was Monday, February 2; the money was due on the ninth, so we sent it out the next day. I had a mere $950 in the bank, so my share just about cleaned me out. It also eliminated any chance of my repaying Aggie in the near future.

The topic of discussion as we three blackmailees trudged back from the mailbox was how long could this situation be allowed to continue? What if he demanded more? Moira, to our alarm, stated quite forcefully that were he to make a second demand she would do things *her* way. No amount of arguing from us would dissuade her from calling in the troops.

As Gilbert and I lay in bed that night, sipping the cocoa Moira had thoughtfully brought us, we tried to plan our future. After the wedding I would go away and wait for Freddy to die. How long could it take? A few years at the most. I'd get a lot of writing done. Then, the threat removed, he would divorce Moira, descend on my hideout, and sweep me away to France or Wales or some quaint midwestern town, and there we'd grow old together, tapping away on twin word processors, composing the great plays and novels we were born to write.

All we had to do was get through the next seven weeks.

Freddy's courtship of the duchess soon ripened into a shameless assault on that winsome noblewoman's weakness for the grand romantic gesture. Flowers arrived daily, as well as boxes containing recently published works of the ripped bodice school. Once a hansom, pulled by white horses, met her in front of the building to take her to Paradiso.

The sheer relentlessness of his campaign forced Gilbert, Moira and me to decide that Winslow *had* to lay off the controlled substances. So far, at least, Freddy had been a perfect gentleman. But what was to say that on some future date, after a surfeit of wine, he might not pounce and find his passion reciprocated by a Winslow too blissed out to deal with the situation sanely? Freddy would come up for air to find his dentures clutching a suddenly disembodied breast, or something far worse. Somehow, Mummy would have to learn to swank without Ecstasy.

It was, of course, Claire who provided the solution to this apparently insurmountable problem. (She remained ignorant of Winslow's continued reliance on drugs but not, of course, of his continued, indeed worsening, panic between appearances.) Claire recommended this: if it was Winslow who was frightened and the duchess who was not, then *get rid of Winslow*.

Once proposed, the sound reasoning behind the approach became clear to all, even Winnie. His nerves, once he was in full drag, were never half as bad as when he was in his own dowdy slacks and cardigans. Then he would stare into the mirror at his small frightened mouth and frail mop of blond curls, and he'd wail in horror at the apparent impossibility of persuading anyone he was a glamorous and confident woman of the world. So, from now till the wedding we would not let him become that frightened man again. He would move out of his apartment, into God's Country, and live every moment as the duchess.

The results of this strategy were immediate and dramatic. Within days the panic attacks had lessened so much that Gilbert and Moira induced him to venture out, completely drug-free, for a shopping trip with Maddie to buy gifts for the bridesmaids and ushers. He passed the test magnificently, denigrating "shoddy goods" and bullying salesgirls with a grandiloquence that matched his most inspired drug-induced flights.

This policy of perpetual impersonation was not without its drawbacks. We had to spend scarce funds for more clothes and nightgowns, but the worst of it was Winslow. He became more insufferable daily. Since all private moments with us were "rehearsals" for the public appearances, he conducted himself at these times with the same imperial hauteur he employed in public encounters with the merchant class. Any exhortations from us to knock it off were met with sulks and comments on how impossible this would be if we were forever forcing him "out of character." So we were left with no choice but to grit our teeth and endure Mummy's running commentary on our numberless shortcomings.

And so February passed. Gilbert, Moira and their parents arranged the final details of the wedding and reception. Caterers were hired, as well as musicians, florists, photographers and a contractor to build a temporary extension onto the Cellinis' sweet little ballroom.

Gilbert and I continued our affair, regularly searching the bedroom for concealed microphones and crouching photographers.

Gilbert selected Holly, Ugo Sartucci and Mike from the restaurant to be the ushers, surely as unlikely a trio as had ever fulfilled this office.

News of the duchess's divorce spread quickly through the famed family grapevine and many called to offer nosy questions in the guise of sympathy. The duchess always said sadly and beautifully that, yes, it was a shame, and, more sadly still, she'd just heard from Lord and Lady Greenfield, who couldn't come to the wedding, poor Maude having fallen in the bath and broken her hip.

We waited for further demands from Gunther and prayed they would never come.

And Freddy continued his gentlemanly and futile courtship of the fair Gwendolyn.

Little did we know that we were not the only ones in whom this romance had stirred profound anxieties. In fact, our tremors of fear every time they dined together were nothing compared to the seismic shocks these rendezvous sent coursing through the very foundation of organized crime's wealthiest and most internecine clan.

Little did we realize that for years the House of Bombelli had seethed with deeply rooted rivalries. The hope of a peaceful resolution and the need to present a unified front to rival families had combined to ensure that these long-standing conflicts remained carefully submerged beneath the placid day-to-day routine of drug smuggling and contract murders.

But now a fictitious duchess batted her eyelashes, sighed "*L'amour, l'amour!*" and sent the whole bloody mess bubbling to the surface.

Twenty-six

"Evenin', boys. You mind steppin' inta the car? I wanna have a little chat with ya."

These bone-chilling words were uttered just outside Paradiso at one a.m. on the first Tuesday of March. A cold rain was falling and Chick Sartucci was leaning out the rear window of his dark Lincoln Continental. A poker-faced, square-built driver held an umbrella over the door so Chick's cigar wouldn't be extinguished by the rain.

Nooooo! Not now! Not tonight! Save me, God! I'll do anything you ask! I'll become a priest and work with the poor in war-torn countries! Just don't let me die!

"Gosh, Chick, it's such a cold wet night. Why don't you come in and have a brandy?"

"Good idea!" said Gilbert, whose prayers were on similar lines and involved reading to the blind.

"Hey! Calm down, guys!" chortled Chick. "I'm not gonna hurtcha! I just wanna chat. I like the car better. S'more private."

"Happy to oblige!"

"How's Ugo?" asked Gilbert, pushing me in ahead of him.

"Great. Just great. He's real fonda you guys."

"Well, we're nuts about him!"

The car cruised slowly toward the park.

"Firs' thing I wanna say is how much I like you two guys. Right from the firs' time I metcha at Maddie's Christmas party, I thought, these are bright kids. Lotta class, lotta talent. What I mean is, you guys and your fiancée an' Moira, too—you're good people. *However . . .*"

He paused unendurably and smoked as the car cruised into the darkness of Central Park.

". . . I can't say the same 'bout that mother-in-law, you're gettin', Gil. Mind ya, no reflection on Moira. She's the best. But her mom . . ." He shook his head sadly. "I don't think she's a nice woman."

"Well, neither do we!" said Gilbert.

"Hell, no! So *pretentious*!"

"We can't *stand* her!"

"I mean," said Chick, scowling righteously, "what can you say 'bout a dame runs off an' marries a duke just to get herself a fancy title, then comes back to the States for her daughter's weddin', meets a sweet rich old guy wit' one foot in the grave and right away drops her husband!"

"Deplorable!"

"Let's call a spade a spade, boys. The duchess is nothin' but a fuckin' golddiggin' old tramp!"

"Gosh, Chick!" I said, realizing that if we kept concurring with everything he said we might soon have Winslow's blood on our hands. "I can certainly see where you'd get that impression, but I don't think the duchess is necessarily after Freddy's money."

"Ya don't, do ya?" he said, his eyes narrowing with suspicion.

"Not *necessarily*. I just mean I think her marriage was on the rocks before she met Freddy. She was going to divorce the duke anyway."

"Yeah? Well, ain't it funny how she didn't come out an' say so till she went to Freddy's house an' got a good look at them marble floors an' the gold spigots in the bathroom? . . . Look, I don't wanna give you boys no grief. You got nothin' to do with it. I just want you to give Her Highness a little message. You tell her she ain't gonna get away with it. It took Freddy seventy years to pile up that dough and he had a lotta help from his family doin' it. She thinks she's gonna swoop down on his det'bed and scoop the whole pot, she's fuckin' crazy! She marries him, she's *dead*! She runs boo-hooin' to Freddy 'bout threats, she's *still* dead. He ain't gonna live forever, though he seems to think so, an' after he's gone they'll be plenty of us an' just one of her. She marries, she's dead. She complains, she's dead. You tell her who said so, *you're* dead. Do we have an understanding?"

"You bet!"

"Absolutely."

"And I want to assure you right now, Chick, that there's no way the duchess is *ever* going to marry Freddy Bombelli. You have my word on that!" said Gilbert.

"I'm glad to hear that, Gil. And I'm sure you won't go troublin' Moira with this. She's a sweet innocent kid and there's no sense worryin' her with stuff she couldn't possibly understand."

Chick dropped Gilbert off at GC and me at my apartment since at that point we were afraid to give even the mildest of indications that our friendship was more than platonic. As soon as Chick sped away I got a cab and went to God's Country.

"Thank God you're alive!" cried Gilbert, embracing me.

"Well he wasn't about to kill me, honey!"

He said he'd already gone to wake Mummy and Moira but they weren't home. They rolled in fifteen minutes later fresh from a night on the town with the lovesick don. We filled them in on the new threat, deciding to honor Chick's request to omit mention of who had made it. Moira demanded to know but we stuck to our guns.

"Look, Your Grace," I said to Winslow, "you understand you can never accept Freddy's proposal?"

"Of course I do, you impertinent pup!"

"Then, please, for your sake and ours, stop seeing so much of him! Say you're busy with the wedding or need your rest. Anything. Just *avoid* him!"

"Love, love!" sighed Winslow, gazing at his new Cartier wristwatch. "It never quite works out, does it?"

We told Claire about the threats the next day. She was horrified but agreed there was no cause for real concern since Chick's fears could never come to pass.

Over the next week, Freddy called daily to arrange dates, but Mummy always had a conflict, though she was willing to chat.

He often asked when she planned to file for divorce. Had she made her intentions plain to Nigel? Did he respect them or was he trying to coerce her into staying with him against her wishes? She always replied that she'd told Nigel and he'd promised not to fight, but they both preferred to wait till after the wedding. And, oh, bad news! Poor Lady Fish would not be able to attend, arthritis having left her all but calcified.

But despite Mummy's efforts to cool the romance, Freddy did not relent. The flowers came so thick and fast that visitors to God's Country would look around quizzically, as if wondering where the coffin was.

With the wedding now a mere three weeks off I was increasingly plagued by calls from various Cellinis asking about the bachelor party which it was my duty, as best man, to organize. This tradition was apparently as sacred to the male side of the family as the public opening of gifts was to its brides. Their admonitions to get the show on the road, coupled with their generally salacious tone, made me realize, to my vast discomfort, that I was expected to host nothing less than a major Saturnalia.

Gay men usually have a fair grasp of the mechanics of heterosexual male traditions. Even if we have never ourselves hunted, attended a prize fight or argued in favor of the death penalty for umpires, these activities are so often depicted in films that we know, more or less, what's what. As for me though, never having seen a popular movie about such an event, the bachelor party remained an arcane and mysterious rite. I sensed there was more to a full-scale job than a mere surplus of liquor, but sensed, as well, that my image of chorines emerging from cakes was somewhat passé.

Mike at the restaurant asked my plans in earshot of Aggie, who kindly butted in to say that Paradiso was not booked for anything the Sunday before the wedding and we were welcome to use it free of charge, so long as we agreed to clean up after ourselves and pay for broken fixtures. I gratefully accepted, but, this detail solved, all other mysteries remained.

Finally, I called Ugo and confessed that I'd never attended a bachelor party and would appreciate any pointers on how to make it a memorable one. He was flattered to think his reputation as a party animal had led me to defer to his judgment, and promised he would get right on to it. I had only to supply the guest list and pay the bill. He would take care of the rest.

One night, the third week of March, as Gilbert and I were leaving Paradiso, we found ourselves face-to-fender with yet another indisputably criminal car, this one a huge maroon Caddy. We were about to turn on our heels and reenter the restaurant, when the weasely figure of Charlie Pastore jumped out of the back seat.

"Hi, boys! I hoped I'd catch you two before you left. How you doin'?"

"Great, Charlie! How are you?"

"Glad to hear it! You look swell, just swell. Handsome! Boy, what I wouldn't give to be your ages again!"

He was a short man with darting eyes and a smile that seemed permanently fixed. He spoke rapidly, racing to the end of one sentence and on to the next, which gave him the maddening habit of asking questions then going on before you could reply.

"Well, I see by your faces, boys, that you're wondering why I'm waiting for you here. Am I right? So, you don't mind I'd like to take you to a little flat of mine round the corner from here. Privacy, y'understand."

Ten minutes later we were sitting in his tiny "P.A. da Tear." His driver, Piltdown Man, served drinks.

"Bet you're all excited about the wedding? Huh? You getting a little nervous? I know I was, but hey, don't be, you're getting a fantastic girl! And the mother! Whoa! Now, that's a Lady with a capital L! Don't make 'em like that anymore. Zamatterafac, that's what I want to talk to you about. Freddy, Freddy Bombelli, is . . . well, I don't have to tell *you*, right! You know more than I do, right! He's just crazy about her and who can blame him? Best thing coulda happened to him, little ray of sunshine in his declining years. Say, she could do a lot worse herself! Freddy's a wealthy man! He'll treat her right, too, not like that rotten duke of hers!

"Now, I'm not going to beat around the bush here. I know what's in the wind. There are certain people don't want to see Freddy happy. They been talking to you, right? They told you to give the duchess a message and you did, and that's why she's been giving poor Freddy the cold shoulder. Now, I ask you, is that *fair*? Two people trying to find happiness and a couple of greedy so-and-sos want to ruin it for 'em! S'enough to break your heart, am I right? So listen—*don't be intimidated!* You're Cellini people and the Cellinis look after their own. We'll protect you. Understand? But if we're gonna give you our protection I think we've got a right to expect something in return. A little loyalty. Is that wrong?"

It took a moment for us to see that he actually meant us to answer for a change.

"Oh, no! Not wrong at all!"

"Fair's fair!"

"Zactly! *Zactly!* So, listen up, boys . . . He's gonna ask her to marry him. I know this, 'cause he told me himself. And when he asks her, see, she's going to say yes. Because there ain't no doubt she was *planning* to say yes, before certain parties started trying to change her mind. Don't take no Ph.D. to see that! Why else would she have suddenly decided to divorce old dukey? Huh? It was a bad thing you boys did, goin' and makin' her back off, leavin' a sweet old man to die alone with no wife to hold his hand. But, hell—I ain't blamin' you. This party leaned on you, right? Got nasty? So we ain't going to get mad at you for making a mistake when there's still plenty of time to correct it."

"But Charlie," I said, "what if the duchess doesn't *want* to marry Freddy?"

"Hey, boys! Don't *insult* me. She was chasin' him like a fuckin' bloodhound up until you told her otherwise! Don't *insult* me, boys, it hurts my *feelings!* And when my feelings get hurt—I don't know what I'm doin'! She wants him! And he wants her!"

"And he's going to *get* her!" said Gilbert, heartily.

"Hey, that's more like it!"

"Those two beautiful old people are going to find the happiness they deserve!" said Gilbert.

"Eventually!"

"They're gonna *tie* that knot!"

"In the due course of time!"

"Who are we to stand in the way of love!"

"*Zactly!*"

We staggered back to God's Country in silence, operating under the ageless superstition that nothing is true till you say it aloud. We got there at two a.m. to find Claire, Moira and Mummy all awake and flapping about in great agitation. The evening's drama was far from finished.

"Where have you *been!*" cried Moira. "I called the restaurant and they said you left nearly an hour ago!"

"We were detained," I said flatly.

"Oh, Gilbert!" she said, throwing her arms around him and bursting into sobs. "You have no idea what I've been through!" She paused dramatically and said: "I was *leaned* on!"

"You, too?" asked Gilbert.

"You, *too*?" asked the duchess, twitchy but still in character.

"Yes!"

"*Again?*" said Claire.

We nodded.

"By the same person?"

"No. A new one."

"Oh, dear! What happened?"

"I believe I'd already begun, Claire," said Moira petulantly, then seated herself on a pouf and breathlessly imparted her tale.

Mummy had decided to spend a quiet night in, and Moira had gone down to SoHo to meet Vulpina and attend the opening, at Concepteria, of Aldo Cupper's "Bags #4." After the opening Moira walked Pina home and was trying to hail a cab when a dark Cadillac pulled up in front of her. The rear window rolled down automatically and Lunch Fabrizio leaned out and asked her if she would kindly step in for a chat.

As the car prowled through SoHo, Lunch told her, in the most offensive terms, exactly what he and his sympathizers thought of the duchess's base attempts to seduce the aging Freddy. "Coffin snatching," he called it, amongst still riper terms. He made no secret of his belief that Moira had put her mother up to the whole thing as part of her despicable plan to become heiress to Freddy's millions and power. His demands were as follows:

If the duchess even *divorced* the duke before Freddy's demise, Moira would have "an accident." This just as a warning to the duchess.

If the duchess married Freddy anyway the duchess and Moira would be killed following Freddy's death. No amount of preemptive carnage would prevent Lunch's loyal survivors from carrying out his vengeance.

If Moira or the duchess breathed a word to Freddy, or to anyone else who subsequently informed him, Moira, Gilbert, the duchess and Freddy would all die swiftly and terribly.

Gilbert and I just stood there, our jaws slack, unable to believe the rock had gotten bigger and the hard place harder still.

When she'd finished we told them all about Charlie, mentioning

Chick now as well, since there seemed no more point in concealing anything. Then it was *Guernica* time again. Eventually the panic subsided due to sheer exhaustion and we agreed to meet again the following afternoon.

Claire and I shared a cab uptown. As it sped up Central Park West she squeezed my hand and assured me there had to be a way out. Nothing more was said till we bade each other good night as I left the cab.

On the way in I checked the mailbox and found another pasted-up note from Gunther, demanding a final five thousand dollars, payable before the wedding.

Twenty-seven

I don't know how Claire, Moira or Winslow managed to make it through those final terror-packed weeks, but for Gilbert and me the preferred sedative was sex and plenty of it. We stopped sleeping over at each other's places since we had an uneasy feeling we were being watched, but our discretion extended only so far as this precaution. We never found ourselves alone in a room but Gilbert would gaze at his watch, then at the nearest door, and murmur, "What do you think?"

Our little group spent hour after hour debating strategies for survival, but none of us, not even Claire, could think of a way to reconcile the demands of Lunch, Chick, Charlie and Freddy. There was only one pathetic tactic available and that was to stall.

If Freddy proposed, the duchess would say she needed time to think. Then, just before the wedding, she'd receive a telegram saying the duke was ill and couldn't attend. Following the wedding she'd return to England, wait a week and announce the duke was dead and buried. She'd not said so earlier because she didn't want to ruin her daughter's honeymoon with such tragic news. She would return to the States (we could hardly have Freddy descending on Trebleclef to console her) and fall back on propriety, saying she could hardly discuss remarriage till a suitable period of mourning had passed. This would do nothing to improve the real situation, but it would buy us time to think of a way out.

If we could.

Which we doubted.

The most immediate problem was Gunther, or, more to the point, what Moira wanted to do to him. When she heard of the new demand she bayed with fury and declared implacably that it was high time we called Freddy's trusty nurse and told him we had a candidate for Sergery.

"Moira," I pleaded, "it just isn't right!"

"I fail to see what's wrong with it. Jesus, Philip! *You're* the one he wants to get killed! Haven't you ever heard of self-defense!"

"It's not the same thing!" said Claire. "This is premeditated murder!"

"Well, of course it's premeditated! How else do we get him first! I don't understand you people at all!"

"Look, Moy," said Gilbert, "he said it's the final payment. And you don't have to pay much! Just five hundred dollars or so! We'll scrape the rest together. Winnie, you've got a lot of jewelry from Freddy you could pawn."

"Pawn my jewels!" twittered Winnie, resplendent in a ruffly purple cocktail dress. "I must say that seems terribly callous when one considers the affection with which they were bestowed. What sort of women would—"

"*Winnie!*"

"Oh, all right!"

Gilbert and I between us could come up with three grand by the end of the week. Claire pledged five hundred.

"Moira," she said, "you can at least put in as much as I'm contributing!"

"No! There's a *principle* here!" she said and, donning her trenchcoat, stormed out, her eyes glinting with terrible purpose.

The moment she left I called Gunther's salon.

"Capelli, may I help you?"

"Listen, Gunther, you've got to stop it! You have no idea how much trouble this blackmail could get you into!"

"Mr. Cavanaugh, I grow weary of these foolish attempts to incriminate me! I will not be duped into saying things that have no basis in truth."

"I'm not trying to dupe you! I'm just saying you have to cancel the new demand. We already paid you once!"

"A paltry sum, when you consider the damage you have done me!"

"Then you admit you accepted the money!"

"I accepted money from you, yes. But I did not *request* it. You took it upon *yourself* to mail it to me. Since I have lost considerable income, I am not so foolish as to refuse just compensation."

"Listen, Gunther, you're playing with the wrong people. If you don't stop this you'll be killed. Do you understand that? *Killed!*"

"Death threats, Mr. Cavanaugh? Perhaps it might interest you to know that I am *also* recording this conversation. So if anything should happen to me I now have a tape which my attorney—"

"*Jesus Christ!*" I said, and hung up. "Oh, *lovely*! Now Moira's going to have Gunther murdered and the only evidence is going to implicate *me*!"

For once, though, mob tradition was on our side. When Moira returned she sourly agreed to kick in five hundred. What prompted her change in heart was not any moral reawakening but an unexpected lesson in the economics of assassination. Having Gunther hit would cost fifteen hundred, to which sum the rest of us refused to contribute a penny. Faced with the choice of eliminating him for fifteen hundred or mollifying him for five she opted frugally for the latter. So, later that week we placed the bills in a heavily padded envelope along with a note Moira insisted on adding which read, "Final payment! Try this again and you're dead meat!" and mailed it to the correct post office box.

My share having exhausted my funds, I was unable to buy a wedding gift for Gilbert and Moira. This was a problem only because of the famed custom of opening the gifts for the delectation of all. Claire hit upon the solution of finding some nice antique from God's Country, wrapping it up, then returning it after the wedding.

As for Freddy's courtship in the weeks before the duke's death, Mummy steered a cautious middle course, neither seeing as much of him as she had before Chick's threat nor as little as she had after it. This, of course, pleased no one, but it didn't leave anyone trigger-happy either.

Given these recent developments, you can, I'm sure, understand why neither Gilbert nor I was much looking forward to his bachelor party, particularly since all three of our prospective murderers would be among the guests. There was no choice, though, but to attend.

It was among the most dreadful nights of our lives, all the more so because neither of us could for a moment betray our revulsion at the bacchic excesses Ugo had so lovingly devised. We had to pretend to enjoy it all—the lesbian porn film, the novelty ashtrays that let you be a rapist every time you extinguished a cigarette, the besotted revelers retching in the john, and the stripper who accepted the ten-and twenty-dollar bills of admirers in a way which gave new meaning to the words "safe deposit box."

This tridextrous miss, we soon gathered, had been leased by Ugo as his own special gift to Gilbert. Gilbert, he announced to hoots of approval, could do whatever he wanted with her. What Gilbert wanted to do with her, of course, was to send her to a vocational school in another state, but he couldn't exactly say so. My heart bled for him as he had to sit there in front of a drunk and applauding crowd, pretending to be inflamed with lust as she thrust her betassled tits in his face. Finally, when she knelt before him and began undoing his belt, he had no choice but to leap up, grab her hand and, amidst whistles and stomps of approval, lead her into Aggie's office and lock the door. There he blushingly told her he'd caught the clap from another of her trade and had only seven penicillin filled days to go till his honeymoon. She was grateful for his honesty and only too happy to bump the door rhythmically with her behind while shrieking in pleasure, to the crowd's roaring chant of "Do it! Do it!! Do it!"

As I said, Lunch, Chick and Charlie Pastore were among the crowd which also included Marlowe Heppenstall, fat Cousin Steffie's hubby George Lucci, Christopher, Mike, Lou the chef, the dishwasher, Lunch's son-in-law Lou, various mobsters and Holly Batterman (who left immediately after Gilbert's feigned dalliance, his dialing finger tumescent with anticipation).

Chick and Charlie drank harder and laughed louder than anyone, letting Gilbert and me know they were on our side. Both found some discreet moment to make inquiries as to whether the romance was proceeding satisfactorily toward fruition or extinction. I informed Charlie that wedding bells were sure to chime eventually, and I told Chick that the royal hussy had gotten the message but was trying to squeeze a few more baubles out of Freddy before reconciling with the duke. Both seemed satisfied.

The party dragged on, endlessly it seemed, but by three or so all had left but Ugo. He was smashed but still offering toasts and waxing maudlin about his new friendship with us. We were different from him, he knew, with different tastes and ways of expressing ourselves, but we were all right and in getting to know us he had broadened his horizons. We assured him that he had broadened ours as well and he happily vomited and passed out on the banquette.

As we began sifting through the wreckage, Aggie showed up.

"Well, well. Look at this place! I'm just getting out of a li'l party m'self and I thought I'd swing by and assess the dam'ges. Not half as bad as I 'spected. You shoulda seen the joint after *this* one's bachelor party," she said, gesturing toward the prone figure of Ugo.

She was very drunk, as were we, but none of us was quite insensible.

"You boys have fun?"

"Yeah."

"It was great!"

We mustn't have sounded too convincing because she threw back her head and roared.

"That bad, was it!"

At that point, after having worn the masks of macho revelers all night long, the temptation to let them drop was overwhelming, and we did. Not that we said anything; we just exhaled mightily and shook our heads slowly in the way one does to convey one has just been tried in the furnace.

A look of motherly concern came over her. She sat at our table and lit up a cigarette.

"My spies tell me you boys have been taking some heat lately."

We eyed each other quickly, each warning the other to exercise caution. God only knew what *her* angle was. So, we just nodded vaguely, noncommittally, and fell silent.

"Want to tell me about it?" she asked.

We shook our heads. She smiled.

"My, oh my! They got you so scared you don't know who to trust, do you? Well, don't worry about me, boys. I'm not on anyone's side. Haven't been for years."

She kicked off her shoes, leaned back, and put her feet up on the table. She puffed dreamily on her cigarette and gazed serenely at the wreckage.

"Got me a nice fat bundle from my first hubby, took over this place and told them all to leave me *out* of it. I said to Lunch and the rest of 'em 'I'm sick and tired of sitting up nights worrying maybe the cousins are getting an edge. Who cares? S'all the same to me. You boys have all the fights you want, just don't have 'em here.' My place is a neutral zone. Isn't that nice? No guns, no grudges. They respect it, too. Wouldn't let 'em in if they didn't. Stand at the door with a goddamn gun."

Another silence fell and Gilbert quietly asked why people were so concerned about the duchess. She laughed.

"S'a long story, darlin', but I'll try to give you the short version. If you'll just answer me a little question."

"What?"

"You two boys are gay, aren't you?"

We sat there tongue-tied for a few seconds and Aggie said, "C'mawwwn, guys, I can keep a secret. I know anyway, from all Chrissy's catty remarks and the way *you*"—she meant me—"used to get so damn flustered when I came on to you. You're gay, right?"

We nodded.

"Then, Gilbert darlin', *why* on earth are you marrying that honey-tongued bitch, Moira?"

"For the gifts," said Gilbert, and Aggie threw back her head and laughed louder and harder than I have ever heard anyone laugh in my life.

"HAH! HAH! HAH HAH! Well I hope you get some *nice* ones, honey!"

When it had finally subsided she poured herself another drink and answered our question.

Freddy was unique among godfathers in that he did not have a "boss," a clear second in command. He used to have one, his son Harry "Gotcha" Bombelli, but Gotcha succumbed to cirrhosis of the liver about two years ago. There was much pressure on Freddy to fill the post quickly but Freddy saw the whole thing as a tremendous opportunity to spur productivity. He told the underbosses who headed the three families, Lunch, Chick and Charlie, that he would choose one of them to fill Gotcha's shoes. He would not, however, choose for one year, his decision to be based on which of the family businesses performed best within that period. This edict was grudgingly accepted and profits predictably zoomed right across the board.

With the rise in profits, however, came an attendant rise in rivalry. While the families continued to socialize and appear mutually supportive there were dark rumors of plans to deliberately sabotage rival cousins' profits. Then the Coast Guard seized narcotics which were earmarked for Chick. Though these things happen in even the best-run businesses and had certainly happened before, now there were whispers of tip-offs. And when Big Jimmy Fabrizio died in a car wreck only two weeks later there were hushed speculations about fixed brakes, despite the coroner's assertion that Jimmy was a walking wine cellar at the time of his death.

Aggie felt that neither the drug incident nor the car wreck were more than unfortunate accidents, but their happening so close together set into effect a chain of discreet sabotages and murderous reprisals. The murders were all meticulously arranged to look like accidents in order to avoid detection and more reprisals (which, of course, didn't work very well, as none failed to result in retaliation). Accusations were sometimes quietly made but were always hotly denied.

This led to a bizarre sort of catch-22. How could the problem be solved when no one could quite admit there *was* a problem? Those who killed and sabotaged knew, of course, that *they* had killed or sabotaged, but could never be one hundred percent sure that the death or business setback they'd avenged was not, in fact, the accident it had seemed to be. For this reason they always took meticulous care to see that their retaliation should *also* seem accidental, leaving their victims in the same state of crazed uncertainty. No one admitted to *anything* and it was generally felt the crisis—*What* crisis?!—would not end until Freddy named a successor.

Which Freddy refused to do. For, despite the occasional setbacks suffered, business had never been better. Freddy got richer every day and no one was happier than he to deny that a problem existed. The deadline came and went, and he announced that he was delighted with all three but wanted more time to think. And so the situation continued. After the electrocution of Jimmy Pastore, however, the tension had grown so great that the three underbosses had gone to Freddy and begged him to make a decision. He'd vowed to do so soon, but then he'd fallen for the duchess, further forestalling his decision and leaving Lunch and Chick Sartucci enraged that a woman so closely allied to the Cellinis had snared Freddy's heart. An actual marriage, they feared, would completely force them out of the running, whatever lip service Freddy might pay to fairness. Charlie agreed with this assessment and was, naturally, delighted.

But why had Chick and Charlie chosen *us* to lean on?

We could thank Christopher for that. He was so pissed at my failure to reciprocate his affection that when the duchess problem arose he informed them both that Gilbert and I were the old girl's closest confidants and advisers, knowing full well we'd find ourselves on the receiving end of their violent and contradictory demands.

So there we were, caught in the middle.

Any advice?

Aggie said that Freddy would probably make Charlie boss. He intended to anyway, and had confided as much to her. Lunch and Chick, whatever they said, would not move against us while Freddy was alive, and once he was dead, Charlie would be so powerful no one would dare touch us. If we sided with Chick, and the duchess jilted Freddy, we'd have *Freddy* against us, for Charlie would be certain to tell him who'd engineered his heartbreak. In the unlikely event that we evaded Freddy's wrath, his successor, Charlie would be equally ill-disposed toward us. Therefore, the safe thing to do was to make sure the duchess married Freddy as soon as possible.

We almost told her but figured, hell, she'd laughed enough for one night.

We imparted this cheery news to Claire and Moira, though not Winslow, who was not, we feared, in a state to cope well with it.

Somehow the five of us stumbled through that week of final preparations. There were tuxedo and dress fittings and family dinners and a premarital conference for Gilbert and Moira with Father Eddie Fabrizio, who would be performing the service. On Thursday the duchess received a telegram from Nigel informing her that he had failed to find a buyer for the property in Africa. He was now back at Trebleclef, suffering from phlebitis and would not be coming to the wedding.

The night before the wedding there was a rehearsal dinner at Casa Cellini. The wedding party, except for bridesmaids and ushers, stayed over. Gilbert came to my room at two in the morning and sobbed convulsively onto my chest for I don't know how long because I fell asleep. When I awoke he was gone and the dreaded day was upon us.

Twenty-eight

"Where's Moira?" I asked at the breakfast table.

"*Silly!*" said Maddie. "Don't you know the bride never sees the groom on her wedding day till they meet at the altar? It's a tradition! I'm not sure why, but I 'spect it's because their feelings would get hurt if they could each see how nauseous the other one looked. I mean, take Gilbert! Give us a smile, will you! . . . Gosh, hon, if that's the best you can do, maybe *you* better wear the veil! Heee, heee, hee! How about you, Gwen? Were you nervous at your wedding?"

"Only the first one, dear," said Winslow.

"I know just what you mean. Gets easier and easier, doesn't it? No offense, Tony love."

I was deeply grateful for Maddie that morning. Her giddy nonstop chatter eliminated the need for us to say even a word.

The schedule for the day called for the guests and the rest of the wedding party to come by the house at noon for a glass or two of champagne. Then the whole party would traipse en masse over to St. Gregory's, which was only a five-minute walk away. The ceremony would begin at one-thirty. Gilbert paced maniacally about the house all morning, annoying the caterers and the men putting the final touches on the heated tent erected next to the ballroom to accommodate the overflow of guests. A little after twelve, as the first guests were arriving, he pulled me aside and said he could not face the rest of the day without some of the chemical assistance on which Winslow had once relied so heavily. I questioned the wisdom of this but it was hard to deny a dying man his last meager indulgence, so we stole upstairs to break sacred tradition by conferring with Gilbert's bride/dealer.

We entered the bedroom and found Claire fussing with her hair at the vanity. Moira was nowhere in sight. Claire explained that she was in the john and Gilbert, spying her purse, swooped down on it and began rifling its contents in search of solace.

He did not, however, find solace.

What he found was a small envelope containing a key which bore the number 723, the same number as the post office box to which we had mailed our seven thousand dollars in hush money.

The three of us stood, staring wordlessly at the key, our brains struggling to digest this overload of input. We had been blackmailed, not by Gunther, but by Moira, who had herself *chipped in* to divert suspicion. That was why "The Avenging Angel" knew about Freddy, and why Gunther had displayed ignorance and anger when asked to negotiate his demands. Of course our statements would have seemed like pathetic attempts at entrapment! And Moira, fiend that she was, had kept us so busy worrying about how she would retaliate that we had not begun to guess she herself was providing the motive for vengeance.

A long minute passed before we could think of anything to say. The sheer enormity of it defied translation into speech.

"But, I don't understand," said Gilbert numbly. "Gunther himself said he'd gotten our money."

"Yes," said Claire, gritting her teeth, more furious, I sensed, at herself than at Moira, "but he didn't say how *much*. She could have sent him a measly hundred and pocketed the rest!"

"That goddamn fucking sleazy subhuman—"

"Gilleycakes!" said Moira, wafting in front of the bath, wearing her gown, "you're not supposed to see me before the service! It's *bad luck*!"

"You bet it's bad luck!" screamed Gilbert, hurling the key at her.

"*Gilley!*" she said, ducking, "what's gotten *into* you!" Then she gazed down at the key where it had landed on the vanity. "Gilbert Selwyn!" she gasped. "You went through my *purse*! How could you! I'll never trust you *again*!"

Gilbert raced toward her, his arms outstretched in a way that left no doubt that strangulation was uppermost in his thoughts. Moira sidestepped him neatly and, hiking up her gown, extended one bare leg and tripped him. He crashed into the vanity sending brushes, jars and tubes clattering to the floor.

"You vicious *bitch*!" he screamed.

"I will not be spoken to that way on my wedding day!"

"Moira, how *could* you!" said Claire, still stunned.

"I had to! My contract with Winnie calls for me to get my percentage of his profits only if I deliver the seed money by *next week*! I was afraid I'd come up short and he'd freeze me out. I mean, he's met a lot of rich people lately! If I don't deliver on time he could borrow from them, and all my work will have been for nothing!"

"But Moira," said Claire, "Winnie's not the sort to do that. Cut you out because you came up a little short!"

"I'm sorry," said Moira poignantly, "but like I told you, I have this problem trusting people! Ever since I was a little girl . . ."

This was entirely too much for Gilbert who rose, snarling, to his feet, seized a nail file from the vanity and advanced menacingly on his bride. Moira shrieked and lunged for the bed where her purse sat open. She removed a small aerosol and pointed it at Gilbert.

"You keep away from me you miserable faggot! I've got Mace!"

"I want that money back and I want it now!"

"Tough shit, Nancy! You'll get it back when I make my fortune and not a moment sooner!"

"Stop it! Both of you!" yelled Claire.

Gilbert pounced and Moira sprayed his eyes with cologne. He fell to his knees sobbing and cursing. Suddenly the door opened and Maddie entered. Moira, without missing a beat, flew to Gilbert's side and embraced him tenderly.

"Gilley, honey! Are you okay, baby! My silly honey, getting perfume in his eyes!"

"Gilbert!" said Maddie. "What are you boys doing here? Didn't I tell you it was bad luck!"

"It certainly was Momma Cellini. He tried to spray cologne on my neck and got it in his eyes! Ooooh! Poor clumsy baby! Let Mummy kiss it!"

She gave him a smooch and backed away suddenly, her lip bleeding.

"Lambkins! Save some for the honeymoon!"

"Couldn't keep away, could you!" gurgled Maddie, wiping a tear from her eye. "Just too much in love to wait!"

She babbled merrily on, but I didn't hear it. I was too busy calculating the ramifications of this appalling development. If it was *Moira* who'd been blackmailing us, then Gunther had not yet made even a *first* move against us! That left only two possibilities: one, that he planned to do nothing, which was hugely improbable, or, two, that he had waited for the ripest possible time to spring his revenge—and what time could be riper than today? I grabbed Claire's hand and begged Maddie to excuse us.

"Sure, kids, you go mingle! Oh, Moira love, your friend Pina's here. That gentleman she's dating is terribly striking in a frightening sort of way."

Eight eyes widened in dread.

"Petey?" asked Moira. "A little Japanese fellow?"

"Oh, no! This one's not Japanese. He's very *tall*. I don't recall the name but it was something German. Gosh—funny, isn't it, how she only dates people we used to be at war with?"

We raced to the bottom of the stairs and there was Pina, dressed in her peach bridesmaid's gown, looking somewhat uncomfortable as it was the first time she'd appeared in public since adolescence not wearing one of her own eye-popping designs. Gunther was nowhere in sight and we prayed for a desperate moment that Maddie had gotten it wrong. No dice.

"Why, yes, I brought Gunther. He told me you weren't quarreling anymore and he wished a chance to patch things up. Pardon my appearance. The sacrifices we make for loved ones."

"Pina," moaned Gilbert, "you said you were bringing Petey!"

"Yes, but he canceled quite abruptly. Then Gunther happened to call and asked if I was free today. He wishes me to design new smocks for his salon. A challenge, no? I am racking my brains for a motif. What an interesting floor this is. Is the mother about? You must warn me so I can avoid her. Our car was followed here. I can't imagine by whom."

We left her babbling to a rather bewildered Sammy Fabrizio, who'd just wandered in, and we raced off to look for Gunther. We found him alone in the dining room. He had a shoulder bag with him.

"Ah, Mr. Selwyn and Mr. Cavanaugh! A big day for you!"

"Gunther, you were not invited!"

"Yes, I was. Vulpina invited me. She is entitled to bring a guest and I am that guest."

"Not in this house, buster!" said Gilbert trying to sound a lot braver than he felt.

"Mr. Selwyn, you would not, I hope, try to prevent me from sharing your day. I might be offended and feel compelled to show your guests *this*."

The last thing we'd expected was anything *worse* than what we'd expected, which was that he'd brought prints of the infamous photo. Alas, Gunther had not confined his revenge to such a tame and predictable gesture. He reached into his bag and pulled out a magazine.

It was one of the raunchier all-male magazines, a photo monthly called *Himpulse*. I had, in the course of my studies, become sufficiently familiar with the periodical to know that, while it mainly featured still photos from recent films of interest, it also included a sampling of candid snapshots submitted by the magazine's devotees. Gunther flicked the periodical open to the ManFan page and, just as I feared, there we were—not merely exposed, but *published*. We stood for a long moment, staring at the photo and those surrounding it, our utter defeat only compounded by the sad truth that we were not the most attractive couple on the page.

Gilbert snatched it away and glanced over his shoulder to make sure no one had entered the room.

"How dare you!" said Claire, blushing crimson. "Taking that photo then having it printed! They can sue you for that!"

"It would make a most interesting trial, wouldn't it?" he asked

Gilbert and I were too dazed to be capable of strategic thought, but Claire, even in the wake of two major debacles, still had her wits about her. With one swift gesture she pulled the bag off his shoulder and, barking "Block him!" to Gilbert and me, fled the room

He snatched at the magazine Gilbert held, but Gilbert sidestepped him and ran from the room, closing the door behind him.

"No need to worry, Mr. Cavanaugh." He smiled. "I have another." And he opened his jacket just enough to let me see that another issue was indeed folded snugly in the inside breast pocket. He clicked his smile shut and strode from the room, his eyes ablaze with evil purpose.

I followed, my heart pinballing around my chest, as he sauntered with long strides past the guests in the living room, through the hall and into the ballroom where waiters were serving champagne. He crossed directly to where the duchess stood regaling Cousin Steffie with fox-hunting stories and whispered in Her Grace's ear. She excused herself, walking out with him through the tent and onto the grounds. I followed at a safe distance.

They stopped at a point near the far end of a long wall of shrubs and small trees, the same wall behind which those ill-fated Magi had made their last trip to Tony's study. I saw that if I could race undetected to the other side of the shrubs I could peek at them through the bushes. I did so and within seconds was spying on their conversation.

"It pains me to be the purveyor of such disturbing news, but I'm sure Your Grace understands that it was vital to prevent this marriage from taking place."

"You're absolutely right, Mr. Von Stroheim!" said the duchess, dramatically. "I've never been so shocked and disgusted in all my life!"

"I knew the man was a depraved fortune hunter, but had no idea *how* depraved until an acquaintance brought that photo to my attention."

"Revolting! Might I see it again? I want to be sure it's really them!"

He handed her the magazine and she studied it intently.

"Shocking! Absolutely shocking!"

"The next page, Your Grace."

"Yes, yes of course," said Mummy, rapt with repugnance. "I want to be *quite* sure . . . Hmmmm . . . Oh, *dear*, oh dear! . . . Well, it's them all right! Might I hold on to this? I think it's best if *I* show it to Moira."

"Of course. You feel she will see reason?"

"She had better! And if she doesn't . . . well, I'll be at that church and when the priest asks if anyone knows any reason why these people should not be married—I shall *speak*!"

"Again, my apologies for being the bearer of such sad tidings."

"Mr. Von Stroheim—"

"Steigle."

"Mr. Steigle. You will never know how grateful I am that you came to *me*!"

And, stuffing the magazine in her purse, she strode majestically off. Gunther followed and I waited till he'd vanished, then dashed back through the tent and into the ballroom. Gilbert was by the gifts table, his face contorted in an unconvincing smile as Chick Sartucci energetically pumped his hand and patted his back.

"Hey! How ya doon!"

"Great, Chick!"

"Don't you two look sharp! Say, ya mind settin' an old man's mind at rest? I heard how *Her Grace*"—and he spat the words out like bad clams—"had a li'l romannic dinner wit' Freddy at Paradiso. She's not still leadin' the poor guy on, is she?"

"No!"

"She's going back to her husband the minute the wedding's over!" said Gilbert. "They're reconciled!"

"Ain't that sweet!"

"There's nothing between her and Freddy! We nipped it right in the bud!"

"Zat a promise?"

"Absolutely!"

"Well, in that case . . ."

He brinned and took an envelope from his pocket. It was a wedding card. He pulled the card from the envelope, removed a check from it and scribbled an amount, presumably generous. He replaced the check and card in the envelope, sealed it, and placed it on top of the others.

"God bless ya!" he smiled and walked away.

"Shit."

"Good news and bad," I said. "Gunther gave Mummy his last copy of the magazine but he's expecting her to—"

"*Hah!*"

"Hi, Aggie!"

Between the drop-dead black silk dress and the knowing smile, she looked like an Oscar nominee who's having a ménage à trois with Price and Waterhouse.

"*Look* at you!" she hooted. "Standing guard on the loot! Fuck, Gilbert, if I had your chutzpah I'd be runnin' this mob instead of feeding it!"

"You wanna keep it down, hon?"

"Well, here you go!" she said, plopping an envelope on the others.

"A grand, baby, and worth every penny for the laughs I'm going to have watching you take my dear greedy family for all they're worth! Have fun!"

We thanked her and dashed for the bridal chamber where Claire, Mummy and Moira were hotly debating the Gunther peril.

"Calm down, Winnie!" said Claire. "You've done very well! You've bought us time that we desperately need."

"Well, what good will it do! I'm not going to stand up in the middle of the goddamn church and denounce Gilley and Philip! And when I don't, *he* will! Or else he'll come back here and start telling everyone!"

Winnie was right. The ceremony was due to begin in only fifty minutes. Gunther, confident of triumph, would make no move in that time. But there was no doubting that following the ceremony he would return to the reception and do what damage he could. Fortunately, he was now lacking evidence, but he could still make quite an ugly scene. Our best bet was to get him ejected from the premises *before* the wedding took place. But how to do this without him spilling his nasty beans?

We sat there, stumped and wordless as precious moments slipped away. Then Claire, who was sitting in the window seat, staring down at arriving guests, said, "Oh, is *that* one here, then?"

Suddenly she leapt to her feet and we could almost see the lightning bolts flashing about her cranium. She swiftly outlined a plan which was, to our surprise, a good deal more down and dirty than anything we'd have expected from our own headmistress.

"Yes," she agreed, "I'm not proud of myself for even dreaming it up, but I can't think of anything else. And unless one of you *can* I suggest we get on with it. We've only got forty minutes."

We went over it several times, ironing out the delicate logistics. I suggested several embellishments which Claire deemed sordid but practical. Then the photographer bustled in and asked Moira if she would stand looking thoughtfully out the window for him, and the rest of us raced off on our bold and dangerous mission.

I sought out the guest Claire had spied from the window and soon found him.

"*Hi*, Leo!"

"Hi," he said, his voice tinged with uncertainty. He couldn't decide whether to snub me for having once resisted his youthful generosity, or to make another go for it.

I apologized for my rude behavior when last we'd met, explaining that I'd been in a surly mood and had wrongly taken it out on him.

"Hey, that's okay!"

"Glad you understand. Say, how about some champagne?"

At the same time, the duchess sought out Gunther and informed him that she'd spoken to Moira, who was now up in her room weeping inconsolably. She was now planning to seek out Gilbert and thrash him soundly. But first, might Gunther consent to do her a small favor?

He was a gay gentleman, was he not? Ah, she'd thought so, though she hastened to add that she could readily distinguish between homosexual gentleman of good character and depraved exhibitionistic gigolos.

The favor was this: a nephew of dear Maddie Cellini's, nineteen years old, rather a good-looking boy, was distressed because he suspected himself to be gay and feared a life of shame and ridicule. What the boy needed, she felt, were a few words of reassurance from a sensitive gay gentleman, someone who could let the young man know that if he did indeed turn out "that way" he could still be a happy and productive member of society. She hated to impose on Gunther, who'd already been *so* kind and helpful, but would he, please, consent to offer the lad a few inspirational words?

Gunther consented and the duchess asked him to wait where he was.

Meanwhile, I'd poured four glasses of champagne into Leo with predictable results. I said I had to go to the bathroom and he leered and said he had to go, too. He followed me to the guest room Gilbert had slept in and immediately got fresh with me. I sat him down and explained, tenderly holding his hand, to observable effect, that, yes, I was gay, but I had a lover to whom I was faithful. Then I went to the bathroom, closing the door and crossing my fingers. When I emerged he had a funny little smile and asked if I didn't mind his staying there a bit "just to think." As he said this he couldn't help glancing at the nightstand where Gilbert had deliberately left the copy of *Himpulse* (minus the damning page) poorly concealed beneath a doily. I pretended not to notice his darting glance and left, racing through the next bedroom and back into the bathroom, where I crouched peeping through the keyhole to make sure that Leo was perusing the magazine. It was hard to see but I heard the unmistakable sound of a buckle being undone. I stood and, gazing down from the bathroom window, signaled to Gilbert, who signaled to the duchess, who then informed Gunther that the troubled youth was waiting for him in the last room on the left side of the upstairs hall.

Listening at the keyhole, I heard Gunther enter and Leo mumble a frantic humiliated apology.

"But you mustn't stop," said Gunther. "I would like to watch."

"Oh?" said Leo. "What else would you like?"

I rose beaming in triumph that our sordid plan had come to fruition. I signaled to Gilbert, who raced into the house to tell Tony that he wanted a little chat with him before the ceremony. Gilbert leading the way, they strode up the stairs, down the hall and, without knocking, into the bedroom.

"Get out!" hissed Gunther, a request Leo would have seconded had he been able to speak. Tony entered just behind him. I bolted from the bathroom and rushed to the scene of the crime.

"Jesus *Christ!*"

"What do you think you're doing, Gunther!"

"You fucking child molester!" bellowed Tony, as the mortified pair fussed with belts and zippers.

The duchess, who'd stood at the foot of the stairs, chatting with Freddy while waiting for just such a commotion above, said, "Goodness, whatever can be the matter?" and, taking Freddy's hand, dragged him to the scene.

"*You* were behind this, Selwyn!"

"What are you talking about Von Steigle?" asked Gilbert blandly.

"I don't know who you are, mister," said Tony, "but I want you out of my house and I want you out now!"

"Not until I've said what I came to say!"

The duchess and Freddy skittered in.

"I don't think there's any need for you to hear this, Gwen," said Tony, fearful of offending the dowager's delicate sensibilities. Gilbert, who had no such compunctions, announced that this lecherous German, Pina's guest, had been having his way with young Leo. Freddy and the duchess gasped.

"Point no fingers at me, Selwyn!" shouted Gunther. "What about this!" he thundered and thrust the copy of *Himpulse* into Tony's hands, the copy from which our photo had been removed. Tony stared at it in horrified amazement.

"How dare you bring such filth into my house on my son's wedding day!"

"Your son is *in* here, you fool!" said Gunther. He grabbed the magazine back but could not, of course, find the picture. He swore that we'd removed the evidence, then, realizing the duchess was present, pointed wildly at her and said, "*She* knows. She can tell you that I'm right! Tell them!"

"Tell them what, you vulgar man?"

"*Tell* them! Tell them about our chat in the garden!"

"I haven't the vaguest idea what you're talking about! Young man," she said, turning to Leo, "you've shown bad manners and deplorable taste."

"He forced me!" whined Leo.

"*I did not!* Liars! You're all liars!" he screamed. "*You!*" he said, advancing on Winslow. "*You* were the one who sent me to this youth! You knew he would seduce me! You arranged it deliberately!"

A shocked silence fell as Freddy, who had yet to say a word, advanced on the furious Teuton and, himself trembling with rage, said: "This is the woman I love. You are calling her . . . a *pimp*?"

"That's *exactly* what I'm calling her, you contemptible dwarf!"

"Do you know who you're *talking* to?" said Tony, stunned. "This is Frederick *Bombelli!*"

"Who cares! I've never heard of Frederick Bombelli!"

Freddy inhaled sharply and, his nostrils flaring, said, "You have heard, perhaps, of Freddy the Pooch?"

All of us staring at poor Gunther in that electric instant could see that the name definitely rang a bell. The arrogance fled his face, as did the color, and a small strangled sound issued from deep in his throat. I was reminded of a Daffy Duck cartoon I'd once seen where Daffy, confronted with some horrific sight, stared, mesmerized with fear, and his bill fell off.

"Gunther," said Gilbert kindly, "I suggest you leave. In fact, I suggest you move."

Gunther wordlessly picked up his suit jacket and, mumbling an apology to his host, fled the room. We never heard from him again, through there were rumors sometime later that he was teaching English at a boy's school in Salzburg.

*   *   *

Our sense of triumph, however, was not long-lived. For, even with the Gunther menace laid at last to rest, where were we but back where we were before, face to face with the Lunch, Chick, Charlie and Freddy menace?

The Gunther incident was quickly hushed up so as not to sully the beauty and spirituality of the day. Inquisitive guests (and there were plenty) were informed that a guest had gotten drunk, behaved badly and left. And in the excitement of the mass departure for St. Gregory's, the matter was forgotten by everyone. Except Holly, of course, who never ceased pleading for details.

I will not dwell long on the ceremony. It isn't nearly so important to my tale as what followed it. Besides, the details, which hewed scrupulously to tradition, are already familiar to anyone who has ever attended a wedding. I will not even attempt to convey to you the feelings I experienced watching my lover marry the woman who had been blackmailing us for the previous two months. These feelings were, and remain, quite indescribable.

The wedding party spilled ebulliently from the church and, since we were so close to Casa Cellini, decided to eschew the waiting limos and instead walk to the house, Gilbert and Moira leading the merry postnuptial parade. At one point I fell behind a bit and noticed the duchess walking arm-in-arm with Freddy. Chick and Lunch were not far behind and I saw that they, too, noted this public display of coziness and were not pleased. More alarming still, though, was the duchess. She looked oddly different.

"Scoping out Mummy?" asked Claire, sidling up to me.

"Is she okay? She's looking a bit wild-eyed, don't you think?"

"She's drugged half-senseless," whispered Claire. "After the Gunther business she staggered into Moira's room and kicked out the bridesmaids. She said her nerves were shot and she couldn't go on without some Ecstasy. Moira was too busy trying to cover the cut on her lip to care, so she just gave her the vial and said 'Help yourself'!"

"Why didn't you stop her!"

"I was in the john! I walked in just as Moira was saying, 'Jesus Christ, Mummy, two's *more* than enough!'"

We wondered fearfully what the results of such excessive euphoria might be. We didn't have to wait long to see. Before the party had quite reached the house, the duchess and Freddy stopped in their tracks and Mummy threw her strong arms about the little mobster and squeezed him jubilantly. He'd proposed.

And she'd accepted.

I have spoken before about the notorious efficiency of the Bombelli grapevine, so you can imagine how swiftly a scoop of this juice quotient became widely known. Within minutes, it seemed, everyone was talking of nothing else. Gilbert and Moira's twenty-minute-old marriage was stale news indeed.

Freddy sought out the newlyweds to apologize for this bit of upstaging. We were all in the ballroom just next to the gift table which was now groaning under dozens of gorgeously wrapped boxes and envelopes. It says volumes about the distance Gilbert had traveled that he gave no more than a glance at that gaudy array. Moira, in contrast, could not unglue her eyes from it for more than three seconds at a time. Even now with her life in immediate peril, the spell it exerted upon her was extraordinary to witness.

"You must forgive me that I do such an impulsive thing on your wedding day!" wheezed Freddy. "But when I see Moira in her gown and the beautiful bridesmaids and I hear the music like from heaven! I am carried away by so much beauty and love! My heart feels like it's gonna bust and I can wait no more! So, forgive an old man who has reason to be impatient!"

"Oh, don't *say* that Freddy, love," cooed the duchess, kissing his cheek. "You have years and years!"

"Gosh, Mummy! I don't know what to say!" said Moira, her index finger twitching as she counted the envelopes.

"Congrats," said Gilbert weakly.

"Look at you," said Maddie to the duchess. "I've never seen a woman so happy! You're eyes are buggin' out with joy!"

I desperately wanted to confer with the others in private, but this would not be possible for a while since they were all obliged to stand in the receiving line—in which line, Cellini tradition dictated, the best man did not participate. With the rest of the syndicate prisoners of politesse I could only wander alone through the crowd, keeping an eye peeled for Chick and Lunch who'd now be tossing a coin to see who got to apply the cattle prod. (Though as Freddy became more familiar with certain flaws in his chosen bride, even these two would be forced to take a number and wait their turn.)

I saw Leo and was suddenly overwhelmed with guilt over how cavalierly we'd used him to get out of our predicament. I offered him my condolences, and he was grateful to receive them, which made me feel even worse. As we stood chatting, I felt a hand on my shoulder. I executed a standing high jump worthy of Olympic consideration. Turning, however, I saw that it was not a foe, but a friend. For the moment at least.

"How ya doin', how ya doin'!" said Charlie, looking more weasely than ever in an ill-fitting tuxedo. "Swell party, huh? Swell! And a beautyful ceremony! Didn't she look nice! How ya doin', Leo? Havin' a good time?"

Leo trickled off miserably and Charlie, beaming, informed me that we had done our jobs beautifully and that our interests would be looked after. This assurance, based as it was on the assumption that Freddy and his bride would find happiness, did little to raise my spirits.

I excused myself from Charlie and headed down the hall to hide in the bathroom till the others were freed from receiving duty and I could once more find safety in numbers. As I reached for the knob the door opened from the other side and I was face to face with Chick Sartucci.

"*There* you are, Chick! I've been looking all over for you!"

"Well, ya found me," he growled and, grabbing my arm, jerked me into the bathroom, slamming the door behind us.

"You got a dictionary at home?"

"I believe so!"

"Good. When you get home tonight, look up *promise*. And when you're done with that, look up *dismember*. When you're done with that, just look up. Look up every chance you get. You still won't see it coming."

And, casually filching a guest soap, he left the room.

"Don't *worry*!" said Charlie when I voiced my concern. "He knows he hits you or Gilbert, I'll get back at him after I take over."

"Thank you, Charlie. I feel *so* much better."

I sought out Chick and begged for another chance to set things right. He informed me coldly that the only way to save ourselves would be to see that the engagement was broken. Today. Before the end of the wedding.

"What if we can't persuade her today?"

"Then do it tomorrow. But, as of tomorrow mornin'—s'open season. Unnerstand?"

As that hellish day wore on I discovered there are few things more difficult to do than keep a good conspiracy cooking at a wedding. Everything works against you. The leading players are forced mercilessly through their paces, from the receiving line, to the traditional dances, to dinner, all throughout which lascivious aunts tap their water glasses to make the newlyweds smooch. Even when the poor slobs manage to evade the glare of communal scrutiny, their footsteps are dogged by drunken relations who've been waiting all day to express the novel view that the ceremony was lovely. With all these pernicious obstacles it was hours before we managed to drag our renegade duchess into the study for a crisis conference.

"What the fuck do you think you're *doing!*" said Moira.

"I'll thank you not to take that tone with me, even on your wedding day!"

"Winslow," I said, close to tears, "you *can't* promise to marry Freddy!"

"Why on earth not?"

"*You're a man!*" hissed Gilbert.

"What a perfectly rude thing to say!"

"Look, Winnie," said Moira, nose to nose with him, "you're blasted up there now, but when you come down you're going to be in deep shit and so am I, *so knock it the fuck off!*"

Winnie rose and glared at her.

"You're a horrible child! I've *always* thought so! I so much wish Claire were mine instead of you! There, I've said it and I'm glad! Don't think you're getting a penny when *I* die, you ungrateful beast! I'm not so old I can't have more children with Freddy! I'll have a nice baby girl and *you'll* be out in the cold. Just you *wait!*"

We regarded each other numbly. Claire said there was no point trying to reason with Winnie till he'd crashed, and the rest of us nodded wearily.

Then he laughed lightly and said, "What are you all so worried about? Is it those awful men who've been making threats?"

Gilbert glumly retorted that, yes, they entered into it.

"Well!" he said, "I'll fix *their* wagons!" And he swept out of the study, the rest of us stumbling frantically after him. He marched through the ballroom and out onto the lawn where Lunch, romantic that he was, stood watching the sunset.

"There you are," smiled Lunch, puffing at a cigar. "I was lookin' for you. I think it's time we had a little talk, Gwennie."

"Your Grace, to you!" said Winnie, pulling the cigar from Lunch's mouth and squashing it underfoot. "I can't abide smoke!"

"What the fuck are—"

"Nor can I abide foul language, so please refrain from using it in my presence. I understand from Moira that you object to my marriage to your uncle."

"She's damn right I object!"

"Well, *that*, my omnivorous friend, is *your* problem. By trying to make it ours you are committing a considerable blunder. You might have gotten away with such tomfoolery when Freddy was running this family alone but now that I am running it with him I assure you such high-handed behavior will not be tolerated!"

"So you're fuckin' in charge now, are ya!"

Winnie smartly slapped his face.

"I warned you about such language! Though I can see now that sterner warnings than that will be required to penetrate that lard-encased brain of yours. I think tonight I'll speak to Freddy regarding a little transfer for you. Bolivia, say. A year or two spent disciplining shiftless coca growers should give you sufficient time to reflect on the virtue of humility. Now, if you'll excuse me, I have more pleasant matters to attend to. Oh, and by the way," he added as he turned to go, "I don't know if you're aware of it but your wife, Sammy, is sleeping with Serge. I can't say that I blame her. Good day, Mr. Fabrizio."

"There, see!" he burbled as we trailed him back to the house. "You just have to know how to talk to these people! Now where's that awful Mr. Sartucci!? Here, Chick! Here, Chick, Chick, Chick! Ha ha ha ha ha!"

* * *

What was there for our little band to do after that but decide to get as drunk as we could? We knew any efforts to rectify the situation could only make it worse, if that were still possible, and oblivion was the kindest fate we could hope for. The gifts were due to be opened soon and the four of us took our seats at the head table to watch the guests glide through the last few dances before the hollow ceremony would take place. We got a few bottles of champagne and sat down to some serious imbibing.

A slow waltz ended and a tarantella began. Tony and Maddie, who were seated next to us, rose to dance. We gazed down and saw the duchess and Freddy.

Freddy drunkenly caressed Mummy's thigh under the table. She pursed her lips and slapped his hand gingerly, a show of resistance so mild as to be an encouragement. He placed a hand to his chest in a "mea culpa" gesture, then grinned impishly and renewed the assault.

The duchess emitted a high, scandalized giggle and, egged on by her clear delight, Freddy extended his hand further under the table where it suddenly encountered the last thing he had expected it to. He pulled it away as if it had been bitten, and stared at the duchess, his eyes brimming with horror. She smiled dreamily in return, and pecked him on the tip of his nose.

Freddy made a gargling sound, clutched his chest, and fell forward onto the table, knocking a bucket of champagne to the floor. The duchess, alarmed, leaned over him, asking tearfully if he was all right. The dancers, hearing the commotion, looked to the head table and gasped in dismay.

"My God!" shrieked the duchess. "Is there a doctor in the house!"

Medicine was not, alas, the family specialty. Half a dozen people rushed the table, including Tony, Maddie, Aggie and Freddy's three would-be successors.

"Don Bombelli," beseeched Charlie, "we're sure you're gonna be all right, perfectly all right, top notch, but who would you like to look after things while you're recuperating? Or supposin' you don't . . ."

"*Who*, Freddy!" echoed Chick.

Freddy raised his head, his eyes full of pain and utter confusion as he wheezed his last words.

"Is a *man*! . . . Is a man, is . . ."

His head fell to the table, his eyes still full of rude surprise.

"The man is *who*!" pleaded Lunch.

But no word came from Freddy. They edged in closer, praying there was just enough life left in him to utter·one single name and so resolve years of conflict. Every person in the ballroom stood poised and breathless.

Everyone, that is, except Gilbert, who was so relieved at the timeliness of Freddy's demise that he could not restrain the urge to celebrate.

On countless occasions since that day I've wondered how that tense situation might have resolved itself had Gilbert not chosen that moment to open a bottle of champagne. We'll never know, however, for he *did* open a bottle, and the pop of the cork pierced the hush of that room like a gunshot. Entirely too much like a gunshot, in fact, for some overimaginative soul at the back screamed in terror and another equally fanciful guest yelled "Duck!" And all the guests, shrieking as one, followed this alarmist's advice.

Within seconds Chick had whipped out his gun and was squinting about madly trying to locate the assassin.

"Wait, you idiot!" said Aggie, chortling drunkenly to Chick. "That wasn't a goddamn *shot*! That was just Gil—"

But she never finished that sentence. For, at that precise moment, a minion of Lunch's, at a middle table, peered up and couldn't help but note that Chick was the only one in the room brandishing a gun. He removed his own weapon, and Chick, seeing this, wheeled and took aim, though not quite quickly enough, for his alarmed prey fired first.

Chick, while not so hefty as Lunch, still presented a target no gunman, even one reeling from champagne and tarantellas, could fail to hit. The bullet found its mark, as did a second, and Chick fell. Chick's son Ugo saw this and, screaming like a samurai, rose and gunned down the assassin.

"Jesus fucking *Christ*!" said Aggie and scrambled under the tablecloth, coming out the other side just between Gilbert and Claire.

"God, honey!" she snapped. "You just *hadda* have champagne!"

From then on we witnessed little, crouched as we were in terror behind the head table, but the constant crackle of gunfire supplied all the information we cared to have as to what was going on in the ballroom. Guns blazed and panic-stricken guests dove under tables or stampeded the exits. Screams of horror and the wails of the newly bereaved filled the room.

At one point I crawled over and peered around the end of the table, gaining a partial view of the tent beyond the French windows. The musicians, who'd been crouching behind the inadequate protection of music stands, had bolted the platform and were charging out through the open glass doors. A man running with a saxophone while gazing unwisely back over his shoulder collided with a support post and the entire canopy collapsed, turning the fleeing crowd into one immense, writhing, red-striped organism which spoke in dozens of voices, none of them calm.

Not that we were, of course. We crouched under the table, Claire, Gilbert, Winslow and I, all hugging each other and finding God. Moira was also crouching with us, or, more accurately, behind us. She said it was our duty to protect her since, with her gown, she made the best target.

"Kee-rist!" said Aggie, philosophically, guzzling champagne from the bottle. "Ain't life a hoot? For two years these murdering bozos have managed to keep a lid on things. Then some bitch and a pair of hungry faggots decide to fleece 'em for some wedding gifts, and it's World War Three!"

"You *told* her!" said Moira, glaring indignantly at Gilbert and me.

"What's the difference?" said Gilbert.

"Oh, none, I'm sure! God, Gilbert, I can't trust you at *all*!"

Gilbert just stared aghast and collapsed his head onto my chest. "Oh, Philly," he sobbed, "I'm *married* to this!"

Just then a bullet whizzed over our heads, shattering a mirror on the wall behind us. Moira shrieked in terror and, grabbing Winslow to pull him in front of her, grabbed too hard and pulled his wig off.

Aggie stared, her eyes growing huger by the second.

"She's . . . *she's* . . . !"

The four of us nodded grimly as Winnie frantically adjusted his wig.

"That's why we were still upset when you said we'd be okay as long as she married Freddy."

Aggie goggled a moment, then out it came in a great loud torrent: "HAH HAH HAH!"

"All right, dear, it's not *that* funny," sniffed Claire.

But Aggie could hear nothing. She was totally convulsed, doubled over and pounding the floor with her fists, as bullets ricocheted over our heads.

"Aggie! *Please!* You're drawing their fire!"

"You did all *this* for some lousy presents! Hah hah hah hah!"

Moira suddenly clambered to the front edge of the table and raised her head enough to see over the rim. What she saw galvanized her enough to make her leap up with a reckless disregard for personal safety.

"*Nooooo!*" she screamed in pure, animal rage.

Unable to imagine what had so moved her, I peered over the table and saw Charlie and four soldiers crouching behind the gifts. Other men were shooting at them from behind tables.

"*No!*" shrieked Moira, as a flashbulb exploded in the middle distance. "Not behind the *gifts!*"

A bullet narrowly missed her and she dropped, cursing violently.

"Gilbert, they're shooting right at our *gifts!*" she wailed.

"*Hah hah hah—!*"

Claire pointed out that there were numerous people here not fond of our little contingent and they now knew exactly where to aim. The tablecloth would not protect us.

Claire leading the way, we all waddled a short distance behind the camouflage of some overturned chairs, Aggie's uncontrollable laughter a beacon for the bullets that whizzed over our heads every inch of the way. We reached the narrow space behind the bandstand. And who should we find there but Holly Batterman, who'd been wooing the flautist when mayhem struck. He knelt there shaking, blood soaking his shirt from a flesh wound in his shoulder.

"I wish you had *told* me it was going to be this kind of wedding!"

Gilbert apologized and we fell silent, even Aggie. Ricocheting bullets struck the metal of the music stands and the wall over our heads.

"Oh Lord!" said Claire. "This is no good either!"

"Well," I said, "I don't see where else we can go!"

"I'm not moving!" whispered Holly.

"There!" said Claire, pointing to the door to Tony's study which stood a few feet beyond the far edge of the bandstand.

"We can't!" cried Holly. "It's too far!"

"Well, we're going to, Tubby," said Aggie, removing a pistol from her beaded bag. "Who wants to ride shotgun?"

Moira immediately offered to take it.

"I'm going to give *you* a weapon! Fat chance, honey. I'll do it!"

Suddenly we heard a terrible crash that sounded like Tiffany's exploding. In an instant the room went dark as the great chandelier shattered on the floor.

"Now!" said Claire, and we all bolted out from behind the bandstand and through the door into Tony's study.

From then on, Gilbert, who knew the house best, took over. He led us to a corridor where there were back stairs to the second floor. We raced through the house, Winslow tripping on his high heels, until we'd reached the safety of my guest room.

"Out!" said Claire, closing the door on Holly.

"*No way*, honey!" he said, charging the door and easily pushing her aside. "You're not leaving me alone in this slaughterhouse!"

She tried to assure him he'd be safe in any of the other bedrooms, but he refused to budge. Finally, Claire just threw up her hands, let him in and closed the door. We all collapsed nervously onto chairs, the floor and the bed.

"Well, so far so good, kids," said Aggie, "but you're going to be in some very hot water when this gets out."

"Whatever do you mean?" said Her Grace, daubing her eyes.

Aggie patiently explained what we had not yet had time to realize. The spectacular self-destruction of the Bombelli clan would, without question, produce a media circus of the first magnitude. It would come out that the fighting had been triggered by Freddy's engagement to the duchess. And in the constant glare of media scrutiny and government investigation, would our little secret stay secret for long?

"What secret!" said Holly, perking up considerably.

Worse still, said Claire, when the survivors found out over whom their loved ones had gone to their graves, they would not be pleased.

We all sat there silently as the horrible truth sank in. The deaths of Freddy and Chick and, we hoped, Lunch had not brought us one bit closer to real safety.

Then Claire stood up and said: "Then there's nothing to do but murder the duchess."

"*What!*" shrieked Holly.

"C'mon, Winnie! Off with the dress!"

"In front of all these people!"

Claire stepped toward him and wrenched the wig off his head.

"I said *off* with it, Winnie, and I mean *now*! We don't have time!"

"Stop it!" cried Winnie.

Claire turned to Gilbert and me, and said, "Strip him."

We advanced on Winnie, who, sensing we meant business, tearfully demanded a robe and undressed himself. He then padded into the bath where he scrubbed his face clean and did what he could with his limp curls.

Holly sat on the bed staring, almost trembling with joy. Here, unfolding before his eyes, was the most spectacular scoop in the history of mankind. It was like he'd died and gone to dirt heaven.

We paid him no heed. We hardly dared for we knew at any moment someone might walk in and see the transformation before it was complete.

The makeup removed, we dressed him in the pants and sweater I'd worn the previous evening; they were extremely tight, but looked acceptable under my trenchcoat. Gilbert's sunglasses completed the disguise.

Claire then took the dress and ripped it in several places to give the impression that its occupant had suffered a violent assault. She then turned the dress inside out, took it over to Holly and, begging his pardon, smeared blood from his shoulder wound all around the tears.

This done, she addressed Holly with chilling authority.

"What you have just seen, Holly, is ours and the Mafia's darkest secret. I don't care how juicy it is or how much you ache to tell it— if you breathe a word to one single soul you're a dead man. Do you understand?"

He nodded, trembling.

"I have to get Winnie out of here. We'll take the back stairs and use my car. I'll leave this gruesome trophy plus one of her shoes behind the bushes on the grounds. The rest I'll take home and burn. Philip, if in the future Gilbert ever assures you you can make some easy money, please ignore him. Good-bye."

Holly had to stay behind to wait for the ambulances which would surely arrive soon. Gilbert and Aggie had to stay behind to see what had become of their family, I had to stay because Gilbert was staying, and Moira was just a wreck about the gifts. Claire and Winslow left, and not a moment too soon, for minutes later the police arrived and no one was allowed to go.

When we heard the sirens we ran downstairs. Gilbert found Maddie and Tony, who were unhurt, and there was much hugging. Moira ran straight for the gift table and what she saw made her crash to her knees as if stabbed straight through the heart. There was not a single unperforated package in the lot. Moira rose and tearfully shoved the body of a slaughtered mobster aside, looking for something, *anything*, that was not shattered, bullet-riddled or soaked with blood. As for the envelopes containing the cash and checks, these had mysteriously vanished.

It was then that the police entered and shouted "Freeze!" Those mobsters who were still alive and unhurt offered no resistance. They seemed, if anything, relieved.

We were all taken in for questioning which went on until seven the next morning. Nineteen men, including Lunch, Chick, Ugo, Serge and George Lucci were murdered, and no one had seen anything.

Gilbert and I told all we had seen without fear of reprisals since no one we'd actually seen murder anyone had not been killed himself. The police, sensing we were out of our depth and only peripherally related to the principals, pressed no charges.

We were ushered out a back door to avoid the clamoring press. Moira looked so ghastly in her blood-splattered gown that we were given a police escort to Manhattan. Gilbert and I asked to be let out on Broadway so we could get a bit of air, and the policeman obliged, taking Moira on to God's Country. As we strolled in the cold morning breeze we came to the newsstand at Eighty-sixth Street. All the morning papers carried screaming headlines about the historic mob massacre.

The *Post*'s, in red ink, read simply BLOODBATH! Beneath this headline was a picture of Moira.

It showed her with her fingers splayed frantically against the sides of her face, her eyes wild with dread and her mouth wide open as she screamed the words, "No! Not behind the *gifts*!"

The caption beneath the photo read A BRIDE'S ANGUISH.

Epilogue

The roar of inquiry has died down now, but for quite a while we were the darlings of the media. Especially Moira, or the "Bride of Death" as the press dubbed her. The interviews came thick and fast, and not a single reporter failed to be charmed by her warmth and obvious sincerity.

Yes, she said, she'd known that her boss, Freddy, had once run a crime empire, but she'd believed, as had so many, that he had become a frail, repentant man who wished only to spend his twilight years sitting in his little garden, hearing her speak the words of the immortal Tolstoy. Yes, she'd known, too, that the Cellinis were widely rumored to be mafiosi, but they'd all been so kind to her, and Mummy had taught her not to judge lest she be judged.

Mummy, of course, was that rara avis for which tabloid editors have been known to light candles and offer prayers: the Mystery Woman. Moira professed tearful ignorance as to why Mum had pretended to be a duchess, though she imagined she'd only wanted her daughter to be proud of her. As for her whereabouts, Moira feared, as did most, that despite the police's inability to locate her remains, the evidence offered little room for hope. This tragic probability sometimes caused Moira to break down in tears, and once she had to be comforted by Sue Simmons on "Live at Five."

Moira's real mother, of course, got wind of it all and hush money was duly paid, though Gilbert and I refused to contribute a penny.

The countless photos published in the days following the event made Gilbert's face so recognizable that I and I alone had to schlep all over Manhattan and the boroughs, buying up every available issue of *Himpulse*. The expense and embarrassment were staggering.

As for Gilbert's media coverage, it was of a less desirable sort than Moira's. Within weeks no fewer than three of his former lovers had come forward and sold their reminiscences to, respectively, The *National Enquirer*, the *New York Post*, and *Torso*. These revelations only generated more sympathy for poor brave Moira, who received mountains of letters advising her to dump Gilbert and find a man more worthy of her unselfish affection.

As the Bombelli trials wore on, Maddie was shocked and disappointed to learn that her beloved Tony had been engaged in money laundering and insider trading. "Think of it, Gilbert!" she said. "All those months I was a moll and never knew it!" Tony's lawyers got him off with a light sentence and Maddie asked for his assurance that once released he would never steal again. He gave her his promise and that was good enough for her.

Aggie fired Christopher but asked us to continue working at Paradiso, for the publicity in those first weeks generated phenomenal business. Later, after Gilbert's former beaux started coming forward in droves, she decided that the abusive jokes and prying questions of drunks at the bar were more than she had any right to subject us to and she let us go.

I don't suppose any of us who survived "Blood Wedding" suffered half so much in its wake as did poor Holly. Faced with daily headlines screaming questions about "Moira's Mystery Mom," he was never more than a breath away from claiming the scoop of his lifetime. Yet he dared not speak after Claire's warning, and dared still less after Moira sent him the threatening note wrapped around a dead pigeon. And so he trudged through his days, a sad chubby Tantalus with a tale he could never tell.

Scentinels, the world's first ingestible deodorant, got off to a promising start. Moira, by contracting lucrative magazine accounts of her wedding, raised the rest of the seed money. With Winnie she formed a company and won FDA approval to run clinical tests. The trials went swimmingly and the subjects were uniformly delighted with the product. But just as it seemed they'd win approval to market it, disaster struck. A small percentage of the subjects found themselves suffering ghastly side effects months after they'd ingested the tablets. People would wake one morning to discover they suddenly reeked of rotting fish or overripe gorgonzola. Lawsuits rained down on the company and it folded faster than a sofa bed.

Claire and I finished our musical. We're shopping for producers.

As for Gilbert and me, well, I hate to disappoint the romantics among you, but things didn't quite work out for us—though the days just after the wedding were about the happiest we ever shared. Nothing, not the strident reporters, or incredulous detectives, or even Moira, could dampen the exhilaration we felt at being alive, together and out of danger.

Rapture at merely being alive is not, however, an emotion one can cherish indefinitely. The sense that death is *not* apt to come crashing down on you any second is a nice one, but after a while the thrill fades. So, with danger no longer spicing our romance, Gilbert and I were forced to occupy ourselves in the same pastime new couples have pursued since time immemorial—the search for fresh incompatibilities. He did not see why I insisted on writing when he was lonely and bored. I did not see why he didn't want to write at all, especially after his pretty speeches about our shared literary destiny. He did not see why I was incapable of "having fun" and I did not see where the fun lay in club-hopping till four a.m. with his wife and the ever-changing army of "new friends" they'd acquired in the wake of their sudden infamy. (Most of these friends were the sort of unspeakably chic trendoids who, asked what they do for a living, reply, without a trace of a smile, "I'm an aesthetician.") There was also the small matter of our sex life, which needn't interest you, since it did not, after a point, interest us.

When the revelations of his checkered past hit the papers, Gilbert suggested we cool the affair for a while. A while stretched into weeks, then months, and we realized that neither of us was exactly crying himself to sleep at night. Each content that he'd gently let down the other "before it ruined our friendship," things returned to their old footing. There was a sticky in-between period, but that receded as these things do. I'm happy, once more, to love Gilbert, not too well but wisely, and to enjoy his bracing company as often as he's willing to share it.

Though I confess that, just lately, I have avoided him assiduously, leaving my machine on and peering down at the street before leaving the apartment. This is because of the last time I spoke to him. My early-warning system was operating well enough this time for me to slam the phone down almost immediately, but the few blood-chilling words I heard before doing so still haunt my sleep.

"Hi! S'me! Philly, I have a little proposition for you, and please don't say no till I've finished—"

READ ON FOR A CHAPTER FROM
JOE KEENAN'S
PUTTING ON THE RITZ

One

I've noticed over the years that Truly Bad Ideas, like flu strains named for Asian capitals, insidiously time their visits to occur during those periods when our defenses, reeling from some previous blow, are at their most tattered and flimsy. I see it all the time. Some friend or acquaintance who'd always seemed the very epitome of Reason will be jilted by his lover or passed over for a promotion, and the next time I see him he's talking about the marvelous career advice he's getting from his astrologer and would I like to buy some nutritional supplements? There are, of course, any number of crises capable of inducing this poignant tendency to grasp at straws. I can, however, say with some authority that few ordeals leave one half so limp and suggestible as the ordeal I had suffered a mere two weeks before my story begins. I refer to the spectacular and highly public demise of a musical play to which one has devoted the last three years of one's life.

The show, a cheeky satire of network television, was called *Here for the Season*. The book and lyrics were by me, and the music was by my longtime friend and collaborator, Claire Simmons.

Its failure, like that of most flops, was the end result of a whole series of dire miscalculations. If pressed, though, to name the one decision that really drove a stake through the thing's heart, it would be my agreement to accept as co-librettist our renowned director's twenty-four-year-old boyfriend.

Claire, whose radar at such times is more functional than my own, argued against it, but I felt that the script needed only minor changes and the youngster, who seemed amiable enough, was not seeking a dominant role so much as a ride on our coattails. This proved incorrect. We soon learned that our coauthor, far from being amiable, was a violently opinionated young man who, when contradicted, displayed a temper that called to mind Caligula with a toothache. To make matters worse, the director's only response to his paramour's screaming fits was to scream louder. If you want an idea of what our average rehearsal was like, rent a martial arts film and watch the last twenty minutes.

Chaos reigned. Actors quit and were replaced with inferior performers. Songs were cut, scenes came and went with dizzying speed, and the whole gossamer fabric of the show unraveled like a congressman's alibi.

The days following the show's closing, which coincided with its opening, were not happy ones. I soon discovered, as one does in these situations, that my friends, however sincerely fond of me, seemed to find my downfall a strangely agreeable spectacle. They phoned constantly, ostensibly to offer support but mainly to hear the grisly details and inform me of such venomous reviews as had escaped my attention. A typical call went like this:

CONCERNED FRIEND: (*cheerfully*) Hi, Philip! (*then, darkly*) How are you?

ME: I'm fine.

C. F.: I just want you to know I'm personally writing a letter to that Siswycz creep.

ME: *Siswycz?*

C. F.: Mark Siswycz. He reviews for *Avenue A*. You haven't seen it, then?

ME: I've never even heard of it.

C. F.: I guess they don't sell it up where you are. Well, I wouldn't worry—any critic *that* vicious must have problems of his own.

ME: I take it he didn't like us.

C. F.: Wait, I'll read it to you—

Now normally when my life begins to feel like an Edvard Munch painting sprung to life, I turn to my closest chums, Gilbert and Claire, and they rally round with inspirational slogans and cheap champagne. But, my little support system had, alas, broken down just when I needed it most.

Gilbert, to give him his due, spent the night after the closing with me, offering quiet sympathy while having pizzas delivered to the director's apartment. In the days since, however, he'd vanished from sight and was not returning calls. That left Claire.

Claire is normally one of those indomitable Mary Poppins sorts of women, who, faced with adversity, grit their teeth and think lovely thoughts. For a week or so after we closed she managed to put up a brave, sardonic front. But then the *Times* critic, trashing some other new musical, conceded that it at least lacked "the numbing incoherence" of *our* show, and Claire gave up, surrendering to that lush despair even the most stoic lady composer will feel when *The New York Times*, having buried her, returns a week later to dance on the grave.

Anyway, this should give you some idea of how pathetically susceptible I was on that fateful afternoon when Disaster, brilliantly disguised as Opportunity, first bade me come closer and listen awhile.

"Hi! 'S me!" chirped Gilbert into the phone.

His bubbly manner was miles away from the penitence I'd have expected from a friend who'd carelessly abandoned me to my burden of woe.

"Hi," I said in my most glacial tone.

"How goes it?" he asked. "Not picking at the scabs, I hope?"

"I'm fine," I said. "No thanks to you."

"Well, I like that!" came his miffed reply. "And here I am working day and night to rebuild your shattered reputation!"

"Oh?" I asked, hope and dread colliding within me. "How've you been doing that?"

"I got you a job!"

"A job?" I asked. If I'd had any sense, I'd have hung up right there and you'd be reading a pamphlet now, but, as I said, I was filled with the blind hope of the shattered and I pressed for details.

"This isn't anything illegal, is it?"

"Philip! You disappoint me. It's a *writing* job. Someone's doing a club act and needs the Cavanaugh touch to make it soar and glitter."

I asked if it was for pay, and he replied that, though fees had not been discussed, the performer was equipped to pay handsomely.

"Who is it?" I asked.

"I'll get to that. But first, what are you doing tonight?"

"Nothing, why?"

"Because we have to celebrate! My divorce came through!"

"*Great!*" I said, my anger entirely forgotten. "Already?"

"Yes! Isn't it grand? She's out of my life, Philly. Gone! Kaput! Extinguished!"

"Congratulations! That's wonderful!"

I should explain, I suppose, that though Gilbert is a contented—some would say devout—homosexual, a year ago he'd married a woman named Moira Finch. Romance was not the motivation. Both he and Moira had large, wealthy stepfamilies, well positioned to shower them with expensive gifts. Gilbert proposed a temporary merger, and Moira, whose scruples cannot be glimpsed without the aid of a particle accelerator, accepted.

Things came off rather less happily than expected, but come the finale the two were, in the eyes of New York State, if not the Lord, man and wife. They set up housekeeping and coexisted with increasingly strained civility for about six months. Then one night Gilbert ate some leftover Chinese food Moira had been saving for her lunch, prompting her to change the locks and file for divorce on a charge of mental cruelty. In the months since, Moira had been traveling and was now believed to be infesting the greater Los Angeles area.

"I'm so happy for you!" I said. "I thought she was holding things up, trying to get all this money you didn't have."

"She was. But now she's got her hooks into some rich sap and wants to haul him in but quick."

"Well, *that's* a break! God, the guy must really be loaded. I hope he's got a good lawyer."

"And a food taster. So, what say we put on our party frocks and celebrate? My treat, of course."

"You're on!" I said. "Thanks a bunch. This is just what I needed. Where do you want to go? There's this new place in Chelsea that's—"

"No, let's eat in. I want you to see my new place."

"New place?"

"Well, it's not mine really. It belongs to the fellow I work for. You'll be working for him, too."

"He's the one doing the club act?"

"No, that's somebody else. A woman. You'll be working for her, but you'll also be working for my boss, only she won't know it."

"*What?*"

"I'll explain tonight. Just come by around eight. I'll stuff you with champagne and caviar and give you the whole poop. You got a pen?"

I fetched one and scribbled down an address on Madison Avenue in the seventies. "This is your *boss's* place?" I asked.

"Right. Wait till you see it!"

"My God, Gilbert—are you telling me you have a *job?*"

"Yes! I'm a working boy again. It's great! I've been at it two weeks."

"Two *weeks?*"

I was frankly stunned. Gilbert and employment have never been on cordial terms. He tends to view jobs the way a rodeo artist views bulls; he's willing, when compelled, to take one on but neither desires nor expects to stay in the position for long.

"Yes, two weeks—you needn't make it sound so miraculous!" he added testily.

"What sort of job is it?" I asked.

"I'll tell you tonight."

"But—"

"*Tonight,*" he said, and rang off.

Annoyed as I was at him for leaving me so fogbound, I had to at least give him credit for taking my mind off my poor deceased musical. So mystifying were his statements that I could ponder little else for the remainder of the day. Apart from his fantastic assertion that he'd been cheerfully employed for weeks, there was this business about having found me a job, too. It worried me. Especially disquieting was his insistence on withholding details until I'd been stuffed with delicacies. A job that couldn't be offered without a side order of caviar was not, in all probability, a job I'd be wise to accept.

With these speculations fermenting in my mind, I donned the as-yet unpaid-for suit I'd purchased for my opening, strolled down to Ninety-sixth Street, and boarded a bus for that exotic faraway land known as the Upper East Side.

It was February and for the past two weeks the city had been pummeled by snow and bone-chilling winds, causing the homeless to flee into shelters and local news anchors to pantomime chilliness in well-heated studios. In the last two days, though, the winds had abated, temperatures had soared to record highs, and the sun had burst forth, inspiring an attendant sunniness in the normally funereal mood New Yorkers reserve for bad Februaries. Even now in early evening the breeze was mild and people wore light jackets and wide smiles. Stepping off the bus on the East Side, I decided to stroll down Fifth Avenue, where, I suspected, the cheeriness that prevailed on the West Side could only be heightened by the addition of twelve-room apartments and trust funds.

I sauntered downtown, exchanging little smiles with passersby, and arrived in due course at the Metropolitan Museum of Art. There was a party being held there that evening to celebrate some much heralded exhibition, and, as usual at such events, the limousines were thick and plentiful. But in the midst of their gleaming ranks there was now unfolding a scene of discord in sharp contrast with the avenue's springlike mood.

Two cars had apparently collided, and one, a stunning silver Rolls-Royce, its front headlight shattered, was now splayed across the avenue, blocking all traffic. Two liveried drivers were examining the damage, and standing next to one was a gaunt elderly woman in a pink gown, the elaborate bottom of which she'd swept off the wet pavement, exposing two unlovely gams. I couldn't hear what she was saying, as the waiting limos were starting to honk, but she seemed to be giving what-for to the other car's driver. Between the pink, upraised gown and the spindly legs, she looked something like an enraged flamingo.

The rear door of the other limo was now thrown open and a statuesque, raven-haired beauty leapt out and entered the fray. She had a loud, piercing voice, and so salty and direct was her mode of expression that the waiting partygoers told their drivers to lay off the horns and stop drowning out such first-rate entertainment. Rows of black limousine windows glided down and elegantly coiffed heads popped out like champagne corks. Bejeweled necks twisted and craned, seeking a better view of the festivities, and even those already ascending the grand stairs to the museum stopped in their tracks and gazed mesmerized at the battle.

Making a mental note to myself to check the columns tomorrow, I strolled on and soon reached the address Gilbert had given me. The lobby had burnished mahogany wainscoting and wallpaper that deep color I've always thought of as wealth green. I told the mummified doorman whom I wanted, and he directed me to the penthouse.

A dark paneled elevator with lovely inlaid designs brought me to the top floor, where there were only two apartments. I rang the appropriate bell and the door was at once flung open by Gilbert, who stood resplendent in a new silk suit. He smirked, curtsied, and yanked me in.

Interior design is not a topic on which I can discourse with anything approaching authority. My own apartment, though comfy by my standards, is not what you'd call "decorated" unless you consider the widespread use of milk crates to be motific. I do make the occasional stab at renovation, though this consists largely of turning over sofa cushions and realizing they looked better the other way. Given these circumstances, I'm inclined, perhaps, to be too easily impressed by such niceties as parquet floors, wall sconces, and armchairs without springs sticking out.

But *this* apartment, I could see, was of a richness calculated to dazzle eyes far more discerning than my own. Everything about it screamed (or, rather, murmured) of England and old money and high tea after the cricket match. I felt I'd stepped out of my own life and smack into the middle of *Brideshead Revisited*.

"Woof!" I said, or words to that effect.

"*We* like it," said Gilbert, yawning lightly, leaving me no option but to pull his hair.

"Ow!"

"Cut the Cecil Beaton routine," I said, "and tell me how you ever maneuvered yourself into this joint."

"That can wait. I have to show you the *rest!*"

Dropping all pretense of jadedness, he dragged me swiftly through eleven rooms, all done in the same Anglican Moneybags style.

There was chintz everywhere and huge fireplaces crowned with richly carved mantels and dark oil paintings. There were marble busts and heavy tables crowded with bibelots and photos in antique silver frames. Ancient editions of Shakespeare and Milton were tossed about like yesterday's newspapers, and thick brocaded draperies, covered with no doubt imported dust, framed each window. Gilbert babbled away, quoting prices on the more valuable tchotchkes, then saying "Think fast!" and tossing them to me.

"Don't do that! God, what a setup!"

"Twembly and Coleman!"

"Huh?"

"Ever-so-classy designers. Hand them a chicken coop and they'll make it look like Somerset Maugham lives there."

"You've actually moved in?" I said, wondering suddenly what had raised him to such opulence. It was not an apartment any young man of Gilbert's means was likely to attain *virgo intacta*.

"I *told* you—I just work here sometimes."

"And who's your boss?"

Gilbert smiled and leaned right into my face. "Tommy! *Parker!*" he said, then pulled back as though to avoid the flying spittle that would attend my screams of envy.

"Who's Tommy Parker?"

He heaved a sigh of exasperated disbelief. "Don't you know *anything?*"

"Well, pardon me for living, but I've never heard of him. Who is he?"

"He's *only* the editor of *Boulevardier!*"

He referred to the well-known men's fashion monthly. I'd heard of it, naturally, though I'd seldom given it more than a glance. I have nothing against fashion magazines per se, but I've never been able to see the point of spending money I don't have to look at men who won't sleep with me modeling clothing I can't afford.

"Sorry," I said, "but I'm not a subscriber."

"Obviously," he said, casting an eye at my suit. "Still, you *must* have heard of 'Nosy' Parker?"

This rang the vaguest of bells. "Gossip columnist?"

"Right," said Gilbert. "He wrote for *Boulevardier* for nine years before he was bumped up to editor. Anyway, Nosy Parker was *incredibly* famous."

"And you work for him?"

"Yes."

"But not at the magazine?"

"No, I work here."

"Oh. . . . Doing *what?*" I asked, and there must have been a certain something in my voice because Gilbert walloped me on the head with a chintz pillow.

"Fuck you! You're always making out I'm some kind of cheap gold digger who'll do anything to lead the high life. I truly resent that!"

"I'm sorry," I said.

"You should be!"

"I am. Where's the champagne?"

"Chilling. Anyway, the reason I work here is because the whole thing's an enormous secret. Tommy's putting his reporter's hat back on to do this major, *major* exposé, and I'm helping with the research and co-writing it."

"Exposé?" I asked, intrigued in spite of myself.

"Yes."

"Of who?"

"*Someone . . . very . . . big,*" said Gilbert, whose specialty is pointless suspense.

"*Who?*"

"I'm getting to it. Normally, of course, I'd never dream of co-writing anything since the results can be—well, I don't have to tell *you*, do I?"

"Champagne?"

"I'm getting it!"

He rose and I followed him down a richly paneled hall lined with little prints and paintings of hunting scenes.

"So," I said, "this Parker guy gives you the run of this place when he's not around?"

"Of course."

"And you're telling me there's *nothing* going on between you?"

He stopped short and exhaled wearily, as one mourning the death of tact. "My dear Philip, it is *extremely* unprofessional to sleep with one's coauthor."

"Ah. Struck out, then, huh?"

"I did *not* strike out! I've barely even tried. He's not the sort you can just pounce on. I'm laying the groundwork."

"And not much else, apparently."

We continued along the hall, snaking around corners as I goggled at the sheer vastness of the place.

"Anyway," he said, "the *important* thing is the story—whatever may happen between Tommy and me, it's something I really *have* to do. Even if it means putting aside the book for a while."

I let this pass without comment, even though such references normally provoked gales of satire from me. "The book" is Gilbert's novel, a steamy and provocative dissection of the urban scene. He's claimed to be working on it for five years now, but as for the actual manuscript, the yeti has been sited more often and reliably. He claims his zealous perfectionism has slowed his progress and seems to view it as a mark of precocity to have arrived so young at that state of tormented inertia it took lesser writers like Salinger and Capote years to achieve.

"I mean," he said, "I figure the book will always be there—"

"Indeed."

"But *this* story," he said, ignoring the dig, "is different. We have to strike while the iron is hot."

I followed him through a swinging door into the kitchen. I paused to take in its magnificence. Not even here, I saw, had stateliness surrendered an inch to modernity. Even the appliances were customized to appear generations, if not centuries, old.

"What are you goggling at?" asked Gilbert, fetching a stunning silver cooler from the cabinet that covered most of one wall.

"I've never seen a mahogany toaster."

"Actually, it's rosewood."

He hauled a magnum of Bollinger out of what looked like Oliver Cromwell's refrigerator, then reached into the freezer and pulled out two champagne flutes.

"Anyway," he said, filling the cooler with ice, "it's a wonderful opportunity! The minute I heard about it I thought, Philip *has* to be in on this. I owe it to him after all the grief I've inadvertently caused him."

"Very sweet of you. So, enough already. Who's this big exposé about?"

His eyebrows danced up and down a few times, and a grin spread across his face as he lovingly enunciated the name.

"Peter Champion!"

"Peter *Champion?*" I said, appropriately awestruck. "Wow! You're certainly gunning for the big game."

"Gunning?" He smiled, meticulously removing the foil from the champagne bottle. "Philip, my dear, we're going to *crucify* the fiend!"

"Well!" I said, impressed in spite of myself. Then I suddenly recalled his earlier statements and promptly broke into gooseflesh.

"Hang on a minute—you're expecting me to *help* you with this?"

"Absolutely," he grunted, pressing both his thumbs against the cork. "You're indispensable to the whole plan. Tommy and I will do the research and the writing. But *you*, Philly—*you* get the *fun* part!"

And with that the cork flew out, rocketing to the top shelf of the cabinet and severing the spout from a very pretty nineteenth-century Crown Derby teapot.